MEG LUDWA

Valkyrie

First edition

ISBN: 978-1-7356394-2-0

Editing by Dylan Garity
Cover art by Satine Zillah

This book was professionally typeset on Reedsy.
Find out more at reedsy.com

To my wife, Rachel. I love you, Gingersnap.

Contents

Chapter 1

Thirteen hours. Dr. Shea Tristan's twelve-hour shift had ultimately run long when a wounded peace officer had burst through the emergency room doors of her hospital wing. The young man was top priority med-transported and needed immediate attention, yet Dr. Tristan's replacement had yet to show in the twelfth hour of her already-exhausting shift. So, despite the ache in her bones and the drowsiness clouding her muddled thoughts, she'd prepped for emergency surgery.

"Don't worry, Mrs. Jeffries, your husband made it. He's going to be alright; His Fortune Shines," Dr. Tristan had said to the patient's sobbing, woeful wife in the waiting lobby after forty-five tiresome minutes in the operating room.

The peace officer had taken a serrated knife to the abdomen while trying to break up a scuffle between two rival gang members in the Middle sector. He was lucky to have been med-transported in time. Few were as fortunate. The surgery ran longer than she'd anticipated, but he would've been lost if the med-transport had arrived only five minutes later.

Patients suffering more gruesome injuries occasionally rolled into the emergency room, particularly when Shadow and the Trinities were directly involved. A peace officer had been lost just the week before after she'd attempted to arrest a Shadow operative caught selling smuggled cigarettes from the Dome. The officer had taken a knife to the throat and died within minutes. Dr. Tristan hadn't been the doctor on call, but she'd come into the hospital that night and found the mourning silence in the halls unsettling. Gang-related violence had become too common over the past few cycles, and although it twisted at her heart to know that another life had been lost, she couldn't afford to let it distract her for long. Too many people, patients and their loved ones alike, depended on her to remain focused.

She'd been so exhausted and focused on saving the poor officer's life that she'd forgotten to wash herself after the surgery. She reached to shake the distraught wife's hand with the man's blood speckled and dried on her pale skin. It took a moment of examining the horrified expression rising across the woman's plump, flush face for her to realize the unfortunate mistake.

Two more shifts, then I can crash in bed all weekend. She closed the office door shut behind her. Her fingers reached to flip on the lights, hesitated, and then dropped again. Her eyes ached. *Dark. Dark is better.*

She pushed herself forward and plopped down in the chair behind a small desk in the corner. Her office, though cramped and no larger than a common patient's room, was wonderfully peaceful and quiet.

Sitting brought relief to her sore feet. She leaned back against the chair, stretched her arms high above her head, and parted her lips to yawn. Her heavy gaze drifted to the computer screen, and she blinked her weary eyes. The small, flashing envelope icon in the bottom corner caught her attention, and she sat up and scooted the chair forward against the desk: an intramail. She clicked the icon and smiled when she recognized the sender.

Shea,

Hey sis, I know we're only supposed to use the intramail for official business, but I wanted to remind you that today is Dad's birthday. He's not celebrating it—you know how he is—but I think it'd really make his day to hear from you. It's been rough out here lately at Apex, but don't overthink it—I don't want you to worry.

Hope you're doing well. We love and miss you.

- Charles

"Oh, no…"

A wave of guilt rushed over her—she'd forgotten her father's birthday. Whether it was due to her busy schedule or mere absentmindedness, she would've let the day pass by unnoticed had Charles not broken official comms-protocol to remind her. A simple intramail message wouldn't assuage her guilt at this point, and although it was against practice to use the ministry's computers and intramail for personal use, she nevertheless slid open the cover to the webcam built inside her monitor.

"Sorry, Uncle Alex," Shea said, motioning absentmindedly toward a portrait of a young, stately gentleman hanging from the adjacent wall. "One personal intramail won't hurt, will it?"

The blue light at the top of her monitor flickered to life when the webcam activated. Her smile waned when her face appeared on the screen, illuminated by nothing more than the pale glow. Not only was Shea exhausted after her thirteen-hour shift, but the arduous hours had visibly taken their toll on her. Dark circles enveloped her tired, drooping hazel eyes and her long brown hair, originally drawn back in a bun at the base of her neck, hung loose to frame her slender, weary face. The longer she peered at her own image, the more she yearned for sleep. She imagined looking at herself through that wife's eyes and figured she may have had the same reaction under similar circumstances; Shea wouldn't want Dr. Tristan to be her physician either, if she looked as terrible as this.

Shea rose from her chair and strode to the sink in the adjacent restroom. She didn't bother switching on the ceiling lights, and instead groped for the faucet handle to twist it open. The water chilled her skin when she rinsed her fingers and leaned forward to splash her cheeks. She yanked on her hair tie to release her messy bun before re-collecting the thick hair into a neat ponytail. Returning to the desk, she strained to smile against her exhaustion. She took a breath and pressed 'Record.'

"Hi Dad! I know, I know, we aren't supposed to use intramail like this, but—" she greeted, then began to sing. *"Happy birthday to you, happy birthday to you, happy birthday dear Da-ad!"* Her voice faltered against the dryness in her throat.

She hesitated, and then spoke again with feigned levity. "My singing voice hasn't improved over the cycles, clearly. But happy birthday, Dad, I hope you're at least doing *something* special with Charles today to celebrate. I wish I was with you two at the facility, but I know you wouldn't have it."

She wavered for a moment and sat in silence, her smile

weakening. "I just miss you two, is all. It's been hard lately without you guys. I'm one of the newer physicians on staff here at the hospital, so they're assigning us the longer night-shifts that no one else wants. But I'm holding up alright. If Mom handled it, so can I. The house is quiet without you two stomping around, though."

Shea glanced up at the clock on the wall—11:35. Her warm, soft bed at home beckoned to her the longer she stayed seated in that office.

"I'll write to you soon, Dad, I promise. Tell Charles I say hello, and that I love him." She strained to smile through her exhaustion. "I love you both. Take care out there and stay safe." With a wave, she ended the recording. Her smile dropped and she sat motionless staring at the screen, waiting for the message to send.

A knock at the office door startled her. Shea slid the computer webcam lens shut.

"Who is it?" she asked, rising from her chair.

"It's Brad, open up," a man answered from the other side, impatient.

Shea took a deep breath before opening the door with a strained, wide smile. "Dr. Wilson, to what do I owe this unexpected pleasure?"

Dr. Wilson, a tall, jowled, middle-aged man with dark graying hair, eyed her up and down with a scowl. "You look ghastly."

And you're a colossal dick. "Just finishing up a shift, actually. On my way home now, if that's alright."

"Sure, not a problem. You're free to go home right after you visit with Secretary Willis."

Shea stared at him, stunned. "Begging your indulgence,

Dr. Wilson, but Dr. Mohan is scheduled to take over and can make the visit—"

Dr. Wilson raised his hand to silence her. "Secretary Willis asked for *you* specifically. He is a Statesman, and is a good friend of your uncle. It would mean a great deal to this department, and me as your supervisor, if you paid Secretary Willis a visit."

Shea bit her tongue against the ire rising through her chest. Her smile tightened. "Of course. I'll head that way immediately."

Dr. Wilson offered a polite nod and turned to walk away. "Please do, Dr. Tristan. His Majesty Guide Us."

"May Strength Remain." Shea's voice remained calm despite herself, and she turned back to shut the door behind her. She marched down the hall, silently cursing her supervisor beneath her breath.

***

A white laundry transport pulled through the security gates outside. It backed into the narrow delivery dock beneath the Ministry of Health and Wellness and idled for a few moments before stabilizing clamps latched onto its bumper. The driver's door slid open. A young man stepped out and rounded to the rear of the vehicle, all while darting nervous glances over his shoulders. He wiped a bead of sweat from his brow and clapped his palm twice against the side of the transport.

The rear double doors slid open and a figure clad in dark clothes, face obscured by a gray scarf, hopped out onto the bay carrying an empty duffle bag.

"You know the drill, Trev. Keep her running, I won't be long." The woman checked the time on her wristwatch and strode across the platform toward the ventilation shaft. The driver had already begun lifting heaps of soiled sheets from the damp bay floor and heaving them into the back of the transport.

He glanced anxiously over his shoulder. "Don't keep me waitin', alright?"

She didn't respond, and he watched her disappear into the shaft, leaving him standing alone among the mounds of dirtied linens. He glanced around again and jumped at the announcement blaring from the nearby speakers:

"Be advised, scheduled rainfall set to begin in ten minutes. Be advised, scheduled rainfall set to begin in ten minutes."

He shuddered and bent down to hoist another armful.

Chapter 2

"Secretary Willis, how're we feeling today?" Shea entered the luxury hospital suite with a soft knock on the door. The room was large enough to house three patients, the corners stacked high with vibrant flowers and lush greenery. A vast window along the far wall offered a scenic view of Valhalla, the lush moon their Odin Prime station orbited. Beyond the cloud-streaked atmosphere, blue seas, and vibrant green landscapes was the planet Yggdrasil, the blood-orange gas giant with its massive, thousands-of-kilometers-wide lightning storms.

Shea had seen this view countless times in her life on Odin Prime, and the sight no longer struck her with the same sense of awe as when she was a child. She took in a breath, expecting some scent of the blossoms from across the room, but instead drew in the aroma of stringent cleaning solution and sour body odor.

Secretary Willis, a heavyset older gentleman with glasses, a receding hairline, and a bulbous, reddened nose, peeked over the top of the handheld Dome news broadcast and smiled at her. He shifted to sit up in his bed, rocking the bed frame as he moved.

"Dr. Tristan, it's so good to see you," he said as he adjusted the pillow behind his back. "I appreciate you taking the time to come see me."

"Of course, it's no trouble at all," she said with a smile, and reached to extract his medical chart from the foot of his bed. She opened the file and scanned the details: cirrhosis of the liver. "It says here that they've found a liver for your transplant. His Fortune Shines."

"His Fortune Shines, *indeed!*" he exclaimed with a widening smile.

"I can't say I've ever seen organs become readily available so quick before." She closed the file and slid it back inside the document sleeve at the foot of the bed.

"Yes, well, dedicating your entire life to the station as a loyal Statesman sometimes has its perks," he said coyly, and adjusted his glasses. "The chancellor is a good man, as well, to take care of us so well. And a good friend."

Shea strained to smile when she recalled her forty-seven-cycle-old patient two floors below, a citizen employed by the State as an accountant for the Department of the Interior. He also suffered from liver failure and had been waiting on an organ transplant for lunars, while the gentleman lying before her now had waited only four days. But the secretary was a Statesman, ranking higher than any typical citizen. There was no higher title that denoted greater loyalty to the State. The title was granted only to Party Assembly members and those closest to the chancellor, and offered a level of privilege not available to other citizens. She brushed the concern for her other patient aside—Statesmen were more valuable to society, after all, and needed the organs more. How could she complain? Shea herself was a Statesman from her familial ties with the chancellor; she would hope the same steps would be taken if she were in Secretary Willis's position.

Shea sat in the chair beside his bed. "Uncle Alexander is a good man. Have you spoken to him lately? I'm sorry to say I haven't seen him since the funeral."

The gentleman frowned. "Yes, the funeral… tragic, what happened. We all still miss her dearly. Your mother was a good woman, a good *Statesman*. Your uncle took it particularly hard." Shea swallowed against the lump hardening in her throat and forced a smile. He continued with a pat of his plump hand over hers.

"But I'm saddened to admit that I haven't seen much of him, either. He's been quite busy getting the criminal matter under control and working through therapy. The last I saw of him, he was just beginning to walk again. I know he's grown quite tired of that wheelchair. Who wouldn't?"

"His Fortune Shines, I'm glad to hear he's walking again. The stroke took us all by surprise," Shea said with a tired sigh. "He refused to let me see him after the stroke. Wouldn't even let me be on his medical team."

Secretary Willis frowned. "My dear, you'd just lost your mother. He didn't want to burden you with his troubles. He is a very proud man, after all. Probably didn't want you to see him in such a state, to worry you further. Besides, with he and the party planning the Peace Accords, it's a wonder he manages to find time to eat and sleep."

The Peace Accords… a disaster waiting to happen.

Shea had overheard bits of the news broadcast the week prior while eating a hurried supper in the break room.

"… *The Party assembled late last night…*" Shea had checked the clock while shoveling a spoonful of sweet oat mash into her mouth. "*… a proposed station-wide Peace Accords, aimed…*" She'd tipped back the rest of her still hot tea, hissing as she nearly scalded her tongue. "*… integration protocol for non-citizens…*" She had missed the rest of the broadcast as she hurried across the room, dropped the dishes into the sink, and rushed out the door to her next appointment.

"I suppose," Shea said, too tired now to think of it further. It was time to leave. Her home beckoned to her, and she'd done as her department asked: used her position as the chancellor's niece to cozy up with the prominent Statesman and earn the hospital brownie points in the process. But then again, this hadn't been the first time such demands were made of her.

She began to rise from her chair but returned fully to the seat when the secretary continued speaking. Agitation plucked at her tired nerves.

"Oh! I must ask how your date with my nephew went! I'd completely forgotten to ask him about it last week."

Shea hesitated for a moment. She blinked, mind drawing a blank. Had the date been so unremarkable that she hadn't remembered, or was it her exhaustion? It suddenly struck her and she forced a smile. "It went… very well."

It had been a disaster. The secretary's nephew was dimmer than a spent light bulb and duller than a butter knife. Handsome, but self-absorbed and insufferable. Their conversation over dinner had been so excruciating that Shea recalled remarking how she'd had more fun earlier that day conducting corrective surgery on a patient's anal fissure.

Anal fissures are more appealing than your nephew, Secretary Willis.

"When will that second date be, then?" he asked with a sly

grin and a wink. "You two would make such a great match, don't you think?"

Shea's jaw tautened behind her thin smile. "I'll have to look at my schedule, Secretary. My shifts have been quite daunting as of late." She stood from her chair. "Begging the secretary's indulgence, but I unfortunately must be going. Is there anything I can get for you before I leave?"

He watched her for a moment, noting the hard chill behind her words. The grin across his thin lips shrank away. "Yes, I'm still waiting on my Cyntrax treatment. The nurse said you'd take care of it when you came to see me."

Of course she did. Shea smiled and offered a quick nod. "Sure thing, let me get that dose ready and I'll be right back."

Shea turned and left the room before he could respond. She walked down the hall, wiping the sensation of his thick, meaty hand on hers against her lab coat. The sooner she could administer the Cyntrax, the sooner she could return home and sleep. Her next shift was in ten hours, and she was determined to spend as much of that time unconscious as she could.

"Shea Tristan," she nearly yawned. She stood with eyes closed and arms crossed before a heavy, locked supply closet door.

Almost done. You're almost done with this bullshit. She yawned again.

The security lock beeped and flashed red. *"Credentials cannot be verified."*

Shea opened her eyes to stare at the door, brow furrowed. She tried again. "Shea Tristan."

BEEP. *"Credentials cannot be verified."*

"… the hell?" Shea tapped the security pad with her finger.

"Shea. Tristan."

BEEP. *"Credentials cannot be verified."*

The agitation plucking at her nerves swelled in a flush of heat in her chest and face. She raised her fists and banged against the thick metal door. "Oh, come on!"

"Hey! Whoa!" A young nurse ran over and placed a reassuring hand on Shea's shoulder. "Dr. Tristan, just calm down—"

"Why won't it open?" Shea barked, and stepped back from the door.

"They ran an update on the security software a few hours ago, and it messed with some of the staff's access credentials. They probably just haven't fixed yours yet. But sure, assault the door, that should fix it."

Shea crossed her arms and took a deep breath against the heat burning her ears. "Sorry, it's just been a long night."

"Don't apologize to *me*." The nurse placed her palm against the door and patted it softly. She smiled. "Apologize to the supply closet."

"Nurse Elliot, are you really asking me to apologize to a closet?" Shea tried to suppress the smile curling at her lips.

"You hurt its feelings."

"It's a closet."

"It's a valued member of this staff and deserves to be treated as such."

Shea laughed. Her annoyance and anger melted from her heavy shoulders as she stepped toward the door and placed her palm against the cold metal. "I'm sorry, supply closet."

"Rebecca Elliot," the nurse spoke into the security pad with a smile and a wink. The red light flickered green, and the door slid open. "See? You just had to ask nicely."

"Thanks." The lights inside the supply closet flickered the life when Shea stepped inside. Her tired, aching eyes searched the wall-to-wall shelving. "Thanks also for shoving Secretary Willis's dosage on me. I don't need sleep or anything."

Nurse Elliot let out a breath and stepped inside the closet behind Shea. "Yeah, sorry about that. I was going to take care of it, but the department was pretty adamant in having you be the main point of care for him. Can't imagine why…"

"It just comes with the territory." Shea pulled down a cardboard box, peeked inside, and slid it back onto the shelf. "I'm used to this sort of thing. I help with favors, I make my superiors look good…"

"… you date Statesmen's sons and nephews." Nurse Elliot peeked inside a small box, her eyebrow cocked.

Shea scoffed with a roll of her eyes. She pulled down another box and looked inside. "Yeah, well… it's expected of me, of us. It's what the State wants."

"And is that what *you* want?" Nurse Elliot's voice softened as she returned the box in her hands to the shelf.

Shea made to reach for another storage box, but stilled. She hesitated, her fingers resting on the ledge of the wire shelf, and sensed a heat rise again through her cheeks and ears. Her heartbeat quickened. Nurse Elliot and she had been fast friends since Shea had begun working there lunars ago. The two often shared the same shifts and exchanged polite smiles and greetings when they passed one another in the hall, each busy with their own lists of tasks to finish. But Shea could always count on Nurse Elliot to cheer her up whenever she'd had a particularly difficult shift. She had always left Shea smiling when they went their separate ways. It had all felt so innocent until that moment, until Shea detected a certain tone in the way she asked that question.

There was always something about the young woman, about the way her eyes lingered longer than most, which suddenly disquieted Shea. The State's moral edict was clear and concise: perverse, repugnant, and immoral behavior deemed detrimental to station society was strictly outlawed. And those found guilty of succumbing to such perversions were not only dangerous, but were enemies of the State itself—chip away at the foundation of society, and it could collapse entirely. It was expected that loyal citizens report such behavior in their peers, and loyalty was rewarded with greater decrees of respect. Many Statesmen earned their titles by holding their peers accountable for their detestable behavior. Nobody asked what happened to those taken into custody. Nobody wanted the answer.

"You know, I can't seem to find any Cyntrax down here." Shea turned and placed her hands on her hips, making sure to avoid meeting the nurse's gaze. She grew aware of the narrow space between them and leaned away to widen it.

Nurse Elliot, her cheeks flushed, crossed her arms and looked away as if suddenly ashamed. "Right… maybe it hasn't been stocked since the last shipment. I think there was another drop-off made this morning, though. You could probably check the shipments office upstairs." Nurse Elliot turned her back to Shea and wiped at her eye with the sleeve of her jacket. "I'll stay here and keep looking in case we missed it."

"Thanks, I'll let you know what I find." Shea turned and hurried from the closet. She glanced over her shoulder a final time; Nurse Elliot merely stood there, her back turned to the entrance, staring at the floor.

Chapter 3

The elevator dinged before its double doors slid open on the seventh floor. Shea stepped out into the hall and tucked her hands deep into the pockets of her white jacket.

Should I report her? I mean, it's reportable behavior, isn't it? Then again, maybe I just read too much into it... maybe she was just being nice and I misread it as something more. I could just ignore it.

Shea glanced at the office directory displayed on the wall and noted that the Shipments Office, Room 724, was down the hall to the left. She turned on her heel and continued, her eyes trailing along the tiled floor. She couldn't shake the sensation of their closeness in the closet, or the heat radiating in her cheeks. Nor could she ignore or quite understand the heaviness in her chest, weighing against her ribs like a stone.

If she wasn't just being nice and was—what would it be called, flirting? If she was flirting and I don't report her, will it only get worse? Shouldn't she get the help she needs to correct the behavior? Isn't it my responsibility? A good Statesman would report her.

Shea stopped, closed her eyes, and buried her face in her

hands with a deep, tired sigh. She'd only ever filed a report once, two cycles prior when she'd discovered a young doctor on her rotation was having an affair with his patient. Shea filed the report with the nearest peace officer station, and both the doctor and patient had disappeared within the week. It took nearly a week to get over the residual guilt from turning them in, but she reassured herself that it was her responsibility as a Statesman to protect Odin Prime's societal integrity. Such sacrifices were necessary.

But Nurse Elliot was different—they were *friends*. They'd laughed and suffered through arduous, wearisome shifts together. She couldn't help but feel reluctance in reporting her. After all, it was only a hunch. Shea wasn't sure if the guilt she now felt was from her failure as a Statesman or for feeling the urge in the first place.

She peeked through her fingers at the clock hung on the wall and groaned against the increasing weight of exhaustion on her shoulders: 12:20. She should've been home over an hour ago, fast asleep in her warm, comfortable bed. Yet here she was, running one final, stupid errand.

"Just get the damn thing and we're done," Shea whispered to herself.

She approached the Shipments Office and noted that the doorway sat open, yet the lights inside remained extinguished. Glancing around, Shea realized that she was alone in the hallway, and all other offices remained shut and locked. She rolled her eyes.

Of course, it's just after noon. Hospital administrative staff are on their scheduled lunch break. Must be nice to have a cushy 9-5 gig. Bastards...

"Hello?" Shea leaned into the office and reached for the

inside light switch. Her fingers flipped the switch on and off as her gaze lifted to the ceiling lights. Nothing happened. "Hey, anyone here?"

Shea hesitated. Had it been any other day, with any other patient waiting on her, she could have easily turned around and request that the nurse or follow-on doctor administer the shot after the staff returned from lunch. But her patient was a Statesman, and such excuses wouldn't be tolerated. Particularly not from her superiors.

Just get in, get the dose, and leave.

One step inside, then two. The office was still and silent, and Shea squinted to peer deeper inside at the tall storage shelves lining the rear of the room.

Can't see anything. Her footfalls were unsure as she groped, arms outstretched, through the emptiness in front of her. The darkness closed in around her; it crawled across her skin. Surely there was a lamp on one of the desks inside that she could turn on, or maybe a computer monitor she could flicker to life. All she could hear was the sound of her own breath, her own heart beating inside her chest, when something moved in the darkness ahead of her: the shuffling of feet, of something being dragged across the tile floor. Shea took a breath, and then scoffed.

"Okay, real funny, guys. I know your jobs are boring and all, but I'm on a schedule. Would you mind knocking it off and turn the lights on already?"

Silence.

Shea wiped her dampened palms against her lab jacket and continued forward. "This is really unprofessional, guys, you know that?"

She couldn't shake the sensation of eyes following her

through the darkness, of the pranksters who were no doubt delighting in the torment. She'd heard of administrative staff playing tricks on one another when work was slow, but the stories were always so innocent, playful: applying post-it notes all over someone's desk, turning monitors down, fiddling with chairs so that they'd lean back farther than normal. But this didn't feel innocent or playful at all—this was malicious, and she'd be sure to file an official complaint to her superior during her next shift.

Her fingertips grazed the chill of a metal desk and she released a breath, her shoulders loosening. When she stepped closer, her feet caught against something solid and heavy on the floor. She cursed quietly to herself and fumbled blindly until she felt the computer monitor and the button along the edge.

The monitor flickered to life and the bright white light enveloped the space around her. She sucked in a breath through her teeth and closed her eyes, still too adjusted to the darkness to see comfortably in the bright glow.

"Fun's over. Come out, guys."

She opened her eyes and peered down at the floor. A security guard lay dead at her feet, his head craned awkwardly above his snapped neck. His eyes, still open, peered lazily past her through the glow of the monitor, his mouth hung wide as if to cry out.

Shea screamed. She stumbled back and tripped over another solid mass on the floor behind her. The fall landed her hard on her back, knocking the wind from her lungs. She gasped for breath and noticed the second security guard, his neck snapped and face lying flat against the cold tile floor, beneath her legs.

Crying out, she scrambled backward until her back pressed against a storage shelf. Her gaze darted around the room, cloaked in thick darkness, lit only by the glow of the computer screen. Her heart raced, drumming hard against her chest and in her ears as she took staggered, panicked breaths.

A glint of metal on the floor drew her attention: a pulse pistol dropped by one of the guards. She lunged forward and grasped at it before standing again. The pistol trembled in her hands as she extended it out ahead of her.

"That's not a smart move, Doc," an unseen woman spoke from the back of the room. Shea turned toward the voice and squinted to see through the darkness. She could only see the vague silhouettes of shadows against the backdrop of shelves and storage containers. "If you're any smarter than those guards, you'll drop the gun and leave. *Now.*"

"Stay where you are," Shea's voice cracked against her dry throat as she spoke. She strained to steady the pistol in her hand. "Don't move, or I'll shoot."

"You think they didn't try that already?"

Shea grew acutely aware of the two dead security guards lying near her feet; she could almost feel the chill from their skin. She still saw the contortion of their neck bones from the corners of her eye in the dim light of the monitor. Reaching out, she took hold of the screen, and twisted it around to illuminate the back of the room.

A tall figure stood beside an emptied box of Cyntrax, a loaded duffle bag slung over her shoulder. She was dressed head to foot in dark clothes with a gray scarf obscured her face. The woman's piercing green eyes lingered on Shea's through the glow of the illuminated screen.

"Drop the bag."

"No. Let me pass."

"No."

The woman appeared to grin beneath the scarf. "Well, then. Where does this leave us?"

"What, are you insane? I have a *gun*," Shea said, incredulous. "Now drop the bag and put your hands behind your head, or I swear I'll shoot."

"Oh no, you'll *shoot*? You even know how to handle that thing?" The woman dropped the duffle bag and rotated her shoulders. "You wanted my hands behind my head, right? Like this?" She slid her palms behind her scarfed head and took slow, exaggerated steps toward her.

"Stop." Shea stepped back and placed her finger inside the trigger well of the pistol. "I said *stop*! Get on the ground!"

The woman lunged forward and sprang over the desk with an agility Shea had never seen before. Shea closed her eyes and squeezed the trigger, firing twice. She heard the thick slap of rounds striking flesh. The woman seized the pistol in Shea's hands, undeterred by her wounds, and twisted it hard from her grasp.

Shea cried out when the woman contorted her wrist and twirled her around. The woman wrapped her arm, the sleeve dampened with blood, around Shea's neck and tightened. Shea thrashed and kicked, clawing desperately at the arm squeezing against her throat. Darkness came over her as she gasped for air and sensed her limbs weaken and become heavy.

Chapter 4

The young driver tapped his foot anxiously against the front bumper of his laundry transport and glanced at his watch. He had completed loading the piles of soiled laundry left on the platform for him over ten minutes ago and was now growing agitated. Darting his eyes around the empty loading dock, he could feel the heavy rapping of his quickening heart in his throat.

Vic was late. They had run this operation every six lunars for the past three cycles, and she had never once been late. If anything, she would turn up a few minutes before their scheduled egress, but now she was a minute behind. He let out a long, muted groan and directed his gaze to the empty laundry chute. He'd forgotten about the State's weekly scheduled rainfall that afternoon, and the incessant tapping of thick raindrops against the tin roof above him now eroded his shaky nerves.

Trevor was already a nervous man by nature, but during extraction days he was nearly useless. He was content with his limited role as the driver and had refused to get involved beyond that. Most operations went down without any complications—Vic made sure of it. The two had grown friendly over the past few cycles, but there was a part of him that still feared her. She was precise to a fault and didn't tolerate his occasional cowardice. But today was different.

What if they were waiting for her? What if... The longer he waited on that empty platform, the more he panicked. *What if they trace it back to me? After what I told them, how could they not? It's my fault. How was I supposed to know that they'd ask me about this shit when they detained me?*

A bead of sweat rolled down his narrow jaw as he vividly recalled the most recent public execution: a young woman had been caught selling black-listed literature in the Dome and was sentenced to death for inciting sedition against the State. All public executions ended with a unified proclamation of the State motto: *May Strength Remain.* He closed his eyes and pictured the executed bodies hung from the Mourning Tower at the center of the Middle Borough atrium, their crimes notated on a placard tied to their ankles. Trevor shuddered and looked at his watch: 12:43.

"Screw this, I can't wait any longer." Trevor triggered the driver's side door and slid inside. Something must've gone wrong. Vic was punctual but was now a no-show, and he wasn't prepared to allow himself and his family to be dragged into any fallout left from a botched operation. The State wasn't known for leniency or mercy, and he refused to put himself in a position that would lead to him standing on that execution platform or hanging from the Mourning Tower.

Trevor turned the engine over and shifted the transport into drive. As he did so, he felt a slight jolt shiver along the sides of the vehicle. Just as he registered the sensation in his mind, a hand reached out from behind his right shoulder and wrapped its stained fingers around his throat.

"You were gonna leave without me, Trevor? You useless sack of shit." Vic emerged from the darkness in the rear of the vehicle. She squeezed his throat before releasing him with a shove. "What would Mama Wilder say? She'd think you turned Statesman."

Trevor gasped for air and clutched at his throat. He coughed and shifted in his seat, then glanced back at her and stilled. "The hell happened to you?" He surveyed her and noticed a dark stain on the right side of her chest, a round cavity in the fabric. "Holy shit, were you *shot*?"

"Doesn't matter," Vic brushed off the question and turned back to the darkness of the van's rear. She drew the scarf away from her face and sneered. "Just get us outta here."

***

Trevor didn't hesitate at the command, and turned toward the steering wheel. Vic disappeared into the back where the drug-stuffed duffle bag sat among the heavy mounds of soiled white linens. She braced herself as the transport jerked forward. She looked down on the unconscious body lying beside the bag and scowled.

She hadn't anticipated taking a hostage during the operation, but she couldn't justify killing the only niece of Chancellor Tristan. Mama Wilder wouldn't have agreed to it. There would've been considerable consequences to face, and Vic knew that Mama Wilder, despite the power she touted in the Anchor, couldn't fend off the fury of the State looking for vengeance. Besides, the doctor was a witness, and in this particular situation a kidnapping was less detrimental than a murder. Vic had two very bad options to choose from and decided on the less risky one. If anything, it'd be safer to kill and dispose of her in the Anchor, but that would be Mama Wilder's call.

Vic crawled along the floor between the piles of linen and pulled a large, thick blanket from beneath a pile of dirty laundry. As they approached the first security checkpoint, Vic situated herself closely beside Dr. Tristan to allow the blanket to cover them both. She reached out beneath the blanket to grab onto a handful of soiled laundry, tugging it so the fabric tumbled over them. The vehicle came to a halt and she heard Trevor's window descend.

"Hey there, Trev."

"Afternoon, Freddie. What's with this rain? You'd think they'd schedule it when everyone's asleep or somethin'."

"Eh, you know them. They wanna make it feel *natural,* whatever the hell that means. How's Stacy doin'?"

"Oh, she's good. We're savin' up to get a place in the Middle sometime soon."

Vic heard footsteps circle the outside of the van: another guard. They hesitated, rattled the latch, and slid the rear doors open. She felt her limbs stiffen beneath the mound of sheets; her breath quieted. She grew acutely aware of the warm body beside her breathing slow and steady against the thick blanket.

"Good to hear! Glad you'll be gettin' outta that shithole." The guard paused and tapped on the van's siding. "Another load so soon?"

"What can I say? Patients are messy. They spill food, piss and shit themselves, sweat everywhere, bleed..."

The other guard hoisted himself into the transport. He took a step inside, slid his baton out from his belt, and prodded into the various heaps of soiled linens. Vic felt the sheets above her shift.

"Well, that's good for business, I suppose. I dunno how you do it, man. That shit's nasty."

Trevor laughed. "You learn to love it."

"If you say so." The guard speaking with Trevor patted his hand against the side of the transport. "We clear back there?"

The slow, methodical probing ended. The guard turned, hopped onto the ground, and closed the doors shut behind him. "Nothin' back here. He's clear."

Once word spread that there'd been an incident in the Ministry of Health and Wellness, station security measures would heighten, and freedom of movement would be heavily restricted. Inter-sector transits and personnel shuttles would be immediately halted and inspected. But at this moment, they were in the clear.

Ten minutes later, Trevor pulled the vehicle forward through the checkpoint into the Middle Borough tunnel transit: a long, flat platform that would draw them and other commercial vehicles through the long tunnel connecting the Dome and Middle sectors. The ride normally took around fifteen minutes depending on the time of day, and Vic prayed they'd reach the Anchor tunnel by the time the peace officers alerted checkpoint authorities.

Vic let out a breath and caught a whiff of Dr. Tristan's lavender perfume mingled with the scent of her own blood. She brushed aside stray strands of her red hair and peered at the doctor. The girl's features were strikingly akin to her mother's in the darkness beneath the sheets, and Vic's anger simmered the longer she examined her face. She'd hardly had enough to dose her with a sedative she'd found in the supply office before carrying her out with the duffle bag, and now wished she'd killed her instead.

The bitch is just like her mother, she thought. *If Mama Wilder has any sense, she'll do me the favor of letting me be the one to kill you.*

Chapter 5

"Iris Hammond."

BEEP. *"Credentials verified. Good afternoon, Chief Hammond."*

The deadbolts sealing Iris's office unlocked with a click before the metal doors parted before her. The inside of the spacious office flooded with warm light from enormous windows that overlooked half of Odin Prime's enormous solar sails. Beyond the radiant sails was the northern hemisphere of the swirling orange planet Yggdrasil. The local star of the Hel Cluster shined bright in the distant darkness of space.

The office was plain and decorated by someone with a simple eye who valued sophistication and practicality over flair. The slate walls remained bare besides framed Peace Academy degrees, certifications, and awards earned throughout the course of a lucrative career. A crimson matte Valkyrie armored suit and helmet were displayed on a mannequin in the far corner. Hanging in the center of the wall, adjacent to the office doors, was the official portrait of Chancellor Alexander Tristan. It was expected that every State official proudly display the portrait to reassure the Party of their unwavering loyalty. And Iris was a proper

Statesman.

The portrait reflected a young, charming Chancellor standing erect before a podium draped with the State flag: a single star hovering above an arch stretching across the bottom corners against a navy-blue backdrop, representing the solitary station above Valhalla's atmosphere. Many State officials who dutifully hung the portrait felt that it was outdated and stale, although they wouldn't dare admit this aloud in front of their peers. Chancellor Tristan's youthful glow and foxish charm, which had been expertly captured in his official painting, had long since atrophied and left him unrecognizable from his boyish portrait, especially after his stroke four cycles before. The last anyone had seen of him, at least in public, he was wheelchair bound and frail. However, no Statesman would ever dare point out this observation, lest they find themselves cast away to the Anchor or the execution platform.

Iris's stiletto heels clicked against the floor as she approached a tidy office desk at the center of the room. She placed her black clutch beside the lamp and ambled casually toward the windows. She crossed her arms, bit her lip, and surveyed the gentle spin of the station.

"… Shit." She breathed between clenched teeth and tapped her heel against the floor.

The intercom resting atop Iris's desk beeped.

"Chief Hammond, the initial report for the incident today has just arrived from downstairs. Shall I bring it to you?"

"Yes, Philip," Iris replied, adjusting her fitted gray dress. "And bring coffee with you."

Philip acceded politely and ended the call. She peered out the window, jaw taut, and restlessly toyed with the set of dog tags dangling from a chain around her neck. Turning away from the planetary view, Iris approached her desk and leaned forward, resting her knuckles on the chilled metal surface. She was impressed, if not also annoyed, that the investigative unit had been so quick to process the crime scene and file a report.

The doors had remained opened since Iris had entered just minutes before, and as Philip approached the office, he knocked lightly with the side of his knuckles. "Permission to enter, Ma'am?"

Iris brushed her short red hair behind her ear and motioned for him to enter with an outstretched hand, waiting for the folder. Philip gently slid the folder into her open palm and set the black coffee on her desk.

"Three officers killed, correct? Not building security, but *peace officers?*" Iris asked, opening the folder and flipping the edges of the pages between her fingers.

"That's correct, Ma'am," Philip began. Iris turned and skimmed through the initial report and examined the crime scene photographs as Philip continued. "Facility security was out for lunch during the incident. The peace officers were inside the security office at the time of the attack, we think around a quarter after twelve. The first two suffered fractured necks, and the final kill was by strangulation. After cordoning off the area, investigators discovered the medical supply closet had been raided, with Cyntrax being the primary target, along with antibiotics and morphine. There *was* blood spatter found at the scene, however none of the officers at the scene are DNA matches."

Iris flipped to the final page in the folder and stared at the photo of a young, stoic woman with short strawberry red hair and green eyes. Iris instinctively found herself counting the freckles on the girl's cheeks. The photograph had been taken at the Peace Academy nine cycles prior when the young cadet had just graduated with honors, soon to be sent to Valkyrie selection. Three small badges of achievement decorated her dress uniform across the left breast, and the name etched across the small black plate on her right breast had been blackened out.

Iris's jawline tautened. "I don't see a name for this girl, who is she?" she asked without removing her eyes from the photograph.

Philip nodded. "About that, ma'am… Multiple attempts were made to scan through our databases to locate her file, or any information pointing to her identity. However, all related files have either gone missing, been redacted, or suffered significant data corruption."

"And the blood was hers?" Iris asked as she closed the file and turned away from Philip.

"It seems to have been a match with what little information we could find about her. The suspect appears to have scrambled our internal and external security recordings before departing, so their escape route couldn't be determined. Although we believe that the suspect had assistance and fled to the Anchor." Philip paused and hesitated momentarily before proceeding. "Some information was also purposefully withheld from the report in your possession, Ma'am."

Upon hearing this, Iris turned and locked eyes with Philip as he continued. "The investigative unit discovered a weapon at the scene, and it had been discharged at the time of the attack. It was a pulse pistol assigned to one of the deceased officers and was laced with fingerprints belonging to Dr. Shea Tristan, the chancellor's niece."

The two stood in silence, his words hung heavy in the air. Iris couldn't help but flash a quick grin at the ridiculousness of the chancellor's niece being involved, and slowly turned and sat on her black leather desk chair. She crossed her legs and tossed the file onto the desk before resting her elbows along her armrests.

"And the status of Dr. Tristan?"

"Unknown, Ma'am. She was supposedly finishing up her night shift and hadn't been seen since before the lunch hour, but records indicate she never clocked out. We've spoken to a handful of witnesses who spoke with her that morning, but there doesn't appear to be any viable information on her involvement."

Iris tapped a fingernail, slow and steady, against the soft leather armrest. This was difficult enough without the chancellor's niece being involved; although the girl was not particularly close with her uncle, her involvement would be disastrous to the State if leaked to the public. Regardless of what her alternative objectives may be, today's events would be a PR nightmare for the State. Her other motives would have to wait.

"Philip, this folder will remain in my possession, and all other evidence and data collected from this afternoon will be sanitized immediately. The involvement of Dr. Tristan has made this case too sensitive for typical protocol."

"But—" Bewildered and dismayed, Philip shook his head. "Begging the Chief's indulgence, what about the peace officers who were killed? The investigators know too much already; they'll ask questions about—"

"Did I *stutter*?" Iris interrupted with a biting sharpness.

Her fiery gaze pierced through him as she rose from her armchair. The taller she stood before him, the more he diminished.

"Surely you remember, Mr. McGovern, that upon appointment to this position as my assistant, you were to follow every directive and order I issue. *Without question.*" Iris paused to let the silence hang between them. Her eyes hardened. "The doctor's disappearance, coinciding with the murder of peace officers and storage theft, is damning enough to this organization's reputation. Do you truly believe that, while the chancellor and his party are publicly seeking a Peace Accords with non-citizens, many of whom are *criminals*, that we can afford to broadcast our ineptitude? Public order hinges on our populace believing in our competence. The accords are unpopular enough without information like this leaking. The strength of our State and Party *cannot be questioned.* Do I make myself clear?"

Philip remained silent and lowered his gaze before offering a quick, affirming nod. Iris, pleased with Philip's submissive state, softened her gaze. Her disposition cooled.

"Good. Now, I expect that task to be completed within the next three hours. Inform my men that I will be out this evening and to be ready with my car at 19:00." Iris reached down and wrapped her fingers around the petite white coffee mug before raising it gracefully to her lips. "You're excused, Mr. McGovern. His Majesty Guide Us."

Philip's face fell blank as he clicked his heels and bowed, his fist pressed to his chest. Iris grinned at noticing his bow was lower than usual, an unspoken display of apologetic subservience. "May Strength Remain." Philip took one step backward before turning away from the desk.

Iris sipped her bitter coffee as she watched Philip hurry from the office, disappearing into the hall. Turning her gaze downward, she flipped the folder open once more to the suspect's photograph and took another sip. She set down her cup and took a long, steady breath.

"Victoria, what the hell were you thinking?" she uttered aloud, massaging her temples with the tips of her fingers. "I don't have time for this."

The late-night Party Assembly meetings had taken a toll on her over the past few days. Iris had earned a reputation for being competent and effective, both qualities that justified the Party and chancellor leaving her much to her own devices. Oversight and micro-managing were for the inept, after all. However, with the Party requiring her expertise and guidance when planning the finer details of the accords, Iris had found herself sitting through extensive, exhausting meetings answering questions and offering counter-arguments regarding security concerns for proposed citizen integration concepts.

The concept was utter nonsense. After countless cycles of bloody inter-sector strife, Chancellor Tristan was seeking to reintegrate non-citizens into civil society. The Peace Accords would grant citizenship to criminals and refugees within a station that didn't want them in the first place. The proposition had met immediate opposition from those highest in the Party's ranks. But Chancellor Tristan was obstinate in his old age, even though it was his own policies enacted decades prior that he was now directly challenging. The Party would reluctantly obey, and so would Iris. She had only just returned from one such meeting that day to hear of the attack in the Ministry of Health and Wellness.

Her head throbbed as she glanced up at the clock on the wall and noted the time; her transport would be ready in less than an hour. Sliding open a desk drawer, she extracted a pulse pistol and tucked it away inside a thin, black briefcase at her feet.

Chapter 6

The first sensation that struck Shea upon waking was the dull ache in her neck and back. Her eyes still shut, she tried to shift her body away from the pain but only invited more. The growing sharpness of the ache drew her further from her daze, and through her wavering grogginess she could hear what sounded like the distant creak of footsteps against wooden floors. Her eyelids and limbs were heavy as she shifted again against the soft, lumpy mattress beneath her. As she gradually regained her consciousness, a feverish desperation began to seep through her mind; her senses grabbed at whatever information they could collect, but confusion still muddied her thoughts. Her surroundings smelled of dust and old wood, and the footsteps that had awoken her moments before had now left her lying in silence.

She opened her tired eyes and found herself in a small, simple bedroom with a few bookshelves and a small desk. The mattress below her belonged to a small twin bed, which shifted awkwardly as she struggled to hoist herself onto her elbows. The room glowed with a warm light that spilled in through a nearby window and cast shadows on the bookshelves overstocked with dusty books. The room was a far cry from her Dome residence, with its smooth metallic shelves and soft leather furniture.

Shea glanced down at her body and froze, mortified at seeing herself in clothes that didn't belong to her. Instead of her hospital lab coat, dress pants, and white button-down shirt that she had worn to work at the Ministry, she now found herself dressed in a long-sleeved gray top and fitted black slacks. Everything, including her muddled mind, felt disjointed and out of place.

A plate of food rested atop the dresser across the room, with a small dinner roll and a cup of minced meat and rice beside it. She frowned and looked away, her stomach suddenly too restless, her nerves too shaken, to even considering eating.

She ignored her lingering drowsiness and clumsily climbed onto her feet. Blood rushed to her head and she stumbled and pressed her palm against a nearby wall for support. Her balance was thrown, her body felt weak, and her heartbeat raced as desperation turned to panic.

Where the hell am I?

Darting her frantic gaze around the room, Shea noticed a pair of boots placed beside the bed. She collapsed forward, grasped the boots, and fumbled with them in her hands. As she rose and slipped the boots on, her attention wandered out the window to the street below. This borough was very poor, with deteriorating brick and wood buildings huddled together for structural support. Some leaning walls had to be propped up with thick wooden beams to prevent their collapse. Shea caught sight of towering stacks of storage connexes beyond the cluster of poorly assembled buildings. Make-shift scaffolding, netting, and staircases connected the towers where countless people strolled and lingered.

Climate-regulating ceiling panels dimmed to an artificial dusk, and women were beginning to unclip laundry from suspended wires between windowsills. Rickshaws parked along the street with their drivers standing idly beside them, soliciting exhausted passersby for an inexpensive ride home. Solar propellant was a luxury few could afford. Quick transportation was offered by those who were strong enough to pull a rickshaw. It wasn't unusual for her to see rickshaws in the Dome either, since authorized drivers would often commute from the poorer boroughs, but she'd never seen so many in one place.

Shea wondered how far she was from the Dome, and how many inter-borough tunnels she'd traveled while unconscious. She wondered how, given the security present at the inter-borough tunnel checkpoints, she had passed through unnoticed. Her gaze peered out across the skyline of the borough; she saw patches of damaged tiling along the ceiling of the station hull that interrupted the displayed image of a setting sun through a mass of violet and rosy clouds. It flickered every few seconds.

An artificial sunset for those who have never actually experienced one.

Having finished tying the second boot and unsteadily rising, Shea caught sight of the wooden door across the room crack open. A tall, dark-skinned young man stepped inside and offered a kind smile. He wore a neatly trimmed, angled beard that faded up his strong jawline to a shaved scalp.

"Before you ask, no, I wasn't the one who changed your clothes."

His voice was calm, and had they met under different circumstances Shea might have found it reassuring. But she now fought off the instinct pestering her to run, and instead reached back and braced herself on the foot of the bed. Her balance had yet to fully return, but her stubborn pride demanded that she not advertise it. Defiant anger swelled in her chest.

"Who are you, and where am I?" Her voice was stern and pointed.

"My name is Simon. Simon Wilder. You're still a bit disoriented, but the sedative we had to give you should wear off within the next thirty minutes or so."

Shea's eyes hardened. "Sedative?"

Simon's smile turned apologetic.

"Do you have any idea who I am? Who my uncle is?"

"I do," he said. His voice remained calm and steady. "If it's your safety you're concerned about, Dr. Tristan, there's no need. You won't be harmed here, I promise. You're safe."

"Safe? I was *safe* in the Dome, not in this—" She gestured toward the window, her anger flushed across her cheeks. *This shithole*. "Wherever *this* is. I demand you take me back this instant!"

"If I had any say in the matter, I would. But I'm afraid I don't," Simon said.

"May I inquire as to why?"

"Mother wouldn't allow it. Nothing goes down in this borough without her permission first."

Shea examined his disposition and mannerisms, looking him over with an uncertain eye. Simon's dark skin left her uneasy and on edge. She eyed him up and down.

"Are you a refugee?" she asked.

Simon's smile tensed. "Would it matter if I was?" Shea parted her lips to speak, but faltered and remained silent. Simon continued, "Listen, I know what citizens think of refugees and their children. But we aren't sick. I know the Anchor has a shitty reputation, but we at least don't have the Ink. Although a lot of you from the Dome behave as though we do."

Shea stayed quiet for a few moments. The tension in the room soured until Shea took a breath and dropped her gaze to the floor. "My apologies. It wasn't my intention—"

"It's fine," Simon said with a sigh and an outstretched hand. His temperament cooled, and the warmth in his eyes returned with a sympathetic smile. "You've never been outside the Dome; you don't know any better. But to answer your question, I'm a non-citizen child of a refugee. Born and raised on Odin Prime, just as you were."

She took a breath and steadied her voice against her simmering anger. "My apologies. May I ask why I was brought here?"

"It wasn't exactly *planned*, if that's what you mean. I'm sorry I can't offer you the answer you're looking for. But you have nothing to fear from me, I promise you."

Shea's drowsiness had been gradually lifting as they spoke, and she wondered again how she'd arrived in that room; how simply existing in the wrong place at the wrong time in the Ministry of Health and Wellness had delivered her here. She'd only yearned, more than anything, to return home after her shift had ended to collapse onto her bed, to sleep away the past thirteen hours. It alarmed her how distant that memory now felt.

She imagined her brother and father receiving her intramail message in Apex, completely ignorant of her abduction. Not knowing that, as they watched her sing happy birthday, she'd been choked unconscious and held captive against her will. They would respond, or send her a letter, and she wouldn't be there. The thought alone made her heart ache, and she yearned for nothing more than to hear their voices.

"Do you feel well enough to walk?" Simon asked, in what she perceived to be honest concern.

Releasing her vice-grip from the foot of the bed, Shea pushed forward and stood tall. Escape wasn't an option, at least not yet. Even if she could run, could push past this hulking man and break free from that building, where could she run to? How would she know the way? It was in her best interest to cooperate, if only for the time being. To bite her tongue and comply.

"Yes, if I must," Shea said.

"Good," Simon smiled at her, "because Mother wants to meet with you."

Chapter 7

Simon led Shea from the small bedroom through a narrow, darkened hallway, lit only by recycled illume bulbs. The plaster walls were cracked, and she peered down passageways and rooms as they passed. Shea hadn't ever seen a facility in such a state on Odin Prime, where most rooms and hallways were cased in clean, polished metal, not cracked plaster and dusty wood. Distant laughter carried through the empty halls, startling her. She trailed behind Simon, uncertain and pulse quickening, to an old spiral staircase at the end of the hall.

At the top of the staircase was a single office, and when Shea entered, her attention was drawn immediately to bright flames dancing in the spacious fireplace on the opposite wall. The warmth of the fire hugged the red brick walls of the dark office and crept across her chilled skin as she stepped further inside. Framed photographs of what she could make out to be a happy, embracing family with smiling faces hung on the walls: a young black couple holding a joyful little girl in their arms. As she scanned the room, Shea caught sight of two soft leather chairs set before an aged wooden desk, and a lush green plant set in the far corner.

The sedative seemed to have finally run its course, and the

haze clouding her thoughts was progressively evaporating with each passing moment. As her clarity returned to her, so too did a swelling, righteous anger. Shea's face flushed hot as she clenched her fists and bit her tongue.

A shift in the darkness drew her attention. An older black woman sat behind the aged wooden desk. Long, salt-and-pepper dreadlocks were pulled back into a neat bun at the base of her neck. She was watching her with a keen eye, smiling. Shea glanced back to the doorway and watched Simon, who offered a final reassuring nod, close the door quietly behind her.

"So, the princess is finally awake."

The woman's voice carried a low rasp that aged her despite a lingering glimmer of youth in her face. She lifted a handkerchief politely to her mouth and let out a deep, bellowing cough. Having carefully patted her lips, she lowered the handkerchief and tucked it away under her sleeve. She cleared her throat and gestured politely to the leather chairs set before her desk.

"Please, have a seat."

Shea remained standing, silent and fuming.

"Don't let those old chairs deceive you, they're quite comfortable. It's not like we had much of a choice in the quality of our housing—this borough used to be Odin Prime's warehouse storage sector, after all. God, you should've seen the mess during construction. Sloppy execution, shit materials, second-hand and broken furniture—for fuck's sake, will you just sit your ass down?"

Shea hesitated only a moment longer before stepping forward. Biting down on the flesh inside her cheek to temper the words creeping up her throat, she sensed the woman watching her as she moved across the room. She slid into the soft leather chair, crossed her legs, and narrowed her gaze on the woman.

"I might inquire as to what purpose you have with me, and why I've been assaulted and brought here against my will."

"I'm sure you would, Dr. Tristan. And we'll get to that, I assure you. But *assaulted*? Surely that is a bit of an overstatement."

"I believe strangulation, kidnapping, and drugging fall within the parameters of assault."

"You seem like a tough girl, I'm sure you'll be fine. I mean, just look at you!" The woman gestured at Shea's crossed legs. "Up and walking around and not even any cuts or bruises from this *assault* you speak of." The woman smiled, clearly amused.

The frustration simmering in Shea's chest boiled over.

"You clearly know who I am, so you must know that what you've done to me is a dire mistake on your part. My uncle will not accept this. I demand you return me to the Dome *at once.*"

"*Demand?* Rather impolite, aren't you, Dr. Tristan? Surely you wouldn't speak to a fellow Statesman in such a harsh tone—why should I be any different?"

"I don't give a damn about being polite! Return me to the Dome this instant, or—"

The woman slammed the palm of her hand against the surface of the desk, rattling its loosely affixed pieces. Shea's limbs locked and her body jerked back at the sudden, thunderous crack. The two sat in a tense silence, gazing at one another for what felt like minutes. Shea's heart hammered against her ribs, the palms of her hands growing chill and damp. The woman watched her, grinned at the fear behind Shea's eyes, and slowly relaxed back into her chair.

"Manners maketh man, Dr. Tristan, and you aren't in the Dome anymore. You are in *my* house now. And when you're in my house, you will follow my rules. Is that understood?" the woman asked. Shea sat across from her, still silent and stiff. The woman's voice hardened. "Is that *understood?*"

Shea cleared her throat and shifted in her seat. "Yes."

"Good." The woman cracked a satisfied smile. "This is how this conversation will proceed: I will ask you questions, and you will answer in kind. It's only proper that we get to know one another before discussing business. Isn't this how you Statesmen go about conversing?" Shea watched her, brow furrowed, and said nothing. The woman proceeded. "So, tell me, Doctor, what kind of medicine do you practice?"

"Internal medicine," Shea responded flatly after a moment's hesitation.

The old woman paused, waiting for additional commentary. When none was offered, she shook her head in disappointment. "And what made you want to enter internal medicine, Dr. Tristan?"

What does it fucking matter? "I like the work. Helping people."

"And what was it that made you want to become a doctor?"

Shea swallowed and gave pause. "My mother was a doctor."

The old woman cocked an eyebrow, intrigued. "*Was?*"

Shea faltered, but took a steadying breath and continued. "She died four cycles ago, before I began my residency at the hospital."

"Four cycles ago." The old woman sounded intrigued and tutted. "How unfortunate, I'm so very sorry to hear that."

A rush of heat turned in Shea's gut and flushed her cheeks and ears. She bit her inner lip and tempered her voice. "I don't like talking about it."

"Hm. Shame."

"Can you *please* tell me what the *hell* I am doing here?" Shea asked, now sounding more exasperated than angry.

The woman laughed sweetly. "Dr. Tristan, formalities aside, let us be honest with each other, shall we?" Her demeanor shifted, and the coldness in her eyes sent a shiver down Shea's spine. "You willingly chose to intervene in a situation that did not concern you. And upon intervening, shot one of *my* people. You can see how this troubles me, can't you?"

"And who are *your* people?"

"*My* people are Shadow," the woman stated as she leaned back and outstretched her arms widely. "And I am Harriet, though most people call me Mama Wilder."

The confidence and strength that had bolstered her up to this point instantly drained away, and Shea's conviction dropped like a heavy stone in her belly. This woman's proclamation had left her utterly, desperately deflated as the stark reality of her situation came into focus. She'd treated countless Shadow victims during her time at the Ministry of Health and Wellness. They weren't shy about their disdain for the State, nor about assaulting State authorities if it meant furthering their agenda: *Abandonedin the Shadow of our oppressors, we shall rise.*

"What does your gang want with me?" Shea asked, her voice softening against the slight tremor in her throat.

Mama Wilder threw her head back and bellowed a deep laughter.

"*Gang?* My goodness, when you say it like that we do sound a bit trifling, don't we? We're much more than just some petty 'gang', my dear." She laughed and arose from her chair. "But I have no doubt in my mind that that is what the Party Assembly would like you to believe."

Shea sank back into her chair, feeling helpless in Mama Wilder's gaze. Her heartbeat quickened as a growing panic seeped through the cracks of her waning poise. The State had defined Shadow as a danger to the public good—they ran the Anchor in the relative absence of State authority. The borough was populated with refugees, non-citizens, and impoverished citizens alike. They were all burdens of the State. Shadow was known, or was rumored, to terrorize Anchor residents into submission and promote 'unhealthy and immoral lifestyles.' Shea had heard plenty of rumors growing up in the Dome of the cruelty in the Anchor, and she'd seen the result of that cruelty first-hand in the operating rooms of her hospital wing.

Mama Wilder continued. "I like to describe our organization as a self-governing body for the malgoverned. Once your shit-stain of an uncle assumed authority after Chancellor Dreifus's death, and threw out his refugee asylum policies, we had no choice but to assume responsibility for ourselves. It's not like we could rely on CoP protection anymore."

"That's nonsense! The Coalition of Provinces were spineless, selfish cowards. They wouldn't even help *us*. Why would they help *you*? Besides, Dreifus's refugee policies failed all on their own long before my uncle took power,"

Shea stated. "His heart was in the right place, but this station never had the space or resources to house so many refugees from Valhalla, especially ones that harbored the Ink and leeched off Odin Prime's rations. You can't possibly hold all of this against him."

"Diseased hoards and leeches? Spineless CoP cowards? Is that the story the State still teaches their children? I can't say I'm surprised," Mama Wilder said, almost laughing. "No doubt they believe that we should've just been left on that god-forsaken moon to die from the Ink, then? Is that much better? To be abandoned on a moon rather than in the lower levels of your shitty station?"

Shea said nothing. She remembered her teacher in grade school instructing them on the turbulent history of their cherished home. Odin Prime had been established to expand the reach of human colonization and orbited a newly discovered, habitable region outside the Coalition of Provinces charted territory: the moon Valhalla, nestled deep within the Hel star cluster beside the swirling gas giant Yggdrasil. The Coalition of Provinces spent decades pooling their resources from their scattered space stations and colonies to fund the ambitious project. Odin Prime's mission was to support ground operations, such as mining, agriculture, and irrigation developments. But neither the CoP or Odin Prime could have predicted or prepared for the Ink. The Ink consumed entire colonized regions, killing hundreds of thousands in a sweeping panic. Chancellor Dreifus was foolish, blinded by misguided empathy, and opened Odin Prime to unskilled laborer refugees fleeing the pandemic, but sacrificed station security in the process. The Coalition of Provinces, consumed by their own cowardice, quarantined Odin Prime and demanded the chancellor do more to ensure the plague wouldn't spread to neighboring stations. Supply shipments were suspended, resources cut. The station remained flooded with those who would in turn suck the station dry of their limited resources. The quarantine was deemed permanent once her uncle assumed power, and all communication with the CoP was severed. Any ship attempting to leave the quarantine was destroyed, and their station was left to survive on their own without aid from those who had sent them there in the first place. In the end, Odin Prime was nothing more than a failed experiment, and Chancellor Tristan alone kept them alive in the cold emptiness of space. This was common knowledge in the Dome and Middle Borough. All children learned this during their early schooling and grew to look upon their station's refugee population, and the CoP itself, with suspicion and contempt.

Mama Wilder continued, "No, Dr. Tristan, the State only provides services to those in their favor and leaves the rest to perish. The resources were always there; we didn't take any more than we needed. The State simply hoards everything they possess like rats: rations, wealth, security… Shadow exists to serve those who are not as privileged as yourself, Dr. Tristan, a well-respected Citizen. A *Statesman.*" This last word she spat like venom, as though it tasted bitter against her tongue.

"I take it, by your criticisms of the State, that you're a refugee?" Shea asked. She tried to imagine the old woman fifty cycles younger, crowded on a personnel shuttle with countless other workers and families from Valhalla's labor communities. Had her parents been in the agricultural facility, or perhaps the mining quarry? In the end it hadn't mattered—everyone fled from the Ink in the end, hoping to find safety within the walls of Odin Prime.

"Don't act so surprised. Most of the Anchor is made of us and our children. Besides those whose citizenship has been revoked, that is. We're all treated the same by the State regardless. It's what makes Shadow so vital to our survival."

Mama Wilder stood and walked around to the front of her desk, her focus on Shea never wavering. Leaning against the desk, she crossed her arms and smiled.

"Of course, nothing is *free*. You can't get something for nothing; everything has a cost, and I accept payments in the form of loyalty and favors. The operation you so heroically tried to cut short was a medical resupply. Had you been successful, you would have inhibited the medical treatment of dozens of this borough's residents, including children."

Mama Wilder's words caught her off-guard, and Shea clumsily stumbled over her words in defense. "Listen, I know that resources are thin and that the State has a strained relationship with the refugee population, but Odin Prime still maintains enough medicine, food, and supplies for everyone, even non-citizens. There may be conflict, but your borough still receives weekly rations, just like the rest of us. The production and distribution of medical services is strictly regulated, and if it isn't reaching this borough then maybe it's because this organization is stopping—"

"Doctor, the State *lies*! Your uncle and his Party Assembly hoard essential resources and distribute them as payment for blind obedience and complicity. Those who fall out of line are cast out like lepers, their citizenship revoked. Who do you think provides care to all those non-citizens in their place?"

"If my uncle cares so little for you here in the Anchor, what interest does he have in pushing for citizen reintegration? Why bother pursuing his Peace Accords, if he supposedly cares nothing for you?"

Mama Wilder chuckled. "Why, indeed?"

"You know what? Fine. Even if I believed you, and I don't, while we're being honest with each other—doesn't your organization do the same as my uncle?" Shea's frustration at hearing the slander against her family boiled over. "Blind loyalty to authority in exchange for a dose of medicine? Or a bag of plant meal? If using the populous to strengthen your authority over them is the way you operate your business, what makes you better than the State?"

A silence hung heavy between them, broken only by the cracking of the fire. Shea's heart drummed deafeningly in her ears.

A coy grin curled in the corners of Mama Wilder's lips. "Who's to say we *are* better than them, child?" Still smiling, she leaned off the desk and strolled back behind it toward a small window at the rear of her office. "Ever since your uncle's refugee segregation protocol, we can no longer afford to wave a banner of moral superiority. We all gotta do what we must to survive, do we not? I have no shame accepting that reality."

Mama Wilder glanced out the window and, upon observing the street below, furrowed her brow, dismayed and bothered. "Speaking of *them*..." She sighed deeply and stepped away from the window. "They've decided to pay us a visit."

Chapter 8

The muted echo of hurried stiletto footsteps in the outer hall reached Shea's ears. Her shoulders and muscles tensed at their approach. The handle jostled and turned before the door was pushed open by an older black gentleman; annoyance and exasperation radiated from his tired face.

"Let her in, Bern," Mama Wilder said, frustrated. "And stick around."

Bern parted his lips to respond, but was promptly interrupted when a woman rounded him and slipped through the space between himself and the doorway. He rolled his eyes, closed the door, and stood silently in the corner.

The woman carried a thin black briefcase in her pale hands, and when she lifted her chin to greet Mama Wilder, her identity immediately struck Shea: Iris Hammond, Chief of Odin Prime Security. Growing up in the Dome as the Chancellor's niece, Shea had been raised among the predominant and influential members of the State. She could never misplace that steeled, freckled face, short red hair, and statuesque poise.

"Chief Hammond! Oh, His Fortune Shines!" Shea leaped to her feet, her voice nearly dripping with relief.

This woman's presence sent a warm rush of reassurance throughout her body, and the anxiety that had been building upon mounds of panic and fear seemed to be flushed away in an instant at seeing her enter. "Has Uncle Alexander sent you?"

Iris responded to this outburst with an uplifted palm, silencing Shea's excitement. Her lips down turned and her eyes darkened in abhorrence. She met Shea's eyes briefly before looking away.

"Sit down. I'm not here for you."

Shea was struck silent and dumbfounded. She stumbled back and took her seat again on the leather chair before dropping her gaze dazedly at the bare wooden floor. She was suddenly deflated, empty.

Iris, directing her focus to Mama Wilder, reached her long fingers into the thin leather briefcase. A moment later, she withdrew a folder and, having approached her desk, tossed it casually onto the rough wooden surface. Mama Wilder held Iris's steely gaze as she pushed herself away from the window and stepped toward her desk.

"Iris, I can't say I'm too surprised to see that radiating face of yours this evening," she greeted the chief with feigned enthusiasm that sounded scratchy in her throat. That same cold smile rested across her face as she sunk into her chair.

"Let's skip the formalities, Harriet." Iris's tone was short, but laced in her words were tinges of exhaustion. "I've managed to do enough damage control in my department to keep this from escalating further. My assistant disposed of the remaining evidence that would've led the incident back to us." Iris gestured absentmindedly at the folder. "This is all that is left."

"And what about this one? She's a loose end, she saw everything." Harriet nodded toward Shea, not once meeting the girl's widening gaze.

"… *Me?*" Shea's heart seized in her chest. Glancing desperately between Harriet and Iris, she watched as both women grew increasingly tired of her presence. She suddenly felt very small and vulnerable. Mouth drying and palms dampening, she steadied her voice through the tremor building in her throat, "I don't understand. H-How am I a loose end?"

"Because you meddled, like a petulant child," Iris said, reaching deep inside her briefcase once more. She extracted a pulse pistol and cocked the hammer back with her thumb. The bag dropped to her feet. Her words were pointed and furious, "And by shooting my *daughter*, you've exposed her to a level of risk that does not sit well with me."

A shot of panic pierced through Shea like electricity, reaching the tips of each limb and setting her nerves on fire. In that moment, the events from earlier that day replayed in her mind like a reel.

The darkened storage room, the murdered guard's weapon resting on the linoleum at her feet, and observing the dark figure lunge at her across the desk …

Shea remembered how unexpectedly heavy and coarse the pulse pistol had felt against her palms, and the sound that erupted when she squeezed the trigger had been deafening and terrifying. That cold voice, and the arms that had engulfed her, had belonged to the daughter of revered Party member Chief Hammond.

Well, that's it. Shea thought. *I'm fucked.*

Iris flipped the pistol's safety off with the side of her thumb and, locking her eyes with Shea's, continued to address Harriet, "I can dispose of her without too much effort. Her father was transferred to Apex last lunar and her uncle is too preoccupied to notice her absence; no one would ask any questions, at least not before we can stage something. She's expendable, unless you can find a use for her."

Shea jumped up from her chair and backed away from Iris. Her wild eyes darted between Iris's pitiless gaze and the pistol resting comfortably in her grip. Edging closer to the open fireplace, she felt the heat from the flames dance across her legs and back. Despite the warmth of the flames, her heart shuddered against the mortifying chill creeping along her skin. She bumped awkwardly against the fireplace mantle.

Harriet pivoted from side to side in her chair, casually observing the scene unfold. She grinned.

"We could use a new doctor around here. We lost Dr. Anders in a run-in with the Trinities last lunar."

Iris stepped forward and pressed the barrel of the pistol firmly under Shea's chin. "You have a very important choice to make right now, Doctor." She nudged the barrel harder against her throat and forced her jaw to lift. "You can find yourself in the gainful employment of Ms. Wilder as this organization's medical provider, or find yourself in a black bag. And I'll make sure you climb into the bag yourself before I shoot you, to minimize the mess. The choice is yours."

Shea swallowed hard against the pressure of the pistol's barrel and firmly closed her eyes. The back of her body radiated from the flame's heat, and she felt a single bead of sweat roll down her neck and back. Her nerves were screaming as her hands began to tremble. The crispness of these sensations was striking to her in that moment, and she grew acutely aware of how alive she now felt. Through the cloud of manic fear muddying her thoughts, of her indignation at being kidnapped and held against her will, what became clear in that present moment was that she wanted to live. The realization had come from somewhere dark and primal deep inside her, and the words burst from her chest like a wild animal.

"Fine!" she shouted, choking down the tears cresting from her closed eyes. "Fine, I'll do it! Just, please don't kill me!"

"Wise choice, Doctor. I'd hate to waste all of that State-sponsored medical training." Iris lowered the pistol and turned away. She switched the weapon back to safe before uncocking the pistol's hammer. "Should you feel the need to renege on our agreement, I shall use the evidence in that folder to prosecute you as an accessory to crimes against the State and publicly execute you myself. Your body will hang from the Mourning Tower until you're nothing but bones. Do you understand me?"

Shea heard the words that Iris had spoken, but they sounded muted and muffled in her ringing ears. The adrenaline that had fueled her body until that point was beginning to wane, and an unexpected dizziness spread through her mind like a creeping fog. She anticipated her knees buckling at any moment and reached up to brace herself against the mantle. Lowering her gaze to the floor, she sensed her breath quickening to suppress the nausea suddenly edging up her throat.

Harriet grinned with satisfaction. "Bern, please escort the good doctor back to her room. Inform Simon that she will be staying with us until further notice. Ask that he keep an eye on her for the next couple days to ensure she's taken care of."

"Yes, Ms. Wilder." Bern, the older black gentleman still standing by the door, complied with a simple nod and moved toward Shea. He placed his hands gently on her shoulders to steady her wavering balance.

"It's alright, now. Come on." Bern's voice was calm and reassuring, but in her current state his kindness fell on deaf ears. She didn't fight or struggle; she had neither the strength nor the conviction to do either. Instead, Shea was led like a helpless child across the room and out the office door. She hadn't looked back once at either woman as she exited, but she shuddered at Harriet's throaty chuckle as the door closed behind her.

Chapter 9

"You're a real cunt, Iris." Harriet's chuckle was harsh and gruff.

Iris rolled her eyes as she lowered herself onto one of the leather chairs, "I don't make threats unless I am willing to follow through with them. I wouldn't have hesitated to take her out, but now I have a silent witness and you have a new doctor. A fucked-up win-win for both of us."

Iris reached down and slid the pistol back into her brief-case before leaning back into the chair. She hesitated for a second, breathed against a brief pang of guilt, then let the moment pass. She hadn't ever thought she'd have to interact with Shea Tristan again, especially after the events that had transpired four cycles ago. Iris's actions that day hadn't weighed on her conscious, and seeing Dr. Tristan again certainly wouldn't change that. She remembered the distant, horrified look in Dr. Lilly Tristan's eyes, and the crimson staining the slick white bathtub. She brushed the memory aside.

Harriet's grin faded, and she tapped her finger anxiously against the closed folder. "Why were your officers there? We've done this operation countless times without a single complication. What's changed?"

Iris's jaw tightened. "They weren't *mine*. Those officers borrowed ministry guard uniforms and were in an area that was supposed to be clear of personnel. I don't know who directed them to take that action, or why."

"That makes me uncomfortable," Harriet said. A low wheeze in her chest suddenly erupted into a hoarse, deep coughing fit. She withdrew her handkerchief and hastily covered her mouth as the fit took its course.

Iris observed Harriet without saying a word. This hadn't been the first time she'd seen Harriet's coughing outbursts. As the fit subsided, Harriet wiped her lips and hurriedly tucked the cloth away again. Iris noted what appeared to be splotches of red against the white cloth, and noticed herself frowning.

Iris retrieved her briefcase and rose from her chair. "I'll handle it as much as I can in my department. I'll do what I can, especially with all this Peace Accords business they're dragging me into."

Harriet chuckled. "What a fucking joke. Peace Accords, my ass. Any idea what that Party of yours is up to?"

Iris glanced across the desk with a sternness in her eye. "Not fully. They're looking to reintegrate non-citizens but disagree on the process. And I don't fault you for your skepticism, especially after what you've experienced. From what I've seen during my sessions with them, the intent appears to be genuine—either that, or they've upped their bullshitting game."

"I'll believe that sack of shit when I see it for myself, my dear." Harriet's grin tightened. "What the State says, and what they actually end up *doing*, tend to be quite different from my cozy lil' corner of the station. I've seen first-hand the sincerity of State promises."

"Yes, well, I suppose we both have, haven't we? But as I said, I will do what I can. In the meantime, make sure you hold up your end of this bargain." Iris turned and began walking toward the door, but slowed to a stop. "If our arrangement becomes compromised, Harriet, I will do what I must to protect my child. Just as I'm sure you would."

Harriet narrowed her gaze on Iris, her smile waning. "Of course. I'd expect nothing less."

Iris nodded and turned again to leave. Harriet leaned forward and took the folder into her hands.

"One more thing, Iris, before you go. I find it hard to threaten Shea with a conviction from what I've seen in these documents. There's no evidence in here linking Shea to the crime scene."

Iris glanced over her shoulder. She grinned. "Yes. But she doesn't know that, does she?"

She exited and rounded down the spiral staircase. Upon stepping into the congregational space, she felt a heated gaze following her. She turned and noticed a figure standing near a pillar, arms crossed and brooding. Iris hesitated for a moment, unsure and disarmed, before stepping toward them.

"Victoria, I—"

The figure broke off and hurried down the nearby basement staircase, leaving Iris alone in silent stillness. Iris lingered for only a few moments, regained her composure, and exited the church.

Iris left Shadow's headquarters as darkness overcame the borough. The narrow street was all but empty except for a few meandering pedestrians, however they were too busy with their own lives to bother with her. Her sleek black transit vehicle remained parked on the curb between two dilapidated rickshaws. A tall, stocky driver in a suit opened the back passenger-side door when Iris approached. He offered her a quiet, knowing nod before closing the door politely behind her.

"You've been busy today, Hammond," a man's voice greeted Iris as the door behind her shut.

Startled, Iris turned to see a gray-haired black gentleman, dressed in a dark blue tailored suit, smiling back at her from across the seating compartment. Her steeled expression and eyes softened with a warm smile that stretched across her lips.

"Jefferson, I didn't expect to see you so soon."

He reached his hand out to her. She took it and squeezed, grazing her thumb against his wrist. "Your face is a welcome sight, as always."

Jefferson offered a reassuring smile before gently squeezing her hand in return, then leaned back in his seat. His eyes lifted toward the office window. "How's Harriet holding up?"

"Oh, you know, as calculating and charming as ever. Although that cough of hers is getting worse each time I meet with her. We may need to arrange for her to see another specialist."

Jefferson scoffed. "She's too stubborn for that. She's always hated doctors; you should've heard her verbally abuse the doctor delivering Simone. Poor guy needed a drink after that night." He smiled, then grew serious. "I assume you handled the situation?"

Iris melted back against the seat. "Victoria is safe, for now. Harriet can use the doctor, so that's one less loose end we'll have to cover. What I find myself hung up on is who directed those peace officers to go undercover in the first place."

"That, I can help with." Jefferson reached into an open briefcase at his feet and withdrew a black folder. "Seems someone within your office got a tip and went behind your back, ordering an undercover operation."

Iris cautiously took the folder from him, frowning. "You know all of this *already*? I must say, Jefferson, you continue to impress me."

"I'm good at what I do."

Iris opened the folder and scanned the documents in silence.

"How certain are you of this information?" she asked.

"Absolutely certain."

Iris turned forward to her driver on the other side of the shaded glass pane. Any softness in her demeanor while speaking with Jefferson had turned rigid and taciturn. "William, please take us back to the Dome. We have an errand to run."

***

Philip McGovern left his office late. He'd followed Chief Hammond's directives and put in the extra-long hours to ensure that the assault on the Ministry of Health and Wellness earlier that day was expunged from any official record. The detectives had to be spoken to, reassured that their case would continue under more sensitive, careful supervision. They weren't pleased, but they had little choice but to accept the order.

Philip wondered how those detectives would've reacted if

they had known their collected and organized evidence now burned in the facility's garbage disposal, soon to be released with the other stations' trash into the emptiness of space. He hated doing it, cringed at each shred of evidence that curled in the hot furnace, but in the end he valued his career far too much to challenge his boss.

Philip blinked his tired eyes and shifted his shoulders as he walked down the narrow sidewalk in the darkened streets of the Dome. The enormous blood-orange gas giant swirled and turned far above him through the glass-domed ceiling. His residential sector was close to the inter-borough checkpoint, and he hadn't the spare change for a rickshaw. His feet and back ached, and he began to quietly curse to himself when a black transit vehicle pulled up alongside him. Philip jerked back, startled.

"Mr. McGovern," Iris greeted him warmly as her window descended. "Are you on your way home?" She was smiling at him in a way he hadn't seen before, and seeing it now made him nervous.

"Yes ma'am, I am." He glanced around, ensuring they were alone. His voice quieted when he leaned toward her. "It's taken some time, but I've completed the task you requested."

Iris opened the door and slid over. "Outstanding work. Why don't I offer you a ride home? It's the least I can do for all the hard work you've done for me today."

"I don't want to inconvenience you, ma'am."

"Nonsense, it's no inconvenience at all. I must insist, since your late hours today are my fault to begin with." Iris's voice spoke with an unusual charm that he had not heard before.

"Thank you, Chief Hammond. That's very kind of you. His Fortune Shines."

"It's nothing," Iris responded with a warm smile and a dismissive wave of her hand. "It's the least I can do."

Looking around, he begrudgingly agreed and stepped into the vehicle. Shutting the door behind him, Philip noticed Jefferson sitting in the front seat and felt his heart drop. The vehicle doors locked.

The three sat in silence as the vehicle pulled away from the curb and drove down the empty street. Philip glanced around nervously and noticed the black folder resting on Iris's lap. He'd already walked most of the way home; it was only supposed to be a short drive down the road to his apartment complex. However, when his stop arrived, the vehicle did not come to a halt. The driver maintained his course and continued until making a left turn down an obscured alleyway along the sector's hull.

"Ma'am, my apartment—"

"Philip, you and I are due for an honest conversation." Iris's tone was flat and cold. The vehicle drew to a halt in the darkness of the alley. The doors unlocked, and Jefferson and the driver exited.

The door beside Philip swung open. "Wait, what's goi—" Philip's shouts cut short when Jefferson reached inside, grabbed him by the collar, and dragged him out kicking. The driver politely opened Iris's door and offered his employer a hand. Philip flailed against Jefferson's grasp as Iris graciously took her driver's hand and calmly exited the vehicle. She adjusted her dress.

Jefferson reached back and struck Philip in the jaw, knocking him to the ground. Iris reached into her briefcase and withdrew her pulse pistol. She shook her head and wagged the pistol disapprovingly.

"Tsk tsk, Philip. You have made me sorely regret my appointment of you as my assistant."

Philip cupped his aching jaw with his trembling palm. He spat a wad of blood onto the pavement. "Chief Hammond, please, I—"

"Who got to you, Philip?" Iris asked, calmly pacing back and forth from one side of the alley to the other. "Not like it matters much, not anymore at least. We already know that it was you who forged my signature ordering the undercover sting operation in the hospital. That it was you who went around behind my back."

Sweat dampened the terrified man's brow. He stared up at her, desperate and pleading, and fumbled over his words. "Chief Hammond, I'm sorry, I—"

Iris reached back and cracked the side of her pistol against his cheek with one hard swing of her arm. He cried out and cradled his bleeding face. "Sorry doesn't cut it, you pathetic weasel!"

"I can explain! P-please!" His lip trembled as he spoke.

"Oh, you'd better explain. Or the next few minutes are going to be very uncomfortable for you."

"If I tell you everything, will you let me live?"

Iris laughed. "You aren't exactly in any position to negotiate, are you?"

Philip took a long, forced breath and lifted his frightened gaze at her. "I was walking home alone from dinner with some friends last lunar when a man stopped me. I thought he was going to mug us or something. He looked a bit rough, you see, beaten up a bit. He definitely didn't look like he belonged in the Dome... but he somehow knew my name, knew that I was your assistant."

Iris narrowed her eyes. "Did you get this man's name?"

"Robert. Robert Bunker," Philip said.

"I know that name," Jefferson said. "He's a Trinity operative."

"Yes, him!"

Jefferson turned to Iris with an unsure look in his eyes. "They found him dead last week—hanged himself in his apartment. Left a note talking about a bad breakup with his girl."

Philip glanced back at him with a sneer. "Yeah, well he wasn't fucking dead when he came up to me, okay?" He returned his attention to Iris. "He knew that I worked for you. I don't know how, but he did. He said he had some valuable information to share with me, information that was vital to the security of the State, to all of Odin Prime, but that I had to swear to keep the information to myself—away from you."

"What kind of information?" Iris asked, her demeanor growing colder.

"He gave me the name of a State-contracted laundryman, said that he was the mover in illegal Shadow supply runs. He warned me that Shadow was planning to tamper with the hospital's medicinal stock during their next drop-off to incite panic in the Dome. Something about a power-move to destabilize the State."

Iris and Jefferson exchanged a quick glance.

"But he was a Trinity. There are POs everywhere in the Middle Borough, with established offices and liaisons between his organization and ours. He could've easily just brought this up to them instead of tracking your scrawny ass down," Jefferson said.

"Not unless our boy here, someone who knows my signature better than anyone else, was convinced that that wasn't a viable option," Iris stated flatly, still staring at him. "Isn't that right, Mr. McGovern?"

Philip refused to meet her gaze, and chose instead to look away down the alley. "He said… that your loyalties didn't lie with the Party Assembly, and that you had spies everywhere throughout the force. That as a prior Valkyrie commander, you were planning a coup to overthrow Chancellor Tristan with Shadow's help." He turned his attention back to Jefferson with a hardened eye. "Robert said the POs couldn't be trusted, that *you* couldn't be trusted. And that's why he came to me."

"And you just *believed* him? Didn't question his motives or his sources?" Jefferson asked.

"If you'd seen the look on this guy's face, the desperation, the *fear*…" Philip frowned and shook his head. "He was convincing. *Very* convincing. But I wanted to be sure, so I sent out a BOLO for the laundryman. They stopped and interrogated him. It didn't take long to break him. We got the date of his next scheduled visit at the hospital."

"Is that when you decided to forge my signature authorizing an undercover sting operation during that next visit? An effort on your part, I must emphasize, that left three good peace officers dead," Iris said.

Philip began to cry. His sobs were quiet, muted in his throat. "I thought… I thought I was doing the right thing, I swear. I thought I was doing what was best for the State."

"You should've come to me after that operative approached you, Philip," Iris said, her voice tinged with a hint of sadness and disappointment. "You could've prevented all of this from happening. Those officers would still be alive; Dr. Tristan would be sleeping safe and sound at her home…"

"I know, I'm sorry," Philip cried. He cupped his hands over his face and wept harder.

"Who else knows about this, Philip?" Iris asked. "Who else did you tell?"

Philip choked against his tears and shook his head. "N-nobody, I swear! Please forgive me, I'm so sorry."

"I know you are."

Iris glanced up at Jefferson, who offered her a knowing nod. She raised the pistol and squeezed the trigger, releasing a single shot into Philip's left temple. His body fell hard onto the cement as the echo of the gunshot ricocheted down the alley.

***

The driver and Jefferson immediately sprang into action, swiftly stepping in to grab Philip's limp arms and legs. Iris popped the trunk of the transit vehicle, lined entirely with a large black plastic sheet, before the two men tossed the lifeless body in. As Iris and Jefferson stepped back inside the seating compartment, the driver removed a bottle of bleach from the back of the trunk and slammed it shut. As he strolled around toward his door, he popped the top of the bottle and doused its components over Philip's spilled blood on the pavement. The driver slipped back into the vehicle, turned over the engine, and drove out of the alleyway.

Iris and Jefferson sat in a heavy, tense silence for a while as the transit vehicle drove out toward the residential neighborhood.

"I don't like this," Jefferson said.

69

Iris scoffed and shook her head. "No. Nor do I." She took a breath and tapped her finger against her kneecap. "Someone knows just enough information to link us with Shadow. But this nonsense about a coup… it's dangerous. I can't see Harriet making a move against the State, even with my support. It's not only insane, it's suicidal. But a rumor like… People have been hung from the Mourning Tower for less."

"Harriet would never make that kind of move. She's content lording over the Anchor, and she would die before putting Simone in that much danger. Anything above occasional disruptive operations that benefit her organization would draw unwelcome attention from the POs, and she doesn't want that."

"Then where the hell did that Trinity get that idea from?" Iris asked.

Jefferson shrugged. "Not like we can question him about that, can we? The dude hanged himself after he spoke with our boy."

"I'm sure he did, but I highly doubt he was the one to kick away the chair," Iris scoffed. "No doubt to cover the tracks of whoever is behind this fucking train wreck."

"Maybe it was Rubio. The Trinities could stand to benefit from Shadow's misfortune. I mean, it's pretty ballsy to make accusations like that against a Valkyrie, especially a prior commander. But perhaps he wanted a reason to push the State against Shadow to consolidate some more power for himself. Eliminate the competition and swoop in?"

"It's possible. But how would he know about our agreement with Harriet? Rubio wouldn't know shit about my loyalties. We've been careful." Iris anxiously bit her inner lip too hard and tasted the slightest bitterness of blood against her tongue. "Regardless, someone out there knows more than they should, and that makes me uncomfortable."

Jefferson's jaw grew taut. "So what's your plan then, Hammond? How do you want to handle this mess?"

"Harriet needs to know that she's got a snitch in her ranks, but we should wait until we have more concrete information. And we need a change in strategy, a drastic one…" Iris's voice trailed off as her eyes gazed out of the passenger side window. "Our agreement with Harriet has worked up until now but I'm not so sure it will work for very much longer after this setup, for either of our children."

"I agree. So what do we do?"

Iris turned her attention back to Jefferson and frowned. She found herself fiddling with the dog tags around her neck, and steeled herself. "We must get our children off Odin Prime. At the end of the day, when whoever is orchestrating this makes their final move, we must ensure that our children aren't here to see it."

Chapter 10

Shea awoke the following morning with sore, puffy eyes. She'd sobbed for hours into her pillow until exhaustion overcame her and she fell into a restless sleep. When she opened her eyes, she couldn't bear to even lift her head from the mattress. She merely stared ahead at the empty chair beside the dresser and longed for the Dome, for the life and peace she'd been torn from. There was a hollowness that ached in her chest, a helplessness she'd never felt before.

She eventually rose from bed and found clean clothes in the bedroom's dresser. She changed, washed her face in the small attached washroom, and peeked out the door to find a cold, stale breakfast plate waiting for her: nearly burnt toast, two hard-boiled eggs, and a mug of chilled mint tea. She had half a mind to leave it there, but the eager growl from her belly overcame her bitter spite.

She'd nearly finished her breakfast when an anxious rapping knocked on her door. A young, energetic girl waited impatiently on the other side, no older than fifteen, with long, dark hair pulled back in a high ponytail. Her smile was wide and eager as she fidgeted from side to side. She was at first excited, then suddenly struck with an unsure perplexity when her eyes fell on Shea.

"You look younger than I thought you'd be. Taller, too," she said. She outstretched her hand in greeting, and Shea reluctantly took it. "The name's Theresa, I'm Tony's lil' sis. You haven't met him yet but there's no rush to, he's sort of an ass. I'm here to show you around."

Shea acquiesced. Theresa escorted her to the organization's medical room, which was nestled in the facility's lower levels. During their brief walk, Theresa offered her an enthusiastic, abridged tour of the building. It didn't take long, wandering down the creaky hall and down the spiral staircase, for Shea to recognize that Shadow's headquarters had been established inside a makeshift church.

Religious diversity was disruptive to social order and detrimental to Odin Prime's cohesion. Long before Shea was born, her uncle had assumed authority and banned all faiths not adhering to the State's new official, unifying faith. Their mysterious deity had no name other than "The Patriarch," and his strength guided them through the turmoil of Ink-ridden refugees and political strife. There were no formal gatherings, no religious rites other than personal prayers and public adoration, but it was enough to bring their people together in a common belief. It took less than two cycles of arrests and public executions for heathen fanatics and their leaders to submit to her uncle's policies. It had all been for the greater good; in the end, their unity gave them strength. All children in the Dome and the Middle Borough grew up muttering their nightly prayers to the Patriarch, and greeted each other with a request for his majesty and strength. Shea was no exception, and touring the church left her with a sense of unease.

The scent of wood and dust kicked up from the creaking floor and drifted in the air as they stepped into the congregational space. Rows of pews stretched along both sides of the room, and an old tattered carpet trailed down the middle between them. She raised her eyes to the ceiling and noticed the hanging, cobwebbed chandeliers with electric candles, some missing their bulbs.

Shea couldn't help but feel constricted within the church's walls. She glanced back toward the entrance of the church and found Bern sitting on a stool, reading a book with an electromagnetic rifle propped against his hip. He guarded a pair of locked, reinforced steel doors, with a narrow sliding hatch at eye-height to peer outside. His eyes, still sharp and keen despite his age, lifted from the pages of his book to meet hers. She looked away and trotted to catch up with Theresa.

"It's like you've never seen a church before."

"I haven't," Shea replied. "We don't have them in the Dome."

"Well, we don't have them here anymore, either. I guess the refugees built this when the neighborhood was set up, not that it mattered much. Works for us, though."

As she passed through the congregational space, her gaze lingered on the rows of tall, blacked-out windows. The edges from the pane-glass window art reached out from underneath the thick black paint, showing only an obscure account of what was hidden beneath. Shea couldn't help but find it haunting, like desperate fingers grasping and groping from the darkness.

***

"Okay, Jacob, say *aah*."

Shea parted and widened her lips with dramatic exaggeration before sticking out her tongue. The young boy seated in an old upholstered chair before her struggled to comply with her instructions through bouts of giggles. He imitated her and stuck out his own tongue, choking back his laughter.

"Oh my *goodness*, look at that snake tongue of yours!" Her hand clutched frightfully to her chest before she leaned forward toward him. She peeked down his small mouth and at the back of his throat with a flashlight, a flat wooden depressor holding down the boy's wiggly tongue.

This was Shea's fourth appointment of the afternoon. Hours had passed since her tour with Theresa, and the helplessness that had filled the cavity in her chest had gradually transformed into a righteous fury. She awoke weighted down by her dread that now burned quietly in anger. Fighting back wasn't an option, nor was negotiation with Harriet. She had to escape and return to the Dome. She needed to reach her uncle, to tell him about the treachery of his chief of security, and the vileness of the Anchor.

It would have to wait. A successful escape required careful, concise planning. It was imperative that she be patient and cooperate for the time being. She could at least provide services to those who needed it in the meantime.

Clicking off the flashlight, Shea slid the tongue depressor from the boy's mouth and sat up to offer him a kind smile. "Good news, Jacob, there aren't any *gnomes* living behind your molars."

She winked at him as he slipped back into a fit of giggles. Her smile weighed heavily across her face, and as she turned away to toss the depressor into the trash, it lingered for only a moment before dwindling.

Her heart sank heavy in her chest when she recounted the boy's symptoms; Jacob suffered from prolonged malnutrition. She'd noticed his condition immediately when he entered her examination room on weak, unsteady legs. He was far too short and underweight for a child his age, and after a short physical examination Shea had seen the symptoms in his swollen and tender gums and decaying teeth. Each of her patients that afternoon had suffered the same ailment, and all had been children.

Shea was relieved to find that her modest medical examination room was surprisingly adequate. That is, for being in the lower levels of an old, run-down Anchor church. It was small, no larger than her bedroom on the top floor, but she found it was well-stocked with the medical supplies she needed. The Cyntrax stolen from the hospital the day before was now stocked inside her cabinets, and she regrettably found herself repeatedly reaching inside to retrieve a fresh vial. Slipping her hand inside the cabinet, she plucked up another vial, silently tamping down on her simmering irritation.

"Your mama works in the agro-spheres, huh?" Shea asked. The little boy nodded. "What does she do there?"

Jacob shrugged. "I dunno. She's dirty when she comes home. And tired. But she sometimes brings me things."

"Oh yeah? Like what?"

"She got me an apple last week," Jacob said with an excited bounce. "I wanted to share with Mama but she said she didn't want any."

Shea strained to smile. "Well, that sounds like a pretty awesome present! What about your dad? What does he do?"

Jacob's smile and shoulders shrank. "Dad worked with the

fish. But Mama said something bad happened, and now I don't see him anymore."

"I'm sorry, buddy." Shea's voice quieted to a whisper. She ruffled his hair. "But hey—you wanna grow up to be big and strong? I think that'd make him really happy." Jacob nodded. "Good! I can help with that. I'm going to give you something that'll help, okay? It's just a quick, little shot."

Jacob's face twisted, quizzical. "What's a shot?"

Shea stammered. "Didn't Dr. Anders give you shots of this before?" She showed him the Cyntrax bottle, and Jacob shook his head. A rueful pang swelled in her chest. "Well, it's a special kind of medicine that helps your body get stronger. Our bodies are pretty good at taking care of us, but sometimes they need a little boost." *Especially when said body is malnourished.* "But it should help you feel better for a little while."

"What does it do?" Jacob asked with widening eyes.

Shea tapped on the bottle with a smile and whispered as though telling a secret. "It's magic." *Nutrient and immuno-booster.* "Special, secret magic."

Jacob stared at the bottle in wonder, mouth agape. "Special magic…"

She didn't know why in that moment, as she pierced the fresh needle into the bottle, her thoughts turned to Secretary Willis. The rotund man had smiled at her from his hospital bed, past a bulbous red nose and fat, drooping cheeks. They had chatted together in his lavish room, rich with vibrant green flora and a picturesque view of Valhalla, the beautiful plague-infested moon. Jacob let out a weak cough, which snapped Shea out from her thoughts. She was left staring at the malnourished boy with a sense of surreal disjointedness.

Shea had every reason to dismiss Harriet's accusations against the State and her uncle. But patients like Jacob gave her pause.

"Odin Prime still maintains enough medicine, food, and supplies for everyone, even non-citizens."

Shea was no longer so sure.

"Alright Jacob, are you a brave boy?" Shea's artificial cheeriness tasted sour through her smile. Jacob didn't seem to notice, and only beamed brighter. She stepped toward him and retrieved a child-sized syringe and band aide from a nearby desk drawer. Jacob nodded silently, his mouth aghast, and stared wide-eyed at the needle now being unwrapped in front of him.

"Do you wanna get big and strong? Like this?" She lifted her arms and puffed out her chest, motioning through various strong-man poses. Jacob's earnest smile melted through his frightened hesitation; he nodded, enthusiastic, and let out a giggle.

"Well come on, let me see those muscles!"

Jacob wasted no time in mimicking her and puffed out his tiny chest and cheeks. As he flexed his frail arms, she pierced the first needle into the vial and withdrew the clear liquid into the syringe. She switched to a fresh needle, tapped the syringe firmly with her fingernail, and sanitized an area of his thigh with an alcohol swab.

The boy's arms were too feeble and bony to administer the dose, which limited the injection to his thigh. Distracted by his own spectacular performance, he didn't even notice Shea inject the needle. By the time Jacob realized what happened, Shea had already tossed the top of the needle into the orange medical bucket and turned to offer him a generous smile.

"My goodness, Jacob, you're just about the bravest and strongest boy I've ever met!" she doted warmly, removing a band-aid from its wrapper and applying it to the tiny wound. Tossing the remnants away, Shea flexed again. "Ready to go home with your mama, strongman?"

Jacob giggled and took her hand before hopping off the plush chair. "Yes. Thanks, Dr. S."

"No problemo, kiddo." His hand felt fragile in hers as she walked him out of the examination room. His mother was waiting patiently in the darkened hallway. The only light illuminating the hall was a single string of tiny illume bulbs strung along the wall. Jacob's mother stepped into the dim lighting and reached lovingly for her son.

"Thank you, Doctor," Her voice was tired but gracious as she took Jacob into her arms. Even in the faint lighting of the hallway, Shea noticed the sunken cheeks and weary wrinkles like creases etched into her face. There was a faded tattoo on her wrist of three straight lines: the designation mark of agro-sphere workers. Despite her visible fatigue, the mother held the boy firmly in her strong arms. Shea couldn't help but notice how frail he looked in his mother's embrace.

"Of course, please bring him back in a few lunars for a follow-up treatment." She offered Jacob a final wave and smile. "He's a good kid. I look forward to seeing him again at his next appointment."

The mother nodded in appreciation and turned to leave. Shea watched them disappear up the staircase and couldn't help but wonder what favor this woman now owed Shadow for the boy's treatment. She was relieved to have helped the boy, but a part of her hated herself for enabling Shadow's manipulations.

The hallway grew quiet. She stood for a few moments and allowed the peaceful stillness to envelope her. Closing her aching eyes, Shea took a deep breath and exhaled the tension building in her shoulders, when—

THUD.

"Motherfu—!"

And just like that, Shea's moment of peace ended. She groaned and noted the tension creeping back into her bones.

She turned and peered down the dim hallway. A door stood cracked open at the very end. A bright light spilled from the narrow gap, where she could now hear muted laughter. Theresa had mentioned during their brief tour that the rooms at the end of the hall were the organization's training and fitness rooms, and that she wouldn't need to enter unless there had been an accident or emergency. Shea had little interest in the rooms at the time, but the swelling laughter threaded and tugged at her curiosity.

She could hear myriad voices inside the room, but Simon's voice carried the loudest. She moved closer and then heard two other distinct voices sound from behind the door. She faltered, and after a moment's hesitation continued on.

Shea passed a closed door on the opposite side of the hall and peered through the narrow window slot. The extinguished lights blanketed the inside of the room with darkness. She noticed what looked to be dummies propped against the far wall with machines positioned near the front and along the sides. A faint scent of burnt plastic wafted from inside. She squinted to get a better look, but soon lost interest and continued down the hall.

Shea adjusted a stethoscope dangling around her neck

and tucked her hands inside the deep pockets of her white hospital jacket. Her steps slowed before approaching the cracked door. Peering inside through the gap, she could barely make out the figure of a young, hulking man lying on his back, writhing against a vibrant blue mat. She leaned closer to get a better view and noticed weight-lifting equipment in the far corner. The musky, stringent odor of sweat swept through the door. Her lips downturned and her nose wrinkled in disgust. She buried it inside the crook of her elbow to shield her lips and nostrils from the stench.

The young man shifted uncomfortably on the mat and contorted his face in a wince. "Shit, that hurt. I think you might've broken something!"

"Tony, the only thing I broke was your glass ego. Now get your fat ass off my mat." A woman's familiar voice broke into a chuckle as Tony rolled to his side and pushed himself onto his knees. He wobbled unsteadily before pushing himself onto his feet and placing his hand against the small of his lower back.

"Fuck off, Vic."

Tony limped out of view with a pained grimace across his face. He must've been over six feet tall with a strong, clean-shaven jawline and slick jet-black hair. The gel used to push his hair back had left a greasy patch shimmering on the mat, which he didn't bother to clean.

"Yeah, I love you too, boo-boo." Vic stepped into view. Her red hair was pulled back into a messy bun that hung heavily over the nape of her neck. Despite being dressed only in loose-fitting black sweatpants and a tank top, her stature and poise made her one of the most intimidating and strong women Shea had ever seen. She carried herself with disciplined authority, and Shea couldn't shake the lingering familiarity in her voice and face.

Vic turned and glanced in Tony's direction with a cocky, handsome smile across her lips. Her sharp green eyes were striking and confident, and she offered Tony a wink after what Shea could only imagine was a response to an impolite gesture on his part.

Those eyes—

"You're being rude, Doc." Vic's voice deepened to a growl; her smile waned and slipped away like shedding skin. She turned and locked her stony gaze with Shea. Shea's heart dropped like a heavy stone into the pit of her gut, and a chill danced up her spine. Those same eyes had stared her down in the Ministry of Health and Wellness the day before, and those strong arms had lifted Shea up and carried her to the Anchor against her will. This was the Chief's daughter, who she had shot at point-blank range and almost lost her life over.

Victoria Hammond. This *is Victoria Hammond... This is 'Vic.'*

"Hey, stranger!" Simon swung open the door and greeted Shea with a warm, sincere smile. He turned and extended his arm, beckoning her inside the room. Her body was rigid, and her joints locked at any attempt to move. Simon observed her hesitation and glanced at Vic, who had just broken her stony gaze and turned away. "Don't worry," he whispered, leaning closer, "she won't be a problem, I've got you."

The curiosity that compelled Shea to approach the door immediately drained. She couldn't peel her attention away from Victoria; she was a predator, and Shea felt like her prey. What fueled her body now was a primal instinct to escape, and her tense muscles ached and begged for her to turn and run. The sweat-stained air that now wafted freely from the open door stung at her nostrils and repelled her even further.

Just leave.

But what held her still in the doorway was Simon's kind eyes and smile. His arm remained outstretched into the bright room, and his calmness was surprisingly soothing against her biting nerves.

Shea reluctantly propelled her body forward. Stepping further into the light, she adjusted her eyes and caught sight of Tony, who sat brooding on a bench in the far corner. He rubbed his large palms along the nape of his neck and held a dejected scowl across his lips, refusing to lift his gaze to meet hers. Scanning her gaze around the room, Shea observed an old set of exercise equipment on the opposite wall, including a rusting squat rack, duct-taped punching bag, and row machine.

"Sorry if we got a bit loud, it wasn't our intention to disturb you. Dr. Anders didn't mind us being noisy, so it's become a bit of a bad habit," Simon said. "I'm glad to see Theresa was able to convince you to start accepting patients today, though. It's been hard helpin' people out lately without a doctor around."

As Simon spoke, Shea's attention lingered on the predator pacing across the room. Victoria leaned against the far wall near Tony and turned her icy eyes back at her. Of course Shea had assumed their paths would cross again, considering she was the newest addition to Shadow's forced labor pool. But she now realized how ill-prepared she was for the reunion. This woman triggered every fight-or-flight impulse Shea's body could muster, and she began to hate her for it. Victoria's gaze was unsettling, and her mere presence left Shea with a lingering discomfort and unease. Despite Simon's reassurance, she felt exposed and vulnerable. In the ministry, she at least had had a pulse pistol to defend herself, but standing in Victoria's presence now, she was defenseless.

Shea froze. Her eyes scanned up and down Victoria's body when the realization struck her: the woman showed no trace of a wound. She'd been certain that she'd shot her; she'd heard it after squeezing the trigger. Yet the skin on the woman's shoulder and chest remained untarnished. There was no trace of a wound along her exposed, sweat-slicked skin.

"How?"

"How, what?" Simon asked, confused and glancing back at Shea.

"That's impossible…"

"What's impossible?" Simon turned his attention to Victoria, who was now grinning.

"I *shot* you. I know I did."

"And I choked you out. What of it?" Victoria chided, cocking an eyebrow. She stepped closer with darkening eyes and a tight grin. "You're lucky I didn't snap your fucking neck after I figured out who you were. Better watch yourself, *Statesman*—that luck of yours may not last too long down here in the Anchor."

"Okay, let's all just take a deep breath, yeah?" Simon moved forward, his hand outstretched in what seemed to be an attempt to referee the situation. He parted his lips to speak again, but Shea turned and exited the training room in a hurry. She could hear what sounded to be Simon calling out to her, asking her to stay as she rushed up the stairs toward her room.

85

Chapter 11

Shea spent that evening seated at the edge of her mattress, her gaze fixed to the brittle glass window. She watched the artificial, damaged skyline darken as the hours passed, listening to the distant sounds of incoherent conversations and Theresa's muted laughter. She closed her eyes and recalled the view from Secretary Willis's hospital room, of the cosmic scene she'd taken for granted. Shea had never believed that after a lifetime growing bored of staring out into the vastness of space, at the star-pocked void beyond Yggdrasil and Valhalla, one night of an artificial night's sky would make her appreciate her life in the Dome.

Like clockwork, Shea would hear Bern's soft-soled shoes shuffle past and hesitate by her door. She imagined his ear pressed gingerly against the door frame, intently seeking any sign of life to prove she hadn't run off. Shea would clear her throat or tap her foot against the bedpost, and Bern would be on his way again until his next visit.

During one of Bern's check-ins, Shea heard the gentle clatter of dishes outside her door followed by a knock. She waited, not hearing his feet shuffle away.

"Just leave it there, I'll get it later," she said. Her stomach growled, as if to protest the very words leaving her lips. The hunger she felt at that moment was real, but she was still determined to at least have the freedom to eat when she wanted, not when she was told.

"It serves you no good to be stubborn, miss," Bern replied. "But suit yourself." She heard the dishes settle on the floor followed by Bern's shuffling feet leaving her alone again in her silence.

When she opened the door ten minutes later, Shea found a bowl of cabbage soup and roasted potatoes waiting for her. She grimaced as she lifted the dish from the ground, her lips turning down at the wafting scent of cooked cabbage. The saltiness of the broth nipped at her tongue as she drank it, forcing it down to suppress the growl of her belly.

This is atrocious.

She gulped down the remainder of her soup before taking a bite of roasted potato. The food her family had eaten on a regular basis as a child was luxurious compared to the dish now in her hands. They'd never gone without fresh crops from the agro-spheres, or fresh fish from the fishery. Shea had never bothered imagining what food in Anchor was like, or of life outside the Dome in general. She was content living her life and minding her own business.

She finished the last roasted potato and rested the plate on the floor beside her bed; staring at the empty dish, she eventually grew appreciative to have had any food at all.

Just a couple more hours until they fall asleep, Shea thought, looking back out the window. *And then I'm getting the hell out of here.*

***

The bedroom window opened with a crack, snapping the dried paint that had sealed it shut. The old wood scraped along the ridges of the windowsill as Shea pressed it up, glancing back every so often to ensure that her movements hadn't awakened anyone. She had waited patiently almost three hours since finishing her supper to attempt her escape, until the only sound of life she could hear was her own breathing.

"Shhhh, you piece of shit," she whispered as the cracking of the wood and shaking glass ripped through the silence. She peeked her head out from the narrow opening and peered down at the empty street below. Her drop would be from the second story, but regardless of whatever injury she may sustain, it was worth the risk. Especially if it meant escaping back to the Dome and getting as far away from Shadow as possible, she would make the jump.

Flipping her jacket's hood over her head, she slid her feet and hips through the opened window and shimmied back until her elbows and wrists clutched to the edge. She glanced down over her shoulder and suddenly grew acutely aware of how high she'd been from the street below. Her blood ran cold as she turned her gaze back inside the bedroom.

Is it too late to pull myself back inside?

Her muscles tensed when she tried to hoist herself back through the window. The lower half of her body hung heavy against the siding of the church, and she felt her grip begin to slip from the edge. A bolt of panic and dread surged through her chest as her fingertips began to lose their strength.

Too late!

"Okay, okay, okay—" Shea closed her eyes tight and took a deep breath. "Just drop."

The sensation of falling lasted longer than Shea anticipated, and she opened her eyes in just enough time to see the window far above her, shrinking in the distance. She fell hard onto her left ankle and rolled into a pile of trash.

The shock of the fall gradually waned, and she suddenly felt the sharp bolt of pain rise from her injured ankle. A scream clawed up her lungs and throat, which she suppressed with a tight clasp of her palm across her lips. She coiled against the rocky ground beneath her and clutched at her ankle, tears stinging at her eyes.

Choking back her sobs, she felt along her ankle for any protruding or misaligned bones. Each touch and press of her fingertips sent another shock wave screaming up her limbs. After a few moments she reasoned that each bone had remained intact and in place. She breathed steady against the pain.

Just a sprain, no broken bones. It's the worst sprain ever, but it could be worse... now get up.

Shea rolled onto her hands and knees and lifted herself onto her right foot. She wiped the tears from her face and leaned against the wall, glancing up and down the street for any sign of life. It remained still and peaceful despite her fall. Lifting her gaze back up toward the open window, she breathed a sigh of relief that the drop hadn't been worse. She'd gone this far and couldn't turn back now, and the sprained ankle was worth enduring if it would lead her back to the Dome and the life she'd been plucked from.

What troubled her now was that she didn't know *how* to get back to the Dome. She figured any direction was better than staying where she was, and limped down the dark, empty street. The farther she moved away from Shadow, the more liberated and empowered she began to feel. Despite the hissing ache from her ankle, she smiled as she turned a corner, leaving Shadow's headquarters behind her.

Shea's gaze lingered over the lines of parked rickshaws along the pot-hole-riddled road. She limped by, occasionally glancing up at the old, deteriorating buildings and makeshift stacked connex towers. The scent of filth, dirt, and urine drifted past her as she meandered along. The stench faded as she grew accustomed to it. She compared what she saw now to her home back at the Dome, and her quiet, secure residential block and lavish flower gardens. Instead of filth, she would smell roses, and instead of rickshaws she would see a line of refined cafes and boutiques.

She yearned for it, and her yearning brought with it an unexpected tinge of shame. The people in this borough were impoverished, hungry, and sick. She'd never been exposed to this much suffering, or even considered the reality of their lives.

It's because we're citizens, and they're not. It's the natural order of things. And it isn't my fault that they live this way. The words sounded almost identical to what she'd heard her uncle say countless times before. *They're non-citizens for a reason. They did something to deserve it.*

She rested against a wall to ease off her strained ankle. She hadn't slept much over the past two days, and the exhaustion was now weighing heavily on her shoulders. Each step felt heavier than the last. Closing her eyes, she remembered the faces of the children who'd visited her in her office earlier that day, and of Jacob as he flexed his frail, weak arms. A part of her wondered if she'd still remember their faces after she returned home.

A throaty growl pulled Shea from her reverie. She opened her eyes and stood paralyzed. A stray dog, fur ragged and filthy, stared her down from across the street. It bared its teeth, drew back its wet lips, and stepped forward with a snarl.

"Oooh hey, look at you... *good puppy...*" She backed away into the open alleyway behind her. Glancing back over her shoulder, she saw a fence with a narrow, jagged opening in the corner. She returned her gaze back to the advancing stray and scoffed. "Can't catch a break, can I?"

Shea turned and bolted toward the fence. Each step on her sprained ankle drew piercing agony, but the barking and snarling advancing behind her pushed her through the pain. She dropped to the stony ground and squirmed through the fence's opening. A broken metal wire on the fence snagged on her shoulder and tore through her jacket. The serrated metal pierced her skin as she dragged herself through.

She cried out, wriggled free from the wire's snag, and pushed through the narrow gap. The dog snapped its jaws around her sprained left ankle before she could pull herself entirely through. Screaming out again, she kicked at the dog with her unimpeded leg, cracking her heel against his snout and eyes. With a third solid kick of her heel, the dog yelped, released her foot, and darted off into the darkness.

After pulling the rest of her body through the fence, she rested her head against the cold, hard ground beneath her. Warm blood seeped from her shoulder and trailed down her back as she curled into herself. She tried suppressing the pain and exhaustion radiating through the length of her body, taking slow, deep breaths as fresh tears rolled down her cheeks.

I'll just stay here for a little bit. Just for a few minutes to rest. And then I'll continue on.

Shea lay with her back against the wall in the darkened alley and wept. Exhaustion lingered in her aching bones and muscles, and her wounds throbbed with each quiet sob. She hadn't ever experienced pain like this before, and enduring it now drained her even more.

Only for a little while longer.

It took only a few minutes of rest before her breath steadied and her eyelids grew heavy. The pulsing ache in her shoulder and ankle subsided as she let go and gave in to her fatigue, eventually falling into an unsettling sleep.

Chapter 12

Harriet let out a deep, chest-rattling cough into the handkerchief clenched over her mouth. She leaned back in her office chair, inhaled deep, and blotted away the crimson blood speckled on her lips. Her gaze lingered on the stained cloth, and she tucked it out of sight at the sound of approaching footsteps.

"You alright, Ma?" Simon stepped through her office door with Victoria, Tony, and Theresa following close behind.

Harriet hesitated and then reached into her desk drawer for a pack of cigarettes. "Yes, I'm fine. Get your asses in here and shut that door behind you."

"Lookin' pale, Mama Wilder," Theresa remarked, taking a seat in front of the fireplace. The young girl scooted closer to the brick to bask in the heat lapping at her neck and back. Theresa did this each time she came into the office, and Harriet always imagined the poor thing getting her hair caught up in the fire. If it did happen, it would be the girl's own damn fault, but she couldn't help but play the mother.

"Shut the hell up, and don't get too close to that thing," Harriet replied, gesturing the pack of cigarettes toward the fireplace.

"So, this all about our lil' escape artist?" Tony asked,

flopping hard into the plush chair in front of Harriet's desk. "Cuz' I'm not gonna lie, I'm not really in the mood to go chasin' down some stupid broad."

"Shut up, Tony." Theresa laughed. "You *love* chasin' down broads, don't even lie. Especially the stupid ones."

Tony glared at her and cocked an eyebrow. "Hey, that's different and you know it. Which, by the way, I don't need lectures from my baby sis about. Gross." Theresa snickered and flipped him her middle finger, which he casually returned.

Harriet cleared her throat to silence the room, then leaned over her desk and slid a single cigarette from the pack in her hands. "Yes, this is about Dr. Tristan's… *departure* last night. It seems she didn't adhere to our agreement, and left without permission."

"Oh, the spoiled Statesman didn't cooperate? I'm shocked, truly," Victoria said through an exasperated sigh.

"Cut the girl some slack, she's just scared," Simon said with a shrug.

"Scared," Victoria scoffed. She leaned back against the wall and turned a scrutinizing eye on him. "Please, she was only here for a day, and all she did was treat a few kids. She wasn't harmed, was offered food, a nice place to stay, a good job helping people… *scared*, my ass. That bootlicker piece of shit bailed as soon as she could to save her own skin."

"Oh come on, Vic, you were a complete dick to her. She didn't deserve that, regardless of who her mom was. I don't blame her for being spooked after that lovely chat y'all had," Simon retorted.

Victoria offered an impish grin and shrugged. "Man, come on. I'm a complete dick to *everybody*; I don't know what you expected from me."

"A modicum of self-control?"

"Dunno, that's a pretty tall order."

"How about some basic human decency?"

"You know who you're talking to, right?"

Harriet massaged her temples, the cigarette pack still in hand. "Both of you shut up. I don't care about *why* she ran off, I just care that the little bitch is a liability and needs to be taken care of. Even if we find her and bring her back, she's sure to run off again."

"You want us to take her out?" Tony asked with a hint of a grin.

Harriet remained silent for a few moments, considering the option, and then shook her head.

"Not exactly, no." Harriet tapped one end of the cigarette onto the hard, wooden surface of her desk. She took a deep breath. "I don't think she made it back to the Dome yet, or even the Middle Borough for that matter. Otherwise we'd be having a little visit from some prying POs by now. Or that mother of yours." Harriet gestured to Victoria, whose playfulness waned as her jaw tightened.

"It'll be difficult for her to pass through the gate and board the passenger shuttle without any form of identification. But she could always plead her case to the gate authority, who I'm sure has been notified of her disappearance. Then it'd be over." Harriet spoke as though she were thinking aloud. Her gaze trailed off ahead of her, past Tony toward the rear wall of the office.

"What do you want us to do, then?" Simon asked.

Harriet pulled her attention away from the rear wall and turned toward Simon with a stern look of determination in her eyes.

"I want our people on each gate, both on cargo transport and personnel, watching for her. She isn't exactly difficult to spot in a crowd." Harriet pulled a lighter from her jacket pocket and rested the cigarette between her lips. "They're to apprehend her without causing too much of a fuss, then bring her to the cellars. We've yet to repay the Trinities for murdering our dear old Dr. Anders—let's see how they like having a dead aristocrat on their doorstep."

Harriet smiled and let out a chuckle at the thought of it. She imagined the look on Rubio's smug face when the girl's body turned up in his territory, and how he'd try to tap-dance his way out of PO interrogation. She laughed again imagining his lifeless body hanging from the Mourning Tower after his public execution. Her chest tensed, and her lungs seized.

Harriet's laughter spiraled into a quiet bout of coughing. She clenched her jaw and let the fit pass, refusing to permit it to devolve further. The room grew quiet and watched her as she brought up the lighter to ignite her cigarette. Simon observed her and stroked his beard, a habit Harriet knew meant that he was bothered. She drew hard on the cigarette, feeling the satisfying burn down her throat and chest, and leaned back against her chair.

Simon's face hardened. "Should you be smoking? You've been coughing more."

Harriet exhaled a plume of smoke from her lips. "Should you be questioning your mother?" He rolled his eyes at her. "Now, you have work to do. I recommend you get on it."

Simon scoffed and shook his head. He turned to exit the office. "We'll take care of it."

Victoria had just leaned off from the wall to follow Simon when Harriet lifted her hand.

"Not you, Vic. You stay. Close the door behind them."

Victoria cracked an amused grin and shrugged at Simon, who shot her a playfully intrigued look before closing the office door. She took her time walking back toward the desk, circled around the plush leather chair, and dropped down with a heavy thud.

The two women sat across from one another in silence for a few moments, only looking at each other through the smoke of Harriet's cigarette.

"Mind if I bum one?" Victoria asked, gesturing to the wrinkled pack resting on the desk.

Harriet let out another puff of smoke. "You *know* these are hard to come by. Apex hasn't had a shipment yet this cycle. And I don't like to share."

"You wouldn't even have them if I didn't sneak them back for you. I think I've earned at least one, if her majesty permits."

Harriet nudged the pack forward and carelessly tossed the lighter beside it. "Because her majesty is feeling *generous* today."

"You're too kind. *His Fortune Shines*," Victoria said through a mischievous grin.

Victoria reached out and collected a single cigarette before falling back into her chair. She brought it to her lips and lit the end, all the while never breaking from Harriet's hard stare through the haze of smoke. She took a long drag and lifted her chin, letting the smoke billow up from her parted lips.

"You gotta be careful with these things. They'll kill you,

ya know."

"Maybe. But not *you*," Harriet retorted, her words pointed and deliberate. She tapped her ash into an empty glass.

Victoria's grin tensed. "No, not me. Aren't I just the luckiest?" She took another long drag as they sat for a moment longer in silence. "So, to what do I owe this honor, *Mama Wilder*? Got an errand for me to run for you? A body to hide? A skull to crack open?"

"You could call this a polite, managerial check-in. With everything that's happened I wanna make sure your head's in the right place."

Victoria laughed. "You mean this thing?" She gestured to the side of her head with her cigarette. "Well, sorry to disappoint but the damn thing's never quite been right since I got out."

"I'm serious, Vic."

"You worried about me, Harriet?" Victoria asked. "I'm touched, truly. I never knew you cared."

"Not overly, no. My sole concern is the stability of this organization. Can't have my best operative losing their fucking cool over a conflict of interest, can I?"

Victoria scoffed. "Your *best operative*? Mama, you say the sweetest things." Another pull from her cigarette. Her eyes hardened against the smile across her lips. "You think I can't handle it? You think I was just sitting on my ass all those cycles of rehab?"

"Oh, I don't know, in the last forty-eight hours you've had a visit from both Iris and Dr. Tristan's daughter." Harriet's voice remained casual despite the sharpness in her eyes. "You've only been in recovery for the last four cycles, Vic, but who knows what'll trigger you, make you snap." She said this last sentence as she brought her fingers up to the side of her head like a pistol, tapping it against her skull.

"Iris doesn't bother me."

"You're full of shit. And a bad liar." Harriet chuckled. "You haven't seen the woman since your arrest and she turns up the same day that Dr. Tristan falls in your lap? Let's be honest with one another, Vic. You're a fucking mess—you're just better at hiding it than most."

Victoria offered an indifferent shrug. "Well, we all have to be good at something, don't we?" She reached out to tap ash into Harriet's glass. "You think that girl has that much of an effect on me?"

"I think that when you look at her, you see her mother. So yes, I do think it has an effect. And that's bad for business."

"Ah, business …" She blew smoke at Harriet. "So, this is about her running off, then? This is somehow *my* fault?"

"You couldn't keep your fucking mouth shut, so yes, it is." Harriet's words were sharp and biting. "I understand why you brought her back. If anything, I think it was the best option given the circumstances. You don't go through the training you've undergone and leave with shitty judgment. But I stuck my neck out and made a deal with your mother to make your judgment call benefit both her and myself. By you acting like a complete ass and chasing her away, an *investment* of mine, an *asset* to this organization … yes, it concerns me."

"So, what? Am I on your shit-list now?"

"Learn to keep your mouth shut or else I'll have to get involved, and you don't want that."

Victoria's nod was cavalier as she tapped more ash into the glass. "If you insist, Mama Wilder. Anything else you'd like to rail me for while I'm here?"

Harriet hesitated, watched Victoria for a few seconds, and continued. "If it comes down to having to *handle* Dr. Tristan, I'm tasking Tony. I don't want you getting involved."

Victoria's jaw grew taut, her eyes steeled. Any lingering hint of playfulness drained away. "No. I won't accept that."

"I don't give a shit what you do or don't accept. You're in *my* house and will abide by *my* rules. Tony will handle her if it comes to that."

"It isn't fair." Victoria sat up from the chair and leaned forward. "Not after what her mother did, it isn't right! I deserve justice after what—"

"I said *no!*" Harriet barked, and slammed the palm of her hand down onto the desk.

Victoria glared at her, biting down her bitter anger. "Why?"

"I'm sure you think that by killing her you'll get some closure, and I can't blame you. Bloodshed feels good if it means feeling vindicated. Hell, I've done it myself enough to know." Harriet tamped out her cigarette along the rim of her glass. "But no amount of killing will help you, dear. You're beyond casual retribution, and slitting her pretty, lily white throat won't assuage any of that shit clanging around in that head of yours."

"*Assuage.*" Victoria chuckled as she tossed the butt of her cigarette into the fireplace and hoisted herself from her chair. Harriet watched Victoria gnaw at the bottom lip of her tense smile. "Whatever you say, boss. We done here?"

Harriet gestured to the door, dismissing Victoria. "You'd better hope they find that girl before she makes it back to the Dome, or else we're going to have another visit from that lovely mother of yours."

Victoria said nothing as she swung open the office door, stepped outside, and slammed it shut behind her.

Chapter 13

"She dead?"

"I think I see her breathing…"

"I dare you to poke her."

"What if she's, like, a *crazy* person?"

"Man, you ain't got no balls. Just do it."

Shea felt a cold, boney finger press gingerly into her cheek. She was awake now, and painstakingly opened one eye to discover two beggar boys, no older than seven or eight, hovering near her. They were filthy, from their hair to their clothes, and looked as though they hadn't washed in days. The smaller of the two retracted his tiny hand as if she were a madwoman ready to bite, clutching it tightly against his chest.

"You look like shit, lady," the taller boy blurted out. "You know you're bleedin'?"

She lifted herself up onto her elbows and felt the rush of pain crash through her groggy daze. Her ankle had swelled, doubling in size overnight, and the wound on her shoulder pulsed and radiated with heat. As her sleepiness waned, she realized that it was early hours and residents were beginning to trickle out from their homes and into the streets. From her alleyway she watched a young man step into his empty rickshaw, hoist the front end, and pull it down the street and out of view.

"Yep, thanks for pointing out the obvious," She propped herself up against the wall, being sure not to press her open wound against the filthy brick surface. Although its cool exterior would bring relief to the radiating heat, she preferred to forgo making the infection worse.

"Need a doctor? I hear Shadow's got a new one," the shorter boy said.

Shea chuckled and shook her head before tugging her hood up over her hair. "Oh, yeah? That's news to me."

"You heard what happened to the last one?" the taller boy asked Shea, as if eager to share a secret.

The smaller boy scrunched his nose as if reaching back into his memory. "What was his name... Dr. Albers? Andrews?"

"Anders." Shea shifted her weight onto her right foot and propped against the wall to stand. Blood rushed to her ankle and sent a lightning bolt reverberating up her leg and back. She leaned against the wall and breathed steadily through the dizziness beginning to overtake her. She was dehydrated and hungry, and what sleep she'd managed in the alleyway still left her feeling restless and tired.

Just get back to the Dome... hell, even the Middle Borough will do at this point. Just keep moving.

"Oh yeah, Anders!" The smaller boy proudly snapped his fingers in recognition. "Wasn't he shanked just a few blocks down—"

"Okay, no more story time, kids. I don't need to be hearing about that." Shea hobbled down the alleyway, hugging against the wall for support with each haggard step. She shot a quick glance over her shoulder and noticed the two smiling boys following her, too amused to leave her be.

"You related to Lauren?" the taller boy eventually asked. "You sorta look like her. Don'cha think, Wil?" The shorter boy nodded.

Shea didn't respond before reaching the corner. She peered in each direction down the street and saw the lines of drawn rickshaws down the road, waiting to progress forward through traffic. Some drivers glanced around irritably and bickered among themselves. Others simply leaned against the rail of the rickshaw and waited it out in silence.

The garbage that littered the sidewalks and street was more noticeable now in the early hour light, as were the dilapidated homes that lined each side of the road. The hint of urine and trash still lingered in the air, although she knew that she'd only just grown accustomed to the stench. The odor was most likely much stronger and had settled into the fabric of her clothes by now.

She imagined in that moment what the citizens residing in the Dome would think of her if they'd seen her like this, standing in the Dome's streets. She imagined the downward glances, the upturned noses, and the indignant sneers. Any stranger looking upon her wouldn't see the chancellor's niece, or a highly trained ministry doctor; they would see a crippled beggar—a *non-citizen*. At that moment, she was no better or different than the two boys hovering behind her.

"Do you kids know where that road leads?"

The shorter boy craned his neck for a better look around the corner. "To one of the inter-borough gates. They're waiting for their turn on the transport tunnel ferry. You really ain't from 'round here, are you?"

"You just get exiled from the upper boroughs or somethin'?" the taller boy asked.

Shea watched as the rickshaws slowly advanced through traffic in what seemed to be a daily, arduous task of getting through the gate's security. They were on their way to the Middle and Dome boroughs, accessible only through the larger transport tunnels that carried vehicles and cargo. The gate she needed was for personnel, the shuttle transports. If she could just get past the gate and find her way onto one of those shuttles-

She took a step forward and suddenly saw a familiar face among the crowd. Tony, with his broad shoulders and slicked black hair, shoved through the congested foot-traffic near the gate. His eyes, resolute and deliberate, scanned through the crowd searching each face he encountered.

She hesitated for a moment and watched him, frightened that the simplest motion or additional step would draw his attention. There was no way she could access the gate with Tony standing in the way. He would seize her the moment his eyes fell on her, and that would be the end of it. She pictured Harriet's cold retribution and imagined staring at the closed zipper from inside Iris's black body-bag. She wasn't sure what Iris would do with her body: bury her in the Anchor, launch her into space with the burned trash? The thought alone made her shudder.

Tony's gaze lifted and trailed down the street, and for a moment Shea thought they had made eye-contact. A brief expression of recognition flashed across his face before she turned to the two boys standing behind her.

"So, who's this Lauren girl I look so much like? I kinda

wanna meet her."

The two boys exchanged a curious look. "You wanna go see her?"

"Yes."

"Right *now?*"

"*Yes*. Right now."

They shrugged, indifferent to her sudden request, and turned to usher her in the opposite direction of the gate. Shea limped along behind them, hissing and wincing at each step on her swollen ankle. She had been too slow in reaching the gates, which she now knew were being watched. She didn't dare turn around or glance over her shoulder. Tony may have been watching her, curious if the face that had just turned away was the very one he'd been searching for. She prayed that he didn't truly recognize her face from a distance, and hoped that the only thing he now saw were three beggars, one crippled, disappearing around a corner.

The smaller boy rapped his knuckle against the wooden front door. Shea glanced around for any sign that Tony had followed them. Not seeing anyone nearby, she turned her attention to the doorway, discovering a single crescent moon etched deep into the wooden frame. She reached out and traced her fingers along the ridges of the imprint before the front door swung open.

The first thing Shea noticed about the young woman standing in the doorway was that she was extremely pregnant. She stood with her hand pressed against her lower back for support, and her globe of a belly protruded between her t-shirt and slacks. There was some likeness between herself and this pregnant woman, both women having long, dark hair, narrow chins, and brown eyes. The woman's slippered feet shuffled along the dusty wooden floor as she peeked her head out to smile at the two beggar boys.

"Hey guys, just stopping by for a—" Lauren locked eyes with Shea, and her face changed. Her smile sank away, and she soon glanced down either end of the street before hastily beckoning Shea inside. "Thanks, boys. Stop by later for some dinner, 'kay?"

The taller boy looked disappointed and threw his hands into the air. "Yeah, but—"

Shea stood motionless in the foyer, growing acutely aware of the sudden, heavy silence around her. Lauren had stepped away, leaving Shea alone without a word. She soon heard the clanking of dishes and cutlery reverberating against the old, cracked walls in the hallway. As she took in a deep breath to calm her quickening heartbeat, she became aware of a subtle, lingering scent of fish.

Lauren reappeared moments later in the hall, smiling sheepishly. "You gonna stand over there all day, Ms. Tristan? Come on in and have a seat." She held up two baggies. "Now, which tea would you prefer? Dandelion or mint?"

Chapter 14

Shea sat on an old, sunken couch in the living room. The cushions were flattened from cycles of use, but she welcomed the softness of the fabric after spending the night on the rigid pavement. The scents of fish and dust lingered in the air. Her gaze scanned the room and went over each little personal touch: a small portrait on the wall of Lauren and a man who appeared to be her husband, a coffee table with a chipped flower figurine, an old book, and a picture frame resting on top. This home was old, maybe even falling apart, but it was warm and strangely inviting despite its flaws.

"Here we are." Lauren entered the room from the hall, shuffling her feet while precariously balancing a tray of cups and a teapot. Shea winced as she leapt from the couch to retrieve the tray from the pregnant woman's hands. She set it on the coffee-table and took Lauren's hands to help ease her back onto the deep couch.

Lauren took a deep breath and rested her hand over her round belly. "Thanks. I can normally get around just fine on my own, but with a whole lunar left this kid is makin' it hard on me."

"No, thank *you*, for bringing me in," Shea said. She made

sure she was settled before turning to take a seat beside her. "I'm a little surprised, to be honest. I didn't expect you to recognize me."

Lauren smiled, her eyes growing sadder, as she reached forward to pour the hot tea. "You don't remember me, do you?"

Shea took the cup of tea from the woman's hands when it was offered. She parted her lips to speak, but hesitated for a moment. "I'm sorry, but I don't."

"Can't say I'm too surprised. My family more or less existed in the background." Lauren leaned back and lifted the steaming cup to her lips. She took a sip, then rested the atop her bulbous belly. "We were gardeners for Statesmen in the Dome. Lived in the workers' quarters down the block from your unit."

Guilt sank heavy in Shea's gut. She didn't have any recollection of this woman at all. She glanced down at the dandelion tea steaming in her hand, too ashamed to meet Lauren's gaze. She caught sight of the picture frame set on the coffee table: an older gentleman with a gentle face, and a woman seated beside him with a child on her lap. The little girl had her mother's features, but none of her father's. There was something about Lauren, both as a child in the photo and seated beside her, that Shea couldn't shake—an unsettling sense of familiarity. Shea stared at the photo as Lauren continued to speak.

"My dad did the more elaborate work, usually. Planting and maintaining the wall gardens in offices and home units while Mom focused more on elaborate interior floral arrangements. I preferred the simpler gardens, though. I liked the smell of the fresh soil and flowers. Most of the station outside the Anchor is all metal, ya know? But the residents there were indifferent to us. I remember your family, though. They were nice. Your mom would make us cucumber water. She'd sometimes sneak me a piece of apple candy, too."

Shea remembered running through the halls of her enormous childhood home and catching her mother in the kitchen, readying tall, chilled glasses of water with submerged slices of cucumber. Her mother would return home from work, exhausted and worn, but would still bring around the refreshments whenever she saw a child working on the lawn crew; she'd always had a soft heart for children. She used to say that children, even unfortunate refugees, belonged in a school instead of sweating in her garden. Shea closed her eyes and recalled her mother opening the towering front door and handing a tall glass to a young, filthy girl with short, dark hair.

"What happened?" Shea asked, finally garnering the courage to lift her eyes. "How did you end up here?"

Lauren shrugged. "Mom told me that some Dome kids got bored and decided to break into some home units, stole some shit. After the POs were called, the thefts were pinned on us to keep the rich kids out of trouble. We got exiled to the Anchor after that. Citizenship revoked." She snapped her fingers. "Just like that, gone."

Shea had heard of laborers who either resided in the Middle or near their employment in the Dome, who had been exiled to the Anchor. Their privileges were revoked as punishment for whatever crime or offense they were found guilty of. Dome residents rarely thought twice about it; no one often questioned the verdict of those beneath them.

Shea was just as guilty of thinking this way, and that thought alone now made her gut churn.

"You were wrongly accused?" Shea asked. Lauren nodded before sipping her tea. Shea then thought of the children she'd treated the day before and their struggling parents. She wondered if they had shared a similar misfortune.

Frowning, Shea recalled the faces of the neighborhood children she'd played with growing up. Had it been Anthony, the senator's son? Or maybe his cousin William? Both had even had the nerve to pull nasty pranks on her growing up that left her running home with tears in her eyes. Shea couldn't recall the pranks themselves, only the feelings of hurt and embarrassment from those she thought were her friends. But it had taken one call to her uncle for the pranks to stop. The two freshly bruised boys had left her alone after that, as had most other children who were now too afraid to accidentally invite the chancellor's ire. Her childhood became much lonelier.

But Lauren's family didn't have powerful connections to call upon when cruel young men wronged them. There was no voice of authority to protect them.

"That's awful. I'm sorry."

"It is what it is. I was upset at first, hit a pretty low point. But I wouldn't've met my husband Toby if I'd stayed, or had this treasure to look forward to." Lauren lovingly tapped her belly and sipped her hot tea. "What I need to know is why the *chancellor's niece* is here in the Anchor when she should be back home in the Dome."

"It's... complicated."

"Humor me."

Shea took a breath. "Long story short, I was at my job

in the Ministry of Health and Wellness, in the wrong place at the wrong time. I saw something I shouldn't've and was brought back here against my will." Shea traced her finger around the rim of her teacup as she spoke. She couldn't tell her about the murdered guards, or of firing the pulse pistol trembling in her hands. It didn't seem to matter as much anymore.

"Ministry of Health and Wellness? You're a doctor, now?" Lauren asked, her smile widening. Shea offered a nod as she took a sip of her bitter tea. "Like mother like daughter. How wonderful, good for you!"

"Well, that hasn't exactly worked in my favor. Shadow's pretty much blackmailing me into working as their doctor now."

Lauren cocked her head and shrugged, indifferent. "Could be worse, honestly. Besides, you can do some real good here, don'cha think? Despite the unfortunate circumstances, that is. Most folks here aren't citizens—they need the extra help."

"What, work with Shadow?" Shea scoffed, indignant. "You familiar with them? They're atrocious."

Lauren gestured to the front door. "That moon etching you saw out front? It means we're under their protection."

Shea's heart hitched in her throat and left her nearly choking on her tea. She coughed and patted her chest. "*You're* under Shadow's protection? Does this mean you're gonna turn me in?" Her voice sounded hoarse in her scratchy throat.

"No, I don't think I will," Lauren said through an amused smile.

"His Fortune Shines." Shea breathed in a sigh of relief. "How did you even come to be under their protection in the first place? They're horrible."

"Well, after coming back to the Anchor, I didn't have a lot of job prospects. I was nineteen, broke…" Lauren's voice trailed off, and her eyes grew sad. "But there was one job I *could* do. Not many people see it as very dignified, but I really didn't mind it. I stopped after I met my husband, though. He didn't really like the idea of *sharing* me like that. Besides, he got his job at the fishery pod thanks to Mama Wilder, so I didn't need to keep working like that."

"Wait, so you were a…" Shea dropped her voice to a whisper. "*Prostitute?*"

Lauren chuckled. "That word has such a negative sting, doesn't it? I prefer 'companion.'" She reached out and poured herself another cup of hot dandelion tea. "It worked well for me actually, since Mama Wilder said that I only had to serve one client: this poor girl who just came in from the Dome. None of the other companions wanted to take her as their client. She was… unstable. Prone to violent outbursts, that sorta thing."

Shea hesitated. She could only recall one other person she'd met at Shadow that had come from the Dome: Chief Hammond's unpleasant daughter. She felt a sudden rush of discomfort at the thought of this charming, sweet woman being another woman's prostitute. The Morality Edict that'd been enacted by the State nearly ten cycles prior had outlawed all amoral behavior, including homosexuality. The punishment for such crimes included lengthy prison sentences or camp labor, even death for extreme cases.

Shea knew of some school acquaintances who had ended up detained after their private activities were uncovered. They'd simply disappeared as is they'd ceased to exist in her world. Just like with exile, this was a fact of life that those in her circle didn't question. At the end of the day, the guilty needed to accept the consequences of their crimes. Unity gave them strength.

She suddenly thought of Nurse Elliot and how close they'd been in the supply closet together. There'd been a hopeful look in her eyes, an invitation in her coy smile. Shea's cheeks flushed hot, and she shifted in her seat while fiddling with her teacup.

"You can't possibly mean *Victoria?*"

The smile across Lauren's face grew warmer; her eyes softened against the flush in her cheeks. "Yeah, Vic! You've met her?"

"You can say that. She's the one who dragged me back here."

"Well, don't let that steely, rugged exterior fool you. She's a sweetheart deep down." The blush tinging Lauren's cheeks deepened. "Mmm. Good kisser, too."

Shea scoffed and brushed aside the flustering image of the two women kissing from her mind. Had Nurse Elliot wanted to—

"You must be joking," Shea nearly laughed. "That woman is insufferable!"

"She's an acquired taste, I'll give you that. I remember when I first came on board, my job was just keeping her company. I talked to her, helped rehabilitate her socially. It was hard though—she was *really* damaged goods, you know? I hadn't seen anything like it, poor girl." Lauren's eyes grew sad again, her smile waned. "As she recovered, our business relationship became more... *physical.*" The woman paused, her thoughtful gaze lingering on the steaming cup in her hands. "The State did a number on that girl."

Shea shuddered at the thought of two women being together, at how unnatural and wrong it felt. The persistent discomfort seemed to vibrate through each limb of her body, beckoning her to stand up and leave the conversation. It went against everything she'd been taught, against what the State said was best for their society. Homosexuals were criminals, deviants, and threatened the natural order. Shea thought again of Nurse Elliot. Her heartbeat quickened as she imagined Lauren and Vic together, and then shivered when her thoughts turned to her and Nurse Elliot being together in that same way. She abruptly threw back the little amount of tea she had left in her cup and placed it on the coffee table.

"What do you mean, the State?" Shea asked, desperate to change the subject. "What could they possibly have done to her?"

Lauren's brow furrowed, and she blinked at Shea in disbelief. "Why do you think they brought her back here to this shit-hole? To hide her from them, of course." She waited, but continued at seeing the confusion across Shea's face. "Have you not noticed anything... *different* about her?"

Shea then remembered the gunshot in the supply room. Victoria had sustained a wound; Shea had clearly heard the impact of the bullet against flesh. At their second meeting, though, she'd seen Victoria's untarnished skin. No wounds, no mark—nothing. She brushed the thought aside.

"Other than being a horse's ass?"

Lauren leaned closer, her voice quieted to a whisper. "I remember near the end of our business relationship, there was a house fire down the road from here. It was a nasty one, took down three buildings. Well anyway, there was a kid still inside and people were just screaming like crazy, shouting for help. Vic sprinted, and I mean *sprinted*, toward that fire and just jumped in. No hesitation, no second guessing. She used to be a Valkyrie, you know that? I guess once a Valkyrie, always a Valkyrie." She saw the clueless look on Shea's face and continued. "Anyway, a few minutes go by and the entire top of the house just buckles. Caves right in." She gestured an implosion, nearly spilling her tea. "So, I think, *Well shit, this is it. They're goners.*"

"What happened?" Shea asked, unsure why she was also now whispering.

"Out stomps Vic, carrying this poor kid in her arms, covered in soot, with a goddamn *metal rod* sticking out of her gut. When the roof fell in, she used her own body to shield him. I thought she was dead for sure… no way anyone could survive *that*, right?" Lauren closed her eyes and shuddered, as if trying to brush aside the unsettling image. "I watched Simon grab that rod and just yank it out of her. Vic walked it off like it was nothing. All that blood loss and she just walked it off! Even saw her laughing afterward, in no pain at all. I wouldn't've believed it if I hadn't seen it with my own eyes."

Shea stared at Lauren, mouth agape. "And you think the *State* had something to do with that?"

"You think they didn't? I thought at first that it just came with being a Valkyrie—maybe they were given some weird medical shit to make them invulnerable? But Simon said that was stupid." Lauren took another sip of tea and gestured to Shea. "But anyway, enough about that. By the look of it, seems like you're having some difficulty getting back to the

Dome?"

"You could say that. I tried reaching one of the shuttle gates, but some of Shadow's thugs were waiting for me." Shea suddenly grew aware of her bulbous sprained ankle and throbbing shoulder wound. The comfort of the living room and warmth of the tea had been enough to distract her for the time being, but the ache now came rushing back.

Lauren shook her head, disappointed. "Listen, I know all you want to do is get back to the Dome, but… I think this borough could really benefit from having you around, Shea."

"And be held here against my will?" she scoffed. "I don't think so."

"Who's to say you can't *choose* to stay?"

"And why would I do that?" Shea felt a hot agitation building in her chest. "Shadow uses people for their own benefit, I can't be a part of that."

Lauren rolled her eyes. "Oh, please. Shadow just plays the same game as the State. They at least keep the peace and try to help us out, for a price. The State's done nothing for us here in the Anchor. They abandoned non-citizens and refugees after the chancellor took power. You've just been too close to the State and your uncle to see it."

"But, my uncle's Peace Accords will change all that—"

Lauren scoffed. "Those Peace Accords are horseshit. Sorry, I know that's a bit harsh, but I won't believe anything they say until I see real action taken. You've seen these kids, right? You see how sick they are? How frail?"

Shea remembered Jacob, sitting and giggling in her office the day before. She could almost still feel how frail his limbs had felt against her hands. "I have."

"Those boys who brought you here? I try to feed them

dinner at least a few nights a week from what Toby and I have left of what he brings back from the fishery. We're lucky. They aren't." Lauren's voice elevated with her mounting anger.

Shea shrugged in resignation. "And how exactly am I supposed to help? I'm only one doctor—"

"Stay. Stay and do your part." Lauren's words were pointed and deliberate. "Yes, you're only one doctor, but there's no one else in this borough who can do what you can. One doctor is enough to make a difference." Hoisting herself from the sofa, the woman retrieved the tray from the table. "And you need to ask yourself if you could live with the guilt of abandoning the station's most vulnerable for your own self-interest. Ask yourself if you can just forget what you've been exposed to here and continue on like it never happened."

Lauren turned and shuffled out of the living room, leaving Shea sitting alone on the sofa, dismayed and silent.

Chapter 15

Shea twisted the handle of the faucet, cringing at the subsequent screech of metal against porcelain. Placing a clean washcloth to soak beneath the steady trickle of water, she gingerly pulled her filthy shirt over her head. She hissed through clenched teeth when the fabric of the shirt grazed along her shoulder wound, sending sharp tinges of pain down her spine.

Dropping the shirt to the tile floor, Shea lifted her eyes to meet her gaze in the reflection of the old, cracked bathroom mirror. The face that looked back into hers was unfamiliar—this strange woman was filthy, her hair greasy and knotted in clumps, and her bloodshot eyes hung heavy with exhaustion. Shea reached out to place her fingertips against the mirror, tracing along the lines of the woman's face.

She wrung the hot water from the washcloth and brought it to her shoulder. Twisting her body to see it in the reflection, Shea saw the gash across her skin, inflamed and reddened.

"Damn dog."

She placed the damp washcloth delicately over the wound, flinching and breathing through the ache now radiating down her back. She knew she needed stitches but was in no position to do it herself.

Shea set another clean washcloth in the sink to soak with warm water, then lifted it to her cheek. Streaks of dirt smeared down her face with each wipe of the cloth until her skin was clear. After lathering a bar of soap into her wet hands, she flipped her long hair into the sink and scrubbed at her scalp, peering occasionally over to the stack of clean clothes Lauren had given her, near the door.

It took longer than Shea had thought to finish washing herself; she was limited by only having that single sink, washcloths, and small bar of soap. She taped a clean gauze over her wound after doing her best to clean it, knowing that she would certainly need additional care soon. Her dirty clothes remained a heap in the corner as she slid into Lauren's pre-pregnancy clothes. She could add their clothing size as another thing they had in common.

Shea stepped into the tiny bedroom and gazed at the modest crib in the corner. Above it hung a mobile, hand-made with sewn planets and stars. She stepped across and reached out to gently tap on an extended arm of the mobile. It turned lazily, its suspended orbs bobbing on bits of string. Her gaze dropped to the crib itself, empty and eagerly waiting for the baby's arrival. She imagined the baby sleeping there on the thin mattress, fast asleep and dreaming of whatever babies dream of.

"There's no one else in this borough who can do what you can."

Lauren's words hung heavy on her heart. The thought of her or her child experiencing any complications during or after the birth made her chest tighten: she wouldn't be there to help them. She'd be back at the Dome by then, working diligently at the Ministry of Health and Wellness for her uncle and the State; it'd be like none of this mess had ever happened, and everything and everyone would be in their right place.

"Think you can just walk away, guilt-free knowing you could've made a difference?"

Shea blinked hard and rubbed at her tired eyes with the heel of her palm.

"Get your shit together," she whispered, now cupping both hands over her eyes. She inhaled deep, held, and then gradually released her breath. "You'll be home soon. Just get it together."

Lauren had laid out a mass of blankets across the floor for her to sleep on until that evening, when Shea would make her way to the gates. After sharing tea together, Lauren had taken her to the bathroom to freshen up. She'd outstretching a hand to place a few coins into Shea's palm.

Lauren had closed Shea's fingers around the money. *"It isn't much, but it'll pay for your rickshaw either way."*

Shea's brow had furrowed. *"Either way?"*

"Yeah, to ride to the shuttle gate," Lauren had said with a smile. *"Or, back to Shadow's. Your choice."*

Shea'd nearly scoffed at the suggestion, but suppressed it out of Lauren's generosity. *"You're being too kind; I can't take your money."*

"It's my money to give, ain't it?" Lauren had waved her hand dismissively in Shea's face before turning to leave. *"Your mama was kind to us when few were, I'm just returning the favor."*

Shea found herself wrapped in a ball of warmth on the floor, tucked tight between layers of thick blankets. She closed her eyes and let out a pleased sigh, the warmth slowly sinking to her bones. Sleeping in the alleyway the night before had left her achy, cold, and weary. She remembered waking to the apprehensive poke from a boney finger, and peering through one puffy eye at the two boys who stood above her. She now wondered where those boys slept night after night.

Eventually, she drifted to sleep and dreamed of Jacob. He sat alone on the upholstered chair in her Shadow office, his small frame hunched over and frail. His eyes hung dark and heavy above his sunken cheeks, and he glanced around the room, eager, as though searching for someone who wasn't there. His body seized, his limbs twitched and shriveled, and his pallid skin began to sag from his trembling skeleton. He lifted his gaze, empty and haunting, before going limp and dropping hard to the cold linoleum floor beneath him. She could hear screams, distant and frantic.

Shea jolted from the floor with a start, her heart pounding hard against her ribs. She rested her palms against her closed eyes, trying to block out the sight of Jacob, nothing but skin and bones, lying lifeless on the floor. Her agitated nerves pricked like needles across her skin, and she felt the sweat on her brow dampen her fingertips as she steadied her breath.

"Fuck…" Her whispers trembled from her lips as she wiped a tear from her cheek. She lifted her gaze to the doorway and found Lauren watching her.

Lauren cocked a brow. "You good?"

Shea hesitated, but eventually offered a silent nod despite the sinking unease in her gut. Things weren't good, and everything suddenly felt wrong and distressing. She turned away from Lauren, unable to hold her gaze.

"Well, it's getting dark now and my husband'll be home soon. Figure it'd be as good a time as any to head out, if you're ready."

A young rickshaw driver helped Shea up into the covered seating of the carriage. The rickety metal rung on the side of the vehicle would've been difficult enough to climb with two good ankles, let alone one. The swelling in her ankle had eased over the course of the day, but any pressure or weight still hurt. She situated against the flattened cushion of the seat and turned her attention to Lauren, who stood smiling on her stoop, her hands resting over her rotund belly.

"Made your mind up yet?" she asked.

Shea hesitated and offered an uncertain shrug. "I'm not so sure."

"Well, I hope you stay. I really do."

"I know."

Lauren's smile waned, and she waved a hand in farewell before turning to disappear back inside her home. Shea would've preferred to thank her again for her kindness, but was sure that Lauren hadn't wanted to hear it again. She instead watched the door close before shifting her gaze to the half-moon etching on the door frame. Her heart sunk like a heavy stone in her chest.

The driver stepped forward and squatted down to grab onto and hoist up the front-end poles of the rickshaw. "Where ya headed, miss?"

Shea swallowed against the dryness in her mouth and throat. She turned her gaze from the front door of Lauren's home to the street ahead of her lined with commuting residents. In the distance she saw the two beggar boys laugh and chase each other around a corner. Behind them was a mother carrying a baby in one arm and a basket of potatoes in the other. She blinked and saw an elderly man returning from work wearing a field-hand's uniform, his clothes and face filthy with dirt and grime. These were the residents of the Anchor, not criminals or deviants; they were just regular people, working to make it through another day.

She thought of Jacob, and of his exhausted mother. Regardless of their citizenship, refugee or not, they deserved better.

Her heart nearly sank into her gut as she parted her lips to offer the driver instructions.

***

"You mean to tell me that *no one* has seen her? Not a *one*?" Harriet growled as she swiveled in her office chair, her gaze lingering on the lapping flames in the fireplace. Simon and Vic sat across from her desk and exchanged a quick and silent exasperated glance. "I assign eyes on each shuttle gate, and still nothing. Y'all are fucking useless."

Victoria scoffed and parted her lips to speak, but was cut short by Simon's interjection. "Maybe she slipped out one of the gates before you ordered us out. It could've happened, depending on how early she snuck out of here."

Harriet rubbed her tired eyes. "Unlikely. If she'd gotten out and reached the Dome, or any PO station for that matter, this place would be crawling with Chief Hammond's officers."

"Maybe she broke her back in the fall from the window and crawled off to die somewhere. Wouldn't that be nice?" Victoria suggested with a shrug and a smile. Simon turned a weary, displeased glare at her. "What? A girl can dream."

"Listen, we gotta rotate the people we have on those gates.

They've been standing watch all day," Simon said as he stood from his chair. "I'll go let Tony know that—"

An outburst of shouts suddenly broke out below on the first floor, followed by the drumming of hurried footsteps up the creaky staircase. All eyes in Harriet's office turned and watched as Shea, limping just out of old Bern's reach, barreled out of breath through the open office door. Victoria rose from her chair and reached for the knife on her belt. Simon saw her make for the weapon and reached out to touch her wrist, staying her hand.

"Easy, now." Simon placed his hand on Victoria's arm until her grip around the knife loosened.

"Dr. Tristan, what a surprise! I must say, you look absolutely *terrible*." Harriet's cold smile curled at the corners of her lips. "You mind tellin' me what the fuck you were thinkin' sneaking out last night?"

"I just—" Shea's voice faltered. She took a breath and trained her attention on Harriet. "I just needed some time to think things over."

Harriet cocked a brow.

"About our arrangement." Shea said.

"*Our* arrangement…?" Harriet rose from her chair, slow and steady, and rested her flattened palms on the desk. "If I am not mistaken, the arrangement that I had was with *Chief Hammond*, not you. You are in no position to bargain, Doctor."

"That's where you're wrong." Shea's voice steadied. "I'm the *only* doctor you have in this borough. You need me and you know it." Shea's words hung heavy in the office's silence. She continued, her voice pointed and deliberate. "Your power hinges on the ability to control the public with promises of protection and services. What will you do without the ability to provide even the most basic medical care? What will you do when the parents of dead children begin to turn against you?"

"I could find another doctor to replace you."

"If that were the case, you wouldn't've taken the risk of accepting Chief Hammond's proposal in the first place. It would've been easier for you to get rid of me from the very beginning rather than keep me around. Sure, you might find someone who could do a few stitches and use a needle sufficient enough for shots, but you won't find someone else who can do what I can. I have training. *Extensive* training. You need me."

Harriet crossed her arms over her chest, her grin widening. "I must admit, dear, I'm a bit surprised by this sudden change of heart. You should tread lightly." Harriet waited for a response, but Shea offered only silence. "In rethinking this arrangement, then, what is it exactly that you want?"

Shea shifted from one foot to the other. "I'll stay here as your doctor, of my own free will. I will stay here and treat your people."

Harriet gestured indifference. "In exchange for?"

"No more treating me like a prisoner or bargaining chip. I'm here to help this borough's people, not to further your ambitions, so you will not use me as such." Shea turned her gaze and gestured to Victoria. "And *she* leaves me the hell alone. Those are my conditions."

"And what about your life back at the Dome?" Harriet asked, now more curious than combative.

"Those are my conditions." Shea repeated. "What's your answer?"

Harriet took her time sitting back in her chair, allowing the silence and tension in the air to thicken. The resolute look in her eyes made it clear that she was pondering, weighing the options of the proposal now on her table.

Victoria watched her for a few seconds, read the look on her face, and jeered. "Harriet, you can't seriously be considering—"

"I accept your proposal, Dr. Tristan." Harriet turned her steely gaze to meet Victoria's. "Is that a problem?" Victoria stood fuming, flared nostrils and jaw tautened, but remained silent. Harriet grinned, pleased with her submission. "Good. Simon, why don't you help the girl downstairs to fix her up? The poor dear looks simply ghastly."

Simon stepped forward to loop his arm around Shea's elbow. "You can lean on me if you need."

Shea said nothing further to Harriet. Instead, she moved with Simon on her arm and hobbled out from the office, leaving Victoria alone with the old woman.

Harriet could see Victoria's anger boil over. Her face reddened when she turned around to meet her gaze. "... are you fucking kidding me?"

"Don't test me, Vic," Harriet hissed. "Or you will regret it."

"How could you just accept her back like that? After what she did—"

"She didn't have to come back, but she did. On her own. And what you're doing right now is holding *her* accountable for her mother's actions with that goddamn grudge of yours. She isn't responsible for your past or what happened."

"Isn't she?"

"No, she isn't. And you'd better learn to get over that resentment real quick." Harriet's fiery gaze narrowed.

"Because you've already fucked up once, Vic. If you go and do anything to fuck this up for me again, I will personally hold *you* accountable."

Victoria shook her head, brow furrowed and tense. "She doesn't belong here."

Harriet scoffed. "And neither did you, Vic. But here you are."

"I was different," she snapped back. She took a step back, inhaled deeply, and shook her head. "You're making a mistake by keeping her here, Harriet." Victoria didn't wait for Harriet to respond, and turned away to exit the office.

Chapter 16

Shea straddled a metal folding chair and braced against the chill on her skin. She rested her chest and arms against the back of the chair, having already stripped off Lauren's shirt and set it beside her on the floor. She frowned at the bloodied stain her wound left on its fabric. Shea felt exposed, now only in her slacks and bra. Her embarrassment dissipated when Simon injected a syringe of numbing solution into her wound. She hissed through gritted teeth and stared intently at the white wall ahead of her.

"You're gonna need to be as still as you can, alright? This'll most likely still hurt; the injection just takes the edge off," Simon said.

"I can handle it." Shea's voice cracked in her throat. She had watched him thread the curved needle earlier from the corner of her eye and knew what was coming.

"That fence sure did a number on you," Simon said. Shea noticed that she was now shivering. Wrapping her bare arms around the back of the metal chair, she braced herself further. "Lucky for you though, doesn't look to be too infected. We'll get you patched up, no problem."

Lucky me. "His Fortune Shines."

"Yeah, I'd keep those citizen sayings outta your lexicon if you're gonna stay with us," he said through an amused smile. "Nothing'll pin-point you as a Statesman faster around here than talking like that."

"Right, sorry. It's sort of a reflex." She lowered her forehead onto the back of the chair and sighed, feeling the cold, hard metal against her brow. Her body flinched at Simon's touch as he cleaned the wounded patch of skin with a saline mixture. She breathed steadily through the chill of sweat dampening her skin; an uncontrollable, subdued tremble reverberated through her arms and back as the needle pierced the wounded flesh. A natural response to pain and trauma.

"You ever get stitches before?" Simon asked. His voice was kind and he sounded particularly curious, as if his only motive in asking was to distract her from the pain.

"Once." She thought of her brother Charles as the needle eased through her skin, and she felt the gentle tug of the thread. "I was eight cycles old and was chasing my little brother around the unit. I remember being so angry all I could do was scream at him." Another pierce into her skin, another tug. "I don't even know what he did to make me so mad, but I chased him down until he locked himself behind this glass-paneled door near my parent's bedroom. He was making this stupid face at me through the glass when I put my fist through it."

Simon chuckled. "You're telling me that you, as a sweet little girl, punched through a glass door?"

"Well, it was a glass *panel* of a door, but yes." Shea couldn't help the smile curling at her lips. "You should've seen the look on his face, though…" She had blacked out after punching through the glass and woken up to her brother sobbing over her, pressing his t-shirt against her arm to stop the bleeding. She remembered the look in his eyes, the fear and sorrow, as tears streamed down his chubby, flushed cheeks. Shea couldn't remember what he'd done to make her so angry, but at that moment it hadn't mattered, and she'd immediately sat up and comforted him. The pain of her wrist and hand wasn't what she remembered the most from that day—it was the panic in her brother's eyes and how all she wanted to do was reassure him that it'd be alright.

"How many stitches that end up getting you?"

Shea lifted her forearm from the metal chair, showing Simon the faded outline of stitches near her wrist bone. "Ten. You can't really see them anymore, not unless you're really looking up close."

"Nice, very hardcore of you," he joked with a smile. "It must be nice to have a brother around."

"Do you have any siblings?"

Simon tugged on the thread. "Nope, just me. Victoria's really the closest thing I have to a sister."

Shea shuddered at the name. "Well, to be honest, I feel more like an only child nowadays anyway. I haven't seen my brother in almost four cycles..."

"Four cycles? Damn. No letters or anything?"

Shea rested her forehead back onto the cold metal of the chair. "We exchange the occasional letter or intramail, but not often. The last I saw of him was at our mother's funeral. He—" Her words caught in her throat. She swallowed and took a breath before continuing. "He was in his dress uniform. He'd just graduated from Peace Officer Academy and was working under my dad. I couldn't believe how much he'd grown since I'd seen him last. He always looked more like Dad anyway, but he has Mom's eyes. The distance makes it hard to keep up communication."

She remembered the press of his navy-blue uniform against her cheek when she'd embraced him after the service. Her eyes had been puffy and red from hours of sobbing, yet he'd remained collected and calm. He was no longer the scared boy behind the broken glass, weeping for his bleeding sister. It was Shea who needed consoling, and Charles was there to hold her while she cried.

"But Dad's been gone, working down on Apex with my brother... There's only me now. Not really much for to go back to, if you think about it."

"Well, at least I know now that being impulsive has been in your nature for a while now. Little girls punching through glass..." Simon chuckled.

"I'm not *impulsive*."

"Shea, you jumped out of a second-story window," Simon stated flatly. "Did you even think any of that shit through or did you just think, 'Screw it, I'm good'?"

She stammered, then fell silent. He was right, she hadn't thought anything through before opening her bedroom window last night and had assumed that it would somehow all work out for the best.

"I mean, I didn't *die*."

Simon shot her a look. "Not yet, at least. Ma doesn't take kindly to people going back on their word. But you came back, and on your own. I think it left a good impression on her."

"A good impression," Shea scoffed. "I doubt that."

"Well, you're at least tougher than you look, I'll give you

that."

Shea smiled but faltered when her thoughts turned to her conversation with Lauren in her living room. Shea wasn't tough. Lauren was so much stronger and had suffered so much more. After all she'd been through, all that she'd suffered. Her thoughts turned to Victoria, and she resisted the urge to fidget in her chair.

"Lauren told me about Victoria."

"Ah, so it was *Lauren* who helped you out," Simon said through a knowing smile. He knotted the stitch and snipped the excess thread from her closed wound. "With that in mind, I'm not too surprised you came back. That woman is tenacious."

"Simon, she *told* me about Victoria…" She looked over her shoulder. "Like how she watched her be impaled and simply walked it off. And I shot her point blank and she doesn't have any kind of wound or scar. How is that possible?"

"It's really no big deal."

"It is a big deal. And if I'm going to be sharing a space with her, I need to know."

"Do you really need to know, or are you just being nosy?"

"Simon, please."

He hesitated and took a long breath. "Vic is…" He lightly dabbed a moist rag over the stitches, wiping away the remaining blood on her skin. "… unique."

"Unique?" Shea scoffed, and turned in her chair to face Simon, interrupting his work. "As a medical professional, 'unique' isn't exactly an acceptable explanation."

Simon returned his soiled, damp rag to the metal tray beside him. "I know it isn't the answer you were looking for. But Vic is complicated, and to be honest, I'm not even entirely sure if I know the whole story myself. I probably know more than most here, except for Ma, but even that has its limits. So, asking me won't give you what you're looking for."

"What *can* you tell me, then?"

"Why're you so eager to know?" Simon's voice tensed.

"I'm a doctor. Call it medical curiosity."

Simon's eyes softened with sadness. He wavered for a moment but eventually broke once the silence became too unbearable. Standing from his stool, he carried the metal tray of bloodied instruments to the sink.

"You've already met Vic's mother, the charming security chief. It shouldn't surprise you that Vic used to be a PO before ending up here."

"Lauren told me she used to be a Valkyrie, too."

"Yep. Following mother's footsteps and all, you know? A true Statesman, through and through." He twisted the faucet to turn on a steady stream of water. "I guess she was really good at her job, with decorations, awards and shit. But something bad happened. It was a few cycles after the morality edict was ratified, you remember all that?" Simon glanced over his shoulder to Shea, who offered an affirming nod.

"Vic was caught up in a morality violation. The State had some kind of medical research program that they put her in instead of the… *alternate* sentence. But it messed her up pretty bad."

Shea recognized that familiar language. An 'alternate sentence' sounded much politer and digestible than a one-way trip to the public execution platform. The verbiage, once so normal and routine back in the Dome, now grated on her nerves.

"A State-run medical program?" Shea asked, brow creasing.

"Yeah, if you're looking for what made Vic as *charming* as she is, you can thank them." Simon's voice carried a tinge of sadness that caught in his throat. "I was on the team that broke her out of the Ministry of Health and Wellness, on Ma's orders. She was nothing but skin and bones when we found her. Just broken and deranged, like an animal."

Simon's gaze and voice trailed off as if remembering the images of her. He mindlessly rinsed the blood from each instrument one at a time and took a few moments to regain himself.

"We learned soon after that she could heal super quick, even being as frail as she was. It took six lunars to get her back to a healthy weight and almost a whole cycle more before she was even close to being considered emotionally stable."

"Rapid healing?" Shea pictured an iron rod impaled through Victoria's abdomen, and Simon yanking it out with one swift tug. She then imagined Victoria shortly after their altercation, brushing off the gunshot like it was nothing more than a minor inconvenience. In both instances, the broken flesh, caked and slick with blood, had sealed shut to leave her skin untarnished and smooth. She shook the images from her mind.

"How did you discover that her body could just heal like that? It's pretty remarkable."

"It was, um, a pretty gruesome way to figure it out." Simon's jaw tightened as he twisted shut the faucet. "But I don't really want to talk about that, if you don't mind. It was a rough time and—I don't really want to relive that."

"No, of course. I'm sorry if I've overstepped," Shea said, her voice quieting.

He turned from the sink and carried a clean pad of gauze at roll of medical tape. Taking his seat back on the stool, he motioned for Shea to turn back around. "It's fine. It's just—every day was hard. It took lunars of me sleepin' next to her, calming her after she woke up with nightmares, before she finally stopped. I kept reminding her that she wasn't alone." He hesitated then and cleared his throat before continuing. "Now, I don't know what they did, and I don't know what she had to endure, but there is one thing I do know." He placed the clean, white gauze onto her line of fresh stitches and pulled a strip of tape. "I love that girl, and the State royally fucked her up. I hold them responsible."

Shea remained silent. She couldn't begin to imagine Victoria as anything other than strong and arrogant. The Victoria in Simon's description seemed incomprehensible, intangible. How could the State possibly be responsible when she, someone who was closer than most on Odin Prime to the chancellor, had heard nothing, not even a whisper or rumor, of this 'research project'? No doubt the State was capable of terrible acts—she had come to learn that during her short stay in this borough. But *human experimentation*? She couldn't imagine her uncle, who prided himself as a respectable, pious man, authorizing such an ethically ambiguous endeavor.

Her thoughts then lingered on the malnourished children whom she'd treated on her first day in that very office, and on the two boys who woke her in the alley. A dread crept across her skin and weighed heavy on her heart. She closed her eyes, choosing instead to focus on Simon's touch, on the gauze resting on her stinging wound; the ache of it was more tolerable than where her mind wandered.

Chapter 17

Shea limped down the spiral staircase in one boot, her other ankle dressed only in a thick sock. It had been three days since her return to the church, and she'd spent most of that time recovering in bed with the help of ice packs and a steady regimen of pain medication.

Theresa and Simon had been sweet to her, making runs to fetch her fresh ice packs or cups of tea, before taking a seat beside her on the bed for some light conversation. After a while, Theresa was content simply sitting with Shea in silence as they both read whatever book struck their fancy from the nearby shelf. Shea liked her company and enjoyed their passing afternoons in silence, flipping page after page of their books.

One evening, Simon had brought up a small game board with black and red pieces, set it over her blanket-clad lap, and taught her to play checkers.

"We only play chess in the Dome," Shea had said, turning the black piece over curiously in her hand. *"But I never quite got into it."*

"Well, checkers ain't as easy as it seems," Simon had replied with a mischievous grin. He'd beaten her each time they played, but Shea had teased that she was at a disadvantage

from the medicine clouding her mind. He'd laughed and nudged her uninjured foot. *"Man, are you just going to make excuses all day or are you gonna actually learn to play the damn game?"*

Tony hadn't taken any time to visit her, nor had Victoria. There was a part of her that was surprised the woman was holding up to their agreement. Given her impression of Victoria, Shea had expected at least some rude or snide comments in passing in the hallway. But none came. She knew she'd eventually have to share a space with her, as bumping into her would be inevitable in the relatively small church. But she didn't mind having those first few days to herself to adjust to the new life she'd found herself hurled into.

Stepping into the congregational space, Shea turned her eyes toward the front entrance of the church. Bern was sitting on his stool beside the locked steel doors, reading another book, with his electromagnetic rifle posted against his hip. When he lifted his eyes from the pages and met Shea's gaze, he nodded his head at her in a silent greeting. She pressed her lips together in a thin smile and offered a reluctant wave before turning to descend to the lower levels.

Simon was the first person she saw upon stepping into the dim basement hallway. He was standing outside the secondary training room, peering through the door's glass window with a stern look in his eye. She could hear a steady, rhythmic, drumming echo from behind the closed door as she stepped closer. Simon noticed her and smiled the harshness from his face. His eyes softened when he lifted his hand to greet her.

"Hey! Look who's finally up and about."

Shea limped past the opened door of her examination office and saw that it was empty. "I was getting a bit antsy just sitting there. Figured I may have some patients that needed to be seen today."

"No, we figured you needed some recovery time. We've got a list of requests, but we wanted you back on your feet before we started bringing people in. No pun intended."

"Pun totally intended. I'm a gimp, but I can still get around." Shea chuckled and limped to Simon's side. "What do you guys have going on?"

"Just some routine training, nothing overly exciting." Simon casually nodded his head toward the closed door beside him. A hard crack and thud resonated from inside the room. "You know, typical day."

Shea remembered peering into the room before her escape a few days earlier. She had paid little mind to the room back then. It had been too dark to truly get a proper view of the interior, which was now bright, loud, and chaotic. She approached the door and looked inside, squinting until her eyes adjusted to the emanating, abrasive light.

The room looked reminiscent of a racquetball court that she'd seen back in the Dome: the walls along the sides stretched far ahead, and down on the opposite end sat four target dummies. They appeared battered and torn from extensive use, with chunks of foam missing from their abdomens and chests. One dummy had half of its face missing, seemingly pummeled to oblivion. Small motorized cannons hung from the halls with a basket of orbs beneath them that fed through a hose. Victoria was in the center of the room with her back to the door.

"Run it again, please," she called out between heaving

breaths. She reached up to tighten her copper ponytail and hopped from one foot to the other in her elastic black leggings and sports bra. Her muscled arms swayed across her chest and sides to stretch and loosen. Her exposed, battle-scarred skin was slick with sweat.

Simon pressed a small button to an intercom outside the door. "You got it, sis."

He flipped a switch beside the intercom and triggered a red light against the interior wall of the room to flash. The machines whirred to life. Their cannons pivoted to aim at Victoria, who now bent forward to collect a fistful of throwing knives.

"The hell?" Shea muttered as Simon moved beside her to also peek inside.

"Just watch."

The cannons fired. Victoria swiftly evaded and dodged the rounds faster than Shea could register them. She ducked one shot and launched a throwing knife toward a dummy, striking it in the chest. Spinning, she hopped to elude a shot at her foot, and hurled another knife at another dummy's throat. An orb grazed her shoulder, and she winced through gritted teeth before landing a third knife in the dummy's gut.

"The hell are those things?" Shea asked.

Simon grinned. "Shockies. Soft like a foam ball, but they pack a hell of a punch on contact."

Shea turned a skeptical eye at him. "A bit sadistic, don't you think?"

"Not at all. The room has varying levels of difficulty to help tune your reflexes and hand/eye coordination. We've got limited resources, so we practice more with knives than live ammo. We start you out with the non-electrical shockies on a slow setting, then amp it up, literally, when you get better. Getting electrocuted is a pretty good motivator to improve."

Shea grimaced. "I guess."

Simon pointed to the adjustment knob beside the intercom. "She completes it on the highest difficult cycle. So, trust me, this isn't typical. She gets in there and it's like something just clicks."

Shea peered through the viewing window and watched Victoria sidestep and duck two orbs with ease. "Seems a bit extreme."

"Vic *is* pretty extreme, in general. But she's damn good at what she does." Simon sighed and crossed his arms. "You can take the girl out of the Valkyries, but you can't take the Valkyrie out of the girl."

"I've heard a lot about them, especially after they stopped that Forsaken plot a while back. But I've never actually seen them in action," Shea said as she watched Victoria move inside the chaotic chamber as though she were a dancer on a stage. Each motion of her arm to hurl a knife, each crane of her spine or neck to evade a round, was frighteningly graceful.

"I guess that's the point of a special ops unit, isn't it? They work behind the curtain. You only see them in action if you're the one they're after, and that isn't exactly good for you."

Shea glanced up at Simon with a frown. "Not to shit-talk my new employer or anything, but I wonder why my uncle hasn't ever deployed the Valkyries against Shadow or the Trinities. Seems like they'd clear them—eh, *us*, pretty effortlessly."

Simon shrugged with indifference. "Dunno, maybe we aren't worth the effort. But you're probably right. Even with Vic on our side, I'm not sure we could hold off a Valkyrie team."

The session ended a few moments later. Victoria opened the training room door, breathing hard and dripping with sweat. She was smiling, but faltered when she noticed Shea standing beside Simon.

"Oh, has the crippled Statesman finally emerged to grace us with her presence?" she asked dryly.

"Vic, be nice," Simon warned as he reached out to hand her a clean towel. Vic snatched it from his grasp and pressed it against her damp, flushed face. She wiped the sweat from her skin and eyed Shea.

"I know you're just trying to get under my skin, but I've got nothing to say to you," Shea said, trying not to stare at the scars across Victoria's bare arms and torso. She wondered how she'd acquired those wounds, if they were tied to her service or State experimentation. Her nose wrinkled at catching the scent of her sweat in the air.

Victoria shrugged and offered Shea a taciturn grin. "It's probably best you don't."

Shea's jaw tautened; her fists clenched. She remained silent despite the bitter words against her tongue and turned to limp down the hall toward her office. There were no patients to attend to, but she preferred it to spending another afternoon in her room. She shut the door behind her and sat in the upholstered chair with a sigh.

"Man, you gotta stop acting like a dick around her. You're only going to make Ma angry." She heard Simon's muffled voice from down the hall.

Victoria seemingly brushed his criticism aside and slapped her open palm against the training room door. "Whatever. It's your turn to get zapped, stud-muffin."

***

Detective Jefferson stepped over the toppled chair in the center of a filthy apartment. He glanced over his shoulder and noted the *DO NOT CROSS* yellow tape affixed across the entryway. The peace officer behind him cleared his throat.

"Begging you indulgence, Detective, but might I ask why you've re-opened this inquiry?" The officer clasped his hands respectfully behind his back. "My superiors insisted this was a simple open-and-close case. Nothing about his hanging appeared unusual."

Jefferson trailed his gaze along the walls, examining the erotic posters pinned beside the small twin bed in the corner. Dirty clothing amassed across the floor, while the laundry bin remained empty at the foot of the bed. He noted the sink and the pile of unwashed dishes, the remnants of food now cemented onto the plates weeks after their owner's supposed suicide.

"Yes, it would appear that way, wouldn't it?" Jefferson said, and meandered around the room. "The suicide note mentioned a love interest, is that right?"

"That's correct. He wrote about a girl rejecting him, which drove him to suicide."

"Uh-huh." Jefferson crouched down to pick up the single clean object in the room: a framed photograph of Robert Bunker with his arm around an older, smiling woman with gray hair. Robert was a hulk of a man, with large, meaty arms that almost swallowed the woman beside him. They had similar green eyes, and the woman appeared tired despite the warm smile across her face. "Any word of this girl that rejected him?"

"No, he didn't mention a name. We asked around the neighborhood, but even citizens in the Middle don't particularly like speaking with us about this sort of thing. Especially considering his connection with the Trinities."

Jefferson tapped the photograph with his knuckle. He stood and turned the image to the officer. "Mother?"

The officer shrugged. "I suppose so. I understand she's been notified and questioned, but wasn't able to provide much information." The officer's brow furrowed. "Begging your indulgence, Detective, but what is this all about?"

"Do me a favor and run a quick address check on her. I'd like to question her myself."

"Right away, Detective". He turned and lifted a comms device to his ear.

Jefferson walked casually around the room, scanning the minor details of the apartment while waiting for the peace officer's call to end. Robert Bunker, a Trinity operative, had somehow known Philip was the chief of security's assistant. He'd also somehow known about Shadow's supply runs to the Ministry of Health and Wellness, Iris's involvement, and whom to pin for interrogation and information. He'd approached Philip as a nervous wreck, presented the damning information, and wound up dead soon after, leaving a vague note about a girl who mostly likely didn't even exist. Jefferson sensed an uneasy sensation swim within his gut.

This is bigger than the Trinities. Much, much bigger, he thought as he toyed mindlessly with the photograph in his hands.

The officer ended the call and turned back to Jefferson with a confused look in his eye. "Well, detective, if you'd like to interview the victim's mother, you'll have to return to the Dome and coordinate with the offices there."

Jefferson blinked, confused. "Why? She resides here in the Middle. Your offices should still have jurisdiction."

"Well, she *did* reside here until last week. She's recently received a Statesman's sponsorship and was relocated to the Dome. I guess she's working as a State Party secretary now. You'll have to coordinate her interview with the Dome offices."

Jefferson stroked his beard and returned the photograph to a table. "Understood. That'll be all, Officer. Thank you for your time. His Majesty Guide Us."

"May Strength Remain," the officer said in farewell as Jefferson exited the apartment, ducking beneath the yellow tape.

Minutes later, Jefferson stepped out onto the sidewalk of the Middle Borough neighborhood. He tapped the comms earpiece embedded inside his ear and strode casually toward the nearest personnel shuttle leading to the Dome.

"Line's clear. What'd you find?" Iris's voice asked through the earpiece.

"Nothing good, that's for damn sure," he said as he tucked his hands deep inside his jacket pockets and turned to peek over his shoulder at those walking nearby. "No word on this girl from the suicide note, but the kid seemed to be real close to his mother. She got sponsorship to relocate to the Dome as a State Assembly secretary shortly after her son's suicide. That's some coincidence, isn't it?"

"Shit. You think he made a deal in exchange for his mother's care?"

"That's exactly what I'm thinking. A broke thug, down on his luck, with no promising future or prospects, can't take care of his aging mother and someone approaches him about an opportunity to lift her out of their shitty life—hell yes he took it."

"The kid passes along sensitive information about our ties to Shadow and then willingly takes the fall, all to get his mother out of the Middle." Iris sighed. *"Jefferson, if the sponsorship she received was from a State Assembly member, then that could mean—"*

"I know," Jefferson interjected, and eyed the inter-borough shuttle gate ahead. "It's best we speak about this in private. I trust the line is secure, but I don't wanna take any chances. I'm on my way to your unit now."

Iris remained silent on the other end of the line for a few seconds as Jefferson approached the shuttle entrance and flashed his badge and identification. The gate guard nodded and gestured for him to pass, and as Jefferson pushed through the crowd waiting for the oncoming personnel shuttle, Iris spoke again. Her voice was quiet, tinged with worry.

"Stay alert, Jefferson. It's a very likely chance that we're already compromised. We need to be especially careful moving ahead with them watching us."

"Understood. See you soon." Jefferson ended the call as the shuttle approached.

Chapter 18

Shea leaned back against the wooden pew in the church's congregational space. An old book rested on her lap, and she tapped the side of her thumb against the cover. While the usual hangout area for Shadow staff was in the large kitchen in the back of the church, Shea hadn't the patience to sit through State broadcasts on local news and developments projected on the wall holo-mount. Shea didn't want to know what was happening back at the Dome, about the life she'd reluctantly chosen to leave behind. It was all still too fresh of a wound, and hearing the familiar voice of the State newscaster over the official broadcast was salt in that wound.

Tony had gibed at her in the kitchen the day before while drinking a bottle of brew. "You hear that, princess? They're reportin' a higher PO patrol presence in the Dome and Middle Borough. Ha! Guess they're trying to look for you, huh? They're sayin' it's to help prepare for those stupid fuckin' Peace Accords, but we know better. The Statesmen pricks."

She let out a breath and rubbed her eye with the heel of her palm.

Just focus on why you're here. You're here for your patients...

you're here to help people, not Shadow.

A week had passed since she'd begun seeing patients on a regular basis. Lauren had come to visit her on her third day for a routine pre-delivery checkup. Both her and her unborn child were healthy, and they'd spent some time casually chatting over mint tea before Shea administered a standard Cyntrax shot. It was visits with Lauren, as well as those from neighborhood children and appreciative residents, that made her employment with Shadow worthwhile. Although she was growing accustomed to her new lifestyle, the days were still long enough to exhaust her by supper.

It's still better than the thirteen-hour night shifts, she thought as she rubbed her closed eyelid with her knuckle. She yawned again and peered up at the small clock hanging from the wall: 19:26.

"Long day?"

Shea jerked up, startled. She clasped her hand to her chest and glanced over to see Bern wandering down the center aisle. He offered a kind, apologetic smile.

"Sorry 'bout that, didn't mean to scare you or anythin'," he said. He carried his electromagnetic rifle in his right hand and rested the barrel against his broad shoulder.

Shea let out a sigh and smiled. "No, you're fine. I think I'm still just a bit… I don't know, uneasy being here. I'm still a bit jumpy."

Bern shrugged. "Fair enough. Shadow does take some gettin' used to. Gettin' along well with the others?"

"For the most part, I believe so. Everyone except for, well… *you know*," Shea said. "I guess I prefer being out here than in the kitchen. It's quieter. It's still taking me some time to get used to the others, too, I suppose."

"We've got our fair share of assholes, believe me. But most are good folk and'll accept you in if you give them the chance." He craned his neck and saw the book on her lap. "Ah, takin' up some readin'?"

"Yes." Shea gestured indifferently with the book in her hand. "I figured it's a good way to pass my off-time. We don't really have books like this in the Dome."

"No, wouldn't suspect they do. Not after they purged everythin,'" Bern said with a frown.

Shea's brow furrowed. "We didn't learn about the purge in school. All they taught us is that the station united behind my uncle's efforts, but they didn't really explain *how*. Not even sure I'd even still believe their side of the story anymore even if they did."

"I'm not even sure you were alive when all that mess went down." Bern took a seat at the end of the pew and rested the rifled across his lap. "What're you, twenty-two?"

"Twenty-six."

"Ah, well. Perhaps still too young to remember," Bern said. "It was after your uncle took over, maybe, what, was it twenty-five cycles ago?" He lifted his eyes to the ceiling, trying to recall. "I know it was a while after we settled here. Took a few cycles to convert this old warehouse supply sector into a livable residential area. Was only supposed to be temporary, you know. What a mess…"

"So, you were a refugee as well? From Valhalla?" Shea asked.

"Was indeed. Came up to Odin Prime nearly forty cycles ago with Harriet. She was still a teenager, you see. Nineteen cycles old, if I remember… I worked with her father on one of the agricultural posts on Valhalla when the Ink spread."

Bern's old, tired eyes darkened. "Poor bastard didn't make it. Made me promise to bring his girl up to Odin Prime, to keep her safe. I didn't have a family of my own at that point. So that's what I did—I dragged her to the nearest shuttle port and begged for them to take us. I did my job, kept her safe. Still am, I suppose."

Shea frowned. "I'm sorry you had to go through that. I can't imagine how hard that must've been for you."

Bern shrugged. "Survival is just about getting through the day. So that's what we did."

"What happened after that?" Shea asked.

"Well, Harriet tried to make an honest living once we settled here in the newly constructed Anchor boroughs. She met a cop, they got married, had a kid."

"Simon," Shea said.

He nodded. "Life was hard, but we were safe from the Ink. But time went on, and the Dome and Middle residents, citizens, got tired of havin' us 'leech off their station's resources.' Despite the prior chancellor doin' his best to strike a fair deal, the tides turned when the CoP started demanding more from us. Your uncle was elected, more or less out of anger in my opinion, and initiated the reintegration protocol. And that was that. They cut us off, refused to govern us, and only keep us around to do their dirty work and menial labor that citizens and Statesmen refused to do." Bern scratched his cheek, his unfocused eyes staring off into the distance. "Harriet is a stubborn, iron-willed woman. But she's also the most resilient, tenacious people I've ever met. She didn't take our abandonment lightly. She founded Shadow as a non-profit support organization, but turned to less-than-legal activities when her efforts fell short. She divorced her PO husband when he threatened to arrest her and take Simon if she didn't stop. You can imagine how that turned out."

"And the books?" Shea gestured with the book in her hands.

"Part of the reintegration protocol was what your uncle called 'unification of thought.' Bastard went on a purge spree with books, films, music… anything that might influence people to think differently or rebel." Bern shook his head and sighed. "The only books worth a damn on this station exist solely because Harriet kept them hidden in this borough."

Shea traced her finger down the spine of the book. "It's such a shame."

"It is," Bern said as he stood from the pew. He tucked the rifle beneath his arm, his face somber. "Shadow gets a real bad rap, especially from those lookin' in from the outside. But we'd've all kicked it a long time ago if it weren't for Harriet. We owe her our lives. Try to remember that when you doubt her or what we do here."

***

"No, you're swinging your arm too much. It has to shoot straight up like an arrow, aligning your bicep beside your ear. See?" Simon took Theresa's arm and held it straight up into the air. "When you swing your arm like that, it takes too much time. Your opponent won't be slow, so neither can you."

Shea shifted against the ache in her back. She sat lounging in the corner of the padded training room, a book resting comfortably against her knees. She adjusted the flattened pillow beneath her and glanced up at Simon and Theresa as they methodically went through the motions of their training. If she wasn't mistaken, she could almost see a tinge of blush touching Theresa's cheeks.

It had been strange at first, adjusting to the routine of their everyday lives. But she was gradually growing accustomed to their likes and dislikes, to the way their laughter echoed against the insulated walls of the training rooms: jarring, at first, but eventually becoming too infectious to not join in. Sometimes their afternoons would pass in silence as Simon, Tony, and Victoria trained, with Theresa reading or resting beside her. Other times Theresa would braid her hair and ask about her life in the Dome.

"Have you ever attended a ball? You have a boyfriend? Ever been kissed? What's it like to have servants? What're your friends like?"

"Two, when I was still small. A few, but no one special. Yes, I was fifteen and we kissed in an empty classroom to hide from Mrs. Stiles, our homeroom teacher. I didn't have servants. And…" Shea's voice had trailed off against the twisting of her hair between Theresa's fingers. She had thought again of Nurse Elliot, of her laughter and smile during her long, arduous shifts at the hospital. *"I don't really have any friends."*

Theresa had paused her braiding. *"No friends? With your last name, I'd've thought you'd be swarmin' with em'."*

Shea's smile grew thin. *"You'd be surprised."*

"Now when that arm goes up, you gotta make sure the opposite foot goes back." Simon, using his foot, slid Theresa's leg back and turned her shoulders. "This allows your body to rotate into the motion. It creates that space you need to follow through."

Shea watched them for a few moments before turning her

attention to Tony, who sat arms crossed, with a scowl etched into his face, on the bench watching his sister. The siblings had been with Shadow for over a decade, long enough for Theresa to not remember the life they'd had before. Shadow was all she knew, and she wanted desperately to be a part of it. But despite Tony's own role in the organization, he refused each request she made to train like him.

"He's such an asshole. He doesn't want me training because he doesn't want me getting hurt the way he does," she had once told Shea with a roll of her eyes. But being as persistent and stubborn as she was, Theresa had brought her case to Harriet, who agreed that the girl needed to at least be trained to defend herself. Suffice it to say, Tony was less than pleased but was in no position to argue.

"Now—" Simon lunged forward and cupped his palms loosely around Theresa's throat. "What do you do?"

Lifting one arm into the air, Theresa contorted her body and whispered the steps aloud to herself. *"Bicep to ear... Opposite leg back..."* she shifted her opposite foot clumsily behind her and swung her arm down, breaking his simulated hold, then turned her back to him. "And then I—" She threw her elbow up toward his face.

"Hey!" Simon blocked the elbow and smiled. "Swing that elbow with enough force behind it and you'll do some real damage." Simon reached out and playfully rustled Theresa's hair.

"Be sure not to harm that beautiful face of his. That's his money-maker." Victoria, who had been taking a rest between sets of pull-ups and barbell squats across the room, shot Simon a smirk and a wink.

"What can I say? It's a gift," Simon grinned, and gestured

along his jawline.

Theresa fussed with her dark, messy pony-tail but eventually pulled out the band, letting her hair hang down over her narrow shoulders. "Simon, you messed up my hair..." she whined, running her fingers through the long locks. She turned her blushing cheeks away from him. "Shea, can you braid my hair for me?"

Shea peeked up from the pages of her book, already too distracted by the goings-on in the room to concentrate on reading. Before she could manage a response, Tony was up from the bench, his meaty hands thrown into the air in protest.

"'Ey! Uh-uh, that's my job, peanut. Get your tush over here." Theresa rolled her eyes and stomped toward him before turning to sit on the floor. "This is a brother-job, you know that. Besides, the doc is readin'." He gently took her hair into his hands and began twisting and braiding the strands between his thick fingers.

"I hate it when you call me peanut."

"Yeah? Too bad, peanut. Speaking of, what'chu readin', Doc?" Tony asked, his eyes not breaking away from the braiding work in his hands.

Shea hesitated and lifted her head to peer over the rim of the book. "It's called *Dragon Lung*. It's about a dragon who's on a quest to obtain a magical form of fire breath to defeat an evil wizard."

Simon paused and peered at her, eyebrow raised. "*Dragon Lung*... Isn't that a kid's book?"

Shea stared at him, blinking. "Um." She flipped through the pages, her face flushing. "That... might the case. I just grabbed the first book on the shelf and started reading. Is it bad that I find it enjoyable?"

Theresa scoffed. "Don't listen to this asshole, Shea, it isn't for *kids*. It's more young adult or something." She turned a scrutinizing eye back to Simon. "Give her a break. That poor, fried Statesman brain of hers needs some well-earned campy fiction."

Simon shrugged and raised his hands in defense as Shea flipped apprehensively through the book's pages, tinges of embarrassment still warming her cheeks.

"What about you, Shea?" Simon asked.

Shea blinked at him, confused. "What about me?"

He gestured to the mat with an inviting grin and a wink. "You wanna hop up here and learn a few moves?"

"You're joking, right?" Shea nearly laughed and closed her book.

"Not at all." The smile across Simon's face waned. His voice became serious. "I've seen a lot of bad shit happen out here to people who couldn't defend themselves. You should at least learn a few basic moves just in case shit turns sour."

"When would I even find myself in that position in the first place? Besides, I'm a doctor. I treat injuries, not inflict them," Shea said. "You really think Harriet would send me out there on my own without at least one of you to tail me? I trust you guys more to protect me than myself."

"Don't even bother trying, Simon," Victoria stated flatly. She ducked under and positioned herself beneath the weighted barbell. "She's used to having others do all the heavy lifting for her. Just like a typical Stateman." She hoisted the bar up against her shoulders, completed three back squats, and returned the bar to the rack. "If she wants to be lazy and get herself killed, that's on her."

"Easy, Vic," Simon said. He glanced back at Shea with an apologetic smile. Shea said nothing, and instead turned away from glaring at Victoria to focus again on her book. While the idea of hand-to-hand combat repulsed her, she could take up the offer in a heartbeat if it meant preparing her to land a punch across that woman's face.

"Whatever, you know I'm right." Victoria completed her final barbell squat repetition and returned the heavy weight to the rack. Shifting her shoulders to ease the tension from the bar, she glanced up at a clock resting against the wall. It was almost 19:20. She glanced back and briefly met Shea's eyes before looking elsewhere.

The two had remained civil, or at least limited their interactions to those brief irksome exchanges, since Mama Wilder had accepted Shea back into the organization. The two coexisted, tolerating the other's presence in a silent disdain for the other. There were a few instances when they'd pass each other in the hall or run into one another in the kitchen. Shea could see the anger behind Victoria's eyes, the venomous words lingering behind her pressed lips. But they exchanged looks, turned away, and went about their lives in silence.

Victoria rubbed her calloused hands together. "Alright, let's clean up. Dinner'll be ready soon."

The training room took little time to straighten up before the crew exited. Theresa had spent the walk up the stairway explaining and reassuring Shea that she shouldn't be embarrassed by what she enjoyed reading. She'd looped her arm around Shea's elbow and walked stride-for-stride beside her, occasionally glancing up to offer a smile. Shea wondered if this was what having a sister was like.

In that moment, Shea realized that their routine felt very normal: the long days of receiving patients, spending her evenings reading while they trained, and walking together to the kitchen to share a modest dinner before bed. She couldn't help but feel the conflict between accepting and rejecting the idea altogether. How could any of this, any of her routine here with this dangerous criminal organization, be *normal*? Shea offered a gentle squeeze on Theresa's arm and returned her smile.

They entered the congregational space before turning toward the kitchen. The aroma of cabbage soup lingered between the scent of dust and old wood, and Shea felt the disappointment rise in her gut. She'd come to despise cabbage soup, which was often cooked for supper when other food rations ran low.

Shea detected the quietest whimper, perhaps a gasp, sift through the chatter of the group as they walked along. She lifted her gaze to the back of the church, expecting to see Bern in his usual spot with a book and his rifle. She instead caught a glimpse of a silhouette slumped in the tall doorway. The figure belonged to a pregnant woman, a swollen belly protruding between a ripped t-shirt and a skirt, clutching weakly to the door frame.

Shea's heart stopped—it was Lauren.

Her skin was pale, and sweat slicked across her brow and hair. Bern stood beside her, his jaw agape and eyes wide in fright, trying to hold her steady.

"H-help m—" Lauren's voice croaked before her thin fingers lost their hold on the door's edge, dropping her hard to the floor.

Chapter 19

"Oh my god..." The words escaped Shea's lips in a horrified whisper. She dashed to the back of the church and fell hard to her knees at Lauren's side.

"She just showed up, I dunno what happened!" Bern's voice was laced with fear.

"Somebody help me!" Shea called out behind her.

She heard the clamor of approaching footfalls as she frantically examined her pregnant friend lying limp before her. Her hands trembled when she grasped onto Lauren's shoulder and rolled her onto her back. She pressed two fingers against her throat, desperate for a pulse. When Shea glanced up to Lauren's face, the first thing she noticed was her yellowish, pallid complexion. She slid her bare wrist across her damp forehead and immediately felt the raging, feverish heat against her skin.

"Lauren, can you hear me? Lauren?" Shea leaned over and lifted one closed eyelid; a glimmer of crimson seeped out from the corner of her eye socket.

I only just saw her last week... she was healthy! How is this possible?

"What can we do?" Theresa asked, her voice thick with

anxiety.

Shea pushed aside the panic pulsing through her veins. Something in her mind clicked, and her hands steadied. She'd proven herself a competent doctor in the Dome's emergency room, and she now fell back into that mindset as though it were driven solely by muscle memory.

"Tony, I need you to carry her down to my office, now!"

"Is it serious?" Simon asked as Tony carefully laid Lauren down on a bed of linens draped across the tile floor.

Shea took a breath and steadied herself before answering. "It definitely isn't good." She turned and gestured to Theresa. "We need to get her fever down. Get me a bucket of cold water and a rag—now." The young girl, now jittery and anxious, darted from the room.

"Lauren." Victoria knelt beside her and took her limp hand tenderly into her own. She reached out and swept away a slick lock of hair from her face and caressed her cheek. Her voice quieted to a whisper. "It'll be alright, just hang in there."

Shea crouched down and glanced over to see worry etched across Victoria's face. There was a tenderness in the woman's eyes that Shea hadn't seen before.

"Lauren, I need you to try to speak or gesture if you can hear me, okay?" Shea leaned over and opened her eyelids; the whites of her eyes were yellowed and bloodshot. The pupils remained dilated despite the light shining from the ceiling. Blood pooled along the lower rung of her eye.

It didn't take long for Shea to identify the most obvious condition. She observed Lauren's skin and eye discoloration, and reconciled that her liver had begun to fail, or had long since stopped functioning. Coupled with the fever, the bleeding—

It can't be that. No. The Ink is isolated on Valhalla, there's no way it's reached Odin Prime. It's impossible.

"M-my ba—" Stammering, Lauren deliriously began to contort her body against the linens beneath her. Both Shea and Victoria reached out to ease her shoulders back against the floor.

"I know, I know," Shea whispered, her voice quiet and reassuring. "You need to try to lie still, okay Lauren? We're trying to help."

"Shea," Simon's voice shuddered.

She glanced over her shoulder to see him, his face growing pale, staring at Lauren's legs. She shimmied down the tile and felt her heart hitch at the oozing crimson stain seeping from the woman's hips.

"What the hell happened to her?" Simon pleaded, kneeling at Lauren's feet. Theresa returned with the sloshing bucket of cold water and a dry rag thrown over her shoulder. She plopped it down onto the tile and dunked the rag into the water, wrung it out, and placed it gingerly onto Lauren's forehead.

"I don't know." A tremble broke through Shea's steadiness. She rolled up her sleeves and began feeling along Lauren's belly with quivering fingers. "She has a raging fever, her liver seems to have failed, and she seems to be suffering internal bleeding. Whether it's from the baby or her, I don't know."

She pressed her hands along the abdomen, her fingertips frantically surveying the surface, seeking both soft and firm spaces to determine the baby's position. She understood where the baby needed to be before the mother could go into labor. She knew that the baby would've had to shift into position, its head angled toward the mother's pelvis. But her fingers couldn't detect any sign that this had happened already. From what Shea could feel, the baby was still feet-first.

"We have a problem."

"What can you do?" Victoria asked; her voice was gentle but firm. Shea broke her focus from Lauren and met Victoria's eyes. Their gazes lingered for a moment before she looked away.

"I can try to treat her symptoms, but they could possibly cause irreversible damage to the fetus. We could risk a delivery, but the fetus isn't in the right position yet. I'd have to conduct a cesarean to physically remove him. However in her current state, I'm not confident she could even survive the procedure." Shea hesitated, the words caught in her tightening throat, before continuing, "The only way I could save her life would be to treat her immediate symptoms, which would mean possibly sacrificing her child."

"No!" Lauren shrieked with a sudden, unexpected show of strength. Victoria held her shoulders down and hushed her, caressing her cheek. "Save my baby, please Shea." Blood-streaked tears now streamed down her pallid cheeks as she reached, pleadingly, to grasp at Shea's shirt.

"Lauren, think of your husband, Toby. You two can try again—"

"Please." Lauren's lip quivered as she tightened her feeble hold onto Shea's shirt. "Please, Shea."

"Your body *cannot* handle labor—either through delivery or cesarean. And you're further risking death by postponing your treatment to have the baby. And there is no guarantee that he's even survived whatever illness this is you have. I may not be able to save him, but I can still save *you*. Please, Lauren."

Lauren's face and eyes hardened. "I choose cesarean."

The room fell silent. Shea glanced up and observed the others in the room staring intently at her, awaiting her next move. The silence grew heavy and thick, as Lauren's decision hung in the air.

Shea swallowed hard and took a breath. "Lauren, we can't numb you, and you've already lost too much blood."

"I don't care. Please, Shea, I want my baby to live." The tears began again. Shea watched the resolve on Lauren's face harden and recognized that this woman had already accepted her fate. Any attempt she could make to sway her decision would be ignored, favoring her child's life over her own.

Shea faltered for a moment, then cleared her throat. She turned to Simon. "I need a scalpel." He complied and hoisted himself up to open the nearby drawer.

"Don't worry, girl. It'll be alright. Just breathe, okay?" Victoria whispered softly, her thumb gently caressing Lauren's neck. Shea watched this exchange and felt her heart sink like lead in her chest. She lifted her eyes toward the ceiling and blinked away brimming tears.

"Should I fetch her husband?" Theresa asked in a whisper.

"There's no time." Shea took the scalpel from Simon's outstretched hand. Informing someone that their loved one had perished during a procedure was the hardest part of Shea's job. She'd seen how much more heartbreak and trauma there was when that person was present when their loved one passed, especially when the passing was a violent one.

This will already be hard. But seeing his wife suffer like this would break him.

She positioned herself on the floor between Lauren's bloodied thighs. Her palms dampened against the cold metal of the knife; her heartbeat pounded against her chest like a drum. A bead of sweat slipped down the back of her neck as she stared at the exposed belly resting before her. Shea's mind walked through each process, step by step, methodically thinking through each movement of the procedure. She'd performed cesareans before in medical school and during her hospital residency, but the circumstances had not nearly been as dire then. Before making her first incision, Shea darted her gaze upward, meeting Victoria's eyes.

It had only taken a thin, fifteen-centimeter incision across Lauren's lower belly to release the dark blood beneath the skin, which now seeped onto the linens below. Despite her ill, weakened state, her screams were jarring and ferocious. Simon pinned her heels to the floor to lessen her thrashing. Victoria's hand remained firm behind Lauren's neck, and she had lowered herself to whisper words of encouragement into her ear through the screams.

The procedure only took a matter of minutes, with Shea gingerly sliding her fingers into the incision to find the baby's tiny feet. Collecting the feet and legs into her palm, she then delicately pulled the baby from the womb and amniotic fluid, using her free hand to maneuver the baby's body up and out from the belly. Her method had been executed expertly, and Shea felt a surge of hope as she pulled the baby onto her forearms.

"Okay." Her hands trembled against the baby's petite, wet limbs. "He's out, Lauren. Your boy is out." Shea took a moment to examine the newborn baby and felt her stomach turn—there was no sign of life in him.

Shea pleaded in silence for him to respond. She silently begged the Patriarch to save Lauren's child, to give him strength. She tapped her palm against his torso, rocked him gently. She held her finger against his neck, desperately searching for a pulse, yet felt nothing.

Hand quivering, she wiped away the smear of amniotic fluid and blood from his body and witnessed, with a breaking heart, that his skin held the same yellowish hue as his mother's. Lauren's infliction had not only taken a toll on her body, but the baby's as well. Her baby boy was stillborn.

All the remaining color drained from Lauren's face, leaving behind only an ashen ghostliness. She'd lost far too much blood and was fading quickly with each passing moment. With chapped, bluing lips, she weakly mouthed breathless, incoherent words about her son.

Victoria squeezed Lauren's arm gently and spoke in a soft whisper. "Lauren, your baby—"

"He made it," Shea broke through with an abrupt hardness that felt coarse in her throat. "He's just fine, Lauren. Your son is alive, he'll be okay." The lie felt sharp and biting against her tongue, and seeing the faint expression of relief easing through Lauren's face and limbs shattered Shea's heart.

It was as if Lauren were simply waiting to hear those words, waiting to hear that her son was alive and well. Her labored breathing swiftly quieted, and her eyes softened while gazing at her son in Shea's arms. The room was still and silent, the air heavy with grief and the scent of blood.

Theresa, choking back tears, reached to draw Lauren's eyelids shut. Shea rose from the sullied linens and stepped forward to set the baby down gently in the crook of Lauren's arm. She backed away, her gaze lingering on Lauren and her baby.

Simon lifted his gaze from Lauren's body and saw the broken expression across Shea's face. "Shea... You did everything you—"

She raised her hand to silence him. Her hand hovered there, suspended in the air, as an oppressively potent grief seeped through the cracks of her jagged, shattered heart. The tears she'd been fighting back only minutes before had dissipated, and she now stood silent and vacant, staring emptily up at the white wall of her office. She'd lost patients before, but this was altogether different.

She was lost, and had faded away, no longer knowing where she was. She had no idea how much time had passed, nor did she care, until Shea realized that her feet had been taking her somewhere. Stumbling forward in the haze, she could hardly detect the sound of her own footsteps or heartbeat. Her body was a machine in motion, moving forward on its own without thought.

Shea felt a sudden rush of heat against her scalp, and a strong shiver traced down her spine. Her clothes felt heavy and thick against her skin, and she soon found her awareness returning gradually the longer she rested in the warmth now cascading over her. As the focus returned to her eyes, she watched a swirl of pink water spin down an open drain. Blood rinsed from her shirt and arms, trailing down her skin and onto the hard shower tile beneath her.

The more she tried to pull her eyes away from the smeared

blood across her skin, the more it drew her in. She scrubbed at her arms, her breath catching in her constricting throat, until her skin was raw and stinging. She buckled forward against the tile wall and slid to the floor, now sobbing uncontrollably into her hands.

Shea sat in the hot shower and stared at the blood that had soaked through her sleeves—it was Lauren's blood, and now Lauren was gone. She felt empty, but broken; numb, yet burdened with a heavy grief. In all her medical training and experience, she'd lost only a few patients due to extreme circumstances beyond her control, but she couldn't shake the idea that perhaps Lauren could've been saved. Yet in the end, none of it mattered, and both Lauren and her child were dead. She'd lost patients in her care, but she'd never lost a friend.

She remembered Lauren's smile as they shared tea together, and how she'd beamed when talking about her husband and their modest life together in their old but cozy home. She remembered the hand-made mobile suspended above the empty crib, and how the sewn stars bobbed lazily as it spun.

"There's no one else in this borough that can do what you can," Lauren had said, and her words and voice reverberated in her mind like a haunting echo. Shea still couldn't save her, even if she was the only one in the borough who could.

The shower shut off, leaving Shea curled and shivering on the floor. When she lifted her aching eyes, she discovered Theresa crouching beside her. Tears streamed down her flushed cheeks as she wrapped Shea in a warm, dry towel.

"It's okay, Shea." Theresa draped the towel around her sopping back and shoulders. The girl continued to sob as she embraced her. Fresh tears fell from Shea's eyes as she leaned into her, accepting her warmth and kindness. "It's okay, Shea. It wasn't your fault."

I could've saved her.

Chapter 20

Shit, this dress is too tight.

Victoria contorted her body, twisting her arms to grope for the open zipper against her back. The fabric constrained and rubbed abrasive against her skin; the pencil dress was a form-fitting halter top that reached down just above her knees, and she despised every single stitch of it. Had she the liberty, she would have set that dress on fire with the cigarette she wished she were smoking. But she needed that dress, so she would swallow her pride and tolerate it.

She managed to zip up the back of the dress before stumbling forward to snatch up a small baggie on the dresser. Fumbling with it between her fingers, she tapped out a dash of the fine white powder onto her wrist and lifted it to her nostril. She went through the motions, having done this so many times since being brought to the borough, and inhaled the dust. She couldn't recall which painkiller it was that she'd just taken, but it didn't matter much. It took the edge off her nerves, which now tinged anxiously beneath her skin.

Lauren was dead, and her death had shaken Victoria to the core. She remembered the first time they'd met, when

Victoria had still been strapped to the bed, wrists and ankles bound to each corner bedpost, all to prevent her from harming herself. Lauren had been afraid of her at first, and could only manage to sit beside her on the chair that now remained empty in the corner. She remembered screaming at her and sobbing before crying herself to sleep. When she awoke, Lauren would still be there, sitting patiently, watching her. Days turned to weeks, and over the course of several lunars, the two grew closer. Lauren had been one of the first to make her feel something again—Simon had been the first to make her smile, and Lauren was there to see it.

Their relationship, as physical and friendly as it had become, was still a business partnership at the end of the day. Victoria had eventually moved on to other girls after Lauren married her husband, but there had always been a fondness that lingered between the two. It wasn't love, Victoria knew that for certain, but it was still a meaningful enough affection that lasted over the cycles. She hadn't been as close to any of the other girls as she had with Lauren.

But there was something else about Lauren's death that unsettled her: it was *how* she died. Death was no longer a concept that made her uncomfortable—if anything, her exposure to it had left her relatively neutral to the idea. It was the circumstances of Lauren's death that now ate away at her nerves. Her symptoms felt disturbingly familiar and close, like a foul breath against her neck. The yellowed flesh, burning fever, bleeding eyes…

Victoria closed her eyes and imagined being led down a dark corridor. She turned her head to peer through a small, square door window as she passed. A man was screaming. He was strapped to his bed, jaundiced skin against his sweat-stained white robes. He lifted his head to meet her gaze, a bloody tear streaking down his shallow cheek.

She opened her eyes and felt her heart drumming hard against her rib cage. A cold sweat broke against her brow. The vision was real, vivid and clear. She took a deep breath and felt the effect of the painkiller steadily settle the tremble in her hands. As she lifted her gaze to examine herself in the mirror, the tension in her reflection's shoulders and brow eased, and she reveled in the numbness seeping through her limbs. The memory faded.

A horn sounded from outside the church and pulled her back from her daze.

Time to get to work.

Victoria opened the passenger door soon after and slid inside, greeting him with a smug smile. "Thanks for the ride, Trev."

Trevor sat in the front seat of his laundry delivery transport, tapping his fingers restlessly against the steering wheel. "No trouble at all! Yeah, my wife and I were just enjoying our anniversary dinner tonight, but hey, I'm glad I could come play taxi for you."

"Oh, don't be such a little bitch. I just need you to take me into the Dome." She turned and stepped back into the rear of the vehicle among piles of clean linen.

Trevor scoffed. "I mean, I figured as much, or else you wouldn't've called. What's the deal?" He swiveled his head around and caught a glimpse of her in her dress, her long, flowing red hair draped down her back. He whistled. "You got a date or somethin'?"

"Tonight is not the night to fuck with me, Trev. Now do your damn job or I'll report you to Mama Wilder."

Trevor shifted uncomfortably in his seat and offered an agreeable nod. He shimmied back around and turned the engine over. "You got it, boss."

A thick silence hung heavy inside the vehicle as Trevor pulled away from the curb, narrowly missing a line of parked rickshaws. Victoria observed him for a moment and felt a pang of guilt; she hadn't intended to snap at him.

"Listen," she said, reaching out to place a hand on Trevor's shoulder. "Sorry I snapped, it's been a rough night and I'm a jackass." Trevor nodded. "I've got a few places to hit up once I'm in the Dome. How about I pick something up for Stacy. Say it's from you, for your anniversary. You'll get some good husband points for it."

Trevor begrudgingly cracked a smile and nodded. "That'd be great, Vic, thanks. Stacy'll love that."

Crouching down in the back of the van, Victoria grasped hold of the thick blanket and dragged it over her the length of her body. The last time she'd lain beneath that sheet, Shea had been unconscious beside her. She suddenly remembered the scent of Shea's lavender perfume, and how much hatred she'd carried with her that day. Closing her eyes, she recalled the look in Shea's eyes after she'd placed the stillborn baby in Lauren's arms. Victoria had hated Shea from the day they'd met, determined that she was just like her mother. She wondered, though, if her mother would've offered Lauren that last kindness.

Victoria slipped out from the rear of the delivery vehicle in the rear of a quiet alleyway. She closed the doors and palmed the siding, signaling Trevor to drive away. He would be back in three hours to bring her back to the Anchor. She watched him turn the corner and wished for a fleeting moment that she could travel like a normal citizen, but then brushed the temptation away when she imagined being pressed against strangers in a rush-hour personnel shuttle.

"You wanna throw yourself right into the hands of Dome authorities?" Simon had joked when they'd first discussed infiltrating the Dome cycles earlier. *"You'd use the iris scans, and every PO in the borough would be waiting for you at the next stop."*

Victoria sauntered down the sidewalk of the Dome, casually toying with her hair and dress. This was a part that she knew how to play: the well-to-do, elitist Dome Statesman. Someone like Simon, who'd only ever seen the inside of the Anchor until he was seventeen, would stick out like a blaring red siren. Victoria physically slipped back into Dome society with ease. She looked the part, spoke the part, and knew how to avoid drawing attention to herself. Peace officers kept a keen eye on personnel shuttles and movement between the boroughs, but less scrutiny was paid to those in the Dome who already looked the part.

She passed an older Statesman sporting the maroon jacket of a Party Assembly member and put on her best polite smile and nodded.

A bit late to be going home from an Assembly gathering, isn't it? Victoria noted a smear of crimson lipstick he'd failed to completely wipe away from his earlobe.

"His Majesty Guide Us," she greeted with a sweet lilt.

"May Strength Remain," he responded with a grin. His gaze lingered on her cleavage before they passed one another.

She imagined sliding a knife across his throat, from lipsticked earlobe to maroon collar.

Victoria walked deeper into the Dome's main atrium as the district's lights dimmed further. She entered the Magistrate's public gardens and lifted her eyes toward the vast, domed glass ceiling. The station's rotation had positioned the shimmering solar sails in view, behind which was the backdrop of the blue and green moon marble, Valhalla. Clouds swirled in the atmosphere above the vibrant green land masses and blue seas. She stood in the center of the gardens, breathing the scent of fresh earth and greenery from the trees and sprawling flowerbeds, and marveled at a sight that used to be common to her. The Dome always faced planet-side and offered that majestic view; beneath the Dome, the Middle Borough had select offices and living quarters other than the transport hub that managed a partial view depending on the station's rotation. But the Anchor, acting as the tail of the station itself, was enclosed and denied anyone a view other than those broadcast across the artificial sky.

As the station continued its rotation, Victoria could see the orange gas giant Yggdrasil peek out from behind the moon. A blanket of stars filled the void behind it. Her gaze lingered on the emptiness of space, and she found she could at that moment see nothing else. She could nearly feel the chill of it against her skin.

"Final PCCs and PCIs, everybody! Check your suits and oxygen, we disembark in T minus 2 mikes. Weapons on amber, we aren't red until we land on the objective. Hammond, Smith, Reynolds, you're first in to sweep and clear, Gallagher and Rodriguez will pull security outside the hull."

"Remember to keep your wits about you, Valkyries. By no means can we allow a Forsaken to step foot on Odin Prime."

"And the hostages?"

"The safety of Odin Prime remains our top priority. We will save as many hostages as we can, but if it comes down to either them or the station, we won't hesitate."

Victoria's chest ached. She clenched her jaw, took a deep breath, and pushed herself forward through the rest of the garden toward the residential and shopping districts.

It would've been better if I'd died, too.

Many shops were closing by the time Victoria reached the district. She peered around at the citizens going about their evening, casually laughing and smiling with shopping bags in tow or slung over their shoulders. A few nearby restaurants served late-night drinks to patrons on their patio, situated near an ornate, flowing fountain. The patio offering its patrons a stunning view of the dome above.

Victoria watched a well-dressed pregnant woman rise from her table with the help of her husband. She closed her eyes and saw Lauren contorting on the floor, wildly screaming through bloody tears. There was the clink of glasses and laughter nearby. Victoria carried on.

She passed a small shop that advertised late operating hours, and hesitated near the door. The window display offered a selection of items for sale, such as basic pharmaceuticals, beauty products, and women's fashion accessories. She was about to continue down the sidewalk when she noticed a bottle of lavender perfume displayed next to a men's shaving kit. She loitered near the window and stared down at the bottle. Victoria once again flashed back to the doctor's scent and the stillborn child.

A young woman and her date walked past her, elbows linked and giggling to each other. The woman's shopping bag struck Victoria's hip as she passed, and she didn't seem to notice, let alone apologize. Victoria realized at that moment, though, that her hands were empty. She flipped her hair, slipped on a smile, and stepped inside the shop.

***

A doorman peered over the front desk of the residence hall's lobby. He rose from his chair and watched Victoria idly walk across the lobby admiring the lush wall garden. Her high heels clicked loudly with each step, and a bright pink shopping bag swayed from her wrist.

"Can I help you, miss?" he asked. "Are you lost?"

"What stunning flora this hall keeps," Victoria remarked, trailing her fingertips across a string of hanging ivy.

"This is a secure area, miss. For Party members and their guests only." The doorman scrutinized her and appeared more confused than concerned. "If you have no business here, miss, I'm going to have to ask you to leave."

Victoria turned a courteous, innocent smile at the doorman. "Of course. I'd expect no less." She crossed the lobby to rest her elbows against his desk. "I'm here to see Iris Hammond."

The doorman cocked an eyebrow. "Is she expecting you?"

"Indeed she is," she said, and gestured with the shopping bag. She spoke with a higher, cleaner diction than she normally used in the Anchor. A part of her hated how simple it was for her to slip back so easily into the habit. "She ordered some items from our shop this afternoon but was a bit too busy to swing by to pick them up. She's a valued customer and Statesman; we of course didn't want to bother her with something so trivial. I informed her I'd swing by after my shift to deliver her purchases."

"You may leave her purchases here with me," the doorman said, eyeing the shopping bag with a hint of suspicion. "I can take them the rest of the way after I inspect the items."

Victoria sucked air through her teeth and scrunched her face. "Oh gosh, she may not like that very much."

"And why not?"

Victoria leaned in closer and cupped her palm beside her lips. She whispered, "It's some… *lady stuff*. Not just the lunar reds, either. She made a rather *sensitive* purchase from our back room, if you know what I mean. I'd rather keep the matter private. You know, customer confidentiality and all."

The doorman blinked at her. "I, uh…" He glanced down at the bag around Victoria's wrist and reached back to rub the back of his neck. "I better call this in, if you don't mind."

"By all means, please do," Victoria said, her voice still sickeningly sweet.

The doorman cleared his throat and activated the intercom on his desk. The line beeped for thirty seconds before there was an audible click.

"I swear to god, Mr. Hoover, you'd better have a damn good reason for waking me up at midnight," Iris snapped through the speaker.

Mr. Hoover shifted from one foot to the other, flexing his hands. "Begging the Chief's indulgence, there is a woman here to see you. She says she's from a shop?"

Victoria leaned in closer to the intercom. "Hello, Chief Hammond, it's Vicky. So sorry to bother you, ma'am." her voice dripped with polite regret. "I'm here to delivery your purchase from earlier this evening."

"… Vicky," Iris stated flatly through the intercom.

"Yes, apologies for bothering you this late, ma'am." Victoria locked eyes with Mr. Hoover. "So sorry Harriet couldn't come by earlier with your purchase. She caught the devil of a cough, unfortunately."

The line was silent. Mr. Hoover creased his brow and turned a curious eye back to Victoria.

"Ma'am?"

When Iris spoke again, her voice was no longer tired. Instead, she was pointed and stern.

"Send her up, Mr. Hoover."

Chapter 21

"Well," Iris said as the door slid shut behind her. She hesitated, her hand still near the door activator, and took a deep breath. "This is… unexpected."

Victoria stepped further into the luxury condo. Her gaze trailed over the fine-leather and hardwood furniture placed throughout the sitting room. There was a familiar scent in the air that tugged at her brain. Her jaw tightened, fists clenched.

Victoria scoffed. "Yeah, well… something's come up. I had little choice in the matter. Don't read too much into it."

She carelessly set the shopping bag atop the coffee table and caught a glimpse of a photograph hanging on the wall: her father's peace officer portrait. He was young, even younger than she was now. He smiled in his neatly pressed peace officer dress uniform. The photograph was taken one cycle before he was killed during a violent uprising over the chancellor's reintegration policy. His blonde hair was clipped short, and his eyes were bright blue. Victoria had only been two cycles old when he died. She had no memory of the man now smiling back at her, and forced herself to look away.

"Care to elaborate?" Iris asked as she strode toward a credenza along the opposite wall. She opened a decanter of dark liquor and filled two short, empty glasses.

Victoria traced a fingertip along the soft back cushion of the leather sofa. "A girl I knew in the lower died earlier this evening."

"Shame," Iris blurted out, apathetic. She moved toward Victoria and offered her the filled glass. "And this is relevant to me, how?"

Victoria glanced down at the drink in her mother's hand. She snatched the glass and promptly turned away. "I need the bitch's research data. I know you have it."

Iris faltered. She blinked, scoffed. "What in the Patriarch's name for?"

Victoria sipped the dark liquor and savored the warmth radiating down her throat and chest. "It may be useful." She shook her head. "Or maybe it won't. Fuck, I don't know."

"Does that doctor have anything to do with you being here?" Iris asked, brow creasing.

Victoria nearly laughed. "No. She doesn't even know I've left the Anchor."

"Then what is it you aren't telling me?"

Victoria tipped the glass back and downed the remainder of her liquor. She placed the emptied glass on the coffee table and felt her nerves begin to waver. Closing her eyes, she saw Lauren again, jaundiced and with bloodied tears. Victoria could hear the man screaming at her from behind the locked lab door. Sweat dampened her brow as her pulse quickened.

"I think the girl died from Ink. Which is crazy, I know—we haven't seen a reported case of Ink on Odin Prime since the purge, but I swear it's the truth." Victoria crossed her arms over her chest to hide the tremor in her hands. She bit the inside of her lip and turned to face her mother. "I know the symptoms. I saw them. I *lived* them. It's Ink, no mistaking it. It felt like the project all over again."

"It's been a while since you were in custody, Victoria. And you weren't exactly in your right mind even when you were. How confident are you in what you remember?"

Victoria's eyes darkened and her voice hardened. "I'm pretty fucking confident."

Iris tapped her fingernails against the glass in her hand. Her jaw tautened. "What are you insinuating, exactly?" Victoria said nothing. Iris continued, "You think the State is somehow involved with this girl's death? That they knowingly released a *deadly disease into the populace*? And while they're publicly pursuing Peace Accords with the Anchor, no less? Do you know how *insane* that sounds?"

"Yeah, no shit," Victoria snapped, and turned a fiery gaze at her mother. "But can you think of any other explanation? Every shuttle from Apex is monitored, all personnel given explicit authorization to enter Odin Prime only after a strict medical exam. All to prevent someone, either knowingly or not, from carrying the Ink infection onto the station. All those controls, all that protocol... So how in the hell did I just see a friend of mine die from it?"

"I don't know, Victoria, but you can't just jump to the conclusion that the State is behind this," Iris hissed, trying not to raise her voice too loud in her mounting anger. "I get why you're eager to blame the State for everything—really, I do. I've seen first-hand how cruel and unforgiving the State can be. But this accusation of yours goes too far. Ink is too unstable. They wouldn't release an asset they couldn't control."

"Oh, bullshit!" Victoria shouted.

"Victoria, take a breath and think about it for a second. Say you're right—what advantage could they possible gain from this? Why purposefully infect a population that you intend to re-assimilate into society? That doesn't make any sense."

"I was their fucking lab rat, mom! Don't even try for a fucking second to convince me that the State isn't capable of worse things than what I'm suggesting!"

Iris was rendered silent. She reached back to massage the back of her neck with the flat of her palm; her fingertips traced the dog tag chain around her neck. She stared at Victoria, at the anger raging behind her green eyes, and drank the rest of her liquor in one swallow.

"Fine. Follow me."

Iris led Victoria from the sitting room to a small room at the end of a hallway. She lingered near the closed door for a few moments, steeling herself, and eventually entered.

"You kept her files in my old bedroom?" Victoria asked, bewildered. "That's fucked up."

She lingered near the opened doorway and peered inside, taking in the familiar, nostalgic layout. Her narrow twin bed lay untouched in the far corner with a nightstand beside it. A single picture frame sat on the surface. Stepping inside, she traced the tip of her finger through a thick layer of dust across the nightstand, and examined the photograph: it was a young couple, a man and woman, embracing one another with wide smiles across their faces. Victoria stilled and stared at the picture, the hardness across her face softening.

"Francis is stationed on Apex," Iris said as she opened the closet door. She reached up to unlatch and remove a false wall from deep within. "Been assigned there for a few cycles now. He's done well for himself, from what I hear."

Victoria promptly returned the photograph, face-down, to the nightstand. "It's no concern of mine." She turned and stepped closer toward the closet. She noticed, tucked in the far corner, the matte black sections of Valkyrie armor. She knelt and placed the flat of her palm atop the dusty helmet, caressing it with the side of her thumb. "You kept it all this time..." She gazed up at her mother with a frown. "Why?"

Iris heaved a box from inside the wall annex and turned to rest it on the floor by her feet. "I had my reasons." She replaced the wall cover and hoisted the box again. When she turned and strode from the room, Victoria took one final glance at her childhood bedroom and followed.

"What the hell good do you think any of this information will do you?" Iris asked as she placed the box onto the coffee table.

Victoria lifted the cover and peeked inside at the stacks of papers and data disks. She scowled and closed it again. "I don't know. Maybe the doctor can make some sense of it."

"She isn't going to take this information well," Iris said. "Stupid girl has no idea what her mother has done."

Victoria stifled a bitter chuckle. "That's rich coming from you."

Iris's gaze hardened, her tightly pressed lips turned down in a frown. "That isn't fair, Victoria."

"Isn't it?"

"I was trying to protect you. I was doing my best for you, given the circumstances."

"Yeah, and that worked out great for everyone involved, didn't it?" Victoria nearly laughed, and bit the inside of her lower lip. She tasted blood against her tongue.

Iris stared at her, exasperated. "I swear to you, if I'd known what Project Stronghold would do to you, to those other subjects, I wouldn't have surrendered you." She faltered, dropping her gaze to the floor. "I'm sorry about Cosette—"

"No! Don't you *dare* say her name!" Victoria snapped. "I will abide many things, especially from you. But I will not abide her name in your mouth"

"Yes. Well." Iris turned away and preoccupied herself collecting the empty glasses on the coffee table. "What's done is done, and I have nothing left to say. I suggest you leave now that you have the doctor's files. I will call my driver to have him return you to the Anchor."

"That won't be necessary. I have my own driver." Victoria hoisted the box and collected her shopping bag.

"Considering the incredibly sensitive information in that box you're carrying, I must insist that my driver take you. Patriarch forbid a peace officer stops you on the street and gets too nosy." Iris stepped toward the intercom, pressed a button along the side, and asked for her driver to be ready in a matter of minutes.

"And what of my driver?" Victoria asked.

"I'll send someone to instruct him to return without you," Iris said. She reached into a nearby briefcase, withdrew a black folder, and stepped closer to slip the folder beneath the box's lid. "I know you don't trust me, but I must insist that you take the offer. It is in your best interest to distance yourself from him."

Victoria's brow furrowed. "Trevor? Why?"

Iris ignored the question and walked across the room to the front door. "I advise you deliver this box and its contents to Harriet before letting the doctor sift through it. It is her borough, after all. It is best that she see it first and decide how to proceed." She pressed her palm against the door activator, triggering the door to slide open. "My driver will be waiting for you downstairs."

"If you insist," Victoria said, and stepped into the dark, narrow hall.

"Be careful, Victoria," Iris said. The two held each other's gaze for a brief, quiet moment before Iris placed her hand over the terminal to shut the door between them.

Chapter 22

Shea traced her fingertips along the ridges of her examination room sink and noted each rough edge across the porcelain surface. Five days had passed since Lauren and her baby had died on the tile floor where she now stood. The scent of acrid disinfectant still stung her nose when she breathed.

Shadow had been nothing but accommodating and gentle with Lauren's husband after he'd arrived on the scene. He'd broken down and sobbed over his wife and child's corpses, both of whom Simon and Tony had cleaned and dressed before his arrival. Simon made sure that not a single spot of blood remained on Lauren's body by the time he burst through the front door. Shea later thanked him for it.

"It seemed like the only thing I could do for her," he'd said to her the next day during breakfast through a tired, strained smile.

Harriet had offered Toby a two-lunar mourning period with his job at the fishery. She instructed the supervisor to contact a recruiter of hers for a temporary replacement, and paid Toby a two-lunar payroll advance. She'd even gone as far as to offer him a warm hug when he began to cry again.

"Thank you, Mama Wilder," he'd sobbed into her shoulder.

"I just... I don't know what to do without her."

"It's alright, dear," she'd responded, and patted a warm hand on his back. *"Just take care of yourself, you hear? It's what your girl would've wanted. Let me know if you need anything else, and I'll see you in two lunars for work, yeah?"*

Shea watched the scene unfold and left feeling unsettled. While Harriet at that moment was the epitome of selfless generosity itself, Shea knew better than to take it at face value. There was always an angle to exploit, always an opportunity to leverage.

There hadn't been time for Shea to think on the subject further. More patients were already waiting for her by the next morning, and three more children succumbed to the same horrific illness within five days' time. Each child had been a patient of hers within the past four weeks, all for routine checkups and minor treatments. They returned to her with internal bleeding, jaundiced skin, and raving fevers; the only reprieve she could offer was a heavy dose of morphine to lift the weight of their weakened shoulders. Each had previously come to her relatively healthy, despite the glaring malnutrition plaguing most of the Anchor. Yet all three lives were lost under her care. She felt like a part of herself died alongside each.

She focused on the sensation of the sink beneath her fingertips.

"Fever above 38.5 degrees Celsius... jaundice points to liver..." Shea's fingertips tapped against a coarse patch of porcelain. "Internal bleeding... could be viral hemorrhagic."

Her hands damped with cold sweat.

You know what it looks like, Shea. You've never seen it in person, but you've read accounts, seen photographs and videos of

Ink victims. Pretending or hoping it's something else won't change the possibility that Ink has found its way onto Odin Prime—

"Shea."

She jumped with a start and clasped her hand over her chest. Theresa hovered in the doorway with two mugs clutched in her hands. She raised the mugs with a sheepish smile.

"Sorry, I didn't mean to startle you."

"No, you're fine. I was just a little caught up in my own head, is all."

Shea noted pity behind Theresa's eyes and realized how weary she must've appeared at that moment. She buried her hands deep inside her lab coat pockets and shrugged the exhaustion from her shoulders. Sleep wasn't something that had come easily to her over the past week.

Theresa stepped forward and extended a mug. "You haven't left this room all day. Figured you'd be thirsty."

Shea took the mug graciously and, after taking a sip, felt the warmth spread across her tongue. There was a burn down her throat that lingered and hit her empty stomach like a stone. She smiled. Theresa had spiked the tea—she didn't know with what kind of alcohol, but she didn't care enough to ask.

"Yes." She nearly coughed at the burn in her throat. "I definitely needed this. I hope you're drinking something a little less strong, young lady."

Theresa offered a cheeky wink before taking a sip from her own mug. Shea chuckled, shook her head, and wagged a disapproving finger. She took a second sip from her mug and felt the warmth radiate out from her chest and down her limbs. She needed this; not just the drink, but the friendly company Theresa provided.

"How're you feeling?" Shea asked. "Feeling feverish at all? Abdominal pain or nausea?"

"No, still fit as a fiddle—we all are. I've been checkin' up on the boys, too."

Shea's lips pulled in a weak smile. "Good, good. Thank you. With what happened to Lauren, and now those kids…" Shea's voice trailed off.

"Hey, don't worry about it, okay? We get why you're bein' always checkin' in with us." Theresa leaned forward and sniffed. She cocked her head with a curious look in her eye. "What is that? Lavender?"

"Did you just smell me?"

"Are you offended that I smelled you?"

"Offended, no. Weirded out? *Maybe*," Shea teased.

Theresa rolled her eyes. "We're surrounded by smelly, sweaty dudes all day, every day. I'd have to be comatose not to notice."

"Aw, so sweet of you to say." Shea chuckled and poked a finger playfully at Theresa's side. "You insinuating Victoria smells like a sweaty dude?"

"She has her days." Theresa laughed, then faltered and blinked. "Don't tell her I said that."

"Lips sealed." Shea mimicked zippering her lips shut before taking another sip of her spiked tea. "If you *must* know, I found this bottle of perfume outside my bedroom a couple days ago." Shea lifted her wrist to her nose to take in the scent, a smile curling at her lips. "I'm not sure who left it there. They didn't leave a note or anything with it."

Theresa gestured to Shea, who then extended her wrist out for the young woman to smell. "That's so nice…" She took another few whiffs of Shea's wrist and smiled.

"Yeah. It's a bit odd, it's the same perfume I wore back in the Dome. I'm not sure how a new bottle ended up here, though."

"Ooo, maybe you got a secret admirer," Theresa teased.

"Here? Doubtful. But to be honest, I haven't really given much of a thought about it. I've been a bit preoccupied."

"It's been a rough week…" Theresa said, her smile waning.

"That, my dear, is an *understatement*." Shea recalled the face of the most recent child fatality and took another swig from her mug.

"Any theories on what's goin' on?"

Shea shook her head and savored the lingering burn of the alcohol on her tongue. "I'm going into this blind. I'm trying to work out the symptoms, but we don't really have the resources to treat something this big. I'm trying to work with Harriet on getting some more medicine in, but—" She watched the motion of the liquid in her mug as she swirled it in her hand.

Don't scare the girl. Maybe I'm wrong about the Ink; it could be something else entirely.

"You can't diagnose with the symptoms alone?"

"Some of the symptoms point to what looks to be a viral hemorrhagic fever."

Theresa's face contorted in fright. "I'm sorry, a fucking *what?*"

"It's a kind of virus that induces a fever and damages blood vessels. Thus, internal bleeding and organ failure."

"Shit." Theresa gulped and took another swig of her drink, her brow tense.

"But there's no way to be certain until I can get an

infected blood sample under a microscope. I don't know its pathology, how it is transmitted, how to treat it…" Shea massaged her forehead and let out a breath.

"Hey, hey." She stepped forward and placed her hand on Shea's shoulder. "You eat an elephant one bite at a time, yeah? Try to eat the whole thing at once and you'll choke. Mama Wilder will come through with what you need. So"—Theresa tapped her mug against Shea's and nudged her shoulder—"in the meantime, enjoy your drink."

"An elephant?" Shea threw back the rest of her drink. She inhaled sharply through her teeth, bracing herself against the rush of heat up her spine, and shook her head. "Oh no, all the booze settled to the bottom."

Theresa shrugged. "I've seen 'em in books. They've got huge ears."

Shea wiped the corners of her lips with the edge of her thumb. She glanced up at the clock. It was nearly 20:00. "I think I'm going to call it. I'm going to swing by the kitchen for a quick something, wanna join?"

Theresa shifted from one foot to the other, fiddling with the mug in her hands. "Let's chat here some more. I wanna hear more about the Dome, the gardens you used to have at your old house. Or maybe about your little brother? I heard the Dome's got a pretty big ceiling-thing where the view is pretty out of this world—ha, get it, *out of this world*? Because, you know, we're in space, and there's a really big planet next-door. And a moon. But you already know that. Gosh, *space*. Huge, huh?"

Shea watched her, curious. "You alright?"

"Of course! I just wanna hang out some more down here. I like our chats."

Shea heard it. A faint reverberation of shouts and screams sifted through the floorboards upstairs. Her eyes darted up past the ceiling, tracing the sound of stomping feet and muted clapping.

"Theresa, what the hell is going on?"

Theresa awkwardly stammered and backed to block the entrance of the examination room, closing Shea inside. Her smile was apologetic and meek. "Sorry, Shea. They asked me to keep you company down here until they were finished with the trial. They didn't want to upset you."

Shea stared at Theresa, mouth agape. "Trial? What trial?" Theresa didn't respond and only stared back at her, blinking. She shook her head slowly from side to side, refusing to speak. "Theresa, *what trial?*"

The shouting grew louder and clearer. She heard a distinct chant emerge through the clamor: *"Traitor! Traitor! Traitor!"*

Shea's cheeks and ears flushed hot. Her pulse quickened as she slammed the empty mug onto the tray beside her.

"Move," Shea commanded, her voice deliberate and steady.

"Shea, you won't understand."

"Theresa, *move.*"

Shea pushed past Theresa and bolted up the stairs. Theresa followed, calling out for her to stop. The two emerged from the stairway into the loud, chanting cacophony. Shea stared in horror at the scene unfolding before her. Screaming men and women packed the congregational area, filling each pew reaching back to the main doors. They directed their abuse at a young man tied to a pole at the church's altar; his eyes were blindfolded, and a gag stuffed deep inside his mouth muffled his shrieking. He jerked and twisted to break free, but couldn't loosen from the ropes binding his wrists.

Harriet sat in a chair behind the bound prisoner. Her hardened, cold gaze peered over the crowd. Standing stoic beside her, with a knife clutched tight in one hand, was Victoria. She appeared numb and indifferent, with a blank emptiness behind her eyes.

Harriet took a deep breath, parted her lips, and bellowed, "Let the trial begin!"

The mob cheered with a fury as fingers gripped around Shea's arm like a vise. They yanked her back, pulling her out of view. She tried to jerk away, but the more she struggled the tighter the hand clenched.

"Let go of me!" Shea barked through gritted teeth. The hand released her once they were hidden behind a wooden pillar. She pulled away and turned back to see Simon peering down at her, his jaw taut and brow furrowed.

"You aren't supposed to be up here."

Shea's anger flared in her face and chest. "Simon, what the hell is going on? What is all this?"

Simon frowned. "This is a trial, Shea. It's our borough's way of maintaining public order. Ma prefers handling these sorts of things subtly. It's less complicated just to clean house and dispose of bodies… but sometimes she has to make an example."

"An example? For what?"

Simon leaned closer to her ear. "Remember that day you were taken from the ministry? Long story short: the guards in the storage office weren't supposed to be there when Vic arrived for the pickup. Normally it's a quick in-and-out operation; easy shit, we do it about twice a cycle. So, when we heard that there were guards waiting for us, we thought it was a bit weird. We got some intel a few nights ago pointing to a snitch that ratted us out to the POs. Turns out those guards were actually undercover officers placed there based on the information he provided—"

"Quiet!" Harriet hollered, outstretching her hands to silence the clamoring mass in the pews. Their voices died down to sullen whispers as she rose to her feet. A scowl crept across her lips as she surveyed the church. Her eyes darkened upon turning her gaze to the whimpering man bound to the pole.

"Ladies and gentlemen, the man before you, Trevor Mills, is guilty of the worst violation of our borough's code: snitching to the fuckin' state!"

The crowd hurled furious taunts and curses once again. Some spat on the floor and gestured with their middle fingers. Harriet lifted her palm to mute them again. Trevor's muffled screams trailed over the murmurs of the crowd, his blindfold soaked from tears.

Shea observed the scene from behind the wooden pillar, her mouth agape in disgust. She watched as Trevor writhed against the ropes binding his wrists, his head hanging low and defeated through muted sobs. Her heart dropped. She'd witnessed similar experiences during her childhood in the Dome when the State televised public executions. Shea had always looked away right before the executioner squeezed trigger. A single bullet to the back of the head was the State's preferred method. Thinking back, she couldn't remember their specific crimes, only vague accusations and rushed private trials. But something she could never forget were the motions and words spoken before each execution:

A peace officer in a pressed blue dress uniform stood, stoic and dignified, behind a hooded figure. Television cameras focused on the pair, who stood on a concrete platform inside the Ministry of Defense's prison. The prisoner's wrists were bound behind their back, and they offered no resistance when the officer pushed them down to their knees.

The guard raised a pistol to the back of the prisoner's skull.

"His Majesty Guide Us..."

The pistol fired.

"May Strength Remain."

"This organization provided Mr. Mills with steady employment, a home, and the luxury of a transport vehicle. These were gifts, privileges, under *my* sanction! And how does he repay me?" Harriet strolled down the altar toward Trevor, who contorted his shoulders against the pole. "My generosity, my *charity*, was repaid with disloyalty. By snitching to Dome POs like an ungrateful rat!"

The jeering and heckling erupted once again, yet Harriet continued above their clamor. "When interrogated by those Statesman pigs, Mr. Mills leaked information that nearly prevented vital medical supplies from reaching this borough. From reaching you and your children. His cowardice endangered your families!"

Someone hurled a bottle that struck Trevor's skull, opening a gash on his eyebrow that dripped dark blood over his blindfold.

Shea gritted her teeth. "This is wrong."

"I'm sorry, Shea. It is how it is." Simon's voice was somber in her ear.

A heavy unease crept through her bones as she watched an empty glass thrown from the crowd, shattering against the man's chest. He buckled and cried out against the slurs and curses.

"You son-of-a-bitch!"

"Traitor!"

"Snitch!"

Harriet raised a hand to the crowd, who complied and grew still. She turned to face Trevor and slid the cloth gag out from between his lips. "How does the accused plea to these charges?"

Trevor trembled and sobbed uncontrollably. Sweat trailed down his flushed neck and cheeks as he raised his chin to spit out the words in a whimper, "G-Guilty. I'm… guilty."

Having heard his plea, Victoria stepped toward him. Her face was barren and devoid of expression, yet the hand gripping onto the knife was white-knuckled and taut.

"I don't understand," Shea uttered. "Why isn't he defending himself?"

"There was overwhelming evidence against him. Mama Wilder offered him his wife's pardon if he gave a guilty plea," Simon said. "Otherwise, Ma would've executed them both."

"There is only *one* form of payment I accept, ladies and gentlemen." Harriet stuffed the gag back inside Trevor's mouth as she addressed the crowd. "Loyalty. The state has abandoned you, mistreated and abused you! Yet I provide you and your children with medicine, employment, favors, protection… and all I ask in return is your unwavering loyalty. This is our code, this is how we survive!"

Victoria dragged the edge of her blade along Trevor's throat. Shea clasped her hands across her mouth, muting the scream erupting behind her lips, as blood spluttered from the corners of his gagged mouth and slit neck. His body jerked and convulsed against his bindings. Victoria took a step back and dropped her eyes to the floor. Half of the crowd cheered, while the other gasped at watching his body twist and twitch in the last moments of his life.

Televised state executions were cold, sterile, and detached. Viewers watched from the comfort of their homes as the hooded figure, a faceless enemy of the State, was put down like an animal with a single bullet. It was quick and clean. This execution was different. The scene that had unfolded in that church was raw, vivid, and intimate. The scent of Trevor's blood pooling at his feet carried through the chilled air in the church.

Shea's gaze drifted to Victoria, who remained still and unwavering despite the chaos erupting around her. Victoria's green eyes, devoid and empty, stared off toward the back of the church.

"Loyalty is the only form of payment I accept for my generosity, and death is the only form of punishment I accept for betraying that generosity," Harriet said. Her voice grew hoarse and fought back a cough erupting from her chest. She withdrew a handkerchief from her jacket pocket and raised it to her lips. Turning her back to the pews, she let out a deep, thunderous cough into the cloth before frantically wiping her mouth. She turned back to the crowd, sweat beads sliding down her neck, and cleared her throat. "Let his treachery be a reminder of what happens to those who betray us and their people. Now, return to your homes!"

Shea couldn't compel herself to move away as the residents rose from the pews. She watched as Victoria turned and strode across the room toward the kitchen, leaving Trevor's lifeless body bound to the pole. He was left hanging limp by his bound wrists, blood cascaded down his chest. She stared at him and recalled the countless hooded figures she'd seen lying dead at their executioner's feet.

"His Majesty Guide Us..."

"May Strength Remain."

Chapter 23

Victoria hurled the bloodied knife into the kitchen's industrial sink and braced her palms against the countertop. She drew in a long, deep breath and reached out to twist open the faucet. Her eyes lingered on the smear of scarlet across the sink's basin, left from her soiled fingers, before snatching the knife up again. As she ran the knife beneath the trickling water, Trevor's blood slid away from the blade's cold, metallic edge.

How could he be so fucking stupid?

She recalled Trevor's unease that afternoon at the Ministry of Health and Wellness. He wasn't normally known for his steel nerves, but he was never as anxious as he'd been during that resupply run. The two had normally shared friendly banter during their drives together, but that day he'd remained unusually reserved and quiet. Victoria could even see a slick sheen of sweat across his brow when she departed the van with her duffle bag.

He almost left without me... that son-of-a-bitch was afraid of getting caught, and almost drove off without me. He knew. He fucking knew!

She ran her fingers beneath the stream of cold water and watched the blood rinse from her skin. Letting the chill creep up her wrist, her gaze pulled back to the blood-stained faucet handle. A tremor crept up her icy fingers as her face and ears flushed hot with anger. Her fingers groped for the nearest empty glass on the counter and hurled it against the wall. Its shattered pieces dropped to the tile floor below.

"What the hell is wrong with you?"

Victoria looked over her shoulder. Shea entered through the kitchen entrance, her body rigid and guarded. She crossed her arms across her chest with a furious, heated stare.

"Oh, so her majesty is *talking* to me now? I'm shocked you're breaking our no-contact rule." Victoria turned back to shut off the water as Shea entered deeper inside the kitchen.

"How can you call what just happened back there a *trial?*"

"It was an Anchor trial, and we had evidence. He admitted to it and faced the consequences. Quick and simple."

Shea scowled. "It's barbaric."

"Barbaric? Really?" Victoria reached out and took hold of a rag to dry her hands. She cocked an eyebrow. "No different than those executions your uncle orders, is it? Or displaying bodies on the Mourning Tower?" Her gaze lingered on her damp hands as she dried them. "Whether it's by bullet or knife, it's all the same."

Shea's face hardened. "I'm not going to stand here and pretend that the State's criminal justice system is fair and impartial. But it doesn't excuse Mama Wilder's cruelty—she should be better than them!"

"You know, for someone who's lived the privileged Statesman life, you sure have a lot of opinions on how Harriet should govern the people here."

"Oh, so I'm a hypocrite now? What about you?" Shea asked. "I thought Valkyries were supposed to serve with honor and integrity? But look at you! You're a glorified executioner at this point. You're just another fucking thug!"

Victoria tossed the damp rag into the sink and stepped closer. Her cold, rigid gaze locked onto Shea. "I strongly advise that until you've taken the time to understand the people residing here and the State's crimes against them, against *me*, you keep your fucking opinions to yourself."

"I could've gone back to the Dome, but I didn't. I chose to stay here, to help these people," Shea snapped back, drawing closer to her. "You don't think I see how these people suffer?"

"You've been here, what, two lunars? And sure, you volunteered to stay here out of the 'goodness of your heart,' but that Statesmen silver spoon is still firmly lodged up that ass of yours."

"You don't fucking know me," Shea hissed.

"I know enough. Not everyone has the luxury of playing the white knight like you do." Victoria sneered and pushed past Shea, knocking into her shoulder as she passed. "And Harriet has a few things for you, if you aren't too busy congratulating yourself for being morally superior to the rest of us."

She exited the kitchen, leaving Shea standing alone and fuming.

***

Shea wrapped her fingers around the doorknob to Mama Wilder's office and twisted it open. On any normal occasion she would offer a courtesy knock, especially considering the old woman's propensity for proper manners. But she was still fuming and tired, and was too impatient for manners.

"Harriet—"

She stood still in the doorway. Mama Wilder was slumped over her desk, an oxygen mask held firmly over her nose and mouth. The salt-and-pepper dreads rested, crookedly placed, on the wig mannequin bust nearby, leaving her scalp bald and exposed. Her tired eyes glanced over to Shea before she gestured to shut the door.

"You always gotta be so damn nosy, don't you. Can't knock?" Mama Wilder said. The mask muffled her words as she spoke. Silence hung between them as they looked at one another. "Rough night?"

Shea observed her oxygen mask and craned her neck to see the small tubular tank at her heels. Glancing at the old woman's hands, she noticed her white handkerchief balled up in her palm. Dark red splotches marked the white threads. She felt an unease rise from her gut at recalling the woman's unyielding coughing fits. Shea made a calculated guess and swallowed hard: *lung cancer.*

"What stage?"

Mama Wilder guffawed. "How'd you know?"

"I'm a doctor. I'm good at making educated guesses, and you smoke more than anyone on this station, I think."

"If you're gonna offer me your medical advice, don't waste your breath," the old woman croaked through the mask still pressed over her lips. The oxygen tank beside her desk groaned, and the mask let out a sharp hiss. "I suppose I'm at the stage right before the jumping-off point."

"Does Simon know?" Shea asked, her voice softening despite the frustration still churning in her chest.

Mama Wilder pulled the mask away from her face and coughed violently into her bloodied handkerchief. She took a breath, turned, and pointed at Shea with the mask still clutched in her hand. "No, and your skinny white ass isn't going to tell him, either. Understand?"

"He's your son—I think he deserves to know that his mother is dying," Shea said, sensing a tinge of anger nip at her nerves. "Take it from someone whose mother is already dead."

The woman pressed the mask over her mouth and nose again, eyeing Shea with a cold, callous stare. "It's none of your business what I do or do not tell my own child. This conversation will not leave this office. Is that understood?"

Shea remained silent in her frustration as she strode across the room and took a seat across from Mama Wilder's desk. There was no point arguing with the stubborn woman.

"Well, here's hoping he isn't the one who has to find your dead body after you're gone." Shea's words tasted bitter. She imagined an arm dangling over the bathroom tub, its bathwater a deep scarlet.

"Tell me, Dr. Tristan, what do you think would happen if word got out in the boroughs that I'm on my deathbed? How do you think the Trinities would react?" Despite the exhaustion in her voice, her piercing eyes burrowed through Shea's with a fiery verve. "I already know what you think about that performance downstairs this evening, but that's how it's gotta be to maintain order 'round here. We can't afford to be perceived as weak, and neither can this organization. Power sometimes has to be a performance."

Shea observed a black folder resting on the surface of the desk near Harriet's elbow. It lay open, revealing a stack of documents and a single photograph of Trevor, the man sagging lifeless from the pillar downstairs. Her anger festered.

"You mean *you* can't be perceived as weak."

She snickered. "I *am* this organization. What do you think would happen here if I wasn't around to keep these people in check? It'd be goddamn anarchy, especially if the State got involved." The oxygen mask hissed with her deep inhale of breath.

"And when you're gone, what then?" Shea asked pointedly. "Who's going to fill that chair and run this place? As you said yourself, you are Shadow, after all. Bern is older than you are, Tony's an idiot, Victoria is insane, and Simon's too kind of a man to pull off cruel performance art like you can."

Mama Wilder leaned back in her chair and inhaled a long, hissing breath from the canister. "Perhaps I'm still working that out, Doctor. Who knows, maybe your uncle will roll out his Peace Accords and everyone here will suddenly live in peace and harmony with the rest of the station?" Sarcasm ran thick in her voice. "But while I do so much enjoy hearing unsolicited advice on how to run my own fucking organization, at the end of the day it isn't any of your damn business."

"It is my business if I'm a part of an organization that's at risk of collapsing after your death."

"Yes, fine. Duly noted. Now what the hell do you want?" she asked with an air of exasperation and impatience.

Shea sat up straighter in the chair. "The lunatic said you had something for me."

"Oh, that's right." Mama Wilder snapped her fingers. "You'll be happy to learn that we have a lead on that illness you've been studying."

Shea's eyes widened, and she blinked. The anger drained

from her face. "What, really? How? From what?"

"Victoria ran an errand and retrieved some of your mother's old research files. We believe they might shed some light on what the hell's been goin' on."

"Wait," Shea stammered, her brow furrowed. "I don't understand… my *mother*? What do she or her research have anything to do with any of this?"

Mama Wilder hesitated, watching Shea's growing discomfort. She cocked her head to the side with an amused grin. "Your mother never told you, did she?"

"Told me what?"

"About her job at the state, her ongoing research? What work she was doing for her brother? The chancellor?"

"She was a doctor. She saved lives."

"I have no doubt that you believe that. And in a way, she was," Mama Wilder said. The oxygen mask hissed with another haggard intake of breath. "But her field, her *project*, was a little more… specialized."

"What do you mean specialized? What project?"

The woman sat back in her chair and peered back over her shoulder. A document box rested in the corner, its lid ajar.

"You see that over there?" she asked, gesturing with her thumb. Shea, confused, acknowledged that she did. "It may be best if you just go through that mess first. Might help sort some shit out."

"What's in it?"

"No doubt you can figure that out for yourself within the comfort of your exam room, bedroom, or wherever the hell else that isn't here," Mama Wilder said, her voice growing increasingly tired. "Now if you wouldn't mind getting the fuck out of my office so I can continue dying in peace."

It took only a few moments for Shea to reach her examination room from the office. The box was heavier than it appeared, and hauling it down the steps was more of a struggle than she'd anticipated. She wondered, during her awkward descent down the steps, just how much documentation rested inside. The idea that it was her mother's research made her both excited and anxious.

She set the box down on the tiled floor beside the upholstered chair with a breath of relief. Slipping off the box's lid, she sat in the chair and peered down at the contents inside. Her eyes trailed over the stacks of papers and charts, her heart fluttering when she recognized the familiar penmanship jotted across the various documents. She reached in and pulled out a sheet of paper, tracing her finger along her mother's signature at the bottom. Her eyes welled with tears.

Shea's heart ached, twisting beneath her ribs, while she tried to force back the last memory she had of her mother before her death.

Shea was sitting in the corner of the medical library, a book spread across her lap, when her comms unit beeped. She jerked up, startled, and tapped the unit in her ear with a smile. "Hey Mom! I'm happy you called. Having a good day so—"

"Yes, sweetheart, everything's fine," her mother's voice cut her off. She sounded weary, anxious. "I just wanted to apologize for being a bit aloof; I know I haven't been around for you much lately."

Shea shrugged and leaned back into the cushioned library chair. "It's fine, don't worry about it. I know you've been busy with work and all. It's been a bit lonely without Dad or Charles, but their work is important, too."

"I know, dear. I miss them, too." Her mother was silent for a few moments, then continued. "I'm wondering, out of curiosity, if anyone's approached you lately to ask about my work?"

"What? No. Why?" Shea asked, nearly chuckling.

"Just curious, is all," her mother said promptly. "Listen, will you be home tonight for dinner? I haven't seen you in a while, and I think it would be nice for us to spend some time together."

Shea glanced down at the book in her lap and frowned. A note was written on a sheet of paper tucked along the spine: group meeting, 19:30, library lobby.

"I don't think I can... one of my classes has a group project due next week and we're meeting tonight to pool all the research we've collected. How about tomorrow night?"

Her mother was silent again for a few moments. She sighed and sniffled. "That would be nice. I love you, sweetheart. Good luck with your project."

"Thanks, Mom. Love you, too."

She'd returned home at 21:36 that evening to discover her mother's body lying naked in a tub of bloody water, her wrists gashed.

Shea removed stacks of documents and placed them on the floor beside her feet. At the bottom of the box, beneath all of the charts and papers, sat a portable disk player. She removed it and popped open the lid; there was a labeled disk inside: *RAVEN. STRONGHOLD.*

Closing the lid, she turned the device on and flipped up the small attached monitor. The screen flickered before displaying a white, sterile laboratory. A woman stepped into view and adjusted her glasses with a hopeful smile across her face. Shea gasped and clasped her hand across her lips.

Dr. Lilly Tristan. Shea's mother.

Chapter 24

05LUN13, C164

Dr. Tristan smiles and adjusts her black-rimmed glasses. She looks straight into the camera, her office arranged neatly in the background. Her eyes are bright, her smile wide and earnest.

"It is 09:38 on the 13th day of 5th lunar, 164th cycle. My name is Dr. Lilly Tristan, and I am the lead researcher for Odin Prime's newest sanctioned endeavor: Project Stronghold.

"It is with extreme honor and pride that I lead this enterprise, and I hope that we can achieve the results our station so desperately needs: a stronger line of defense against biological threats to our home station and colony. I am struck with the immense importance of our ambitions, and I cannot emphasize enough how vital our success will be for the survival of our people. Too many have already been lost to the Ink, and we will cease to exist should our efforts fail again. All previous endeavors have ended in failure, but I am confident in our team's expertise and tenacity.

"I will be making occasional video entries, more for my own personal use in organizing my thoughts as we progress, while also maintaining written notes and records for documentation. I pray to the Patriarch that our work leads to a more prosperous, stable, and healthy society. May His Majesty Guide Us."

08LUN25, C164

Dr. Tristan stands in front of the camera with a surgical mask across her face and goggles over her eyes. She adjusts the camera, tilting the screen with agitation behind her hazel eyes. She curses under her breath and manages to straighten the camera angle.

"We've been at it for a little over three lunars now. It's taken some time and considerable effort, but we've managed to successfully, *and safely*, transport a sponge fungus specimen from Valhalla for further research and experimentation. His fortune shines."

She turns and backs away from the screen to reveal a quarantine chamber behind her. She steps forward and slides her hands through two gloved holes along the side. The video feed switches to an angle from within the container, where Dr. Tristan picks up a small petri dish inside.

"We are able to safely handle the specimen through this quarantine chamber. Apex researchers insist that the Ink is transmitted through direct contact with infected blood, or after the fungi's liquefied spores evaporate. These vapor spores leave humans vulnerable to inhaling the toxic material. You can see here how the liquefied spores secrete from the sponge-like exterior are black, resembling thick, viscous ink. Appropriately named, I think."

She slides a gloved finger along the soft, malleable surface of the fungus. It is the size of a closed fist, and the pressure of her touch releases a bead of thick, black ooze.

"Perhaps with further research on this strange species, Project Stronghold can develop a vaccination to mitigate the spread of Ink. We can not only preserve the safety of those on Odin Prime, but also enable our return to Valhalla. We can finally continue our colonization efforts and fulfill our destiny on the moon that gave our lives meaning and purpose in this devoid corner of space."

Dr. Tristan glides her gloved finger across the bead of Ink before the video cuts out.

11LUN18, C164

Dr. Tristan sits in front of the camera. She appears tired; strands of hair have fallen from her bun and lay draped over her slouched shoulders.

"It is 23:51. We've made strides in understanding the sponge fungus, and the viscous spores it produces. We've discovered that the Ink can only infect its victims through inhaling airborne fungal spores or direct contact with the mucus through unprotected skin." She takes a breath and shakes her head.

"My heart breaks for those victims we exterminated for the sake of public safety, when no such action was needed. So many innocent people… lost due to our lack of understanding of the disease. My solace comes in the belief that our work will prevent such needless loss of life.

"On that note, our research team struck a bit of a wall in recent weeks on how to proceed with our research. We've reached the point where many feel we are ready for experimentation. And while I may agree to this point, we were at a juncture regarding by what means that experimentation will proceed. I made the case for sticking with rat test subjects, but my suggestion was opposed by my colleagues, whom

I shall not reveal in this recording out of respect for this project's integrity."

Dr. Tristan sighs and rubs the heel of her palm against her forehead. "It was decided to proceed with human subjects. Convicts, specifically. It was made mention that Odin Prime does not have the luxury of time on its hands, and that certain measures must be taken to ensure the prosperity of all, even at the expense of others. I disagreed and tried to push back against the decision to experiment on human subjects, but I was reassured this was the best course of action moving forward.

"I'm at least relieved that the subjects will be criminals and enemies of the state. Most would have faced a fate on the Mourning Tower anyway. At least we won't be wasting innocent lives in the pursuit of scientific discovery. I suppose the sacrifice these convicts will make for Odin Prime is more than enough to make up for their respective crimes. The subjects arrive tomorrow, and I would be lying if I said I was comfortable with this. But if it will help save lives, it must be done. May His Majesty guide us."

03LUN30, C165

Dr. Tristan stands in front of the camera, leaning her hands against the edge of her desk, head lowered. She sniffles and lifts her gaze to reveal red, puffy eyes.

"It's only been a few lunars and we've already lost half of our subjects. We started with five hundred. And now…" Her empty gaze looks out past the camera. She shakes her head. "Two hundred and forty left. What a waste of resources. To so easily lose half our testing population… We have to find a way to keep them alive long enough to test of vaccination samples. But so far nothing's worked. The human immune system just… can't handle it. We must find a way to fortify our immune system against this disease.

"Each subject's experience is the same. It begins with a mind fever, followed by gradual liver failure and jaundice. The body continues to shut down, and the final symptoms lead to rapid deterioration: internal bleeding, the worsening fever, organ failure… and then it's over.

"We'll have to find another way. We have no choice. Failure is not acceptable when the entire fate of Odin Prime and our presence on Valhalla is at stake. So many projects have failed before… I refuse to accept failure with ours. There has to be another way."

Dr. Tristan turns her eyes to the camera. They are tired, but there is a determined, driven anger behind them.

"At this point, the only thing that matters is Odin Prime. And we'll find a way. We have to."

05LUN09, C165

Dr. Tristan appears on-screen with a wide, hopeful smile across her face. She is excited, and she claps her hands together.

"I think we've finally done it! His Fortune Shines! I've developed a plan last week that may save our research. I'm proposing we use stem cell therapy on our subjects to fortify their immune systems against the Ink. I've broached the idea with Dr. Samson, and he is skeptical but willing to try. Whether the treatment alone will pave the way for resistance to the Ink, or assist in developing a possible vaccination, we aren't yet sure. But it is at least *something*! We couldn't afford to lose more subjects to this research at the rate we were going and still hope to produce meaningful results.

"Dr. Samson and I have been working on compiling a list

of subjects we feel would benefit most from the stem cell therapy. We're hoping that those who have been suffering the most from the illness, and require the treatment the most, will be the first on our list.

"We are nearly one cycle into the project and I feared that we would perhaps fail, given our previous trajectory. But this gives me hope. I believe we may yet yield positive results to present to the Party Assembly. We can only hope and pray. His Majesty Guide Us!"

09LUN13, C165

Dr. Tristan appears unsure and conflicted. Her lips are turned down in a frown; her brow is furrowed and creased. She looks over her shoulder for a moment, then directs her attention back to the camera.

"I am not entirely sure how to explain all that's happened in the lunars following my last recording. It's past midnight, and most of my research fellows have gone home for the night.

"My stem cell therapy was, not to brag, a *magnificent* success. Harvesting the necessary cells from healthy subjects' bone marrow was… unpleasant, but the results were—*are*—extraordinary. Not only have the test subjects successfully resisted Ink fatality, but their bodies have… *changed* somehow. It's not only their immune systems that have improved, it is their overall resiliency and healing. It's remarkable, actually, to see the human body mend itself so quickly.

I brought the results forward to the Party Assembly yesterday evening and suggested we move forward using the stem cell therapy to help fortify the entire Odin Prime population. Imagine our entire society strong enough to return to Valhalla—to properly colonize the moon without fear of the Ink. Imagine the immense productivity and efficiency of a labor force that needn't be restrained by the worry of deteriorating health?"

Dr. Tristan faltered. Her jaw tautened. "Chancellor Tristan promptly ended the assembly meeting and requested a private meeting." She looked over her shoulder again, then back at the camera. Her voice quieted. "The State feels that Project Stronghold should shift its priorities. My research fellows are to continue their vaccination progress with the Ink, per our previous guidance, and Dr. Samson and I are to break off into another branch of research. There seems to be a particularly elevated interest in the discovery the stem cell therapy experimentation yielded.

"We have yet to be briefed on how we shall move forward with this new focus of research. But I have faith that my brother's guidance is for the greater good of Odin Prime, as it has been since his inauguration." She paused, took a deep breath, and forced a smile. "May His Majesty Guide Us."

01LUN10, C166

Dr. Tristan's face is stoic. Her eyes have hardened as she gazes into the camera. The office behind her is cluttered with scattered documents and stacks of papers and books. Her back is straight and rigid, and her hands rest clasped in front of her.

"I will keep this brief, as I am not authorized to continue recording research findings outside of official channels. This is merely a recording to provide some sense of closure to this series. It didn't feel right having my previous video act as the final representation of our progress.

"I cannot divulge the direction our research has taken, Dr.

Samson and I, nor can I offer any insight on the possible implications of our work. I will state, however, that no greater endeavor has ever come to fruition within this department, and I am honored in the work that we do in both the name of science and station security. It is my hope that future generations will look back at the steps we've taken as necessary for the betterment of our society.

"This is Dr. Lilly Tristan, signing off as senior project leader for Project Stronghold. May His Majesty Guide Us."

[CLASSIFIED/SECRET] 09LUN02, C166
[CLASSIFIED/SECRET]

The camera flickers to life to display three individuals inside an examination room. Dr. Tristan stands beside a male colleague peering down at a thin woman sitting at the center-placed table.

"Subject Raven, place your hands on the table."

The bald woman seated at a cold metal table complies without hesitation and slides her thin, pale hands onto the metallic surface. She looks to be in her mid-twenties, however any youthful glow left in her face has long since passed. Her pallid, sunken cheeks are marked with faded freckles. The only striking feature that remains is her vibrant green eyes, which now stare into the empty space ahead of her. Despite the fragility of her stature, her piercing gaze and tense jaw denote a lingering strength that existed before and has not yet diminished.

The tall older gentleman, with peppered hair and a trimmed beard to match, reaches deep into his lab coat to withdraw a black pocketknife. Placing the opened knife on the table beside the woman's hands, he reaches in his pocket once more and retrieves a pulse pistol. His forefinger wraps around the pistol's trigger as he steps back from the subject.

Dr. Tristan stands in the far corner and peeks up at a surveillance camera hung from the ceiling. "Commencing Project Stronghold Obedience Trial, Series 09 on Subject Raven. Time is now 15:00 on the 2nd day of the 9th lunar, 166th cycle."

"Subject Raven, take the knife into your right hand," the male observer commands. The subject does as she is instructed, robotically taking the hilt of the pocketknife into her right hand. She doesn't break her empty forward gaze even once. "Subject Raven, raise the knife in front of you." Again the woman complies and extends her right arm to hold the knife out in front of her chest.

"Very good, Raven." Dr. Tristan steps farther into the center of the room. Taking measured steps, she enters the path of the subject's empty gaze. The subject never raises her eyes to meet her observers. She remains passive and vacant. Upon allowing herself to have a few quiet moments to visually study her subject, Dr. Tristan continues cautiously, "Subject Raven, stab yourself in the chest with the knife in your right hand."

The subject doesn't hesitate. She plunges the knife deep into the left side of her chest above her breast. Hunched over, the subject does not cry out or scream. Dr. Tristan's jaw tightens, her gaze steady. Their subject is clearly in pain, but she doesn't verbally express that pain or fight against it. Her jaw and teeth clench, and the throbbing veins on her neck and forehead surface against her sickeningly pale skin. She doesn't remove the knife, even as dark red blood slips over the hilt and dances across her tightened white knuckles.

A grin cracks at the corner of the male observer's lips. "Subject Raven, remove the knife from your chest and place it on the table in front of you."

The subject slides the knife's blade from her chest and places the bloodied weapon calmly on the metal table. A quiet sigh escapes her dry, cracked lips. An expression of momentary relief flashes in her eyes, and then fades. Blood trickles down her chest and stains her white tunic, but soon ceases as the open wound gradually closes shut, leaving the bloodied skin untarnished. After the knife wound has mended, the subject returns to her passive, vacant posture in her cold metal chair.

The observers exchange a quick, knowing glance. The male steps toward the table and places the pistol in front of the subject. Dr. Tristan once again turns her attention to the hanging surveillance camera in the corner. Her voice cracks briefly before regaining composure. "Subject Raven has passed the first phase of the obedience trial. Subject did not hesitate in following self-inflicting commands, and now qualifies for the final phase of testing. Please send in the variable."

A few quiet moments pass before a door opens in the back corner. Two dark figures drag a small, thin woman from the door's entrance toward the metal table. A sack is draped over her head, and long blonde curls hair hang from underneath. Sitting the woman down in the chair opposite of Subject Raven, one of the guards peels the sack from her head and steps away. The young woman has a youthful, bright face with dark blue eyes that are now filled with terror. A strip of duct tape binds her mouth, and when her eyes meet with the battered and bloodied woman sitting across from her, she lets out a muted, stifled shriek.

A flash of recognition registered on the subject's face as she looks at this woman, whose sorrowful blue eyes are now filled with tears. The woman's wrists are bound behind her back, and her shoulders and arms contort in a struggle to break free. Between her jerking and twisting against her restraints, the woman darts quick, desperate glances at the subject sitting passively in front of her.

"Subject Raven," Dr. Tristan begins, her voice slow and deliberate, "pick up the pistol with your right hand and aim it at this woman."

The subject again does not falter, despite what seems to be a hint of doubt in her eyes. Taking the pulse pistol into her right hand, the subject raises the weapon and points the barrel directly at the woman's forehead. Tears now stream down the bound woman's flushed cheeks as she looks at the subject, shaking her head mournfully. The woman's inaudible sobs fill the quiet examination room.

"Subject Raven has passed the visual variable obedience phase. We will now commence the audible variable phase," Dr. Tristan states flatly as she writes notes onto her clipboard. She glances nervously at the video camera in the corner with white knuckles trembling against her clipboard. The male observer steps forward and takes the young woman's jaw into his hands. He grabs the tape across her lips and peels it off with one, quick motion.

"Baby, please!" the young woman shouts, tears streaming down her face. "Please don't do this. Don't listen to them. You're stronger than this, you're stronger than them!"

"Subject Raven..." Dr. Tristan watches her subject's resolve begin to waver. The subject's brow begins to furrow, her lips twitch. As the subject locks eyes with the desperate woman sitting across from her, the hand grasping tightly to the pistol begins to softly tremble. Her jaw clenches and her eyes begin to fill with tears, despite the emptiness across her face.

"Subject Raven, shoot and kill this woman," Dr. Tristan instructs flatly.

The subject does not comply.

Dr. Tristan glances up at the camera before turning her attention back to the subject. The young woman's sobs hang heavy in the thick, tense air. "Subject Raven," she continues, "you were instructed to shoot and kill this woman."

The young woman sobs and watches in anguish as the subject wraps her finger around the pistol's trigger. "Please… Victo—"

Subject Raven squeezes the trigger.

Red sprays against the clean white wall. The round caught her between the eyes, silencing her sobs in one thunderous gunshot. A tear rolls down the subject's cheek as she continues to hold the pistol ahead of her, awaiting instruction.

The room falls silent and still before Dr. Tristan finally steps forward; she turns her face from the camera to wipe away a tear from her eye. Her quiet voice masks a quiver. "Very good, Subject Raven. Very good. Now, return the pistol to the table."

The subject complies immediately and places the pistol on the metal table. The male observer retrieves the weapon as his partner glanced upward once more at the surveillance camera. She continues, vacantly, "Subject Raven has passed all phases of the Project Stronghold Obedience Trial. The time is now 15:09, making the trial the slowest on record for all subjects. Recommend continued conditioning."

The two guards break the zip tie restricting the dead woman's wrists and drag her lifeless body from the room. The subject does not break her empty forward gaze to watch the body disappear behind her. Another tear drops from the subject's eye as Dr. Tristan places a reassuring hand on her bony shoulder. As she speaks, the subject stares at the blood spray against the white wall; her face hardens, and the remaining tears lingering in her eyes sink away.

"Good job, Raven. Very good."

The camera feed abruptly cuts.

03LUN02,C167 – *Final Entry*

The room is dark, lit only by the glow of the computer monitor. Dr. Tristan leans close to the camera. Her bun is loose and hanging strands of hair across her pale, weeping face. She's removed her glasses to cover her eyes, tears streaming down her cheeks.

"We were wrong! God, I knew it from the start, but I couldn't say no. We were so wrong." She weeps quietly and rocks back and forth. She sniffles, wipes the tears from her damp cheeks, and turns her bloodshot gaze toward the camera.

"I don't know where to start, but I know I don't have much time. I think… I think this will be my final recording. My confession, if you will.

"We've been found out. I don't—I don't know how, but she knows what we've done. What *I've* done. I promised her that admittance into the program would be better for her daughter than the other punishment that awaited her, but I'm not so sure anymore. She's coming for me, I can feel it, like a cold breath on my neck. Nothing I can say or do will absolve me of the terrible things we've done to these people, even if it all started in the name of keeping the station safe.

"But god, it went wrong… all wrong… I thought I'd be safe as long as I was under the protection and guidance of the State, that it would free me of my guilt. Dr. Samson is actually proud of the work we've done. Fucking *proud*! And why shouldn't he be? His plan actually worked. His vaccination actually *works* now. So now the State has both an Ink vaccination and… god, whatever the hell those monsters are that we created in the process."

Dr. Tristan glances over her shoulder with frightened eyes. Her movements are quick, jumpy.

"I don't care that they were criminals. They were still human, *are* still human. Or maybe they no longer are, I don't know anymore, after what we've done to them, after what we've turned them into. Maybe they're just monsters now. Hollow and mindless. Soulless killers. None of it was my idea. But Dr. Samson, and the State… what else would they do when they discovered they had a population that could heal like that?

"This shall be my legacy. Not my medical practice, or dedication to helping my community. Not as a loving wife, sister, or mother. No, my legacy will be one of immoral, feckless corruption. Instead of preserving life, I have delivered nothing but death."

Tears trail down her cheeks, and her bottom lip quivers as she continues, "I can only pray that the Patriarch will have mercy on me, and that my loved ones will not pay for my sins. With every broken piece of my damned soul, I am sorry. Please, forgive me."

Dr. Tristan reaches a trembling hand toward the camera.
The screen goes black.

223

Chapter 25

"Hey Francis, I'm home," Victoria called out when she closed the front door to the modest two-bedroom residential suite. "Sorry it's so late—I had to stay at the office to finish up some last-minute paperwork on the Montgomery case."

She tossed her keys into a ceramic basin resting on a nearby table and glanced at herself in the mirror hanging from the wall. Her red hair was too short to pull into a bun while in uniform. She still had at least seven centimeters to spare before it reached the edge of her jacket collar, which, per peace officer regulation 600-7, meant that she then had to wear it up in a bun. She'd seen other female officers struggle to keep their buns looking neat throughout their long work hours and decided to keep hers just short enough to be within standards. But she preferred it this way anyway, resting just below her ears, layered and hanging. She smoothed a few stray strands before peering at her neck, checking for any blemishes surfacing to her pale skin. A chill ran up her spine thinking of the lips pressed against her skin just an hour earlier.

"Hey there, beautiful," Francis said through a smile. He approached her and wrapped his arms around her waist to pull her body against his. His lips and trimmed beard brushed against her cheek. She shivered when he kissed her hair. His cologne, although sweet, soured her stomach. "Thought you said that case was all wrapped up?"

The smile she returned through the reflection of the mirror was taut and strained. She rested her hands on his wrists and she leaned against his chest, sensing his warmth radiate through her back. It was striking how Francis, with his tall and solid stature, compared to Cosette's smaller frame. She thought of Cosette's smooth skin as she glided her fingers along Francis's hairy, muscled forearms; his skin was darker and coarser. Her fingertips trailed to the wedding ring on his left hand, and she grew acutely aware of the weight of her own. He'd been sure to not buy her a large ring; she'd wanted it to be simple and uncomplicated, like their marriage was meant to be. But it felt heavy now and irritated her skin. She closed her eyes and took a haggard breath.

He's too good a man to deserve this. This is unfair. To both of us, it's just... cruel.

"One of the greenies messed up the evidence inventory receipts. I had to sit with him and supervise as they re-did *every single one*," she said, exasperated.

That part had been true, but she'd only sat with the rookie for a total of one hour, assisting with the re-documentation. The rookie was her responsibility, after all, and she couldn't be expected to assign them a corrective task without staying to ensure the work was done properly. But after that initial hour, she'd spent the following two with Cosette in her studio apartment in the Middle Borough. She closed her eyes again and recalled the feel of the twin mattress beneath them, the brushing of the sheets against her bare skin, the warmth of the woman she loved filling her with every breath. She suppressed the smile creeping across her lips.

"Oh, was it Barnes? He seems kinda flaky," Francis said, making a pitiful face. Victoria's urge to smile sunk away when she saw the look in his eye. She pitied him.

She laughed. "Yeah. God, he's fucking hopeless. And my schedule is hectic enough with Valkyrie assembly to play babysitter. I should have Mom transfer him over to *your* squad, so he can be your headache instead of mine."

Francis reached down and gave her butt a quick squeeze. "You wouldn't dare, you cruel woman." She felt her body stiffen. "He's lucky you went easy on him. I would've assigned him pod duty for at least two weeks."

Pod duty. Of all the extra duties assigned to peace officers as a form of punishment, pod duty was the dullest and most menial. Victoria had experienced it a handful of times. She'd arrived late for two shifts and lost a radio in the same week, much to her superior's ire. The punishment was an entire lunar of daily four-hour shifts, after the duty-day, spent checking inventory and maintenance for the state's fifty emergency evacuation pods beneath the Ministry of Defense. She'd breathed a sigh of relief when she submitted her final shift log; she was never late to another shift again. She couldn't imagine wishing that upon another officer unless they truly deserved it.

Francis leaned in to kiss her neck and lingered, breathing in her scent. "Mmm, did you get a new perfume? You smell a bit different."

She faltered for a few moments before turning to step away from his embrace. She removed her officer's jacket and opened the nearby closet door to hang it.

"Yeah, figured I'd try something new. Do you like it?"

Francis shrugged. "You could smell like a heap of dog shit and I wouldn't mind."

"Oh, dog shit, eh? Well aren't you a charmer."

Victoria closed the closet door and turned to discover she now stood alone in the foyer. She glanced down the empty hallway and peered around the corner to the dining room. The air had turned foul, rank with rot. She lifted her hand to cover her nose, her brow furrowed, and turned her gaze to the dining table. Two plates of rotted food sat on the table, the dishes gathering dust below the hanging, cobwebbed ceiling fan. A lingering unease crawled up her spine, and she felt a sinking dread creep through bones.

"Francis?"

There was only silence.

The sour air felt thick against her throat and lungs as she breathed, tasting the stale dust with each inhale. She walked down the long hallway and entered the dim kitchen. An overwhelming stench of spoiled food hit her, released from the refrigerator, ajar in the corner. Gagging, disgusted, she clasped her hand across her mouth and nearly tripped when backing away into the empty hallway.

"*Subject Raven.*"

Her blood chilled in her veins. Victoria spun around and reached for the firearm at her waist, only to find her holster empty. Her hands trembled, and when she lifted her gaze she discovered Trevor, a deep gash across his throat, staring back at her through clouded, milky eyes. The open wound seeped with dark, crimson blood onto his chest and feet, staining the carpet beneath him. He parted his lips to speak, but what escaped his lips was a choked gurgle, a sputter of fluid. He reached for her and took a step forward. His dead gaze held hers and filled her now-hammering heart with terror.

She turned and bolted up the nearby stairs, screaming against the sound of Trevor's feet scuffing across the floor in close pursuit. Running into the bathroom, she turned and slammed the door shut behind her. She fastened the lock and backed away from the sound of creaking stairs. She was shaking now, a cold sweat breaking out on her brow.

BANG. BANG. BANG.

"Hammond! Come in, Hammond!"

Victoria spun around to discover herself standing in a darkened shuttle. Pulsating, crimson emergency lights ran along the ceiling, offering momentary glimpses through the shuttle's narrow, pitch-black corridor. She breathed steadily through her helmet and recognized the comforting weight of her Valkyrie air-tight, pressurized armor. She peered ahead with the butt of her rifle pressed into the crook of her armored shoulder, at the ready to fire.

The voice spoke again from inside her helmet. *"Do you copy, Hammond?"*

"This is Hammond. Send it," Victoria whispered, and moved forward with slow, calculated steps. Her eyes remained trained down the barrel of her weapon.

"Report operation status."

"We've breached the shuttle undetected. Outer corridor is secured. Approaching the center chamber now."

"Roger. Lethal force has been authorized. You are a go for weapons red. Initiate contact when ready. Support elements are on standby."

"That's a good copy," Victoria replied, and switched off her rifle's safety. "Will report back on mission complete."

She pressed her back against the wall and eyed the main door ahead of her. Her heart drummed in her chest, and she took a deep breath as she unclipped a flash-grenade from her belt. She primed the grenade and threw herself forward, kicking the doors open with one solid strike of her boot.

There were screams before she even tossed the grenade. The doors swung shut just as the grenade detonated with a deafening, blinding crack in the darkness. Victoria pushed forward once again through the doors, rifle raised, and shouted for the civilians to drop to the ground. But what Victoria found inside the chamber left her stunned, frozen in place with her rifle at the ready.

Every man, woman, and child lay dead on the floor. The deafening screams of the citizens had fallen silent, and the quiet that now fell upon her weighed heavy against her ears as she willed herself to move forward. Her eyes darted from victim to victim, tears welling in her eyes at each new tragedy spread across the ground. Each was riddled with gunshot wounds, many in their backs, as if they'd been trying to flee.

Victoria's breath and pulse quickened. She strained to control her breathing despite the spiraling sensation of hopelessness clutching her chest.

"W—what..." She breathed and steadied the tremor in her fingers. Gritting her teeth, she scanned the room for any remaining Forsaken. Victoria needed to stay focused; she needed to finish the mission. "This is Hammond, something's happened. The passengers... they're... they're gone. They've killed them all."

Silence.

"Home station, this is Hammond. Respond."

Silence.

All she could hear now was her heaving breaths inside the helmet and the thick throbbing of her pulse in her ears. She blinked away the look of horror in the victim's eyes, trying instead to stare ahead at the opposite entry to the chamber. A bead of sweat trailed down the bridge of her nose inside her helmet.

A gun cocked behind her. She spun, dropped to one knee, and leveled her rifle at the target. A tall Forsaken man, clad in ragged clothes, aimed a pistol at her. Blood trailed down from his eyes, his lips curled in a snarl. She squeezed the trigger.

"... Victoria?"

Victoria blinked. Instead of the Forsaken terrorist, she found Cosette standing at the opposite end of the chamber. She watched Cosette, hands trembling, gingerly touch the fresh gunshot wound on her forehead. Tears spilled down her cheeks from deep blue eyes. Cosette met Victoria's gaze, closed her eyes, and toppled over onto the body-littered floor.

"No!" She dropped her weapon and threw herself toward Cosette's body.

Victoria jolted up from her pillow with a gasp. Her heart beat heavy in her throat. Her bedsheet clung to her bare, sweat-slicked legs as she lifted her palms to cradle her face. She shivered against the evening air blowing through her cracked window. The chill lingered, whether from the dream or the air, she couldn't tell. She forced slow, haggard breaths between her pursed lips.

"Fucking hell," she whispered. Wiping away a bead of

sweat from her brow, she turned and noticed the warm, shifting body sleeping soundly beside her. Bethany was supposed to have left already, but had instead fallen asleep after their time together. Victoria watched her now, observing the rise and fall of her bare shoulders as she slept, and felt a sudden irritation crawling beneath her damp skin.

She slipped out from the sheets and strode, naked and shivering, to the heap of clothes lying on the floor across the room. After dressing in an old pair of sweats and sports bra, she turned and exited the room, being sure not to wake the companion girl still asleep in her bed. She pressed her back against the cold wall and reached into her pocket to extract a small baggie of white powder. She clumsily tapped a line onto her wrist in the darkness. It was messy, but it would be enough to calm her nerves.

Her bare feet padded along the wooden floors of the congregational space downstairs. Trevor's body was gone by now, dragged away by Tony for dumping in the fishery on the other side of the borough. But she couldn't help but feel a strange, eerie pull from the pole that still stood erect near the altar. The darkness in the church should've obscured her vision, but that didn't stop her from seeing the blood still stained against the wood when she passed by. In the darkness, the stains looked as black as tar.

She needed to sweat out her nightmare. It gnawed at her nerves, scratched around beneath her skin like a burrowing insect. Her punching bag often did the trick, bearing the brunt of her many sleepless, agitated nights. She knew that if it hadn't been for her unique abilities, her knuckles would have been bloodied and raw after the hours she'd spent pummeling the bag. But instead, they would be pristine and untarnished come morning, despite the obvious abuse marked on the bag itself. Victoria needed the release that exercise offered her. She needed to lose herself in training; she needed to forget their faces. She needed relief.

When Victoria reached the basement level, she hesitated when she saw the door to Shea's examination room open. Stepping closer, she peered inside to discover Shea asleep on the upholstered chair. An empty box sat at her feet with sheets of paper, folders, and charts scattered around her on the tile floor. The scent of cheap liquor, tinged with lavender perfume, carried across the air. A nearly emptied bottle sat cradled in Shea's arms. Just as she began to turn away to walk toward the training room, a photograph lying on the floor drew her attention.

Victoria stepped inside, crouched, and took the photograph into her hand. The photograph was of her during Peace Academy graduation, suited in her pressed formal uniform. She'd graduated with honors that day and wore her decorations proudly on her chest. Her fingertips trailed along her name tape, *DeLeon*, and felt that bitter pang of guilt again. But there was something else twisting around with that bitterness, too palpable to ignore: resentment. She considered the eyes of her former self, saw the blind optimism and arrogance, and scoffed.

Victoria lifted her gaze from the picture and found Shea awake and watching her. She'd expected to see that seething anger from the kitchen hours ago, but instead detected pity behind her bloodshot, puffy eyes. Shea looked to have spent most of the evening sobbing, and now uncurled herself on the chair and rested her elbows on her knees, still clutching the neck of the bottle in her hand.

Victoria could smell the liquor on Shea's breath as she spoke, her words slurred.

"I need to talk to you."

"Is that so?" Victoria jeered. "About what?"

Shea swallowed hard and fidgeted with the bottle in her hands.

"About what my mother did to you."

Chapter 26

"Y ou're drunk." Victoria carelessly tossed the photograph back onto the pile of scattered documents on the floor. Irritation nipped at her patience. "And emotional. Emotional and drunk. Not a good combination."

"I'll admit, it's probably not… the wisest or most well-adjusted coping mechanism." Shea took a deep breath and lazily toyed with the bottle in her hands. The remaining liquid sloshed about at the bottom. "But when you're faced with the bitter reality that the person you loved and cherished the most is… *was*… a fucking monster, and a liar, and… and everything you thought you knew about your world, your whole life, just turns out to be one giant fucking lie after another—"

Shea's tired voice cracked as tears brimmed in her blood-shot eyes. She pressed the heel of her wrist against her forehead and forced slow, measured breaths though quivering lips. Tears streamed down her flushed cheeks despite her most earnest attempts to keep them at bay. Victoria watched her and said nothing.

"This is all just so… fucked up."

Silence hung between them for a few moments, until

Victoria couldn't bear it any longer and cleared her throat. "Do you expect me to pity you or something?"

Shea failed to suppress the chuckle rising from her churning, unsteady gut. *"Pity me?* For what, being a gullible idiot?" She sniffed and wiped a tear from her cheek. "No, I don't want that. Especially not from you, of all people."

"Me of all people, huh?" Victoria shook her head and reached out to sift through the various documents across the floor. "Listen, I can go get Simon if you're looking for a shoulder to cry on. I'm not that good at this sorta thing—"

"No," Shea interjected. "No, I… wanted to talk to *you.*"

Victoria let out a tired sigh and leaned back on her palms. "Alright. Talk, then. I won't stay long."

Shea hesitated for a moment and, after swallowing another mouthful of liquor, steadied her intoxicated gaze on Victoria. "I didn't know what she'd done to you. To…" She gestured clumsily with the bottle at the scattered papers. "To all of them."

A tear rolled down Shea's cheek. Victoria could see Shea brush moisture from her face from her peripheral, but said nothing. She instead fixed her attention on a single spot on the floor ahead of her with darkening eyes and tightening lips.

"I watched the recordings. All of 'em. It was so unreal, ya know? Seeing my mom again after all these cycles. I thought I'd be happy seeing her face again but… what she was said and did… it wrecked me. But the video of you and my mother, with that girl." Shea choked back tears. "I wouldn't have believed it if I hadn't seen it for myself."

Victoria dropped her gaze to the papers strewn about the tile floor and leaned forward to lazily sort through them with the tip of her finger. "I'm so sorry, Victoria. I had no idea. I've been an ass this whole time to you, but I didn't know. I'm *so* sorry."

Victoria glanced up and parted her lips to speak, her unsteady nerves panging against a sudden flush of anger. Yet when her gaze fell on the bloodshot, tear-filled eyes staring back at her, she faltered. Her jaw grew taut, and she swallowed down the bitter venom edging up her throat. All she'd ever felt for Shea was anger. Shea was a product of her mother's upbringing: spoiled, entitled, ignorant. But here she was, apologizing for it all, even when it was never her choice to be born into that environment or control her mother's actions. Victoria didn't know what to say, didn't even quite know how to react.

She fidgeted and cracked her knuckles. She clenched her fists, then released. The punching bag was waiting for her down the hall. The nightmare still lingered on her nerves, and she yearned to clobber it from her mind, blow by blow against the battered duct tape and plastic surface of the bag.

Victoria dropped her gaze. "Stop apologizing."

"How did you know her? The girl in the tape, I mean."

Victoria's heart hitched, and she took a deep breath. "She was, uh..." She wavered. Her words caught in her throat. "Someone very important to me."

"I'm sorry," Shea said, brushing away another tear. "I can understand why you hated my mother so much. And me."

"I don't... *hate* you. You just—" Victoria stammered. Her gaze lifted to meet Shea's before dropping again. "You remind me of her."

"I figured," Shea said.

Shea moved from the chair and sat on the floor with

Victoria, still distant enough for both their liking. She picked up a few papers and sifted through them one by one, flipping through the sheets and charts with a keen, albeit tipsy, eye.

Her words slurred as she spoke. "I've read through all of these documents, about Project Stronghold and the trials, but it still feels so, I dunno, disjointed somehow. It's all horrifying, that's for certain. I can't believe that she would've agreed to be a part of this."

Victoria scoffed. "It started as medical testing for public health—simple enough to justify to any reasonable person. No one wanted the Ink to make its way to Odin Prime, but they wanted a way to protect themselves if it did. Horrific, but necessary. And when you're using criminals and non-citizens as subjects, why feel guilty about the work you're doing? It was for the greater good. You probably would've done the same."

"That's… presumptive. But yeah, well, still." Shea let out a sigh and pressed her palm against the side of her head. The sharp scent of cheap liquor tinged her breath. "How did you even find yourself in the program in the first place? I mean, I've known plenty of Statesmen to have been found guilty of moral edict violations, but—"

"I, uh…" Victoria interrupted, then faltered. "Iris volunteered me for the program, actually. She understood it the same as your mother did—for the 'greater good', ya know?" She offered a scornful smile and shook her head. "She saw my other options as worse off for me, anyway."

Shea frowned. "We didn't exactly win the 'good mother' lotteries, did we?"

Victoria's lips cracked the faintest of smiles as she shook her head. "No. Far from it."

Shea skimmed through the paperwork, looking over her mother's handwritten notes in the margins of research documents and medical charts. She looked through photographs of the subjects in various stages of the process and seemed to steel herself against the horror of it all. Her lips were downturned, her brow knit and eyes darkening. The color in her skin drained from her face, and she took a breath as if to subdue her alcohol-filled belly from retching. She met Victoria's gaze for a moment, and Victoria could read the discomfort crawling across the girl's skin.

"It's too coincidental, isn't it?" Shea said, tapping at the documents in her hands. "What happened to Lauren, what's been happening to these kids—their symptoms are straight out of these reports. The hemorrhagic fevers, liver failure, jaundice, internal bleeding…"

Victoria's jaw tautened. "I doubt it's coincidence."

Shea met her set gaze. "But I don't understand… the Ink my mother used was *contained*. Otherwise it would have spread throughout the entire station cycles ago. There has never been a reported Ink case on Odin Prime—*ever*. So why now? Where did it come from?"

"I don't know why the hell you're asking me. I haven't a goddamn clue," Victoria said.

Shea went silent for a few moments with her gaze lingering over the scattered documents. She eventually took a deep, nervous breath. "Would you feel comfortable working with me?"

Victoria cocked an eyebrow. "In what capacity?"

"These notes, these documents smuggled from my mother's lab. They're part of a larger puzzle that I can't figure out on my own. You survived the trials… and if this *is* Ink"—Shea faltered and gestured toward Victoria with an uncertain look in her eye—"you may be what we need to make sense of it all. You're a common denominator."

"What are you suggesting?" Victoria's voice was cold and tense.

Shea stammered. "Just—I don't know…"

Victoria's face flushed hot, her brow creased. "You want to experiment on me, too? Is that it?"

"People are dying, Victoria" Shea said, exasperated. "I understand your reservations, but even if working together only leads to a better understanding of what it is we're dealing with, then it'll be better than where we stand now. All we have to work from now is disjointed video recordings and old notes."

Victoria watched Shea in silence for a few moments, regarding her with an unsure eye. The heated anger eventually drained from her face, and her fists and jaw relaxed.

"Why are you doing this?"

Shea blinked, confused. "Doing what?"

"Helping these people. Non-citizens. You don't owe them anything. You had a life back in the center you could've escaped back to, and been protected by your uncle. Why do any of this?"

Shea blinked back a fresh swell of tears in her eyes and shrugged. "None of this would've happened if it weren't for my mother, right?" She sniffled and wiped a fallen tear from her cheek. "I can't just walk away from it, can I?"

She cleared her throat and continued, "Besides, what kind of doctor would I be if I turned a blind eye to human suffering?"

Victoria considered her for a few moments. She noted Shea's bloodshot, swimming eyes and the exhaustion weighing down against her shoulders. Victoria had seen her after each child had died in that last week, had watched each loss break her further. She couldn't blame the girl for drinking herself numb after the week she had endured. But there was a genuine look in Shea's tired, pleading eyes that gave Victoria pause.

She abruptly stood from the floor.

"You should get some rest, maybe drink some water first." Victoria turned and walked out of the examination room, leaving Shea sitting alone among the scattered papers.

Shea called out behind her. "But, what about-"

Victoria answered from the hallway with a stark tone of finality. "We can begin tomorrow, if you haven't already given yourself alcohol poisoning."

Shea said nothing more as Victoria entered the training room. The lights above flickered to life as she stepped across the mat to rest her forehead against the patched heavyweight punching bag. She closed her eyes, pressed her closed fists against the fabric, and leaned into its reassuring weight. Her nerves were on edge and pricked at her unsettled mind like a fingernail to a scab.

What the hell are you doing? Why are you helping her?

Victoria clenched her jaw and breathed steadily.

Why are you going out of your way after what her mother did to you?

She counted each breath calm herself as her thoughts turned to Cosette. A hint of a smile curled at her mouth as her eyes stung with tears. The tension in her shoulders eased as she remembered the way Cosette's blue eyes brightened when she laughed, and how she remained tenaciously warm and gentle despite the sharp cruelty around them. She couldn't help but see that same tenacity in Shea, in how gentle she was with the children she treated despite their stark realities, and knew without a doubt that Cosette would be fond of her. She would approve of Shea's thoughtful, albeit naïve, persistence.

A tear trailed down her cheek as she opened her eyes again to stare at the punching bag in front of her. She stilled for a moment before wiping the moisture from her cheek.

Because she would want me to.

Chapter 27

"**A**m I hallucinating, or is that Vic I see sitting in Shea's examination chair?" Shea heard Simon chuckle from the basement hallway. She glanced up from her work tray to watch him lean against the door frame. He regarded the two women with an amused, curious eye.

"Oh, I dunno. Why don't you come a little closer for a better look?" Victoria shifted uneasily beside her in the upholstered chair and gestured to him with her middle finger.

"Nah, I'm good. This view is better enjoyed from a safe distance." Simon smiled and nodded his head to Shea. "Everything alright here?"

"Hm? Oh, yeah, everything's fine," Shea returned to the task at hand and slid across the tiled floor on her stool, wheeling a tall metal standing tray with her. The instruments resting on the tray jostled as it moved. "A bit hungover, but I had worse after graduating from medical school. We're just about to get this ball rolling."

"And what *ball* is it that we're rolling, exactly?" Simon asked.

"Oh, you didn't hear? I'm the prized guinea pig. *Again,*"

Victoria replied, deadpan.

Simon stepped into the room and moved toward Shea. His voice dropped to a whisper. "Wait, hold on—did Ma sign off on this?"

Victoria scoffed. "Don't be such a mama's boy. It's fine."

Simon straightened his back, indignant. "I'm not a *mama's boy*, it's just that I can't imagine Ma being thrilled about back-alley science experimentation happenin' inside her business."

"Relax, all we're doing today is taking some blood samples. That's all," Shea said, as she tied a thin rubber hose around Victoria's firm bicep. She motioned for her to flex her hand as though she were squeezing a ball, prompting a plump, ripe vein to surface in the crook of her elbow. "Besides, she wants this outbreak contained as much as we do, so I doubt she'd protest. Good vein, by the way."

Victoria raised her eyebrows. "You hear that, Simon? I have a good vein."

"And you think this'll help figure out what's goin' on 'round here?" Simon asked, more serious now as he watched Shea prep the exposed vein with an alcohol swab. He glanced over to Victoria to see the discomfort behind her eyes.

"That's what I'm hoping." Shea turned and tossed the used swab into the trash. "At least to help identify whatever the hell *it* is. I've already collected some blood samples from a few of the victims to compare with hers."

"Why?" Simon asked.

"Long story," Victoria replied. She closed her eyes and took a steady breath. "One that I don't care to get into at the moment, if you don't mind."

"And you're okay being poked at again?" Simon asked.

Victoria let out a nervous chuckle and shook her head. "Am I okay with it? Sure. Do I like it? No way in hell."

Shea unwrapped the sterile needle from its packaging. The sound of rustling plastic drew Victoria's attention and she recoiled, pressing against the side of the armrest. Her eyes remained affixed to the sharp point of the needle.

"Whoa, are you fucking kidding me? Can't we use something a little smaller than *that*?"

Shea froze, baffled. "Are you… being serious right now?"

"Yes, I'm being serious right now."

"I could literally shoot you in the gut right now and you'd be fine. Hell, I *did* shoot you! It's just a needle," Shea said. Victoria remained silent and tilted her chin up in childish defiance. "So, what, you want a butterfly needle?"

"First off, pump the brakes on that judgment, Doc. Secondly, I don't like needles. Sure, I can heal, but shit still hurts."

"You're being ridiculous."

"Butterfly needle or no blood, period."

Agitation flushed warm against Shea's cheeks as she forced a smile. She threw the needle into the garbage. "Okay, fine, I'll just throw away this perfectly good sterile needle when we're already in a supply shortage."

"I'm sure we'll manage," Victoria retorted, her voice dripping with sarcasm.

"I've treated children who're better with needles than you." Shea opened a nearby drawer to retrieve the butterfly needle pack. "I'd figure a person who couldn't die would be a tad braver with needles."

"Yeah, well, I doubt you've met children who've been poked more times than a lab rat. And don't be ridiculous, of course I can die," Victoria chided, eyeing up the plump vein under her skin. "It just takes a little more effort, is all."

"*More effort?* That's cryptic." Shea tapped lightly on the vein and used her thumb to pull down and tighten the skin. She pierced the vein with the thin needle. Scarlet blood siphoned through the narrow tube and into the syringe. "So, what, if you're hurled into space? Fell into a meat grinder? That sort of thing?"

"I would pay good money to see you try to throw Vic into space," Simon snickered.

Victoria grinned. "Why d'you wanna know? Planning on getting rid of me?"

Shea couldn't help the smile pulling at her lips. "If you keep asking for butterfly needles, maybe. Besides, without you here it'd be too pleasant. And we wouldn't want that, would we?"

She released the knot on the rubber hose around Victoria's arm and switched out the filled vial for an empty one. They needed to collect three full vials of blood, and she was pleased to see how willing Victoria's vein was to supply it. When Shea glanced up from the filled vial to Victoria's face, she was surprised to see the hint of a smile.

"I can die just like anyone else, I'm just a little more durable, is all. I can heal, but I can't grow back limbs or anything," Victoria explained. "So, in case you wanna kill me, try decapitation, disemboweling, drowning, being blown to bits—"

"Yep, I think I got it Victoria, thanks." Shea sealed the filled vial and used her teeth to pull off a marker's cap to jot down the time and date onto the glass. She penned a "V" beside the date and recapped the marker.

"I've seen Vic heal from getting shot, stabbed, impaled, bones broken, burns..." Simon said. "I almost saw a decapitation once, that was pretty rad. Terrifying, but rad."

"I don't mean to break up the party or nothin'," Tony barked as he thundered through the doorway, clutching his blood-soaked hand to his chest. His face grimaced, and his lips curled in a snarl. "But could I get some goddamn help here?"

Shea was switching the final empty vial into the syringe when she noticed Tony's large knuckles caked red with drying blood. A thick shard of glass was wedged deep into his meaty palm, which now dripped crimson droplets onto her white tile floor.

"The hell happened to you?" Victoria stifled a chuckle, clearly amused by Tony's sporadic wincing.

"Some dumb broad wasn't making good on her security fee this cycle, so I had to go have a little talk with her. Her husband wasn't particularly cooperative." He left a trail of blood droplets as he stepped further into the examination room.

"Serves you right for having that stupid 'security fee' in the first place," Shea muttered under her breath.

"What was that?" Tony asked.

"Hm? Oh, nothing."

Shea thought back to the Shadow marking on Lauren's door frame indicting that she was under the protection of Shadow. Lauren had paid her security fee acting as Victoria's personal 'companion,' but she wondered how other residents paid their dues. She couldn't help but feel a tinge of satisfaction at Tony's trivial suffering.

She directed her attention to Simon and shrugged, motioning with the filled vials in her hands. "My hands are a bit full at the moment, you mind?"

Simon gave a knowing smile and stepped toward the supply cabinet. "Yeah, I got you."

"What in god's name are you guys doin' down here?" Tony asked as he followed Simon toward the cabinets, eyeing the butterfly needle pierced into Victoria's skin.

"Just trying to get a handle on this illness going around," Shea responded absentmindedly as she removed the last filled vial of blood. She placed a cotton ball in the crook of Victoria's elbow and slid the needle from her vein, disposing it in the nearby orange bucket.

Tony frowned. "Oh, right. Poor kids—"

"Aw, damn," Simon uttered as he rummaged through the open supply cabinets. "Looks like we gotta make another supply run. We've only got a couple Cyntrax left."

"Hell, we may not even *need* a supply run if our people keep dyin' off like this," Victoria said.

Shea heard them speaking and stilled. A blood-chilling dread crept up her spine, her pulse quickened.

Kids. Cyntrax.

She reached out and placed the last vial of blood beside the others on the counter. Her gaze lingered out into the emptiness ahead of her as the bitter realization sank into her gut like a heavy stone.

Victoria watched her for a few moments with a look of concern in her eyes. "Looking a bit pale, Doc."

Shea crossed her arms and swiveled around in her stool to face the others. She cleared her throat and shifted her shoulders, a pitiful attempt at feigned calm.

"Why has it only been children who are affected? Why

not adults, too? The parents would otherwise be the most exposed, but they're not ill. Why?"

"Lauren wasn't a kid and she still kicked it," Tony responded with an indifferent shrug.

Shea shook her head. "But what if it wasn't *Lauren* who was initially infected? It's possible that the child she was carrying suffered the infection first, making Lauren's death secondary. But, there's something that Lauren and the children have in common. What's the pattern?"

Victoria hesitated; her jaw tightened. "You can't be serious."

"Oh, I am." Shea stood from the stool and paced the length of the office. She met Victoria's hardened gaze. "Tell me I'm wrong."

"What the hell are y'all talking about?" Tony asked through clenched teeth, wincing as Simon plucked the embedded glass from his skin.

"The Cyntrax." Victoria's voice was resolute and steady. She still held Shea's stare as she spoke. "Children and pregnant women have priority for Cyntrax treatments. They're the most vulnerable to malnutrition and immunodeficiency."

"Wait." Simon raised his palms, head shaking in disbelief. "Are you insinuating that the *Cyntrax* is making people sick?"

"Like Victoria said, children and pregnant women are given priority. We've been short on supply, so they have been the only ones receiving the treatment. But they're also the only victims of this disease. The Cyntrax treatments are the single discriminating factor that connects them." Shea returned to her stool and rested her elbows on her knees to cradle her face in her hands. "So, either the Cyntrax itself is killing these children, or specific vials are contaminated."

"What does that mean?" Tony asked.

"It doesn't mean anything good," Victoria stated flatly.

Tony scoffed and looked around the room, agitated. "Yeah, no shit. And what the hell are we even supposed to do about it?"

"I got an idea," Simon said, peering at a clear vial of Cyntrax between his fingers. "I think it's time we make a visit to our friend, Mr. H."

Chapter 28

"Absolutely not!" Mama Wilder snapped, tapping her finger on her desk with each enunciated syllable. Simon rolled his eyes. "But Ma—"

"Don't 'but Ma' me, boy. I said *no*. And my word is final."

Shea stood silent, hands clasped in front of her, staring off to a vague point at the corner of the office. She noted Victoria looming near the door in her periphery, her bare arms crossed over her chest. Whether she was angry or worried, Shea couldn't quite tell. But Shea could tell, from the occasional sway from one foot to the other, that Victoria was at least uneasy.

"If we can get Mr. H to—"

"Mr. *Henderson*," Mama Wilder corrected.

Simon faltered. "… Mr. Henderson to speak with us, I think we can get better situational awareness of this illness we're facin'."

"Absolutely not," the old woman repeated through gritted teeth. "It's too damn dangerous to be waltzin' into Trinity territory. I won't risk you goin' and startin' trouble when shit is already tense. The Trinities are already on my shit-list for interferin' with our Dome supply run, and takin' out Dr. Anders in our own goddamn jurisdiction!" She slammed her fist against the table. A hot cup of tea jostled at the force. Taking a breath, she gathered her composure, and continued in a calmer tone. "They've obviously got an agenda, and I'm not willin' to tempt inviting any further attention until we have our bearings and are ready to defend ourselves."

"It's important," Simon stressed, leaning his palms against the surface of his mother's desk. "People will die before we get our bearings. *More children* will die."

Mama Wilder coughed into her handkerchief and abruptly wiped her lips. Her voice grew hoarse and strained. "People die every day. And you being willin' to put yourself in a position to easily provoke the Trinities into an all-out war will cost even more lives. No, my decision is final."

Simon parted his lips to bark back, his eyes burning, brow furrowed, but instead swallowed his words and remained silent. He let out a frustrated growl as he spun around and struck one of the leather chairs with his clenched fist, not waiting for his mother's dismissal before storming from the office.

Shea wasted no time in following him, leaving Mama Wilder and Victoria alone behind her. She felt Victoria's eyes follow her as she slipped into the hallway.

Hurrying down the spiral staircase, Shea found Simon sitting on an empty pew. He buried his face in his hands, breathing slow and steady to calm himself. She approached and sat beside him, resting her palm on his shoulder. His anger burned hot through his thin shirt.

"I'm sorry," she said, her voice almost in a whisper. "What'll we do now?"

"I'll tell you what we'll do," Simon answered, lifting his fiery gaze to meet hers. "We fuckin' go anyway."

***

The rickshaw jostled side to side when its wheel struck a broken brick on the cracked pavement. Shea cursed under her breath as the force pushed her against Simon's shoulder. She scooted back onto her flattened cushion and adjusted the shawl draped around her shoulders and hair.

"First time ridin' one of these?" Simon asked.

"No, I rode one back from Lauren's place." Another harsh bump against the wheels. Shea's jaw tautened, and her nostrils flared. "But that ride was much smoother than this one. And comfortable."

The cushion beneath her was old and flattened from cycles of use, and she braced herself, clutching onto a suspended leather strap above her, from the sharp turns and sudden jolts of the wooden carriage. The stench of trash lingered in the stale air. She lifted the shawl to cover her nose to conceal her face and repel the odor. They'd ridden the poorly maintained transport shuttle train from the Anchor and caught the first rickshaw parked outside the transit. Shea remarked how similar the Middle Borough's transit area was to the Anchor in both smell and visual poverty.

"What about the Middle Borough? Been here before?"

"First time, actually," Shea responded through the cloth covering her nose and lips.

Simon chuckled. "Well, then, you're in for a bit of treat. The standard of living isn't quite like you're used to in the Dome, but it's still nicer than what we have in the Anchor."

Shea knit her brow together and shot Simon a scrutinizing eye. "I remain unconvinced." She noted an excitement across Simon's face that she'd never seen before, and grimaced recalling the argument he'd had with his mother earlier that morning. "Simon, are you sure this is such a good idea? Harriet was pretty adamant about—"

"Ma is just stubborn." Simon waved a dismissive hand. "She'll be eatin' her words after we get back with the information we collect from our guy. You'll see."

"Have you ever done this before?"

"Done what? Blatantly disobeyed my psychopathic mother?" Shea merely held his gaze, waiting for his answer. He cleared his throat and adjusted his jacket collar. "Whatever, I'm twenty cycles old, a grown-ass man. I don't need my mother's permission for everything."

"You don't sound too confident, Simon."

"Whatever, stop being such a goody-two-shoes Statesman."

"Jackass." Shea playfully jabbed her knuckle into his ribs.

Simon licked the tip of his finger and made to stick it in her ear. "Princess."

The rickshaw turned a corner and the driver, shrugging his shoulders against the weight of the wooden poles, began to slow his pace to approach the routine security checkpoint along the road. Shea dipped her chin deeper into her shawl as Simon reached into the inside pocket of his jacket to retrieve a small black badge. She peeked over to discover a white crescent moon etched into the dark leather.

Simon met her curious gaze and smiled. "I like your perfume. What is that, lavender?"

"It is, yeah. And thanks. But how in the hell can you even smell my perfume over"—she gestured around them—"*this*? All I can smell is trash."

Simon laughed. "You get used to it. But I'm glad she picked that out for you. It's nice."

"Wait, who?"

Simon shushed her silent as they drew into the checkpoint.

The security guard approached the rickshaw and outstretched his hand. "Identification." His brow arched at Shea's obstructed face. She blinked and looked away, suddenly interested in the faded crimson pattern on the old carpet stapled to the carriage floor.

Simon lifted the badge and smiled kindly at the guard. "Is there a problem, sir?"

The guard, still eyeing Shea, took a moment to glance down at the leather badge. He hesitated and cleared his throat before returning it to Simon. "Of course not. We simply request that Shadow respect the terms of the inter-borough ceasefire and that you return by nightfall."

"Of course, don't we always?" Simon slid the badge back into his jacket. The guard, clearly uneasy, gestured to the tall, lanky driver to proceed down the road. When they pulled away, Shea turned and nudged Simon with her elbow.

"The hell was that about? An inter-borough *what*?"

"An inter-borough ceasefire. We have a precarious agreement with the Trinities: they control the Middle Borough, we control the Anchor. So, you can understand how each can be, hmm, *territorial*. Whenever we're entering the other's space, we're supposed to notify the gate security and keep to ourselves. Of course, that's not always the case," Simon explained.

Shea noticed the bumpiness of the paved road smooth when the driver pulled them deeper into the borough. The stench lingering in the air diminished the farther they moved away from the checkpoint, whose guard had now turned away to address another commuter. She looked out from the carriage and observed the increasing level of cleanliness of the streets and sidewalks. The homes, although still quite modest by Dome standards, were well-maintained and sturdy. Small shops and cafes lining the street serviced polite, well-dressed civilians who were just now beginning their lunch hour. Although this borough was still much less refined and wealthy than the Dome, it was most definitely a step up from her new home with Shadow.

"And if you *don't* keep to yourself?" Shea asked. Her thoughts fell on her predecessor, Dr. Anders. She shuddered and felt Simon shrug beside her. He grinned and pulled open his jacket to reveal a black handgun strapped to the inner lining.

"I keep my head down, but if one of the Trinities wants to start something, I'm prepared to finish it."

"Right here, please." Simon motioned for the driver to pull off to the curb. They came to a halt after turning inside a quiet alley. They dismounted from the rickety, tottering carriage. Shea was grateful to be back on her feet and glanced about, peering down each length of the alley, as Simon paid the exhausted driver.

They had arrived in a quieter residential area of the borough. Shea peered above her and noted thin window slates against the roof revealing occasional glimpses of orange gaseous clouds against a backdrop of inky-black space. There were no opportunities to peer out into space from the Anchor. She couldn't bear to look away now that she was given the chance to marvel at the sight, if only through a distant, narrow window. Her heart ached at the sight she'd grown too accustomed to in the Dome, and she yearned for the plentiful scenic views her previous life had granted her.

"You alright?"

Shea peeled her gaze from the sky and turned to notice Simon staring at her. There was a curious look in his eyes as he also lifted his chin to gaze above him.

"D'ya see something?"

"No, it's nothing." Shea scratched her nose and turned her attention to the towering apartment buildings around them. "So, why did Mama Wilder choose the Anchor over this place?"

Simon tucked his wallet back into his rear pocket. The rickshaw pulled away from the curb, leaving the two standing alone in the alleyway.

"It was a trade-off." Simon started walking toward the nearest apartment complex. Shea followed close behind him, making sure to keep the shawl wrapped across her nose and mouth. "Don't get me wrong, the Anchor is shitty, but we love that the state more or less wants nothing to do with it. It's a re-purposed warehouse and storage sector populated with refugees and non-citizens; not exactly prime real estate, ya know?"

"A bit too dirty for the refined tastes of pampered Statesmen," Shea uttered to herself as they stepped through the entryway.

"POs also don't have the manpower or resources to police-up our 'troublesome' borough while also maintaining control of the Dome and Middle. So, the unspoken arrangement is that Mom can govern as she sees fit as long as she keeps the order. And keeps non-citizens from flooding the rest of the station."

"I can't imagine her being overly excited about my uncle's

supposed 'Peace Accords,' then."

Simon frowned. "We joke that it's just the State talking outta their asses again, but I'd be lying if I said it wasn't costing Ma some sleep over it."

They stepped further into the complex's ill-lit foyer and moved toward the elevator platforms. The apartment building lacked the modest cosmopolitan vibe that Shea had witnessed throughout the rest of the Middle Borough, with its cute cafes and tiny goods shops. The old yellow wallpaper along the corridor peeled at the edges of the elevator and molding. There was a lingering scent of dust, cleaning detergent, and cooked onions in the air.

Shea watched Simon press the up button, unsure of exactly where he was bringing her. Or why.

"What do the Trinities get for having this borough?"

"They get a nicer territory, sure, but they have to deal with state presence. POs patrol the streets, it's wealthier, and most of the residents commute to the Dome for lower-to-mid-end jobs." Simon shrugged disapprovingly. "So yeah, it's a nicer place to put up your feet at the end of the day, but you've got the POs breathin' down your neck every goddamn minute of the day. They don't have the same autonomy as we do, workin' in the background and all. It's why they aren't as influential—they gotta stay under the radar."

Shea hesitated for a moment and bit her tongue. "Hm. Okay."

"That's unlike you."

"What is?"

"Not having an opinion about something." Simon grinned at her and leaned to tap her foot with his own. "Go on and say it, it's killing you."

"You think that State presence is a disadvantage, and I get that. You guys can do what you want, when you want, to whomever you want without consequence. Any kind of state interference would derail that. It makes sense, to a point." She turned and met his gaze. "But in the end, Harriet still rules under the State's consent. And I'm not so sure the Trinities are as disadvantaged by the State's presence as you think they might be. Things don't always appear as they seem."

"You insinuating somethin'?" Simon asked, cocking an eyebrow.

The elevator dinged as the metal doors opened with a squeak.

Shea shrugged and stepped inside. "Not particularly. I've learned in the past few lunars that not everything is as black and white as we may think it is."

The elevator carried them to the twenty-eighth floor of the complex, where Shea noted the broken, flickering ceiling lights trailing both directions down the hall.

"Who exactly is this Mr. H and why are we here to see him?" she asked in a hushed whisper as she followed Simon's footsteps.

"Mr. Gerald Henderson, or as most of us like to call him, Mr. *H*, works in the packaging department of the lab that manufactures Cyntrax." Simon halted in front of a door labeled *28-14* and shot Shea a smile. "And I'll give you one guess as to why I brought *you* today."

Shea stared at him, bewildered, as he raised his knuckles to knock on the door. There was a brief, heavy silence before they heard the approaching shuffling of slippered feet. A shadow cast over the door's interior peep-hole, and Shea imagined one squinted eye peering at them from the other side.

"Ahhhh, wha'd'you want?" The old man's voice sounded too muffled, even through the thick door.

Simon offered a warm smile and waved at the peep-hole. "Hey there, Mr. H, long time no see! Sorry for droppin' in like this, but I wanted to swing by to introduce you to our new resident physician, Dr. Shea."

The old man scoffed. "She any better than that jackass know-it-all Dr. Anders?"

"Oh yes, *much* better," Simon continued, his smile unwavering. "She's received the finest medical training available on the station, so I have no doubt that she can help you with your unique condition."

Unique condition? Shea shot a reproachful look at Simon.

The deadbolts securing the door released one after the other until the doorknob twisted and opened. Standing before them was a short, balding old man dressed in dress slacks and a button-up shirt. A surgical mask rested over his nose and mouth, and he wore powder-blue latex gloves. He fully swung open the door and outstretched his arm to welcome them inside the apartment.

One step into the apartment and Shea counted the stack of prescription bottles and antibacterial wipes on the kitchen counter. The realization as to why Simon had brought Shea that day suddenly struck her. The newest doctor, fresh out of medical school, was there to meet "Mr. H":

Mr. Hypochondriac.

Chapter 29

"Mama's gonna be mad when she finds you stole another one."

Victoria peeked one eye open and watched Theresa approach through the haze of cigarette smoke. It was midday, and she'd spent most of the morning training in the basement. Many sweaty hours later, she decided to shower up and relax in the rear of the empty church, stretched out on a pew with one of Mama Wilder's prized cigarettes. That particular spot, nestled near the back wall and a wooden pillar, offered some quiet and privacy in the usually busy meeting space. She found solace in the occasional seclusion of lying there, gazing up at the chipped, painted ceiling.

"You gonna tell on me, T?" She smiled and brought the cigarette back to her lips.

Theresa lay down farther along the pew, the crown of her head touching Victoria's. "Not if you let me try it?"

"Oooh, I don't think so." Victoria chuckled and let the smoke billow from her lips.

"Tony won't find out."

Theresa was sounding more like a rebellious teenager each day, and Victoria wasn't sure how she felt about that.

260

Theresa had barely been a teenager when they met, but she'd been inclined to toe the line and not rebel against her brother or Mama Wilder. That hadn't been the case since Shea landed on their doorstep and blatantly challenged nearly everything. A hint of a smile curled her lips.

"Swing and a miss, kid."

"*Simon* won't find out?" Theresa lifted her chin to peek back at Victoria.

"There ya go. And he most certainly *will* find out." She took another drag, holding the satisfying burn in her chest. "I don't foresee the doc being too pleased, either."

Theresa fell silent for a few moments, and the two lay still in the quiet, staring up through the smoke. "Has she figured anything out about what's going on?" Her voice, despite the forced courage, still carried with it a hint of apprehension.

"I know she's working on it. The girl's stubborn," Victoria replied, and tapped ash onto the floor. "It's just a bit slow-going, is all."

"I just haven't seen her all day and it's made me a little nervous. I mean, this is a big deal, right? Shouldn't she be working in her office? Combing through those samples or whatever?"

Victoria stopped mid-drag. "What d'you mean she hasn't been around?"

"She's been gone all day. You haven't noticed?"

Victoria let out a dismissive scoff. "Why would I have noticed? Besides, I was in the dummy room for most of the morning."

"Well, she's just *gone*. Not in her office, or bedroom. Just, poof." She gestured with her hands. "Simon, too. Oh god, you don't think they're, like, out together, doing stuff? Like… *adult stuff*?" Victoria could hear the distress in Theresa's voice and rolled her eyes.

"I doubt it, T. And even if they are, it's their business."

The two fell silent again. Victoria was sure that Theresa was busy being consumed by foolish, adolescent jealousy. She'd seen the way Theresa watched Simon and blushed when he instructed her in self-defense, or laughed extra hard at his terrible jokes. When Victoria thought on it, she remembered Theresa showing affection for Simon even before his transition, when he still went by 'Simone' and had a feminine, softer face. The passing cycles had only served to make the girl's crush deepen.

But Victoria hadn't noticed that the two were gone. The last she'd seen either of them was in Mama Wilder's office the night before, when Simon stormed out after his mother's refusal to acquiesce to his request. Venturing into Trinity territory could be dangerous, especially with how contentious affairs were between the two parties. Mama Wilder understood this and wasn't willing to risk provoking them further. Victoria couldn't blame her.

"They're just trying to help," Victoria had said to her after Shea exited the room. *"You can't fault them for that."*

Mama Wilder had patted at her lips with the handkerchief and tucked it away. *"And he's going to get himself killed in the process. And we can't risk the doctor falling back into State custody. I'm just tryin' to protect the stupid boy."*

I know. Victoria had thought at the time. *So am I.*

Victoria took one final puff from her cigarette and reached back to give what remained of the short butt to Theresa. The girl had too much on her mind, far too much for any teenager to reasonably handle, and one cigarette wasn't going to kill her. There were too many real, immediate threats to worry about. Victoria sat up from the pew and heard Theresa break out in a coughing fit behind her.

"Where you going?" Theresa asked between harsh, thick heaves. The girl gasped and patted at her chest.

Victoria offered a wave as she walked off.

"Out."

***

The interior of the apartment was as clean as Shea had expected it to be, considering its occupant's condition. It was a modest single-bedroom home with simple furniture and bare walls, and smelled faintly of astringent cleaning solution. She removed the scarf from her nose and took in a breath of artificial pine.

"That son-of-a-bitch told me I was crazy. Threw me right out of his office, told me never to come back. Can you believe such a thing? Heartless." Henderson threw his gloved hands in the air.

"You threatened him with a surgical knife, Mr. H," Simon said as he took a seat on the man's plastic-lined sofa. Shea sat beside him and felt the squeak of the plastic against her pants. She shifted and squeaked again, trying with no success to get comfortable.

"He deserved it, the bastard. Turning away a poor, sick old man…" Henderson sat down on the recliner across from them, also lined in clear plastic. Shea couldn't help but flinch at the sound his bottom made when he sat. "Don't tell me, Anders was caught in some kinda malpractice thing, right? Got fired for bein' a horse's ass?"

"He's dead, actually," Simon said matter-of-factly. "Got stabbed in the Anchor while doing a home visit."

Henderson snorted with laughter. "Serves 'im right. The bastard got what was coming to him." He gestured indifference and crossed his arms over his barrel chest, turning his attention to Shea. "So, what the hell're you doing working in the Anchor? Harriet drag you into it with one of her deals?"

"It's complicated. But yeah, it's something like that," Shea said through a forced smile, still acutely aware of the sensation of the cold plastic beneath her.

"I wouldn't doubt it. Ms. Wilder is a damn crook with her deals and *arrangements.*"

"Easy there, Mr. H, that's still my mama you're shit talkin'." Simon's voice was calm but pointed. Henderson offered an apathetic shrug in response. "But I got a proposition for ya, if you're interested."

Henderson turned and glanced up at the clock hung on the wall. "Impressive, a whole *four minutes* before getting right to the point. I like that—chit chat is just polite horseshit that wastes time, am I right? Alright, what is it? I'm listening."

Simon leaned forward to rest his elbows against his knees. "We need some more information about the Cyntrax shipments."

Henderson scoffed through his face mask. "Oh, you want *more* information! Of course, I haven't risked enough already, now you want more?" He shook his head and wrung his gloved hands together, making the latex squeak. The flesh of his neck and cheeks crimsoned. "Once your little team started picking off our supply deposits, guess whose office they started poking around looking for answers? You think that was easy for me? The stress alone made my symptoms flare up; the rashes were *unbearable.* And god, the stomach cramps!"

Simon remained calm and only smiled. "To which you've profited handsomely, as you well remember. Ma paid ten cycles advance for this place."

"It's not nearly enough, my friend. What's your payment this time around, huh? What could Mama Wilder possibly offer me that's worth sticking my neck out for again?"

Simon leaned back against the sofa with a knowing grin and gestured to Shea. "How about some much-needed medical attention?"

Shea clenched her jaw and fought the urge to slap the smug look from Simon's face. She willed her smile to remain affixed across her lips as she took in a deep, leveling breath. *You asshole.*

"What, and you think that's enough?" Henderson sounded genuinely offended at such an offer.

"I *know* it is. No doctor in the Middle is willing to see you anymore—you've threatened them all. Way to go on that, by the way. Amazing interpersonal skills."

"What's your fuckin' point?" Henderson's irritated gaze trained on Simon, and Shea could see his scowl behind the surgical mask.

"You're sick, no one in this borough will treat you, and you're too low on the social pole to get any kind of treatment in the Dome." Simon nodded toward Shea. "Our doctor is your only option if you want to get proper diagnosis and treatment. And she won't turn you away like the others have."

Henderson turned his attention to Shea and scrutinized her, eyeing her up and down to get a measure of her worth. Hot anger flushed against her cheeks. She felt like a bargaining chip, again. Simon must have learned this tactic from his mother.

Shea would have been apprehensive even if she'd agreed to this arrangement prior to their arrival. She had worked with hypochondriacs before, but always in coordination with a behavioral health specialist. Antidepressants helped these patients, along with consistent cognitive therapy, but she hated to admit that these resources were only available for citizens with considerable influence and wealth. Shea didn't imagine Henderson having either readily available.

She couldn't blame Dr. Anders for turning the old man away if he'd threatened him; she would've most likely done the same under the same circumstances. Treating hypochondriacs took a certain level of patience and tact, and overworked, exhausted doctors rarely had the compassion required to properly treat them. Hypochondriasis was an anxiety disorder, after all, and when an impatient or ill-prepared physician rebuffed a patient and failed to treat the psychosomatic conditions, it rarely ended well.

The old man finally spoke up after a long, tense silence.

"Fine," he blurted out. "But she comes to me. I don't wanna trek all the way to that hellhole of yours."

"No," Simon stated flatly. "It was a huge risk to even come out here to see you in the first place. We can't afford to continuously send her out like this. You come to us, and we'll reimburse you for the rickshaw and shuttle costs. Deal?" He reached his hand out across the open space between them. Henderson glanced down at the extended bare palm and recoiled. Shea noticed the disgust lingering in his eyes.

Shea couldn't exactly blame him for his paranoia, particularly in his line of work at the state lab. The more she observed the old man, with his gloved hands, affixed mask, plastic furniture, and sterilized home, the more her annoyance waned to pity.

Henderson let out a grumble. "I suppose we have a deal. What the hell you wanna know?"

Simon retracted his unshaken hand. "The Cyntrax shipments. Has anything seemed unusual within the past couple lunars?"

"Unusual? Like what?"

"Maybe in the way that they sort the doses before shipping them from the lab, or how they segregate the doses before packaging?" Shea asked, setting aside her frustration to focus on the task at hand.

Henderson shrugged, uncertain. "I mean, the only thing I can think of was the trial announcement, but that wasn't a big deal."

"Trial?" Simon asked. "What trial?"

"They notified our department that they'd be releasing a Cyntrax upgrade. Guess those hoity-toity scientists found a way to make it more potent or something, I dunno." Henderson scratched at his face as if lost in thought, then continued. "But of course we can't just distribute it out with the original ones. We gotta do a trial run before releasing it fully to the public. We usually ship those vials out to monitored control groups, then shift production for general release once it's received final approval. It's standard operating procedures, nothing unusual."

Shea's brow furrowed. "Who does the State use to test the trial doses for safety?"

"Do ya really gotta ask?" Henderson answered.

Non-citizens desperate for care, I'm sure.

"Do they keep the trial doses segregated from the older ones? Like, in the Ministry of Health and Wellness, would there be any chance of the vials getting mixed up?" Shea asked.

Henderson chuckled, genuinely amused by such an audacious question. "You kiddin' me? You think I'd still have a job if I mixed those up and improperly distributed them in the Ministry? I'd get canned, or worse."

There was silence between them for a few moments. Shea sat deep in thought, running her fingers through her hair. She closed her eyes, let out a sigh, and crossed her arms.

"Mr. Henderson, I have an additional request, if you don't mind. For your first appointment." Shea hesitated and considered what she would say next. "I know it'll be a risk, and I know it's asking a lot, but I need you to bring two sample vials of the Cyntrax, one old and one trial. Do you think you could do that for me?"

His jaw grew slack and dropped behind his mask. He faltered and threw his hands into the air. "Are you out of your mind? They keep a log of lot numbers for each shipment manifest—they'd notice if any were missing. I'd be putting a goddamn target on my back!"

Simon outstretched his hand to calm the old man. "We understand, but can you *alter* that manifest?"

"I don't think you can appreciate how breathtakingly fucked I'd be if I were caught doing any of that mess."

Shea's temper flared. "Mr. Henderson, I don't think you can appreciate how breathtakingly fucked we'll all be if we *don't* get those samples. The lives of everyone on this station are on the line, not just yours."

He watched her for a few moments, curious and unsure.

His eyes narrowed. "Is there somethin' going on in the Anchor that I should know about?"

"You get me those vials and I'll let you know."

A silence fell over them as the old man sat and watched them. He rose from his recliner and turned to pace the length of the room, his gaze trailing along the carpet before him.

"Alright, I'll get em for you," he said finally, halting behind his recliner. "But don't think I won't hesitate to throw y'all under the bus if it's my ass they start comin' after."

"We wouldn't expect anything less, Mr. H," Simon said, standing from the sofa. "It's a pleasure doing business with you."

Chapter 30

Simon took a triumphant step into the opened elevator and turned to Shea with a smile. "Well, that went well."

"You're such an asshole!" Shea swung a punch at his arm. The hit tweaked her wrist, and it throbbed as she tucked it beneath her armpit. She turned away from him, too angry to even look at his face.

"Whoa, what the hell's the matter?" Simon asked, bewildered but unfazed by the sudden outburst.

"What the hell is wrong with *you*?" Shea yelled. Her face flushed hot as she shoved him against the wall. "You didn't think to maybe, oh I don't know, *ask* me about all of this before dragging me along as fucking *leverage* in this idea of yours?"

Simon stammered and blinked, confused. "I'm sorry, I didn't think—"

"No, Simon, you *didn't* think!"

She crossed her arms and faced the closed doors, burning in her anger as they descended to the bottom floor. She couldn't begin to explain to him the risk she would take treating an unstable old man with violent tendencies, or how betrayed she felt by his failure to even discuss his plan with her.

"I really am sorry," Simon said, his voice softening. "I don't understand why you're so mad, though. I was afraid you'd say no, but to be honest I figured you'd be happy to help."

"I *am* happy to help." Shea measured her words, careful to not let her frustration get the better of her. "But you could've asked me. I would've agreed. Keeping me in the dark out of fear that I'd say no? Using me like that, you're no better than your mother." Shea swallowed the ire rising in her throat. "It shows you don't trust me, and it's a slap in the face."

The two stood together in the silence of the elevator until it came to a stop on the ground floor. When the doors parted, Shea felt the weight of Simon's arm lay across her shoulders. He pulled her close against his side as they stepped off into the lobby together.

"I can be a dick sometimes, I know. And I'm sorry. But let me make it up to you." His voice was kind, and when she looked up at him he was smiling down at her. "Let me get you a brew—my treat."

***

Shea leered at the tall mug of warm, dark brown liquid resting on the tilted old wooden bar table. She leaned against the stool beneath her and could smell the earthy, sweet scent of it. By the looks of it, the cafe owner had merely gone outside and scooped up a mug full of filthy street water and served it directly to his patrons. She lifted the glass to her eyes to test if she could see through the liquid, feeling dismayed when she discovered that she couldn't.

"Simon, what the shit is this?" When she turned, she saw that he was already half finished with his own, having downed the beverage in three mouthfuls. He smiled at her.

"I still can't believe you've never had brew. You Dome cats don't know what you're missin'." He gestured for her to try it, subduing his amusement at the grimace in her eyes when she withdrew the shawl to take a sip. "The Anchor has their own brew, too. But the middle makes the best, in my opinion. It's smoother and they can afford to mix it with better ingredients, like honey."

It was tepid and thick against her tongue, with an abrasive bitterness that sent her recoiling in her stool. She swallowed and felt her face contort against the bitterness but eased when a smooth honey aftertaste coated the back of her throat and tongue.

"Well it's… much different than anything I've had in the Dome, I'll give you that."

Simon shrugged. "Maybe it's an acquired taste. What do you typically drink back home?"

Back home. Shea breathed against a sinking weight in her chest and compelled herself to smile.

"Well, we use the same grain alcohol base, but we mix it differently. Some like theirs with citrus or fruit juices, or with flower teas and some cream instead of"—Shea eyed the mug in her hand—"instead of this… particular recipe."

"God, it's no wonder you aren't a fan of brew! I'd be spoiled too if I was raised with options like that," Simon said through a well-meaning smile before taking another sip. "Of all the ones you've tried, which is your favorite?"

Shea closed her eyes and heard the distant echo of her mother's voice congratulating her on her acceptance into medical school. The memory arose of her, smiling warmly with tears in her eyes, reaching out across the restaurant table to hand Shea a long-necked glass filled with a chilled, violet beverage.

"Lavender and citrus, I think. It's sweet but not too sweet that it feels like your teeth will rot right out of your mouth after one glass," Shea said with a light chuckle.

"Sounds nice. Maybe you can buy me a glass of it someday," Simon said before downing the rest of his drink. "But all this talk of drinks makes me want another. You good?"

Shea gestured for him to go back to the bar without her and smiled when he nearly skipped back to the bar with his empty mug.

This was the closest cafe to the inter-borough transit gate and was one of the dingier places Shea had seen during their short visit in the middle. The tables and stools leaned and wobbled from side to side depending on where their user applied weight. It was almost as if the furniture were as drunk as some of the customers, tottering off-balance with questionable stability. Nevertheless, the patrons seemed pleased with their friendly chatter and laughter, breaking only to take in a mouthful of whatever drink filled their glasses.

Simon had seated them near the rear of the establishment for privacy. They sat tucked behind a waist-high wall decorated with various hand-written notes and photographs left behind by happy patrons. Shea eyed one photograph of the chubby bartender lifting his shirt to expose his belly, while two drunken old men laughed and drew tiny penises on his gut. Scribbled along the margin in red ink: *Ralph lost a bet.*

The two couldn't stay but for a short while, only long enough to enjoy a quick drink before they'd have to return to the Anchor. Despite the usual coolness of Simon's demeanor, Shea had noticed him consistently looking over his shoulder, scanning their surroundings for what she assumed was possible PO or Trinity presence. His nerves had calmed some since the two sat down at their table, hidden with some privacy behind the barrier, but she could see him standing at the bar and waiting for his second drink, glancing over his shoulder again.

An unease thickened the air. She suddenly grew aware of the lingering sensation of being watched, and tucked the scarf around her face again. Her gaze scanned the cafe's late-afternoon crowd. There hadn't been anyone looking in their direction; the patrons had all seemed too interested in their own affairs to bother with them.

"Ma would kill me if she knew I was on my second drink," Simon said shortly after with a steaming mug in his grasp. He plopped down onto his unsteady stool and grinned.

"Mama Wilder would kill you—and me—if she even knew we were out here in the first place," Shea said. "But I do appreciate you bringing me here before heading back. It's been nice to just relax a bit, and despite the dick move earlier, you're a sweet guy." She placed her hand over his and squeezed. "Thank you."

"Oh, he's a *sweet guy*!" A young woman laughed as she rounded the waist-high barrier. She wore her thick, black hair in a ponytail that trailed down the back of her gray jacket. Shea shuddered when the woman tilted her face and gazed back at her with solid, black eyes. "What a quaint little date we have here. So sorry to interrupt you two lovebirds."

Shea scoffed. "I'm sorry, who—"

Simon lifted his hand to silence her. His disposition had

steeled and gone cold. "We're on our way out, Julep. Just one drink, then we're gone."

Julep clicked her tongue then turned to retrieve a nearby stool. She dragged it across the floor to their table with purposeful noisiness and plopped down on the seat with a grin.

"*Just one drink*," she mimicked. Her empty gaze lingered on the tabletop. "I'm impressed, Simon. No POs have stopped you. Your pigment is a bit... *dark*, for this community."

"Speak for yourself," Simon said with bitterness. Julep laughed. The sound left Shea disquieted, her nerves on-edge.

Although the Middle Borough's residents had more diversity than the Dome, most were still predominately white. And even Julep, whose skin tone was lighter than Simon's, was still dark enough to stand out. Shea had noticed some sideways glances during their walk to the cafe, but she'd thought nothing of it, and now felt ashamed to have been blind to it.

Simon leaned back and crossed his arms. His hand rested near the weapon strapped to the inner lining of his jacket. "I assume you didn't come alone?"

Julep chuckled, still gazing vacantly ahead of her. She blinked and her pupils flashed a scarlet glow before they returned to black; the next moment she reached out and snatched Shea's mug of brew. Shea merely stared at her.

"You assume correctly. I'm not stupid, after all. No offense to present company." She took a healthy mouthful from Shea's brew. When she drew it away from her lips, only half of the drink remained.

Shea sunk lower against her stool and turned a side glance

to Simon. He nudged his foot against hers beneath the table. A show of reassurance, she figured.

The table sat in heavy silence for a few moments before Julep broke it a sharp chuckle. She threw back the remainder of Shea's beverage, downed it, and returned the empty mug to the table. She wiped her lips and directed her ear toward Shea.

"I'm sorry, how rude of me. I don't think we've been properly introduced."

Again, Simon lifted his hand, silencing Shea before she could speak. "She's with me, and she's none of your concern."

Julep feigned offense. "Now Simon, don't be impolite. I bet she can speak for herself." She extracted a pistol from her jacket pocket and rested her wrist beside the empty glass, the weapon's barrel trained on Shea. "Ya know, I've heard this lil' rumor goin' around that there's some drama in the Dome. Something about the good ol' chancellor's family. Who doesn't love some messy royal drama, eh? Well, word is that a niece of his has just"—she gestured an explosion with her free hand—"*poof*, gone. POs have been out tryin' to find leads on where she might've gone, but nothin's popped up yet. Now isn't that somethin'?"

Shea gazed at the mouth of the pistol and strained to steady her quickening breath and pulse. She lifted her eyes to meet Julep's, whose own gaze trailed emptily over her shoulder. What were supposed to be the whites of the woman's eyes were entirely black, just two dark, blinking orbs. Except for that moment she'd blinked, and those pupils flashed as if on fire, before blackening again. Shea had seen prosthetic eyes before back in the Ministry, but they'd been manufactured to be indistinguishable from real eyes. Julep's eyes, unlike anything she'd ever seen before, unsettled her.

Julep tapped the pistol handle against the wooden tabletop. "I don't suppose you've heard anything about this strange disappearance, have you?"

"N-no, I haven't. I'm sorry." Shea's gaze flickered between the pistol and Julep's face.

Julep paused and tilted her head, curious. "Your voice sounds a bit muffled, like you're coverin' up with somethin'—I wonder why a nice girl like yourself would be hidin' her face in public. Unless you had somethin' to hide, that is." Shea felt Simon tense beside her. "You got somethin' to hide? Nice perfume, by the way. Lavender, if I'm not mistaken. Not very common here in the middle. You get that from the Dome?"

Sweat broke on Shea's brow and dampened her palms. "I—"

Simon shifted in his seat. "Just let us go, Julep. We aren't looking for any trouble."

"Us ladies are talkin', Simon," Julep scoffed, and turned the pistol toward him. She tilted her ear toward Shea. "Oh! I forgot to mention *why* some think that the State hasn't found the bitch yet. You wanna hear? It's riveting shit, I gotta say." Shea was silent, blood running cold as she stared at the weapon pointed at Simon's chest. "Some think they haven't found her yet because she's exactly where the state *can't* see: Odin Prime's dirty taint of an Anchor. So I'm sure you can understand my interest when the Anchor prince himself just happens to pop up at the closest bar to the inter-borough shuttle. With a new girl who smells like the inside of a Dome boutique, no less."

"Let him go and I'll come with you," Shea blurted out. "Just lower the gun."

Silence fell over the table. Julep took a breath and parted her lips to speak when Simon jerked forward, lunging across the table to grasp the pistol from her hand.

The pistol fired.

Chapter 31

Shea couldn't help but remember squeezing the trigger in the Ministry of Health and Wellness. Her ears rang through muddled deafness; her heart pounded in her chest, throat, and head. It was frightening enough being behind the weapon when it fired; terror shackled her joints now that she was on the opposite end. Her vision splashed crimson as Simon fell back with his hand clutched at his ear. He fell against the wall behind him. Blood trickled between his fingers and down his wrist, dripping to the floor. When Shea reached up to wipe her face, her palm came away wet with his blood.

"Simon!" Shea fell to his side on the floor.

Julep stumbled back and clumsily kicked aside her stool. Alarmed, if not partially shaken, she aimed her pistol toward the ceiling and fired twice into the air. The cafe erupted in a cacophony of screams.

"Everybody out!"

Patrons shrieked and darted from their tables, bolting out the front door past three of her Trinity companions who entered with pistols drawn. The plump bartender was the last to sprint out into the street, hauling with him his cumbersome, large cash register.

"You good, boss?" the older of the two men asked.

"I'm always good." Julep waved a dismissive hand. She blinked and activated scarlet-blazed pupils as she moved across the cafe. "Bring the girl back to Rubio at once."

"Whata 'bout the prick?" the other thug asked with a nod of his head toward the back of the cafe. "We could kneecap Shadow right now if we just—"

"No, we leave him alive," Julep growled with brows furrowed. After a beat, she glanced over her shoulder and shrugged indifferently. "As a warning. Harriet needs to learn that if she wants to keep fuckin' around on our playground, there'll be consequences. Now, get her so we can get the hell out of here before the POs show up."

When the thug rounded the barrier, Simon had already drawn his pistol. With a bloodied hand still clutched to his wounded ear, he steadied his aim and fired, catching the Trinity goon in the chest. The gun slipped from the man's fingers as he stumbled back and buckled to the floor.

Julep startled and spun around to return fire. She moved behind a nearby table and flipped it on its side to take cover. "For god's sake, we weren't gonna kill you, Simon! You fuckin' idiot!" Two more shots—her remaining Trinities fired back. "But now we have to. I hope that bitch was worth it!"

Simon and Shea huddled behind the short barrier near their table. They pressed against the adjacent wall as rounds whizzed above and struck the rear of the cafe. Decorative lights hanging above them shattered, spraying the two with falling shards of glass. Shea curled into herself, burying her face into her arms to brace against the glass and spray of gunfire. The remnants of photographs and notes taped to the barrier fluttered to the floor, torn apart and shredded by incoming fire.

Simon lifted himself to his elbow and pointed his pistol over the wall to blindly return fire. They were pinned, trapped, and unable to move or escape without taking a hit.

"Just let me go with them!" Shea cried out, hands trembling around her face. She lifted her eyes to see his exposed, wounded ear: a mess of blood, cartilage, and broken flesh. Blood seeped down his cheek and soaked into his beard as he reached into his jacket to withdraw a full clip.

This is my fault; they're only here for me. This is all my fault.

"Stay down, Shea," Simon instructed firmly, and dropped the empty clip to the floor. He inserted the new one with heavy slap of his palm.

Julep crouched low behind the flipped table and dropped her own empty clip to the floor. She reached into her pocket to retrieve another but hesitated, pausing for just a moment before turning her ear toward the entrance of the cafe.

Victoria swung and cracked a wooden stool across her face. Julep collapsed unconscious to the floor. Blood spilled from her shattered nose and busted lip.

The oldest Trinity thug peered over his shoulder to see Julep on the ground. He spun and turned his weapon on Victoria. She lunged, ducked low, and knocked his pistol aside to throw her elbow up into the man's jaw. In the next moment, she'd grabbed his head and pulled him down into her thrusting knee. His nose snapped against her kneecap. She kept hold of his shirt collar as she lifted her eyes to the remaining Trinity who had turned his pistol on her. She dipped behind the body in her grasp just as his partner squeezed the trigger, unloading the remainder of his clip into his associate.

Peeking around the barrier, Shea watched as Victoria let the dead Trinity fall to the floor. The last assailant tossed the empty pistol aside and slid a serrated knife from his belt. He lunged and thrust the knife, but lost footing when she swiftly dodged aside. She snatched hold of his wrist. She rotated his hand and contorted his arm back against his spine, twisting at his wrist until he screamed. The weapon fell from his twitching fingers. He dropped to one knee in a hopeless attempt to unwind himself. Victoria simply released him and reached around to snap his neck with one swift twist of his chin.

Victoria pressed the bottom of her boot to his back. He collapsed forward, dead and limp beside the other Trinity. She turned her attention to the back of the cafe and met Shea's fear-stricken gaze.

"You alright back there?"

Simon grabbed onto Shea's arm for support as he lifted himself from the glass and shell-laden floor. "More or less."

When Victoria saw him, with his blood-soaked shirt and gored ear, Shea saw a distinct flash of panic in her otherwise calm green eyes. Victoria's jaw tautened as the panic in her eyes subsided to anger.

"We need to get you back home. There'll be more of them soon." She gestured to the entrance of the cafe, beckoning them to hurry. "We've gotta make a break for the shuttle, *now*."

The inter-borough shuttle was only two hundred meters down the street. They ran with Simon leading and Victoria trailing behind at Shea's heels. Shouting erupted behind them as the transit gate drew nearer. Shea felt the air pass across her face, chilling the wet blood and sweat against her cheek. She dared not look back or stop pushing forward despite the pained rigidness of her limbs and joints. Her heart drummed hard against her ribs; her lungs reached for breath with each powerful, harried stride. The shouting behind them grew louder, clearer.

"Stop or we'll shoot!"

Shea couldn't tell if the commands came from a Trinity or a PO, but at that point it no longer mattered. They barreled through the open gate toward the awaiting passenger shuttle train. The brash beep of the passenger train sounded across the station, indicating the doors would soon close. They darted past pedestrians, knocking some off-balance as they pushed past. Some shouted back, cursing them or exclaiming when their belongings fell to the ground.

"We made it." Shea gasped for air as they slowed their pace to enter an empty car. "I can't believe we—"

POP-POP.

A hand seized Shea's arm and pulled her aside just when two gunshots fired from behind them. She felt the impact of each round thump against the body braced against hers. Arms wrapped tight around her. The car doors beeped a final time and slid shut moments before the train lurched forward and pulled away from the platform. Their two bodies leaned against the graffitied metal interior wall of the moving train with Shea still held close in a secured embrace.

"Oh shit, you alright?" Simon asked. He stumbled toward them as the train rocked side to side.

Shea tensed. Victoria's embrace loosened, allowing Shea to back away across the width of the train car. Crimson blood seeped between Victoria's lips as she turned and pressed her back against the wall, wincing at the sting of her wounds.

"You—" Shea wavered and fell silent. Victoria spat a wad of blood on the filthy tile floor and wiped the corners of her mouth with her wrist.

"I'm fine, but you sure as shit aren't." Victoria pushed off from the wall, smiled at Simon, and continued down the train car. "You need patching up, and some morphine."

"Morphine would be nice," Simon groaned and followed, cradling his wounded ear.

Victoria draped her arm across his shoulder and pulled him into a hug. "You're gonna need it when Harriet rips your fucking head off." She looked over her shoulder. "You comin', Doc?"

Shea's gaze lingered on the blood stains left on the metallic surface. When she turned to follow them through the train car, her gaze rested on the bullet holes torn through the back of Victoria's jacket. Beneath those layers of clothes, she knew that the skin was closing shut, soon to be left untarnished and smooth.

Chapter 32

Knuckles rapped from the other side of Shea's bedroom door. She remained seated on her bed, unmoved by the repeated summons. She sat, arms wrapped tight around her legs, which were drawn to her chest, and stared at the bare wall opposite her. Since returning to the church, her body felt both tense and exhausted. She dropped her gaze and began counting the threads on her comforter, hoping this alone would be enough to calm her nerves.

"Doc, Ms. Wilder wants to see ya." *She sent Old Bern to collect me.* "She's waitin' in her office." *She can keep waiting.*

The knocking repeated, more urgent now, but Shea remained silent and still. Bern eventually turned and scuffled away, dragging the soles of his feet along the floors as he left. He would most likely be back later at Mama Wilder's request, to demand an explanation on how everything had gone so terribly wrong. Shea already knew the questions the old woman would ask, demanding to know why they had disobeyed a direct order to stay out of the Middle. Those questions could wait; their answers wouldn't change in the time it took for Shea to collect herself.

It had been over two hours since their return to Shadow,

and Shea had decided to retreat to the solitude of her bedroom after treating Simon's ear. She wasn't sure how much of his ear remained, but he would be lucky enough to have only lost his hearing when he could've easily lost his life instead. The last she'd seen him, Victoria was carefully easing him into his bed with fresh white gauze taped to the side of his head and a healthy dose of morphine coursing through his veins.

Shea could still hear the deafening clatter of the pistol firing beside her, could still smell the thick scent of blood and gun smoke. She closed her eyes and rested her forehead onto her knees. The floor had felt cold had against her clammy skin when she'd pressed herself low behind the barrier, trembled as rounds whizzed above them. A chill ran up her spine at recollecting the dense slapping of gunshots striking Victoria's back.

She covered her ears and rolled into a coil over her sheets. She dragged her pillow over her ear and breathed steadily, listening to the drumming of her own heartbeat, until she eventually drifted to sleep.

Shea startled awake and jerked up from the mattress out of an uneasy, troubled sleep. The room had grown dark, and the church was still and quiet. It was late, perhaps only a few hours until their artificial sunrise, and she found herself wide awake in the darkness.

Standing from the bed, she rubbed her face with the flat of her palms. Running her hands through her hair, damp from sweat, she turned and stared at the locked bedroom door. She grew aware of the dryness of her tongue and the empty growl of her stomach. She hadn't had anything to eat or drink since that morning, right before her and Simon departed for the middle. And she'd only managed a few sips of brew before Julep snatched her drink away, but that no doubt wouldn't have made her feel much better anyway. Shea wondered when the kitchen had last been restocked, and if she could slip in and out without drawing attention.

She stepped into the hallway and closed the door behind her. Padding along toward the spiral staircase, she noticed a dim light spilling across the floor from beneath Victoria's bedroom door. Shea hesitated, detecting movement from inside the bedroom.

The door swung open. A short young woman with long blonde hair stumbled giddily into the hallway. She tugged her tight black dress down her thighs and giggled, reaching for and tugging on Victoria's hand to draw her close. She lifted onto her tip-toes and brushed Victoria's long, red hair aside to plant a heady kiss against her lips. Victoria, herself only in baggy sweatpants and a sports bra, playfully wrapped a muscular arm around the girl's waist and grinned into the kiss.

Shea's cheeks flushed hot as she froze, gaping at the scene unfolding before her. She stammered, unsure if she should turn back, hesitating at the persistent growl rumbling from her stomach.

"Um…" Her words choked in the dryness of her throat.

The girl let out a squeak and pulled away from Victoria's lips. She turned a sheepish eye toward Shea, stepped back, and adjusted her dress. She wiped a smudge of white powder from beneath her nostril.

"Oh, sorry, didn't know someone was out here," she said, cheeks flushed pink. She turned to Victoria with a grin. "Be back in a few days, yeah?"

Victoria feigned a smile and leaned against her doorway. "Sure. Want me to walk you back?" The girl politely declined before turning to descend the spiral staircase. She took a final glance over her shoulder before disappearing downstairs, leaving the two in silence together in the hall.

"I'm sorry, I didn't mean to—" Shea said, her words felt as though they were tripping clumsily over her lips. Her cheeks grew hotter. "I wasn't snooping, I promise. I just wanted… uh… hungry."

"What're you doing up this late?" Victoria brushed the apology aside, seemingly unoffended by Shea's presence outside her door.

Shea crossed her arms. "Trouble sleeping, more or less. Today's been…" She faltered, her heart suddenly heavy. Her throat grew tight as she swallowed. "Arduous, I guess."

"That's a fair assessment. It's not every day that you're shot at."

Shea couldn't help the chuckle that burst from her lips. She recalled the splatter of Simon's blood and forced back the urge the cry. "No? Gosh, and here I was thinking I was just starting to get the real Shadow experience and all."

Silence fell over the hallway as the two stood together. There was a change in Victoria's eyes that Shea could see even through the darkness of the hall.

"Wanna talk about it?" she asked. Shea scoffed and looked away.

What the hell is there to talk about? About how the debacle this afternoon was my fucking fault? That Simon was nearly killed, that I could've been killed, for… what, exactly? Even you got shot in the back for me. It was a fucking mess, and it was my fault.

Shea parted her lips to speak, to let her thoughts spill

out like a running faucet. But she fell silent. Her throat tensed and stifled her words, trapped them in her lungs. She blinked away hot tears welling in her eyes.

Victoria's face remained stoic, although something behind her eyes softened. "Meet me down in the training room. We'll have more privacy there."

Shea sat on the bench inside the training room, lazily scrutinizing the exercise equipment along the opposite wall. Her heart ached, and her tired eyes stung from suppressed tears. She had no desire to eat even a single slice of bread despite the incessant growling from her stomach.

Footsteps in the hallway drew her attention to the door just as Victoria entered, carrying a steaming mug in each hand. She had pulled her hair back into a loose, messy bun at the nape of her neck and donned an old, baggy sweatshirt. Shea took a moment to absorb the image of Victoria in this disheveled, if not domestic, state. A hint of a smile touched her lips.

"I don't know what kind of tea you like, so I just made what I liked. Hope that's alright," Victoria stated flatly, awkwardly extending a mug to Shea.

"That's fine, thank you."

The two women sat together in a long silence, sipping their dandelion tea, both staring ahead to the far wall. Shea remembered the first time she'd had dandelion tea in the Anchor with Lauren. That moment shared in her friend's living room felt like ages ago, despite it having only been a few lunars. Her heart ached. It seemed impossible for so much to change and upend in so little time.

"Harriet's been asking for you." Victoria's voice broke through the stillness, jerking Shea out from her haunting reverie. "She's pretty pissed about the whole thing. I told her she should just calm the fuck down, but…" She shrugged.

Shea let out a chuckle. "Doubt that went well." She reached up and rubbed her aching eyes with the heel of her palm. "Do you think they'll retaliate?"

"The Trinities?" Victoria glanced over to Shea, who offered an affirmative nod. "Well, I'm sure that Julep bitch woke up wanting some serious retribution, but Harriet's been able to talk them down before. Rubio, their boss, is a bit more level-headed than his goons—he's a businessman at heart. It's what makes him so good at handling the POs. Besides, when he ordered the hit on Dr. Anders, we didn't retaliate. I'm sure Harriet can use that to our advantage."

"And what if they do? Retaliate, I mean."

"They'd be stupid for trying."

"I can't help but feel—" Shea's voice faltered and caught in her throat. She hesitated before urging herself to speak. "Like, it's *my* fault, ya know? If we hadn't have stopped at the cafe for that drink, if we'd just come back, none of this would've happened. They were looking for me." She massaged her tense forehead with her fingertips.

"There was no way you could've known what was going to happen," Victoria stated flatly. "Besides, Simon should've known better than to stay in the Middle longer than necessary. He knew better than to go out there with you in the first place, especially after Harriet forbade it. The responsibility ultimately falls on his piss-poor judgment." Silence again, until Victoria let out a measured sigh. "And you shouldn't think that way. Feeling sorry for yourself isn't going to help you, let alone anyone else."

Shea took a sip of her bitter tea and returned the mug to

her lap as a tear rolled down her cheek.

"Thank you," she said. Victoria turned her eyes to meet Shea's troubled gaze. "For stepping in when you did. On the train, I mean. I probably would've been hit if it hadn't been for you."

"I wouldn't be doing my job if I let our only doctor get herself killed." Victoria returned to staring at the opposite wall and took another drink from her mug.

"Well thank goodness you're good at your job, then."

They drank their tea in the silence that followed. Victoria shifted on her flattened bench cushion and took a breath, glancing around the room as if to direct her gaze to anywhere but Shea.

"Sorry, I'm not very good at"—she shifted again and gestured between them—"*this*. Talking and all."

"No, it's fine. We don't have to talk, just having some company helps," Shea said. She dropped her gaze to the mug resting on her lap. "I honestly didn't think I'd be this shaken by what happened. It feels ridiculous... it's not like I was even hit."

Victoria returned her attention to Shea and hesitated, as if she were compelled to move closer but decided against it. Instead she cleared her throat and shifted awkwardly on the bench.

"My first shootout was only a few days after I graduated from the academy." A pause, reluctance, before she continued. "We got called down to this disturbance down in the middle, some kind of domestic dispute, I dunno." She waved away with her hand the memory like it wasn't quite clear. "Turns out the dude was an ex-Trinity goon with a warrant out for his arrest. When the bullets started flying, I just—"

Victoria said with an unfocused forward gaze. She shook her head and fidgeted with the mug between her fingers. "It was the first time I ever felt terror. *Real* terror. Like I was gonna die. That shit is scary for a young twenty-cycle."

"How'd you cope with it? After it happened, that is," Shea asked.

Victoria's manner shifted. Her face and voice gradually softened. "My husband."

Shea nearly choked on her tea, managing to swallow a mouthful before letting out a cough. "Husband? Like, a *man*?" Victoria kept staring forward and took a sip of her drink without responding. Shea stammered. "I'm sorry, I didn't know you were—I thought you only liked—"

"We graduated at the academy together," Victoria calmly interjected. "He was at home when he got the call that I was involved in the shooting. When I got back, all I could do was cry on his shoulder." Victoria took another sip of her tea and fidgeted. "After that it got easier. You get used to it after a while, ya know? A few cycles later, I was a Valkyrie and those kinds of missions became the norm."

Shea stared at Victoria, still astounded. "I had no idea you had a husband."

"Because I sleep with women?"

Shea faltered. After a few moments of tense quiet, she shrugged. "Simon said you'd been arrested under the moral edict. I'd assumed—and, well, with the visitors you keep…"

"You assumed correctly." Victoria's voice sharpened as she spoke. "You're stupid when you're young; you don't know what love is. You see everyone around you in normal, happy relationships and you think, *Well, I guess that's what I need, too.* So, that's what you do. It's expected, especially as the daughter of a respected Statesman."

"Ugh, isn't that the truth…" Shea groaned. She couldn't count on two hands how many awkward, disappointing dates she'd been coerced into with Statemen's sons over the past decade.

"Francis and I were very close," Victoria continued. "And I *did* love him, just not in the way he wanted, not in the way that was expected of me. But I thought that was how it was supposed to feel, even though I didn't feel anything at all." She shrugged. "Figured that maybe, if I'd give it enough time, that feeling would finally come."

"And that girl in the video?" Shea asked, her voice tinged with apprehension. She could sense Victoria tense beside her and immediately regretted asking.

Victoria hesitated and smiled through saddened eyes. "Her name was Cosette. She worked in the cafe down the street from our station. And god, her smile each time I walked through the door…" Her face brightened a bit as she spoke despite the tears rising to her eyes. "She was the first person to make me feel something *real*." Her smile grew before faltering, curling into a frown. "And I let it get the best of me and paid the price for it. We both did, in the end."

Shea recalled the expressions across Victoria and Cosette's faces in the video recording. Cosette had pleaded and wept, begged for her not to listen to her handlers. Not to listen to Shea's mother… and Victoria had ended up squeezing the trigger anyway. Whatever Victoria and Cosette had shared together, for however long, was gone with a single gunshot.

"I'm sorry. I can't even imagine—"

"Not your fault, stop apologizing," Victoria stated firmly.

"But it *is*. It's *my* uncle who enacted the edict, it's *my* mother who ran the project…" Shea felt warm tears trail from her tired, stinging eyes. The mug slipped her fingers and dropped to the mat, spilling what tea she had left on the floor beneath them. She curled into herself, cupped her face into her palms, and wept.

Simon's near-death experience. Cosette's murder. Victoria's cycles of torture. Each event connected to her, stuck to her like a web spun by those she had loved and trusted most.

"I can't even begin to understand what you've gone through, or express how sorry I am that my family caused it all."

"Shea, stop." Victoria's voice softened. She put down her mug and awkwardly reached out to take Shea into her arms, pulling her close in a tight embrace. "Just, stop, okay?"

She pressed her forehead into Victoria's shoulder. "I'm sorry," Shea repeated through choked sobs. "I'm so sorry, Victoria. Please forgive me."

Victoria stiffened and wavered before eventually resting her cheek against Shea's hair and whispering back with each apology. "It isn't your fault."

Chapter 33

Iris's dress uniform boots clicked with each step down the long corridor of the chancellor's estate. She adjusted her black gloves and peered at herself in a mirror hanging from the wall as she passed. She eyed her fitted dark blue jacket, the three medals pinned to her left breast pocket, and tucked a loose red strand of hair behind her ear. Pressing her hand to her chest, over where her dog tags hung, she muttered what sounded like a prayer under her breath: "Help me through this one, Daniel."

Her mouth ran dry, and she'd hardly slept the night before. Concealing makeup couldn't mask the sluggish exhaustion in her eyes. She bit the inside of her cheek until she tasted blood, and her otherwise tired mind sharpened. All of her planning hinged on her meeting with the chancellor.

The steel door at the end of the hall slid open when she approached. She took two steps inside before halting and clicking her heels. She bowed low with the palm of her right fist pressed against her chest.

"His Majesty Guide Us, Chancellor."

"May Strength Remain, Chief Hammond." A woman's voice, not the chancellor, responded from across the room.

Iris lifted her gaze to see an older woman, short and

rotund, smiling at her from the chancellor's desk. She wore thin purple spectacles, and her coarse white hair was pulled back into a large, tight bun. Iris hesitated, noting how comfortable the woman appeared seated at the chancellor's desk. Odin Prime's flag framed her from each side like she was posing for an official portrait.

"Madame Secretary Herrington," Iris stated, straightening her posture. She held her hands behind her back and clenched her gloved fists.

Bethany Herrington was one of the most senior Statesmen in the station. Her ascent to secretary of the interior a few cycles back had been marred with old-fashioned backstabbing and backroom deals; many competing Statesmen fell prey to unearthed, damning information that implicated them in morality offenses. The secretary of the interior was practically second in command to the chancellor himself and demanded nearly as much respect. So many cycles of kissing the chancellor's ass paid off.

"I must beg pardon, Madame Secretary, I was under the impression that the chancellor had summoned me today."

"You are correct, Chief Hammond. Unfortunately, Chancellor Tristan had an unforeseen engagement to attend to and is unable to meet with you presently. He's asked that I address you in his place, as is proper."

Iris offered a nod. "Certainly, Madame Secretary."

"Please, have a seat."

"I prefer to stand, Madame Secretary, if that is acceptable."

The old woman's smile tightened. "Of course." She opened a folder on the desk and glanced down to read the documents inside. "I'm sure you are wondering why the chancellor has asked for your presence today." Iris remained silent, so she continued. "As you well know, there was an incident in the Middle Borough yesterday afternoon between the rabble."

"Yes, Madame Secretary, it appears to have been a territorial dispute between the Trinities and Shadow. No citizens were harmed, thankfully. The only casualties were those criminals involved. I received the report late yesterday evening from Lt. Wiles following his local investigation."

"And his findings?"

"Madame?" Iris faltered but maintained her steeled composure.

"Lt. Wiles's report, did you find it to be adequate?"

Iris's joints grew rigid, her face warm. She knew where this was headed and braced herself. "I regret that I have not yet read the report in full, Madame Secretary. I understood the incident to be unremarkable and not requiring my full attention, as the local lieutenant appeared to have managed the situation appropriately."

That was the wrong answer, and Iris knew it. Had any of her officers given her that same answer, they would have been harshly reprimanded for their lack of accountability. Iris would appear incompetent to the Secretary, would look like an irresponsible fool for failing to read the full report. Except that she *had* read it. She'd gone over it line by line, and had hardly slept as a result. A lingering sense of dread had weighed on her that morning when the chancellor himself beckoned her to his estate for a meeting.

Secretary Herrington adjusted her purple spectacles and turned a keen eye to Iris. "Surely, Chief Hammond, when a lieutenant from a local municipality has taken the time to personally bring you a report, you must find it prudent to read it thoroughly."

Iris bowed her head slightly, turning her eyes to the floor beneath her. "My most humble apologies, Madame Secretary. It won't happen again."

"No, it will not. Not unless you wish to lose your appointment," Secretary Herrington stated curtly. Iris remained silent, choosing to swallow the anger crawling up her throat rather than speak. "Now, had you actually *read* the report, you would know that the chancellor's niece, Dr. Shea Tristan, was involved in the shooting."

"That *is* unsettling news, Madame," Iris said with feigned alarm. Of course she'd known that Dr. Tristan was there. When she'd first read that information in the report, she'd nearly gone down to Shadow headquarters and slapped the doctor senseless. *What the hell was Harriet thinking, allowing that stupid girl out of the lower?*

"Indeed it is, Chief Hammond. It was reported that Trinity operatives attempted to capture her in a cafe. The intervention provoked the violent response from the Shadow escorts. Lt. Wiles was quite diligent in attaining eyewitnesses that positively identified her. The witness also observed Shadow members returning her to the lower. The chancellor has been informed and is *quite* adamant on retrieving her from their captivity. Governor Tristan has already been notified down on Apex and shares the chancellor's sentiment and concern regarding his daughter." Secretary Herrington turned a cold smile to Iris. "Do you have anything to say about this predicament, Chief Hammond?"

Iris's face remained calm and unchanged despite the anger turning in her chest. The report in the secretary's hands should have never reached the estate in the first place. All law enforcement reporting was submitted up to the chancellor through her office, and she would've been sure to edit Dr. Tristan from the report before submitting it. Unless the secretary had directly requested the report from the local office, that is.

"I both understand and appreciate the concerns of the chancellor and governor, Madame Secretary. If Shadow is behind Dr. Tristan's abduction, however, then our next move must be precise and deliberate. Harriet Wilder maintains a firm hold over the Anchor. The residents are loyal to her, and will defend her against any suppressive force we deploy into the borough. It is a tenuous situation that could easily incite violence."

"And why should that matter?" Secretary Herrington asked, genuinely curious. "We have enough peace officers to seize the borough, do we not? Should any resident actively resist, we need merely remind them that the ultimate authority on this station is the State, *not* Harriet Wilder." She adjusted her glasses again. "Besides, dealing with them shouldn't prove too difficult—many of them aren't even citizens."

Iris knew what this meant, and hearing it sent a shiver up her spine. She had been a young peace officer, only a cycle after graduating from the academy, when the tumultuous unrest within Odin Prime boiled over. Drastic, violent suppressive action had been required. The officers appointed above her had reassured her that this was for the greater good, and she hadn't dared question them. And at the end of the day they weren't going after true, loyal citizens anyway. Cracking skulls was easier after that, and more frequent. Violence had little effect on her now. Iris imagined meeting Madame Secretary on the front lines of those riots; she would have been sure to introduce the back of the woman's skull to her baton.

"You are correct," Iris spoke slow and calm. "Begging Madame Secretary's indulgence—a considerable amount of time and resources have already been invested toward the chancellor's Peace Accords initiative. The accord's sole objective is garnering *voluntary* conscription for Apex labor; no one will be willing to work with us if we barge into the Anchor attacking our target audience. Or worse yet, making their leader a martyr. I must insist that we approach this in a more calculated manner."

"What are you suggesting then, Chief Hammond?" Secretary Herrington asked through pursed lips.

Iris took a breath and thought of her daughter, of finally freeing her from her prison: Odin Prime itself. She then wondered, with a grin curling at her lips, if the incident in the middle the day before had instead been a blessing in disguise. The grin was gone in an instant when she returned her attention to the old woman at the desk.

"Madame Secretary, due to the sensitivity of the Peace Accords initiative, I would prefer to continue this discussion with the chancellor and the Party Council."

Secretary Herrington cocked an eyebrow and flared her nostrils, visibly irritated. "Surely this is not necessary, Chief Hammond. Many Party members live very busy lives; I doubt that they want to be inconvenienced with such a meeting."

"Begging Madame Secretary's indulgence, but it surely *is* necessary. I guarantee, Madame, that my solution, if approved by the Party Council, will not only guarantee the safe return of Dr. Tristan"—Iris took a breath and smiled—"but will also cripple Ms. Harriet Wilder's authority in the Anchor beyond redemption."

Chapter 34

"Psst, Shea—"

Shea awoke with a start to find Theresa's wide brown eyes peering back at her. She jerked up from her pillow with a gasp.

"Don't do that!"

Theresa stepped back, stifling a giggle. "Do what?"

"Creep around like that. You could've knocked or something, like a normal person." Shea swung her feet out from beneath the covers and rubbed her tired eyes with the heel of her palm. She yawned and blinked. "What time is it?"

"Just after seven," Theresa said. "Mama Wilder wants you to get ready."

Shea stretched her arms high above her head, and felt her spine and shoulders loosen. She dropped her arms heavy beside her and squinted through the artificial morning light spilling through her bedroom window. "Oh, is her majesty going to let me outside, now? What the hell for?"

Theresa shrugged. "Dunno. But she said… how did she put it?" The girl lifted her eyes to the ceiling, searching for the words, "'Tell that girl to get her skinny white ass ready and out the door by noon,' or somethin' like that."

"Did she say where to?" Shea stood from the bed and

strode to the open closet. She peeked inside and tugged the light string dangling in the dark. The single bulb flickered to life.

"She mentioned somethin' about a house call, but I dunno what for," Theresa slid past her into the closet and began sifting through the button-up shirts and slacks hung from the rack. She pulled down a white blouse and held it up against her chest, peeking down the front before turning to Shea with a smile. "You think Simon would like this?"

"Okay, well." Shea took Theresa by the shoulders and turned her body, easing her out the closet and toward the bedroom door. "I'd prefer to get naked *without* company, if you don't mind."

"Can I keep this?" Theresa asked, her eyes dropping to the blouse still clasped tight between her fingers.

"You don't think it'll be too big on you? You're still a bit small."

Theresa hesitated. "I mean... I'll grow into it, right?" Her cheeks flushed. "Can I, please? All of my clothes are old and for kids, but I'm not a kid anymore. I'm almost sixteen—practically an adult."

Shea smiled and nudged Theresa out the door. "Sure thing. Feel free to borrow anything you like from the closet." The girl's eyes brightened as Shea began to close the door. "Just make sure to wash em', okay?"

"'Kay!" Theresa departed down the hall with a bounce in her step. Shea watched her for a moment, smiling, before closing the door to change.

***

"I wanna go," Tony said, folding his arms over his chest. He trailed his gaze from Simon to Shea, both busy packing an empty backpack with medical supplies, and gnawed at the toothpick between his lips.

"You're joking, right?" Simon scoffed and tossed a roll of bandage tape at Tony, who caught it and chucked it back at him.

"You see me fuckin' laughin'?" Tony clenched down on the toothpick and scowled. "Come on, you guys got to have your bit of fun a few days ago, let me have mine."

"I lost part of my ear, dipshit. It wasn't *fun*," Simon frowned and gestured to his wounded ear, still covered with white gauze and tape.

Tony shrugged. "Irregardless—"

"*Regardless*," Shea chimed in, still too focused on arranging the materials inside the backpack to look at him. "Irregardless isn't a word."

Tony grumbled. "Regardless… I can look out for her just fine, she's only goin' to the edge, after all. No Trinities or nothin' to worry about."

"The answer is no," Victoria said as she entered the examination room. She adjusted her brown leather jacket and reached back to draw her long red hair into a ponytail. "This isn't only my decision, it's Harriet's. It's best you don't question it."

Tony crossed his arms again, frowning. "Gee, you think I'm that incompetent I can't escort the doc here to a simple fuckin' house call in our own goddamn borough?"

"That's exactly the case, yes," Victoria said with a breath of exasperation. "Both the Trinities and the State will be gunning for us now that they know Shea is working here. We can't leave her safety in the hands of just anybody, particularly those whose backs are so accustomed to hitting training room mat as yours. She's too valuable to us."

Shea's hand froze as it motioned to fasten the backpack shut. She darted her gaze to briefly meet Victoria's, who seemingly took only a quick second to turn her attention to Shea before looking away again. She swung the backpack over her shoulder and stepped toward Tony, whose face now flushed crimson in anger.

"Tony, we need you here." She placed her hand on his thick bicep and smiled warmly at him. "Simon's hurt, Theresa is still going through training… what if something were to happen while we were gone? Wouldn't you prefer to be here protecting Theresa than out there with me, bored during some stupid house call?"

Tony rested his hands on his hips, indignant. He struggled to hide the pout sinking across his face. "I mean, yeah, I guess."

Shea clapped her palm assuredly against his back. "I wouldn't expect any less from a good big brother. Hold down the fort till we get back, yeah?"

A hint of a grin curled at the edge of Tony's lips before he turned away, lifting his hand to shoo them away. "Yeah, whatever. Get the fuck outta here already, geez. Losers."

Shea flipped up the dark hood of her jacket over her hair as she trailed behind Victoria up the basement stairs.

Outside, she peered at the wooden rickshaw parked on the curb and shuddered. She'd only ridden the carriages a handful of times by this point, but her experiences hadn't left her with an overwhelming desire to hop back into the passenger's seat, regardless of who chaperoned her.

"Can't we just, I don't know… walk?" Shea asked with a shrug.

"They're clear on the other side of the borough, it'd take too long to reach them by foot." Victoria approached the side of the carriage and extended an open palm to her. She cocked a brow. "Unless you'd rather the patient suffer *longer* to suit your preferences?"

Shea parted her lips to speak, but faltered and remained silent. She adjusted the hood over her hair, stomped forward, and accepted Victoria's assistance in climbing up into the carriage, where she plopped down on the worn, flattened cushion. Victoria stepped up and took the seat beside her before the driver hoisted the front end and briskly drew them away.

Closing her eyes against the rough jostling of the carriage, she felt its rickety wheels bumping up against rocks, potholes, and pieces of strewn trash. The unsteady motions left her gut queasy, made worse by the scent of garbage and urine faintly lacing the air. She covered her mouth and nose with the sleeve of her jacket and breathed the scent of her lavender perfume. When she opened her eyes again, she noticed Victoria turning a side-eye at her.

Shea blinked. "... What?"

"You aren't used to it yet?" Victoria asked, gesturing toward the street. *"Eau de proletariat?"*

Shea turned her gaze out toward the lower residents as they passed. She watched the two little boys who'd discovered her in the alley scamper around a distant corner, laughing together in their filthy clothes and greasy hair. Guilt weighed on her.

"I am... *was*, used to it. But I was cooped up for the past week thanks to Harriet, so I doubt that helped. Not sure it's a smell any of us can really get used to, though. Or *should* in the first place, for that matter."

Victoria was quiet for a moment, considering her. "Is that why you wanted to walk? Because Harriet wouldn't let you outside?"

"That's part of it, yeah. Don't get me wrong, I understand *why* she did it. Security reasons an' all, and I'm sure also just to spite me, but you get stir crazy, you know?" Shea offered an impartial shrug and crossed her arms. "That, and the last time I rode a rickshaw the day ended like shit."

"You think today's gonna end in shit?"

"Depends—you gonna *let* today end in shit?" Shea retorted.

"Careful, I wouldn't go around threatening me with a good time." Victoria reached into the inside of her jacket pocket and withdrew a pack of cigarettes. Shea glanced over to see her place a cigarette between her lips, which, if she wasn't mistaken, held back a quiet smile. She looked away again when Victoria lit a match and raised the flame, cupped in her palms against the passing breeze.

The two sat in silence while Victoria smoked. Shea again directed her gaze to the pedestrians on the sidewalks, occasionally catching the scent of drifting tobacco. The rickshaw jerked and rattled with each pothole and bump in the road, and each motion left Shea reaching to a handle-strap hanging from the roof for support. She closed her eyes once more and prayed for the ride to end. Nearly five minutes had passed without a word between them before Shea felt Victoria shift beside her.

"Harriet did the same thing with me," Victoria said casually as she flicked the short butt of her cigarette out onto the street. "After they smuggled me back from the Dome, they confined me to the same room for weeks. She was worried I'd run off the first chance I got, or hurt others in my escape. Simon had to convince her that I was stable enough to venture out to the rest of the church without bolting before they finally let me out."

"I'm so sorry, Victoria. That's... *horrible*." Shea watched Victoria, who kept her gaze fixed ahead of them on the road. She imagined the frail woman she'd seen in her mother's research footage strapped to a bed inside the church, Simon at her side, holding her as she sobbed into her pillow. An aching heaviness rested on Shea's heart at the thought. Looking at Victoria at that moment suddenly became unbearable, spurring Shea to direct her gaze elsewhere. "How long did it take for her to let you out?"

"Long enough to appreciate how shitty it is to be feel cooped up, from one prison cell in the Dome to another here. Enough time to know how you felt leaving the church today."

Shea frowned. *It's hardly comparable, is it?*

The rickshaw's wooden frame rattled as it came to an abrupt halt. Shea braced her palm against the flattened cushion beneath her but felt the sway of momentum pull her out from her seat. She gasped and felt her chest press against Victoria's arm, extended out to prevent Shea from tumbling forward out from the carriage.

"We're here," Victoria said flatly.

Shea leaned against the backrest of the carriage and grew acutely aware of the sensation of Victoria's arm against her chest. She brushed a stray lock of hair from her warming cheek and gently pushed the arm away.

"Clearly."

The rickshaw driver rounded the side of the carriage to extend a hand to Victoria, who ignored the gesture and stepped down onto the curb. The driver, a boy no older than seventeen, blinked and turned the offer to Shea, who scooted toward the sidecar ladder. She, too, ignored the offered hand and hopped down onto the curb and hurried after Victoria, who had already begun striding down the property's stone path. The driver watched the two women stride away toward the entrance of an apartment complex with an empty hand and a scowl.

"Aren't we going to pay him?" Shea asked when she caught up to Victoria's side. She'd looked over her shoulder and watched the driver kick a rock on his way back to the front of the rickshaw.

"We're here on Harriet's orders, it's covered," Victoria replied, lifting her hand to rap her knuckles against the closed wooden door. "Besides, Harriet is the only reason that kid has a rickshaw in the first place. He can afford one free fare."

Shea watched the rickshaw draw away down the road before returning her attention to the tall housing unit stack in front of them. A young boy stood at the base of the makeshift scaffolding staircase with tears streaked down his flushed cheeks. The boy wiped a gob of runny snot from his nose and let out a whimper when they approached.

"A-are you th-the doctor?" he blubbered.

Shea crouched down to one knee and smiled at him. "I sure am. How can I help, little man?"

"D-daddy fell and hurt hisself at work, can't move or nothin'," the young boy cried and wiped fresh tears from his eyes. Shea reached out and took his hand into her own despite the sticky wetness of his tiny fingers and offered a reassuring smile.

"Well, why don't you show me to your daddy and I'll patch him right up, okay?"

Victoria watched as the young boy guided Shea up the rickety staircase, clutching her hand tight into his own. She smiled when she noticed the hint of panic in Shea's eyes at the first wobble of steel plating beneath her feet. She followed close behind.

"Which, uh, unit is yours, kiddo?" Shea asked, masking the uncertainty in her voice and gripping tight to the rail. Another steel plate groaned beneath her feet. "One of the lower ones? Or middle ones?"

"We're at the top," the boy said between sniffles.

Shea let out a nervous laugh. "Fantastic!"

Chapter 35

"This'll hurt, but I need you to lie still for me."

Shea felt along the patient's shattered kneecap, at the shifting bones beneath his swollen, purpled skin. He sucked in a sharp breath of air between his gritted teeth at her touch, yet remained still through the pain. His wife knelt beside the couch where he lay, squeezed his shoulder and patted a damp brown cloth across his sweat-slick forehead. Her makeup smudged beneath her puffy, red eyes.

Shea frowned. "How did this happen?"

"He was just about to leave his shift at the fishery," the wife said, her voice quiet and thick with worry. Her eyes never left her husband's agonized face. "He went to check the feeding lines a final time before clocking out and…" Her gaze trailed down his body to rest on the injured knee in Shea's hands. "One of the feeding lines snapped, was probably an old rope that needed replacing."

Shea shifted another bone beneath the inflamed skin and the man jerked against her grasp, hissing through his chapped lips. She released the knee and offered an apologetic smile.

"He went to grab for the broken line, lost his footing, and

fell onto the bottom platform. Poor dear can't even manage a limp. A few coworkers had to carry him back here; we're citizens, you see, but can't afford the medical care in the Middle. He isn't paid enough at the fishery. So—"

"So you called Mama Wilder for help. I completely understand, I assure you," Shea said with a kind smile. "And I promise to do my best for your husband. Unfortunately, the kneecap is completely shattered; he'll need a cast and to keep weight off of it. It'll take some time and patience, but he'll be up and walking again soon enough."

"H-how long?" the man asked through haggard breaths. His face was slick with sweat; he'd drenched through his undershirt and had begun to soak the cushions of the couch beneath him. "I-I need to support my family. How long t-till I can walk again?"

Shea considered him for a moment, weighing the severity of the injury, and sighed. "Six weeks. Maybe eight, at the latest."

"Six weeks?" the man said, nearly choking on the words as they crossed his lips. Tears brimmed in his eyes. "What am I supposed to do to support my family? I *need* to work! I can't just lie around here for six weeks!"

Shea fell silent as the wife and husband began to sob. The wife leaned in close to him, and his arms wrapped around her shoulders to pull her close against his chest. Shea heard the wife reassure her husband between choked sobs, uttering in broken whispers that it would be alright, that they would think of something to get them through. Shea's heart ached. She turned her gaze away from the couple and noticed Victoria watching her from the nearby hall. The couple's young son sat on Victoria's shoulders, his hands propped atop her crimson hair, staring with mouth agape at his distraught parents.

"Hey kiddo, how 'bout we go play on the roof?" Victoria said. She took hold of the boy's ankles and bounced her shoulders up and down, jostling the young boy until he giggled.

"What's on the roof?" he asked through his tittering.

Victoria swayed him playfully. "We can throw pebbles at people on the street, how does that sound?"

The boy laughed again, and Shea watched them exit the front door of the housing unit. Victoria met her gaze before disappearing outside.

***

Shea climbed the rickety steps to the roof nearly an hour later, tired and worn down. Her fingers ached from setting the cast on the husband's knee, and she massaged her knuckles as she stepped onto the platform. Victoria and the young boy were sitting near the edge, tossing pebbles over the short wire barrier. Victoria kept a tight grip onto the back of the boy's shirt in case he got too close to the edge.

The boy turned and offered Shea a wide, endearing smile. "Dr. Shea, look! Vicky got one in a trash can!"

"Oh, did she?" she asked with a smile in return. When Victoria looked back at her, Shea couldn't help but feel some of the heaviness on her shoulders lift. Victoria's eyes were kinder and softer than she'd normally seen them. "Well, your dad is all fixed up now if you wanna see him."

The boy trotted across the gravel platform and threw his arms around her legs, squeezing her in a tight hug. "Thanks, Dr. Shea!" He let go and disappeared down the staircase behind her.

"*Vicky*, huh?" Shea said as she stepped closer to the edge. "And your pebble-tossing game is on point, apparently. Quite impressive."

"It is, actually. If you saw far that trash can was, I think you would be pretty impressed."

"Only if you can do it a second time, *Vicky*."

Shea took a seat on the loose gravel beside Victoria and gazed out across the Anchor cityscape. The housing stack nestled against the 'edge,' the physical boundary of what used to be Odin Prime's largest converted storage warehouses. Shea gazed over the top of the borough and absorbed the bleakness of it. She squinted and watched silhouettes of men and women climbing sets of stairs, descending ladders, or passing one another on rickety metal walkways connecting adjacent stacked housing unit towers.

Artificial sunlight waned into a burnt-orange sunset as the end of the day drew nearer. One of the old, damaged panels in the distance sputtered, went blank for a moment, and flickered back to life. Shea shifted her attention to the glassy ceiling and saw where the ceiling and wall joined, how it seemed to curve into one, continuous boundary separating them from the frigid vacuum of space. She closed her eyes.

"You alright?" Victoria asked, her gaze still turned toward the skyline.

"Been a long day, is all. I told the wife I'd speak to Harriet about getting her a side-job until her husband was well enough to work again." Shea sensed the heaviness in her shoulders return as she thought of the conversation to come with Harriet. "Which should be fun, seeing as I'm not exactly her favorite person since the incident in the Middle. I've been trying to avoid her, but I can't really do that on this one."

"That's good of you," Victoria said. "I look forward to being a fly on the wall for that shitstorm conversation."

Shea took a breath. "I guess. It's nice being up here, though. It's so quiet."

Shea thought back on the previous week, trapped inside the Shadow church and unable to leave under Harriet's orders. As artificial as the sunlight may have been, she nearly soaked in it now. She'd been caged, confined while the dust from the cafe incident settled. For her own safety, supposedly, but Shea had her doubts given Harriet's tendency for self-preservation above all else. But there were no walls on that roof, no crowds of people or rustling rickshaws. It was peaceful. She took a long, deep breath that filled her lungs before letting it out through a slow, measured sigh.

"I got you something," Victoria said after a beat. She reached beside her and retrieved a crinkled paper bag, extracting the small bottle of brown liquid inside it. She offered Shea a quiet grin. "Figured you needed it after the week you've had. But I guess you can think of it as liquid courage before you speak with Harriet."

"Oh god, is that brew?" Shea took the bottle when it was offered and lifted it to her nostrils. The stringent odor caught her off-guard and she coughed. "Where'd you even get this?"

Victoria shrugged. "I traded for it with a kid downstairs who works as a busboy in the middle. He brought a six-pack back with him and I managed to snag this one from him."

"What did you trade?"

"Don't worry about it."

Shea smiled and pressed the rim of the opened bottle to her lips. She tipped the bottle back and tasted the sharp burn of the liquor against her tongue. It warmed her throat and belly, her mouth tingled long after she downed it. This variety of brew didn't have the honey aftertaste of her first drink, but at that moment she didn't seem to mind.

"Oh shit, that is… *strong.*" She nearly coughed, and returned the bottle to Victoria, who also took a drink. The woman closed her eyes, clearly enjoying the liquor's potency.

"It'll put hair on your chest, that's for sure."

"Simon is gonna be pissed when he finds out that I drank brew with you and we didn't save any for him."

"He'll get over it." Victoria handed the bottle back to Shea, who enjoyed another sip. "Besides, I think he'll just be happy to see us getting along."

Shea shot Victoria a sly grin. "Is that what we're doing? *Getting along?*" She swirled the liquid inside the bottle before handing it back. "Are you insinuating that you don't actually mind my company now?"

"I'm *insinuating* that I have less of an urge to kill you than I did when we first met, yes," Victoria responded.

"I'm going to go ahead and take that as a compliment, Vicky." Shea chuckled and turned her gaze back toward the skyline.

The two sat beside one another in silence, passing the bottle back and forth between sips, staring out across the tops of lower borough buildings. After a few minutes Shea closed her eyes and reclined back to lie on the gravel. The liquor warmed her belly and chest, swam through her mind like a calming haze.

"I'm surprised you haven't had a cigarette yet," Shea said.

"This seems to be the perfect place to enjoy one."

Victoria took another sip, screwed the top back onto the bottle, and lay back to rest beside Shea. "Like I said, I traded."

Shea opened her eyes and turned her head to stare at Victoria in disbelief. "What? Why?" Victoria said nothing and instead closed her eyes and motioned with the bottle in her hand.

Shea smiled and watched Victoria, realizing that this was the most peaceful she'd ever seen her. She observed her chest rise and fall with each breath, noted the slight curl of a smile on her lips, and watched her slender fingers adjust around the neck of the brew bottle.

"Have you ever brought your girls up to these roofs?" Shea asked abruptly. "Your companions, I mean?" The words tumbled from her lips before she could stop them. She immediately regretted it, unsure why the question manifested in the first place, and stared up at the ever-dimming ceiling.

Victoria turned a curious eye at her, cocked an eyebrow. "What? No. Why?"

"No reason. Just curious, I suppose. It's a nice spot."

Victoria returned her attention to the ceiling. "I took Cosette to a garden rooftop once, back in the Dome. It ended up raining while we were up there. You would've thought the rain would've ruined it, but…" She closed her eyes and handed the bottle of brew back to Shea. "Here, you keep it."

Shea took the bottle and paused, her gaze lingering on Victoria for another few moments. She closed her eyes and toyed with the bottle in her hands. She was in no rush to return to Harriet's house-arrest, or to the Cyntrax research that awaited her. But she knew she had to return eventually, and the thought alone exhausted her. There was nothing she wanted more than to stay on the rooftop with Victoria, to share the calm with her where it felt, if only temporarily, as though their worries were few. But she'd already been away from her research for too long that day, and she knew she'd already be staying up longer that evening to make up for the lost time.

"We should be getting back."

Victoria let out a sigh and sat up from the ground. "I suppose so." She rose to her feet and dusted herself off as Shea stood. "Luckily there shouldn't be any trouble finding a carriage this late in day."

"Or, we could just walk back?" Shea asked as the two made their way down the squeaking, wobbly staircase. "I know we gotta get back, but… it's nice to be out, if only for a *bit* longer."

They reached the ground floor and stepped toward the street as the pavement lights flickered to life. The streets were quiet except for the occasional carrying voice from inside the surrounding apartments.

"I mean, it isn't entirely safe," Victoria said.

Shea nudged Victoria's arm with her elbow. "Yeah, well, that's why you're here, right?"

Victoria scoffed. "What, so I can get shot or stabbed saving your ass again? I don't think so."

Despite her reluctance, Victoria continued walking down the sidewalk, passing an available rickshaw waiting across the street. Shea smiled, flipped her hood up over her hair, and hurried forward to keep her pace.

"I was thinking—I was pretty opposed to the idea of doing

any sort of self-defense training when I first got here, but I think I should start. That way I wouldn't have to rely so heavily on you guys, ya know? I mean hell, even Theresa is doing it, and she more or less has the threatening disposition of a cupcake." Victoria let out an amused snort and tucked her hands into her jacket pockets. Shea eyed her. "What do you think?"

Victoria shrugged. "Just amused thinking about a pampered Dome girl like you taking a punch to the face."

Shea waved her comment away with her hand and continued. "Anyway, Simon is pretty banged up at the moment, so I can't reasonably ask him. Maybe Tony can—"

"No," Victoria firmly interjected. After a beat, she cleared her throat and fidgeted with her hands inside her jacket pockets. "Tony's a creep. He'd probably end up copping a feel on you before the end of your first session. You don't want him."

Shea side-eyed Victoria as they walked together down the dim sidewalk. Victoria didn't return her gaze and instead kept her focus ahead of them, taking a few passing moments to peer down alleyways and around corners.

"Well then, what am I supposed to—"

"I'll train you," Victoria blurted out. "Since there's no one else who can. It'll be an inconvenience, but I can find the time."

Shea said nothing for a few moments as they walked. She slowly nodded and let out a resigned sigh. "Well, alright. If there's no one else, then I guess it can't be helped." A few more moments of silence passed between them. "And when would we—"

"Tomorrow."

Shea focused her attention farther down the sidewalk. "Then it's settled, I guess. Tomorrow it is."

"Fine," Victoria said.

Shea nodded. "Fine."

The two remained silent for the remainder of their return walk to the church.

Chapter 36

"Shea, you ready for another run-through?" Victoria asked impatiently through the intercom.

Shea stood hunched over inside the dummy training room with her palms pressed against her knees, straining to catch her breath. Her mess of dark brown hair lay in a disheveled bun at the base of her neck. Stray strands clung to her flushed, sweat-slick neck and cheeks.

"Just—" she heaved and pointed a single finger in the air. "Just, one sec, okay? I'm not… good at this sorta stuff! I'm gonna… I need a…"

Victoria rolled her eyes. "It's only been two circuits. Give me at least one more run-through and I'll give you a rest."

"I'm new to this! Give me a fucking break!" Shea shouted over her shoulder.

Victoria lifted her finger from the intercom button and snorted with laughter. She heard footsteps descending the basement stairwell and turned to see Simon with a wry smile across his face.

"How's she holdin' up?" he asked in a whisper as he pointed to the dummy room door.

"I mean, she hasn't passed out yet. So there's at least that."

He approached her side and peered inside the door

viewing window. "Oh, she looks *pissed*!" He laughed. "That's good though, better to be pissed than to quit, right? How many days has it been?"

"This is her second day," Victoria said. "We've been doing one hour in the mornings before she sees patients and another hour before dinner."

Simon clicked his tongue. "Damn. She's gonna be hurtin' pretty bad with a schedule like that, if she doesn't hurt already."

"She can handle it," Victoria said. "Besides, we can't afford to go easy on her. Like it or not, Harriet's right about the Trinities and POs coming after us now that they know we have her." Simon reached up to touch his still-patched ear. His smile sank, but he said nothing. Victoria continued, "We can't always be around to keep her safe, and to be honest, I'm not sure how much longer we can keep this up."

"I'm sure Ma has something sorted out. She's always got a plan."

Victoria let out a sigh and peered through the door's window. "Yeah, well, that doesn't necessarily give me warm fuzzies either."

"Be nice," Simon warned as he leaned against the wall, arms crossed.

"I'm *always* nice," Victoria stated with a sly grin and a wink.

He nodded his head back toward the stairwell. "Speaking of Ma, you hear about McClintic's Bar hosting her birthday party tomorrow night?"

"Hold on," Victoria said, palm lifted to silence him. She leaned toward the intercom and pressed the button. "Return to the starting position, I'm resetting the circuit."

A fresh outburst of curses and shouting erupted from

inside the dummy room. Victoria rolled her eyes. "Oh, shut up! It's still only the basic conditioning program. Just wait until we get to the shock-rounds. *Then* you can shout at me all you like."

Simon chuckled. "God, you're so mean."

"No, I have standards." She flipped a switch on the control panel against the wall, triggering the cannons to whirl to life again inside the room. She sighed and turned her attention back to Simon. "Sorry, you were saying?"

Shea's muffled shouting broke through between the rapid thudding of the cannons.

"Ma's birthday party. Tomorrow night. McClintic's Bar."

A loud thud from inside the room, followed by a furious scream. Victoria and Simon remained unfazed.

"So soon? I thought her birthday wasn't for another few weeks."

Simon shrugged. "Guess she wants to celebrate a bit early this cycle. Maybe with tensions being as high as they are, she wants to be sure to get some celebrating in before we don't have as much flexibility."

Another shout and thud behind the dummy room door.

"Sure, why not?" Victoria peeked through the door window to see Shea dodge an orb. She smiled watching the woman duck beneath another before being pelted in the face and rolling back onto the floor. Stifling a giggle, she returned her attention to Simon. "I'll ask Tiffany if she wants to go in case she doesn't have any other clients that night."

"Oh, you know she'll accept your offer over any other proposition she may have," Simon said with a knowing smile. He tapped the side of his knuckle against the door before turning back toward the staircase. "Don't be too hard on her, Vic. I know how you can get. Be nice!"

Simon ascended the stairs as Victoria called back to him. "I'm *always* nice!"

***

Shea winced at each measured step down the basement staircase the next day. That morning had only constituted the third training day, but her joints, muscles, and nerves felt as though they'd endured much more than three days of strain. She'd showered the night before and discovered more bruises on her body than she'd ever had during the entire course of her life; the projectile orbs, albeit not yet charged with an electric current, still left evidence on her body that she was, despite her best efforts, still too clumsy and rigid. Her skin, otherwise pale and smooth, was now pocked with aching clusters of purple and blue.

She moved toward the training room at the end of the hall and sneered at the dummy room as she passed. Her lower back popped when she twisted and contorted her torso, the muscles in her arms and abs aching and begging for reprieve.

Victoria was waiting for her on the training mats when she stepped through the door. She sat barefoot on the mats, casually stretching and humming to herself. Her hair was pulled back into a loose bun, and she wore only a sports bra and mid-calf leggings; a 'uniform' of sorts that Shea learned Victoria preferred to wear when engaging in any sort of rigorous exercise. Shea took stock of her own training clothes, borrowed from Theresa earlier that week, and frowned: an old tank top and sports bra with baggy, stained sweatpants.

"Good morning, sunshine," Victoria greeted flatly.

Shea offered a sarcastic smile and stepped onto the mat after removing her shoes. "Ready to torture me today?"

"Only if you're ready to be tortured." Victoria rose from the mat and tried offering Shea a sympathetic smile. "How do you feel?"

"Do you have to ask?" Shea retorted, her words laced with irritation.

"No, I don't." Victoria didn't miss a beat, and crossed her arms over her chest. "But this is me being civil."

Shea exhaled and stepped closer. "Fine. I feel like I've been pummeled half-to-death by a gang of vindictive schoolchildren. *Repeatedly.*"

Victoria resisted the amused smile stretching across her lips. "Ah. Well, how'd you sleep?"

"Like I was dead," Shea said as she lowered herself to the mat. She extended a leg and stretched, reaching her fingers toward her bare toes and grimacing at the tightness in the back of her thigh. "Sleep is the one thing I've not had to worry about since we've started… I'm exhausted and out like a light three seconds after hitting the mattress."

Victoria moved toward the folded rowing machine in the corner and eased it to the floor. "That's a good sign. It means you're working hard enough to earn a good night's rest. You should've seen me after the first few nights of basic training," she scoffed, and pulled the rower's handlebar back to lock it into place. "There are days I can't even remember my head hitting the pillow."

"Yeah, you keep talking about that experience like it was a good thing?" Shea said as she switched legs.

"You ready for your warm-up?" Victoria asked, gesturing to the row machine.

"No."

"Five-hundred-meter row, one minute on the jump rope, repeat five times." Victoria clapped her hands together. "Let's go."

***

"Now, there are two basic kinds of choke-holds: a blood or sleep choke, and airway choke," Victoria motioned the length of her neck with her fingertips. "I can guess you already know the difference."

The two sat kneeling across from each other on the mat. Shea's hair and neck were damp with sweat.

"It seems pretty clear, yeah," Shea said as she rubbed her thumb against her sore, wrapped knuckles. Victoria had had her train on the punching bag after warming up on the row machine, and her fists already seemed bruised and scrapped despite the tape around her hand. "The blood chokehold restricts blood flow to the brain and the airway restricts the trachea."

"Exactly—yes. The blood choke feels like falling asleep, thus the 'sleep' nickname. The airway choke is nastier and hurts like hell." Victoria stood from the mat and motioned for Shea to do the same. "Here, let me show you."

Shea furrowed her brow. "You're going to choke me? *Again?*"

Victoria rolled her eyes and sighed. "What? No. God, are you *still* angry about that? How long ago was that?"

"It still happened!"

"Whatever, just shut up and come here."

She squatted low and motioned for Shea to stand behind her. "Okay, we're going to focus on the blood chokehold. I want to show you how this actually works before I show you

326

how to get out of it. Just put your arms—" She took hold of Shea's arms above her shoulders and wrapped the right one around her throat. Then she hooked her right hand in the crook of her elbow and moved her left hand behind Victoria's head.

"This… feels weird," Shea said. She cleared her throat as heat flushed her cheeks.

"Yeah, well, sometimes violence is weird. Now—" Victoria situated the crook of Shea's right elbow directly beneath her chin. "It's important to get your elbow directly beneath their chin, see? That way all you gotta do is constrict your arm to cut off bloodflow." She motioned for Shea to squeeze her arm against her throat until both her bicep and forearm pressed tight against her skin. "You're essentially pinching around my throat. And you use your left arm to help you constrict and maintain control. It only takes a matter of seconds if done right. Okay, now try it on me."

"Are you sure?"

Victoria chuckled. "I'll be fine. I've been choked out more times that I can remember."

Shea rolled her eyes. "That explains a lot."

It took almost ten minutes for Shea to correctly situate her arms around Victoria's throat and apply the necessary pressure. Victoria eventually tapped on Shea's arm, signaling for her to release. Shea couldn't help but feel satisfied, if not empowered, by having learned how to perform a chokehold—especially on someone who had used it on her when they first met.

"See? You're getting it," Victoria said with a hint of a smile that reflected more in her eyes than her lips. Shea returned her smile and felt something stir inside her chest.

She brushed it aside and moved back into position behind Victoria, her arms wrapped around her neck.

"Alright, so now that you got the basics down, you gotta know how to get out of it. This right here is the danger area. You see how easily you have access to my throat when my chin is this high up?" Victoria demonstrated by lifting her chin into the air. Her hair flitted back against Shea's cheek.

Shea was listening, but suddenly found herself distracted by the warm scent of Victoria's hair. She glanced down at the length of Victoria's neck, and her face flushed. She blinked and took a breath.

"Are you listening?"

"Yeah, high chin. Throat. Danger area."

"Good, because this is the first thing you gotta do to prevent a successful chokehold. If you tuck your chin"—Victoria tucked her chin low against Shea's elbow, and by doing so, brushed her lips against her skin—"then you can't get a proper hold around my throat. That's step one. Now, regardless of whichever is being used against you, it's important that you don't lean backward, or else you'll easily be pulled to the ground. So, you want to drop forward—"

"Right, okay. Don't lean. Low chin, don't lean, drop forward."

"So, if you keep your chin low and—" Victoria leaned forward against Shea's grasp and pulled Shea along with her. Losing her balance, Shea stumbled onto her sparring partner's back. "See? You prevent them from getting a good hold, and you can disrupt their balance."

Shea rested against Victoria's back, jaw taut and eyes staring straight ahead to the opposite wall. "Uh-huh."

"And from here, you can reach back at their eyes." She

motioned up toward Shea's face but merely bopped her nose with her knuckle. "Or, you can reach down and knock 'em in the balls." Victoria swung her arm down between Shea's legs.

Shea quickly released her arms and backed away, heart pounding and hands sweating. "Yeah, cool. Makes sense."

"Okay, now you try. Don't worry, I won't choke you out." Victoria rose from the mat and moved behind Shea, who stood motionless. "You alright?"

She took a breath. "Uh-huh."

"Okay, I'm going to move to put you in a chokehold, and you do as I instructed, okay? I'll go slow at first."

Victoria pressed her chest against Shea's back and reached her arms out around her shoulders and neck. Shea knew that she should have been dipping her chin low and moving forward against Victoria's constricting arms. She imagined Victoria walking through the steps and understood the mechanics of each calculated motion, but she could now only recall the way the woman's neck had sloped against her arm, the way her lips had brushed against her skin, and the sturdiness of her back when Shea had fallen against her. She then lost herself in Victoria's breath against her ear and froze. In the next second, Victoria's arm was tight against her throat, constricting. Shea shuddered, gasping at her fading vision.

Victoria released her embrace and backed away.

"Come on, Shea." Victoria let out an exasperated sigh. "At least make an effort."

"I just—" Shea waved at the warmth radiating off her face with the flat of her hand and averted her gaze. She swallowed against the dryness in her throat and took a breath. "Sorry,

I just… maybe I need to have you show me again."

"Fine, but pay attention." Victoria stepped closer and met her gaze for a moment but paused, her brow knit. "You sure you're alright?"

Shea could barely manage to meet Victoria's eyes. She offered a dismissive laugh and wave of her hand. "Yeah, of course. I'm fine."

Victoria positioned herself in front of Shea once again. Her spine pressed against the front of Shea's chest, and she knelt lower to allow for an easier reach.

"Okay, try to choke me out."

Shea stretched her arm out around Victoria's throat. Just as she had instructed moments earlier, Victoria dipped her chin and dropped forward with a force. Instead of landing squarely on Victoria's back as she had done before, Shea fell further forward. Her gut bottomed-out as she unexpectedly and clumsily tumbled over Victoria's shoulder. Victoria reached out in a feeble attempt to catch her, but instead awkwardly cracked the heel of her palm against the side of Shea's jaw.

Shea cried out and collapsed to the mat at Victoria's feet, cradling her jaw with her tape-wrapped hands.

"Ah! What the fuck!"

"Oh shit!" Victoria reached down and helped Shea to her knees. "You alright? I didn't hit you that hard, did I?"

"You fucking punched me!"

"I didn't punch you! Your face hit my hand."

"How is that *not* the definition of punching someone?!"

"Here." Victoria moved closer and cupped Shea's face in her hands. Her joints and limbs locked into place, frozen, as Victoria studied her face with a concerned, focused gaze. Her thumb trailed along Shea's jawline, grazing the reddened surface of her skin with a smirk. Her eyes grew kinder. "See? You're fine."

Victoria hadn't retracted her hands. She remained kneeling in front of Shea, thumb caressing her cheek. The two didn't speak, didn't move or even seem to breathe. The silence was unbearable. Heat radiated from Victoria's hands and fingertips. Shea couldn't help but glance down at her lips, and—

"I have to go!" Shea blurted out as she knocked Victoria's hands away. She stood from the mat and backed toward the door. "I'm done. This, this is done. We're done."

Victoria parted her lips to speak, but Shea lifted a hand to silence her.

"Thanks for the lesson, I'll see you later."

And with that Shea was out the door and hurrying up the basement staircase. She ignored her sore muscles and joints as she hurriedly ascended each step, not wanting to stop pushing forward until she'd reached her bedroom door.

Chapter 37

McClintic's Bar was nothing more than a refurbished basement of a local repairman's shop halfway across the borough. The owner of the bar, Michael McClintic, also owned the repair shop and had used his craft to decorate the walls and low-hanging ceiling with mended ornamental lamps and lantern fixtures. The mix of yellow, blue, and red bulbs saturated the cozy area with a warm, ambient glow as residents sat around short tables and stools, chatting among themselves over drinks and plates of crusty bread.

Shea sat alone with her back against the wall. She held her second cup of chilled brew in her hand, balanced on top of her knee, and breathed away the lingering ache in her muscles. A subdued discomfort throbbed in her head.

"You should've seen the look on that son-of-a-bitch's face when he turned around and saw me standin' there!" Tony's bellowing laughter carried across the bar. "One hit and he was out like a fuckin' light! He didn't even know what hit him!"

Both of his arms draped over the shoulders of the two escorts who stood on either side of him. A small group of young men had gathered around them, and they joined in his laughter. The smaller of the two companions, a darker-skinned young woman with black, curled hair, smiled and shot a discreet wink at Shea.

Shea's face flushed with warmth. She took another swig from her bitter drink and rose from her seat to stride across the bar to where Simon was waiting at the bar.

"Tony is being insufferable," Shea said as she rested her elbows against the bar.

Simon snickered. "Tony is always insufferable." He wrapped his arm around her shoulder and squeezed her into a side-hug. "I'm glad you decided to come out with us. I know you and Ma aren't the biggest fans of one another."

Shea rested her head on his shoulder. She welcomed the embrace but winced a bit at the sudden shot of pain from her shoulder joint. "Yeah, well, I needed to get out." She gestured with her cup. "And maybe drink a bit."

"Everything alright?"

She let out a long, tired sigh. "Mr. H is late bringing me the vials I need. It's got me stressed out, just… waiting and doing nothing. I'm beginning to wonder if he's gotten cold feet."

Simon frowned. "Have we lost anyone else?"

"Two children last week and one a few days ago," Shea said. "Ten total since it's started."

Simon gave her shoulder another reassuring squeeze. "Try not to think about it tonight. Not like there's much you can do about it right now anyway. Allow yourself to have fun tonight and worry about all that tomorrow."

"I guess," Shea said, resigned.

"To be honest, I thought it was Vic that was bothering you." Simon chuckled.

Shea jerked back and shot him a look. "Why? What do you mean?"

"I mean, you guys have never gotten along, and I know she's been going hard on you these past few days. I thought that was why you were sulking," Simon said, brow furrowing. He observed her face a moment longer. "Did… something happen that I should know about?"

Shea let out a breath she didn't know she was holding and laughed. "No! You're right, it's just… you know, Vic being Vic. I think these training sessions are just a veiled attempt to kill me." She turned away from him and took a long drink from her cup.

"Hey, look who's here!" Tony shouted drunkenly toward the stairway entrance.

Shea and Simon both turned to watch Mama Wilder enter the bar, dressed in a vibrant red pantsuit, her salt-and-pepper dreadlocks hanging down over her shoulders. She raised her hands and smiled warmly at the round of applause and celebratory cheers shouted her way. Simon joined in the clapping and yelled, "Happy birthday" as Victoria followed close behind with her own escort close at her side. Shea recognized her immediately as the same blonde she'd discovered leaving Victoria's room weeks earlier.

Victoria wore a navy-blue button-down shirt beneath her leather jacket. Her loose auburn hair appeared an even deeper red in the warm lighting of the bar, and Shea couldn't help but hold her breath when she watched Victoria smile and offer a wave in their direction. Shea turned her back to them when they approached, choosing instead to stare at the wall of brew bottles and take another long gulp from her drink.

"Simon!" Tiffany, Victoria's companion, welcomed with a happy clapping of her hands. She gave him a hug and kissed him on the cheek. But she hesitated and recoiled when she noticed the bandage on his ear. "Oh honey, what happened?"

Simon strained to smile and shrugged. "A haircut gone bad, I guess." He turned and nudged Shea's arm. "Hey Shea, have you met Tiffa—"

"We've met," Shea interjected with feigned enthusiasm. She looked over her shoulder and raised her cup to the smiling blonde, ignoring Victoria, who was watching her with a concerned look in her eye. "Nice seeing you again! Glad you could make it to the party."

"Well, if you excuse me, I gotta go be a dutiful son," Simon said, and pushed himself away from the bar.

Victoria playfully slapped her palm against his ass as he passed. Shea watched him hurry to his mother's side and give her a loving kiss on her cheek. She thought of her own mother and frowned into her drink.

"Shea—" Victoria began to say, but Shea stood from her stool and moved back toward her previous seat without looking her in the eye.

"I think I'm going to, um—get some space." She gestured to the empty chair and left the two women standing in baffled silence.

Twenty minutes and one additional brew later, Shea still sat with her back against the wall. She closed her eyes and focused on the music played by an elderly man in the far corner, strumming happily at his guitar. People danced to the upbeat tune, or at least did their best around the collection of short tables and chairs. She tried not to think of the children who had passed away in her office over the past few lunars, or of Mr. Henderson's failure to bring her the Cyntrax samples. Shea couldn't conduct her comparative tests without those samples, couldn't isolate the cause of the strange sickness killing innocent children in her borough. She was worthless, just sitting and waiting... sitting and waiting... sitting and waiting. Her jaw clenched; her breath grew shorter as the palms of her hands dampened with sweat.

"Allow yourself to have fun tonight and worry about all that tomorrow." The memory of Simon's voice pulled her from the spiraling panic. She opened her eyes, took a deep breath, and pressed her face into her open palms. She rubbed her eyes and let out a long breath.

The guitar tempo slowed and relaxed. When Shea lifted her face from her hands, she saw Simon dragging his smiling mother to the dance floor. He pulled her into her arms, laughed, and danced with her to the melodious guitar music. Shea smiled watching them and, despite her dislike for Mama Wilder, couldn't help but feel happy for the joy across her face in that moment. Her smile faltered, however, recalling the speckle of blood on the old woman's handkerchief and lips, and her deep, bellowing coughing fits. What happiness she felt gave way to dread, made worse by Simon's unknowing smile as they danced.

A shattered bottle drew her attention back to the bar, where she again made eye contact with Tony's dark-haired companion. Tony cursed at the broken bottle at his feet; Victoria laughed at him with Tiffany wrapped in her arms. Tiffany lifted onto her toes and pressed a kiss against Victoria's neck, leaving Shea with a sudden, sunken sensation in the bottom of her gut.

"Allow yourself to have fun tonight..."

Shea propelled herself from her seat and marched toward the gathering by the bar, making sure to maneuver past patrons without drawing too much attention to herself. Her nerves begged her to turn back, to return to her seat by the wall for the rest of the evening. But the three bottles of brew flowing in her blood pushed her through the anxiety.

Shea slipped in beside the dark-haired companion. She rested against the bar and leaned toward her ear. Her hair smelled faintly of roses.

"What's your name?" Shea asked.

A coy smile spread across the woman's lips. "Melody."

"Melody," Shea repeated to herself. She shifted on her feet and fiddled with her hands. "I'm Shea."

"Pretty name you've got, Shea." Melody leaned her elbow against the bar and scanned Shea up and down with a quick glance. "I've noticed you sittin' alone for most the party."

"Yeah, well… would you like to come sit with me? I think I'd like the company," Shea asked through a volley of rattled nerves.

Melody regarded Shea for a moment and nodded toward Tony. "You're cute, but I'm already spoken for, unfortunately."

Shea looked past Melody's shoulder at Tony, who was too busy drunkenly kicking shards of broken glass beneath the bar and stumbling in the process. His other escort, a beautiful pale woman with braided blonde hair, strained to suppress palpable signs of annoyance and frustration. She rested her hand on her hip, feigned a smile, and rolled her eyes whenever Tony turned away from her.

"Ah, fair point," Shea stammered with a laugh. She

swallowed and stepped around Melody to tap on Tony's shoulder. "Hey, Tony? *Tony.*"

Tony sluggishly spun around and reached out to clasp onto the bar for balance. He blinked at her and grinned with a nod. "Hey Doc, what—what's up? You here to give me a check-up? Eh?"

Shea grimaced at him. "You wish."

"I do. I do wish," Tony muttered and reached for another drink.

"I was wondering if I could borrow Melody for a little bit," Shea said, her voice raised to get through his drunken daze. "And since, well, I don't want to interfere with, you know, business and all. I figured I'd ask if it was alright."

Tony was no longer paying attention. He was deep in a fresh cup of brew and mumbled an incoherent response before chugging the beverage.

"Right. Cool." Shea turned back to Melody and thumbed toward her empty table. "What do you say?"

***

"So I go into the examination room and my patient is just… *gone,*" Shea laughed. Melody sat beside her, also laughing between sips of her drink. Shea fanned her flushed face as she continued. "I start freaking out, because this is my second week as a resident, right? I think they're going to murder me. So, I *run* out of the room looking for this guy and end up finding him fifteen minutes later, butt-ass naked in the dining hall, waving a broom around like a sword!"

Melody nearly spit out her drink. She wiped her lip while laughing, "Oh my god, what happened?"

"Turns out he paid one of the janitors to slip him some extra meds, and he may have gone off the deep end a bit. It took me, another doctor, and three nurses to subdue the poor guy."

"I still can't imagine what it's like to come from the Dome and live here," Melody said. "I've lived here all my life and I can't stand it. I've always daydreamed of what it's like to live in the Dome—going shopping, having a fancy luncheon with other ladies in the center square."

Shea shrugged. "I mean, yeah, the Dome is nice in some ways, but… I actually prefer it here. People are more, I don't know, real? It's been better if only for the people I've met along the way."

Shea smiled and failed to resist the urge to glance down at Melody's lips. She cleared her throat and looked away to notice Victoria sitting with Tiffany across the bar. Tiffany was seated on her lap, giggling while running her fingers through Victoria's hair. Victoria, however, appeared tired while feigning a smile. After a few moments, Victoria lifted her gaze from the floor to meet Shea's.

"So, what was it, exactly, that brought you here?" Melody asked, pulling Shea's attention back.

Shea faltered and let out a breath. "Uh, well… they ended up revoking my citizenship and exiling me here."

"What'd a sweet thing like you do to get exiled?" Melody asked. A mischievous grin curled her lips. "Although, I think I have a hunch."

Shea dropped her gaze to the drink in her hands. "Um, well, there was… a girl. She was a nurse I worked with and—well, we were pretty close as coworkers. Always cracking jokes and making each other laugh, you know? The kind of person whose smile alone makes you want to smile too."

Melody moved closer and reached to tuck a strand of hair behind Shea's ear. "Did something happen?"

Their closeness sent a shiver down Shea's spine. Nurse Elliot had almost been this close to her in the supply closet. Looking back at that moment, Shea regretted not closing that distance.

"I flirted and tried making a move, in my own way, but—" Shea shrugged and let out a sigh. "She freaked out. I think she may have felt something for me too, but she was more afraid of the edict than acknowledging her own feelings, of feeling that… attraction."

"Did she report you?" Melody asked, her voice low. Shea offered a silent, solemn nod. Melody reached her hand to gently caress Shea's cheek. "Is that why you've asked me to keep you company tonight?"

Shea lifted her gaze to meet Melody's, leaning her face into her touch. Tears pooled in her eyes. "I don't know. That's the thing, I don't know what I want. *Who* I want. And I don't think there's anyone here I can really talk to about any of this. So that's why—" Shea gestured sheepishly at Melody. "You know.

"You gotta just follow your gut feeling, honey. Your heart knows what it wants, you just gotta pay attention and listen," Melody said with a reassuring smile. "Have you ever slept with a man?"

A burst of laughter escaped her lips. She wasn't prepared for that question.

"I have, my first cycle of residency. I wasn't into it at all. We tried it a few times, and I just, I don't know, gave up and chose to focus on my career instead. But I always thought it was just because I was doing it wrong or that he just sucked in bed."

Melody laughed and shook her head. "Oh no, no honey." She rested her hand on Shea's leg. "Don't get me wrong, sex can definitely be disappointing, and some men really are just… awful. But"—she leaned closer and lowered her voice—"there's a more obvious reason why you didn't like it."

"What about you?" Shea asked, her own voice now in a whisper. "Do you like women… you know, *that* way?"

Melody's smile grew across her lips, her eyes softened watching Shea. "I do. Why else do you think I was eyeing you from the bar?"

"But… you—"

"Entertain men? I do, yes. But it's just to pay the bills. And there are days when I can entertain women, too." Melody leaned closer and traced her finger across Shea's bottom lip. "And those are the days I truly love my job."

Heat flashed across Shea's face and neck, her heart pounding in her chest. "I… I don't know what I'm doing."

"That's alright, sweetie. I do," Melody smile turned playful as she brushed a stray strand of hair from Shea's forehead. "Your place or mine?"

Chapter 38

Melody stepped inside the bedroom behind Shea, surveying the modest setting with an amused smirk across her lips. A single light bulb hung over the sink against the wall, leaving the two in a warm glow against the darkness. Shea closed the door and hesitated, her hand still clutching the handle. Melody plopped down onto the mattress behind her with a chuckle, startling Shea from her daze. She loosened her grip and turned to press her back against the door, watching Melody shift against the bed.

There's a girl on my bed. No, not just a girl. There's a companion *on my bed... and she—*

"You've got a cute setup here," Melody said. She ran her fingertips along the soft blanket. "Nice bed, too. Cozy."

Shea let out an anxious laugh and stepped away from the door. She crossed her arms. "Yeah, it's not much but," she shrugged. "It's something, I guess."

What am I saying?

"Do you want to come sit by me?" Melody asked. Her voice was level, calm, as she patted the space beside her.

Oh god.

"Do you want something to drink first?" Shea gestured

toward the door, then fidgeted with her hands. "I could get us something from the kitchen if you want."

Melody stood from the bed and crossed the room with a sympathetic smile. "I'm fine. I think that…" She reached to tuck Shea's hair behind her ear and stepped closer. Her voice quieted as she dropped her attention to Shea's lips. "You should just relax. Loosen up a bit, let yourself have some fun. You're tense enough to snap."

Shea let out a breathy laugh and unclenched her damp hands. "I'm sorry, I just… I've never done this before. Well, I have, obviously. But, you know, not *this*."

"That's alright," Melody moved closer and wrapped an arm around Shea's waist. She caressed Shea's cheek with her free hand and whispered. "We don't have to do anything if you don't want to. I can leave if—"

"No," Shea blurted out and lightly took hold of Melody's hips, keeping her in place. She closed her eyes and sighed. "I want you to stay."

Melody grinned and leaned into Shea's grip. "I'm glad to hear that. I want to stay, too."

"I—" Shea stammered. "I don't know what I'm doing."

"Then let me show you," Melody said, and leaned to press her lips against Shea's.

Shea's belly flipped, her face flushed at the warmth spreading from her mouth, her cheeks, her neck. A tightness seized her chest, and she froze in place, unable to move or breathe. She wavered, suddenly dizzy, at tasting the sweetness of Melody's soft lips. All the boys she'd kissed before had had a roughness to their touch; there'd be too much pressure from their dry lips as their hurried, firm hands gripped onto her too tightly. Shea had merely been another thing to consume, to use to satiate an unspoken primal hunger. But Melody's touches were soft, from her delicate lips to the way she lightly trailed her fingertips up the side of her neck and into her hair. Her movements were slow and patient, as if every motion, every breath was to be savored to its fullest.

Melody pulled away just slightly, leaving only a narrow space between their lips. "Is this okay?"

Shea couldn't bring herself to speak, and instead kept her eyes closed and body tense against Melody's touch. She let out a breath and nodded. Melody ran her fingers through Shea's hair and kissed her cheek.

"If it helps, pretend I'm her," she whispered before pressing her lips against Shea's again.

Pretend she's... who? Nurse Elliot?

Shea imagined her closeness with the her in the supply closet and felt the pang regret roil in her chest.

"*Is that what* you *want?*" she'd asked Shea that morning. She imagined, instead of speeding out in confused panic, putting the Cyntrax aside, shutting the door, and reaching out to draw her into a kiss. Melody's lips had become Nurse Elliot's, as the two stood inside the supply closet in each other's arms. Shea wondered what her lips would've tasted of that morning and smiled into the kiss at the thought of recalling the nurse's favorite tea.

Her lips would've tasted like peppermint.

Shea lost herself in the reverie, and leaned to press her lips against Nurse Elliot's. But when she ran her fingers through the nurse's hair, she discovered locks of crimson instead of golden blonde. Nurse Elliot was taller now, and stronger, with lean, muscular arms that wrapped around her waist and drew her closer. Shea caught the lingering, tangled scent of lavender and cigarette smoke in the heat between them. Their kisses grew heady, their grips on each other tighter.

"Is this what you want?" Melody asked as she trailed her fingers down Shea's spine, around her hips, and along the front lip of her slacks. Her touch sent shivers and goosebumps across Shea's skin.

But Shea didn't hear Melody's voice; there was someone else's voice whispering in her ear, and she imagined their green eyes meeting hers in the warm light of the bedroom.

"Yes," Shea managed a whisper as they moved, entwined, toward the bed. "I want this."

***

A light, incessant knocking stirred Shea from her sleep. She raised her head from the pillow and peered, eyes heavy and squinting, over Melody's bare shoulder toward the door. The knocking continued with increasing urgency.

"Shea," Theresa whispered through the door. "Shea, are you up? Can I come in?" The door handle creaked and started to turn.

"No!" Shea launched herself, bare naked and fumbling, over Melody's body. She stumbled over her feet as she padded across to the clothes-littered floor to press her palm flat against the door. "No, no, don't come in. I'm, uh, not decent."

"… Is there someone else in there with you?" Theresa asked, her voice laced with curiosity and excitement.

Shea glanced over her shoulder to see Melody sitting up from the bed to stretch her arms high into the air with a yawn, her chest exposed and bare. Her face flushed hot as she turned her attention back to the door.

"What do you need, T?"

"You've got a patient waiting for you downstairs. He's pretty insistent that you see him as soon as possible."

Shea rubbed her eyes and peeked at the clock on the wall: 06:23. "This early? Is it an emergency?"

"He didn't say. Honestly, he was sort of a dick when I asked."

"Well, did you catch his name?"

"I think he said his name was Gerald something..." Theresa paused for a moment before continuing. "Henderson, I think."

All drowsiness clouding Shea's mind slipped away in an instant, and she stood staring wide-eyed at the door. "I'll be out in a minute, go down and tell him I'm on my way."

Shea heard Theresa turn and stomp down the hallway. "I'm not a fucking butler..."

"Off to work, then?" Melody asked as she stood from the bed and reached for her clothes.

Shea offered an apologetic smile. "It appears so. I'm sorry I can't stay longer."

Melody slipped her dress over her head and shimmied it down around her hips with a smile of her own. "No need to be sorry, *Doctor*. I've got to be gettin' back home anyway."

"I had a lot of fun last night," Shea said through a timid grin. Melody approached her and, leaning in close, caressed one cheek and kissed the other.

"Me too. It's clients like you that make this job enjoyable," she said with a playful wink. "Maybe we can do it again sometime."

"And maybe next time I won't have to steal you from Tony,"

Shea chuckled.

Melody laughed and walked toward the door. "Next time you won't have to." She looked over her shoulder with a charming smile before stepping out into the hall. "See you around."

A flush of heat tinged her cheeks with the last passing thought of the night before. Shea peeked out the door to watch Melody leave and caught the baffled, yet delighted, expression across Theresa's face.

I knew it! Theresa mouthed silently to Shea.

Shut up! Shea mouthed back before shutting the door.

Shea was dressed and out of her room five minutes later, with her dark hair pulled back into as neat of a bun as she could manage in her hurry. She'd spent those minutes not thinking about the heated night she'd spent with Melody, or the unexpected, impassioned fantasy that had seized her. The thoughts gripping her now were of the old, eccentric man pacing her examination room; she imagined him with a facemask affixed across his scowling lips.

Her heart sank when a troubling thought struck her: maybe he was only there to bring her bad news. Perhaps he was there that morning to admit failure and call the whole thing off, and was too spooked to carry on with his end of the bargain.

What if we can't get those samples? What if he's been caught and now the State knows? How many more innocent people-—children—will die if we fail?

Henderson was waiting for her in the examination room with his latex-gloved hands clasped behind his back; his fingers twitched and fidgeted as she stepped through the door.

"Good morning, Mr. Henderson," Shea said with the most earnest smile she could manage. "How can I help you?"

He scoffed and fidgeted with his hands. His voice was shaking as he spoke. "Cut the bullshit, you fuckin' know why I'm here."

He continued to pace from one side of the room to the other, his attention darting around to different, minute details of the walls and floor. Shea saw tinges of disgust in his eyes as he noted particulars he found distasteful or not to his liking. But he seemed distracted despite his scrutiny, and swiped a bead of sweat from his pallid forehead.

"I didn't want to assume," Shea said, her smile faltering. "But let's just cut the formalities, then, for yours and brevity's sake. Do you have the samples or not?"

Henderson stopped pacing and shot her a fiery glare above his facemask. She held his gaze for a few tense moments, unwavering, until he finally reached into his jacket pocket and withdrew two small vials. His fingers trembled.

"Do you know the trouble I went through to get these? Hm? Do you have any fucking idea the risk I took?" Henderson gestured with the vials between his fingers as he spoke. Shea could see his mouth contorting into a snarl beneath his facemask. "I manipulated the shipping manifests as best I could, but you cannot possibly fathom how closely they've been monitoring us these past few lunars! Internal audits, document and logistical reviews, screenings—one tiny slip-up from me and I'm completely, royally fucked! Do you understand that? I'll be swinging on that fuckin' tower 1 by the end of the quarter when they find out."

"Mr. Henderson, please calm down—"

"You don't get to tell me to calm the fuck down!" Henderson snapped. His face reddened. "I keep my mouth shut and tolerate my elitist Dome snob bosses tellin' me what to do every damn day, but I won't accept that shit from the likes of you or anyone else."

"I can appreciate the tremendous risk you took bringing those samples here, Mr. Henderson. You're absolutely right—what you've done is extremely dangerous, but I can also appreciate the role those vials will play in saving countless innocent lives on this station," Shea spoke evenly and calmly despite the sweat rising against her palms. She took a slow, measured step toward him. "What you did was very brave."

Henderson scoffed. "Fuck bravery, I want to live! I fed information to Harriet for countless cycles because she agreed to pay for my apartment—if you'd seen the shithole I was living in before, you'd understand why it was a deal I couldn't refuse. I scratched her back, she scratched mine. But this?" He gestured with the two vials between his fingers. "What the fuck am I getting for this, huh? You agreed to treat me, sure, but that won't fuckin' matter when I'm dead, will it? What the hell is this all worth?"

Shea hesitated. Her attention moved to the spot on the floor where Lauren's pallid, jaundiced limbs had lain still against the floor, holding her lifeless child, lunars before. "I don't think you would be asking me that question if you've seen what I've seen."

"Oh?" He peered at her with a skeptical eye. "And what *have* you seen, hm? You know, you never told me what shit was going on down here in the Anchor when I first asked. You said 'bring me the vials' and that you'd fill me in. So maybe you should start talking as I make up my mind on what to do next."

"You're serious?"

Henderson slipped the vials back into his pocket. "Start talking."

Shea stared at him for a few moments, simmering in her roiling anger, before moving across the room to take a seat in the upholstered examination chair. She leaned forward to rest her elbows on her knees, clasped her hands, and stared ahead at the area on the tile floor where Lauren had died.

"A pregnant woman died in this room a few lunars ago. Right there, on the floor." Shea nodded forward with her chin and bit her lip. "I'd given her a dose of Cyntrax a week before—I wanted to be sure that her and her child had the necessary nutritional and immuno supplements they needed. That's what we do, after all. We reserve the Cyntrax for children and pregnant women down here in the Anchor, since they're the most vulnerable to malnutrition. But she was in her third trimester when I first started seeing her, and there wasn't much else I could do for her at that time except give her that treatment and monitor her progress. I didn't really have much reason to worry; she seemed to be relatively healthy, all things considered when you're a lower-borough non-citizen."

Henderson didn't say anything, and only crossed his arms as she continued.

"I almost didn't recognize her when she came to us for help that night; her skin was jaundiced and feverish, blood in her eyes… she already looked dead." Shea's voice trailed off, her eyes unfocused as she gaze forward. "All she cared about was saving her baby, but I couldn't save them both. She made me promise to save the child, but he was already lost. He'd succumb to the same illness as her, if not before. She died thinking he made it… her name was Lauren, and she was my friend."

She strained to suppress fresh tears and sniffed. "We've lost ten children since Lauren's death, all with the same symptoms: liver failure, internal bleeding, fever. *Ten children*, Henderson. All that I'd unwittingly administered a Cyntrax treatment to. It's the only common denominator between them, the only thing that connects them or makes sense."

When Henderson spoke again, his voice was steady but gruff. "And how does this relate to this suicide mission you've sent me on?"

"I believe the answer to these deaths lies in the trial Cyntrax, but I'm stuck without samples of both the regular *and* trial versions of the drug. With those vials"—Shea gestured to Henderson's pocket—"I can get a handle of what's going on, maybe even identify specifically what it is within the trial doses that's killing these people. And what we can do to stop it."

"If this is all true, and the State, whether accidentally or purposefully, tainted the trial doses, then you're playing a very dangerous game with some very dangerous people. One that you're not likely to survive," Henderson said. "Is it worth it?"

"If my work prevents even one more loss of life, even at the expense of my own, then it is well worth it," Shea said. "I remember each of their faces, Mr. Henderson. Lauren, her baby, and each sick, frail child who sat where I'm sitting now… I can't bear to lose another. I couldn't live with myself knowing there was something I could've done to stop it."

The two remained in still silence for a few moments before Henderson leaned off the wall. He briefly hesitated, groaned, and dug his hand inside his pocket. Without saying a word, he paced forward, placed the two vials on the sink counter, and swiftly exited the room. Shea listened to his footfalls ascend the stairs and exit into the meeting space before lifting herself from the chair. She crossed the room and delicately took the two vials into her hands: the two were nearly identical except for a small 'T' marked on the bottom of one.

Shea let out a long sigh and felt the uncomfortable tension in her shoulders and back ease. She merely stood at the sink for a few moments, holding the two vials in her hand, before Theresa poked her head inside the doorway.

"Just so you know, we had to hold Simon back from running in here to kick that guy's ass," she said.

Shea let out a shaky laugh. "You all heard that, huh?"

"Yeah, from the training room. We didn't wanna cramp your style, but we also know he's a bit of a dick." Theresa approached the sink and peered at the vials between Shea's fingers. "You know, Vic was ready to kill the guy if he didn't hand them over. She doesn't much like him anyway."

Shea rolled her eyes and suppressed the smile at Victoria's name. "I'm not surprised."

"So, what do we do now?" Theresa asked.

"Now we get to work," Shea said with a growing smile as she nudged Theresa's arm. "And I've got an extra special task for you."

Chapter 39

"*Rats.*" Theresa's voice dripped with disgust. "When you said you had something 'extra special' for me, the last thing on my mind was *fetching rats.*"

Shea was too busy counting the stocked inventory in her office to bother with Theresa's tantrum. She tapped a fingernail against the clipboard in her hands and furrowed her brow at the dwindling numbers of supplies.

"Yeah, well, what else can I test on?" Shea asked absently as she peered into a cabinet to count bandage rolls. "I can't exactly just pluck someone from the street, can I?"

"But rats," Theresa whined. "Do you know where I had to go to get these little bastards? I smell like a garbage chute! Oh no, what if Simon walks by and smells me? God, I could just die!"

Shea blinked and stopped her counting. She turned her attention to Theresa, who was now anxiously sniffing her shirt with a revolted expression across her flushed face.

"You've got them already? Way to go, T!" Shea placed the clipboard on the counter and stepped toward Theresa with an apologetic smile. "I know it wasn't the most glamorous assignment, but it's important, you know? I can't even do the experiment without them."

Theresa rolled her eyes. "Yeah, no, I get it. But why'd it have to be me? Why not Tony?" Shea answered with only a doubtful raise of her eyebrows. Theresa let out a sigh and shifted on her feet. "You're right, that would've been a disaster. But you owe me for this."

Theresa pulled a shoebox from behind her back and extended it toward Shea. Tiny claws scurried along the bottom, and their shifting weight swayed the box in her hand. Shea eyed the container for a moment before taking it and prying the lid slightly open. Two sets of beady eyes peered up at her from inside, and long, hairless tails curled around lumps of dark fur huddled in the corner. A pang of guilt rested against her heart, knowing what she had planned for them. She closed the lid and cleared her throat.

"How about I ask Victoria to pick you up something special the next time she's in the Dome? Maybe some perfume or something?" Shea asked.

A knowing smile crossed Theresa's lips. "Yeah, I think that'll do. I'm sure she knows the right places to go, after all. That's lavender you're wearing, right?"

Heat flushed Shea's cheeks. She turned away and moved back toward the counter. "That'll be all—go be a hormonal teenager somewhere else."

"Uh-huh," Theresa said through a smirk. "I'm going to go scrub the nasty off me now. It might take me a week."

"Goodbye, T," Shea said, louder now and with a hint of annoyance.

Theresa hurried out, rushing up the stairs toward her room to most likely gather her shower items, and left Shea alone to stare at the box sitting on the counter. She heard a muted squeak, and the box shifted again.

"I'm sorry, lil' guys." She sighed and rested her palm on the lid, caressing the side with her thumb. "I know it isn't fair, or entirely humane. But I don't really have another choice. At least it's for a good cause, right?"

Another squeak and shuffle from inside, as though one of them were scratching itself. Shea frowned, reached up into a nearby cabinet, and extracted the two, tiny vials of Cyntrax.

Shea told herself not to get attached and to push away her guilt. She mirthlessly labeled one rat *A* and the other *B*, but soon began referring to them as 'Alfred' and 'Benjamin' while absently chatting at them. Alfred and Benjamin each resided in their own shoe box, which Shea had been sure to fill with bits of stale bread and a small dish of water. Alfred's box, just as his vial of trial Cyntrax, was marked with a thick red X. Benjamin, whose vial and container were marked with a blue X, had won the test rat lottery and received an injection of regular Cyntrax. Both rats sat in their respective new homes after the administered injections, nibbling mindlessly on old breadcrumbs and scratching at the injection sites.

Shea hated operating in these limiting conditions. She would've preferred a proper facility, better equipment, sterile test subjects, and appropriate protective gear considering the complexity and possible danger. If the disease were going to latch on and choke the life from her, it would have happened already. But there she was, without symptoms and healthy, spending her afternoon staring at two rats inside her examination room. She watched Alfred poop in the corner of his box and waddle over to lap water from his shallow dish.

She sighed and rubbed the heel of her palm against her

tired eyes. "This better work."

If Shea were honest with herself, she would have preferred to not be responsible for this experiment in the first place. The State's medical school led courses in research and experimentation, but she'd only taken a few and hadn't much enjoyed the practice. Those courses were her only practical experience, and she now felt like she was groping blindly through the dark. Someone else should've been leading the project, a doctor who knew what they were doing; someone like her mother.

I wonder what Mom would've done differently with all of this. Her heart ached recalling her mother's face in the research tapes. She reached out and traced the edge of the rat's box with her fingertips and wondered if her mother had given a name to Victoria other than 'Raven,' as Shea had done with her rats.

Shea's heart sank like a heavy stone in her chest. She took a breath and closed her eyes, beckoning the image of the videotape now replaying in her mind to disperse. Instead she thought of Victoria, holding her in her arms as she wept, reassuring her that none of it was her fault.

"S'cuse me—"

Shea jumped, startled, from her stool and spun to discover a tall, middle-aged man standing in the doorway of the examination room. His face was pallid and damp with sweat that ran down his neck and stained the collar of his old work shirt. His tired, dark eyes lingered on her from a distance.

"Sorry, miss, I didn't mean to scare you."

"Oh." Shea let out a breath and rested her hand over her heart. "No, I'm sorry I didn't see you come in. How can I help you?"

"Was told Shadow had a doctor that was offerin' help to borough-folk. I ain't a citizen, see, so I can't go to the Middle doctors. I ain't feelin' very well." His voice was wary as he spoke. He couldn't have been any older than his mid-thirties, but streaks of gray peppered his dark hair. His sunken, ashen cheeks and dim eyes aged him.

"Of course, I'd be glad to help." She outstretched her arm toward the armchair with a smile. "Please, take a seat and tell me what's bothering you."

His eyes glanced around the room as he took slow, careful steps toward the chair. Taking a seat, he lowered his gaze to the tile floor, his hands still wringing in his lap.

"I, ehm, think I have a fever. Been feelin' a bit achy and all. Shivers."

"How long have you had these symptoms?" Shea asked, turning her back to him to reach up toward her cabinets. She wondered, since he was suffering from a fever, if maybe he was inflicted with the same illness she was now testing for. He was older and wouldn't have received any Cyntrax, though, which gave her pause.

Shea reached into the cabinet and collected the thermometer. "Sir? When did you start noticing the symp—"

A solid push from behind threw her hard against the counter. A sharp sting pierced the side of her neck. She parted her lips to scream but her lungs failed, leaving her in a muted agony that coursed through her blood like fire.

"I'm sorry, miss," he spoke in a whispered tremor. He pressed himself against her, pinning her to the edge of the counter, and extracted the syringe. "They took my kids, ya see… And if I don't bring you with me, they're as good as dead. I can't let that happen."

Panic seized her. A flash of a memory crossed her mind at that moment, of her and Victoria sparring on the training mat, and she steeled herself against her gripping fear. Shea twisted and threw back an elbow into the man's face but missed her mark and was met by the side of his knuckles against her jaw. Large hands grabbed onto the back of her collar and threw her against a nearby wall, knocking over a metal stand of instruments. Her skull struck against the tile wall and stars blanketed her eyesight. When she felt his hands on her again, she turned and blindly reached out against him with frantic, clawing swipes. When her vision cleared, she discovered her fingernails dragging down across his slick face and neck, leaving a trail of torn skin and blood.

The harder she struggled to break free from his hold, the more weight he pressed into her. The pressure of his forearm against her ribs squeezed the breath from her lungs. Shea gasped and thrashed against him, but felt her limbs gradually grow heavy and weak. His hand reached across her mouth, silencing the scream now crawling up her throat.

"I'm sorry, miss. I'm sorry, but please don't struggle, it'll be over soon..."

Tears streamed down her cheeks as she slumped forward, burdened now by her own weight. Her senses obscured, as though she were fading, slipping away despite her will to stay awake. Her heartbeat slowed, drumming loud and sluggish in her ears.

"Easy does it." The man's voice quieted as he withdrew his clammy palm from her lips.

The drug surging through her veins was potent. The man eased away from her as her limbs settled, heavy and weak against his embrace. The strength in her legs failed, and she soon realized she'd slid down the wall to the tile floor below. Her fingertips fumbled blindly along the tile until they grazed an abrasive metallic instrument. Taking it into her hand, she felt the sharp edge of a blade press against her palm: a scalpel, knocked to the floor from her metal stand.

She felt the cold, slick sweat of the man's skin against her cheek when he leaned down to hoist her drooping body from the floor. Her eyesight faded to black, the world around her muted in the haze that engulfed her as he lifted her from the floor. A voice reached her through the darkness, the voice of her father. He sounded distant, but drew closer as she lost herself in the memory.

"Oh Shea, what happened?" Her father knelt before her and tucked a loose strand of dark hair behind her ears. Shea's fists ached, her swollen eyes stung from prolonged crying.

She sniffled and felt her face begin to coil with the swell of fresh, new tears. "T-Tommy pulled my hair and made fun of me, daddy. I told him to stop b-but—" her voice faltered and choked in her throat as warm tears streamed down her fat, flushed cheeks.

"Shh shh, it's okay, baby." Her father brushed his thumb against her cheek to wipe away the tears. "So he teased you and you hit him?"

Shea nodded.

"And gave him a nosebleed?"

She nodded again. "He started crying."

Her father subdued a chuckle behind his dark, trimmed beard, biting his bottom lip and forcing a frown. Reaching out, he gently pulled her into an embrace. Her sobs quieted, her tears ceased.

"Don't tell your mom I said this, but you're right for fighting back. You did good, okay?" Shea nodded and sniffled against his chest. "A lot of boys will tease you because you're a girl, and they

think girls are weaker than they are. But you know what?" She pulled back and looked up into her father's warm, smiling face. "You aren't weak. Don't let those little assholes push you around. You keep punching back, okay?"

The blade sunk deep into slick, warm flesh. She felt a warm, wet spray against her face as the arms holding her up loosened, dropping her to the floor. His muted screams reached her through the engulfing darkness.

A swift kick from his boot cracked against her jaw as he stumbled forward, grasping desperately at his sputtering throat. The bloody scalpel he'd yanked from his neck seconds earlier slipped from his slick fingers and dropped to the floor. She felt his body collapse over her, the bitter scent of copper the last thing she remembered.

***

THWUP.

Simon's knuckles met the padded glove on Victoria's hand with a hard, solid blow. She swung at him with the other glove. He ducked away and threw another punch into the mitt. Another swing, another hit. He was growing sluggish and dragged, and she could feel the weakening impact of each strike.

"Okay, you need a break," she said.

Simon's nostrils flared; his lip twitched as he shifted his shoulders in his fighting stance. "No, I'm fine."

Sweat dripped from his beard after throwing an uppercut into her padded hand. His right ear, what was left of it after the gunshot blast, was bandaged with thick cloth and medical tape. It was damp with sweat, but within the last five minutes had begun showing signs of seeping, oozing blood. Victoria knew his stitches had opened again, for the second time that day.

"*No.* You're bleeding again. We're done," Victoria snapped, tearing off the padded gloves and tossing them to the corner.

Simon shrugged, bewildered. "What the hell, Vic? I said I was fine."

"You're pushing yourself too hard. That ear of yours won't heal properly if you keep fucking doing this to yourself."

"I can handle it." Simon crossed his arms, defiant. Victoria scoffed and rolled her eyes, to which Simon responded with a snarl. "I swear to god, you've been acting super fucking weird lately. What the hell's gotten into you?"

Victoria didn't respond as she stepped across the mats to snatch a towel from a rack. She recalled the shy smile that had flashed across Shea's face as she'd left the bar on Melody's arm. A rush of bitterness spread across her chest.

"Besides," Simon continued, "I can't afford to be out of commission, not with the Trinities acting up as they are. Hurt or not, I gotta keep training. Not all of us are lucky enough to be like *you*, are we?"

Victoria turned a heated, furious eye on him. "Lucky? Is that what I am, Simon? Am I fucking lucky?"

Simon took a deep breath and closed his eyes. A tense silence lingered in the space between them for a few moments before the tightness in his shoulders relaxed in resignation.

"I'm sorry, I'm just..." He lifted his gaze to meet hers. "I'm just *frustrated.* About getting myself into this situation in the first place, about getting hurt and setting myself back, about almost getting Shea hurt... about worrying you. What use am I to anyone if I'm like this?"

Victoria's face softened, and all her anger dropped away as she stepped forward to pull him into a hug.

"You're such an ass, man," she said, her arms tight around his shoulders. "But you don't get to start questioning your use, especially to me. You understand?" Simon wrapped his arms around Victoria's waist and nodded silently into her shoulder. "But you can't keep pushing yourself like this… your body doesn't work that way."

Not like mine. She wouldn't wish that on him, not after what it had cost her.

Simon sighed and rested his good ear against her shoulder. "I know, sis. I'll take the rest of the afternoon off, how about that?"

"I suppose that'll do."

They moved to take a seat on the bench and sipped on tall glasses of water. Simon fidgeted with his ear's moist, bloody bandage.

"Stop." She reached to swat his hand away.

Simon leaned away from her reach to scratch at his ear. "But it itches!"

"Alright, but you'll have to answer to Shea after I tell her you've been messing with it."

Simon grew serious and peered down at his glass of water. "You think it'll work?" he asked as he itched around the edge of tape.

"What will?"

"Shea testing your blood for whatever the hell this disease is. Testing on those rats Theresa caught."

Victoria ran her fingers through her damp, sweaty hair and sighed. "Who knows. Seems to make the most sense, though. Enough of the pieces seem to fit."

"I just can't figure out *why.* What'd be the point in the State purposefully creating something like that and contaminating medication with it? Why kill your own citizens? It's seems too cruel, even for them."

Maybe because it wasn't meant for citizens. "She'll figure it out."

"I hope so, I'm not sure how much longer we have until—"

A man's scream broke through the quiet of the hall outside the training room door. The two froze in an instant, looking in the direction of the blood-chilling sound.

"Was that… from Shea's office?" Simon's voice lowered to a whisper.

Victoria sprang to her feet and darted from the room. Simon followed, trailing her as she sprinted down the hall and broke through the open doorway of the examination room. Two bodies lay in a tangle on the white tiled floor in the far corner surrounded by strewn medical instruments. Crimson blood pooled beneath them and soaked through their clothes.

"Shit!" Simon lunged forward and grabbed the back of the man's jacket to hoist him from Shea's body. Thick, sticky blood trailed from the dead man's punctured throat as Simon tossed him aside. Shea lay on the floor beneath him, streaks of red marked across her face and neck; even her dark hair appeared saturated and slick.

"Come on, Shea," Victoria uttered in a desperate whisper as she crouched over her. "Please be alright. Please, please be alright…"

Shea's vacant eyes remained partially open, her heavy eyelids drooping. Victoria's blood ran cold as she brushed the blood-damp hair from Shea's face and cradled her wet cheek in her palm.

She pressed her fingertips against Shea's neck and felt

nothing. Her fingertips frantically searched, exploring Shea's skin in a desperate pursuit until she detected the slightest, faint presence of a heartbeat. She breathed a heavy, relieved sigh and leaned forward to rest her forehead against Shea's chest. The weak rise and fall of Shea's breathing against Victoria's brow brought warmth back to her veins, and she couldn't help but caress Shea's cheek before pulling back again.

"She's alive," Victoria said as she stood and turned her attention to the dead man beneath Simon. Her eye caught a glimpse of his discarded syringe. "I think she's been drugged."

Simon stepped to Shea's side and knelt to rest a hand on her shoulder. "God, he sure did a number on her. Looks like she put up a good fight, though. Got him with the scalpel before he could carry her out—good girl, Shea."

Victoria loomed over the dead man and peered down at his lifeless face. "Get Theresa to help clean her up and get her to bed."

"What about you?" Simon asked over his shoulder.

Victoria didn't look back as she stepped over the man's body toward the doorway. When she responded, it was in a guttural, chilling growl. "I'm going out."

Chapter 40

Shea awoke with a start, frantic and disoriented from an uneasy, troubled slumber. She strained to open her sore eyes but found her vision still hazy. She gasped for air as she reached, hands trembling, to the radiating ache on her throat where the syringe had met its mark. Her heart raced, pounding in her chest, and she felt the sudden chill of sweat against her brow. Tears filled her eyes as she began to weep and cry out.

"Hey, shh, it's okay," Theresa was with her, now standing beside her bed. The girl gently eased her back onto her pillow. "Just take deep breaths. You're safe."

Shea recalled the desperation in the man's pale face when he entered her examination room. She shuddered at hearing the tremor in his voice as he spoke, replaying in her mind like a record. But she also still felt that fear, overwhelming and palpable, pinging her nerves at the force of his body against hers, the taste of the sweat on his palm when he silenced her. She closed her eyes and could still smell the lingering scent of blood in her nostrils. She breathed deep and gradually recognized an ache throbbing in her skull and jaw.

"What—" Shea's voice cracked in the dryness of her throat.

"What happened?"

Theresa pulled up a chair beside the bed. "You sorta got the shit kicked outta you. But you gave that dude a hell of a fight, to put it lightly."

Shea swallowed hard against the growing lump in her throat. A tear rolled down to the pillow beneath her and she let out a long, measured sigh. She, a doctor sworn to protect human life, had taken one. It had been in self-defense, of course, and she would've been foolish to not fight back. But the guilt churning in her gut didn't much care for that fact.

"It was pretty badass, actually. You caught the guy right in the jugular," Theresa continued, gesturing a stabbing motion on her own neck. "Simon and I got you cleaned up and you've been up here ever since."

"Oh god, Simon saw me naked?" Shea imagined him having to remove her soiled clothes and cleaning the blood off her skin and hair. She tried to smile, but winced at the pain in her jaw. "You should've just let me die to spare me the embarrassment."

Theresa smiled despite the sadness in her eyes and shook her head. "No worries, that was mostly me. He just helped carry you around, mostly."

"How long've I been out?"

"About five hours. Whatever shit that guy stuck you with was pretty damn strong," she said. Her gaze softened as she brushed a strand of hair away from Shea's brow. "How're you feelin'?"

Shea let out a choked laugh as another tear fell. Her body had never felt so broken. "I... could be better. But I could also be dead, so I'm not complaining."

"Thank god for small miracles, you aren't complaining,"

Theresa nudged Shea's shoulder.

Shea's smile dwindled. "Do we know who he was or where he was gonna take me?"

"Mama Wilder wants to have a meeting about that later," Theresa said, pulling the blanket over Shea's shoulders. "In the meantime, just try to get some more sleep, yeah?"

***

Harriet wheezed and bellowed a cough into the handkerchief balled inside the palm of her hand. She tasted blood on her tongue and wiped her lips, glancing around her office to see the eyes of her son, Tony, and Bern fixed on her.

"You alright, Ma?" Simon asked. "That cough of yours isn't getting any better."

She brushed his concern aside with a wave of her hand and tucked the cloth back into her sleeve. "I'm fine, just sit down already." Simon watched her for a moment, worry in his eyes, before taking a seat on one of the two plush chairs across from her desk. Tony sat beside him in the other and Bern, as always, stood stoic in the corner.

"What's Dr. Tristan's status?" Harriet asked.

"Theresa said she woke up for a little bit but then fell back asleep. She's banged up all to hell, but she'll be fine," Simon explained. "She should be well enough to start work again in the next two days or so."

"And the intruder?"

"He ain't a Trinity, if that's what you're wonderin'," Tony said as he chewed on a toothpick protruding from between his lips. "He lived here in the Anchor with his kids. Got exiled three cycles ago. I had to ask around a bit 'bout him, but I guess he mostly kept to himself."

Simon crossed his arms. "The Trinities figured since they

couldn't get one of their operatives inside the church, they'd use one of our own to slip by unnoticed. They took his kids hostage and told him to bring Shea back in exchange for 'em. That's how he got that syringe."

Harriet's lips curled in a sneer. Even she didn't stoop so low as to use children as leverage. "We get them back yet?"

"Vic took care of it."

That was all Simon needed to say. Those in the room had known what that meant, and there was no further explanation needed to understand what violence took place following Shea's assault. Tony would most likely be carrying more dead bodies to the fishery that evening, much to his displeasure. He seemed to understand this and chewed his toothpick with greater aggravation.

"Good." Harriet breathed and tapped her index finger on the desk's surface. Her gaze shifted to the fireplace and lingered on the remaining charred edges of torn paper tossed inside only minutes before their meeting was called. She hesitated before returning attention to her son. "I've decided to schedule a meeting with Rubio to discuss our respective indiscretions as of late. We're scheduled to meet tomorrow afternoon in a secure location in the Dome."

The silent tension that fell over the room was thick and palpable. Even Bern, with his stoic stature, shifted from one foot to the other and dropped his gaze to the floor. Simon gaped at her, astonished.

"You're joking. Tell me you're joking."

Harriet cocked an eyebrow. "You see me laughin'?"

Simon stroked his beard and sat up in his chair. "You're really going to negotiate with these assholes after they pulled a stunt like this?"

"A stunt that failed. And they've lost their own operatives in the attempt, once Vic got ahold of 'em," Harriet said.

"You can't possibly think that's a sane idea, ma. Even if negotiations were reasonable, it's too dangerous for you to go to the Dome. There's gotta be another way to do this."

"Yeah, I gotta side with Simon on this one, Mama Wilder," Tony added bluntly. "It ain't smart."

"Tony, 'smart' isn't something you're familiar enough with to lecture me on." Harriet turned a cold eye on him. "Besides, what would you have me do, bring the Trinities *here*? Rubio would be mad to agree to that, and I'd be mad to accept meeting on their turf. The Dome is our only option—it's the most neutral space available for both of us."

"But again, why meet at all? I understand thing's've been tense lately, but why?" Simon asked, exasperated.

Harriet glanced at the fireplace again. The flames had consumed the last remnants of the unsigned note left on her desk that morning. The message written in black ink lingered on her mind*: It's happening.*

"How long do you think we can last like this? They kill Dr. Anders, we trespass and kill some of their own, they turn around and threaten our residents, we kill them, they kill us… back and forth, back and forth." She sighed and felt another urge to cough tense in her lungs, which she now suppressed.

Harriet thought again of the note and sensed a chill run up her spine. "Sometimes meeting in the middle, finding a compromise, is more important than winning. At the end of the day it's about survival, and you need to understand that."

"Then let *me* go," Simon pleaded. "Let me be a representative for Shadow. You're too vulnerable in the Dome."

"Oh yes, no doubt they'd love to see *you* representing us." Harriet chuckled. "They'd call off the meeting before it even started, after what you did in that cafe. That's the fastest way to torpedo any hope of a productive discussion."

"Ma, I don't like it." Simon's jaw grew taut. "It isn't safe."

"We've agreed that neither party is permitted to bring weapons, and Vic will be joining me for security. She'll be by my side the whole time. Surely that's enough to placate you?" Harriet asked.

"You *and* Vic in the Dome? In broad daylight? God, I don't like this, Ma." Simon rose from his seat and walked around the office with his hands resting atop his head. "And you think Rubio will actually abide by that no-weapons agreement? He's broken promises before."

Harriet offered a weak smile. "With Victoria with me, will it matter?" Simon remained silent in his anger. "So instead of worrying about me tomorrow, why not offer Theresa some more combat lessons? She's been buggin' the shit outta me for more training and you're still useless to me with that busted ear of yours."

"Whatever." Simon threw his hands in the air and turned to leave the room. "Maybe one day you'll actually listen to what I have to say and take me seriously."

Harriet watched him leave the office and felt her heart tighten in her chest. She watched the emptiness of the doorway for a few moments and wanted to call out to him. But she remained silent and shifted her attention to Tony, who was now glaring at her.

"I've told you before, I don't want Theresa in trainin'," he said, his arms crossed defiantly over his chest.

"Well, it's a good thing that I don't care about what you want, Tony. Now get the fuck outta my office."

***

Shea slept through the remainder of the late afternoon with the help of medication Theresa brought up from her examination room. Her body and skull ached, throbbing with each shift against her mattress and pillow. But the medicine was designed to help her sleep, not dull the pain. Theresa protested, insisting that she take the pain pills to help with her recovery, but Shea refused. Besides the fact that others would need it more than her, the narcotics riled her uneasy gut and left her too nauseous to rest.

Theresa remained in the bedroom for a few more hours into the evening, reading in the corner chair while she slept. Shea would wake through a medicated haze and notice the girl, nose deep in her book, before closing her eyes to slip away again.

Shea awoke later, still foggy from her induced sleep, to the sound of the bedroom door opening. Her eyes peeked open to find Theresa had fallen asleep in the chair, twisted awkwardly between the wooden arms, the book draped open over her chest. A tall figure entered and glanced down at the girl before hunching over to scoop her up. The figure departed with Theresa still asleep in their arms. Shea drifted to sleep again only to waken again when the figure returned sometime later.

When Shea opened her eyes she discovered the figure seated in Theresa's chair, leaning forward on their elbows with hands entwined. Long, red hair hung down from their shoulders and tired, green eyes lifted from the floor to meet hers.

***

Victoria felt Shea's tired gaze rest on her and fidgeted in her seat.

"Sorry, I tried not to wake you." Victoria rose from the chair and stood awkwardly for a moment before gesturing toward the door. "I'll head back to my room and let you—"

"No." Shea's voice was weary but resolute. "Please stay. I want you to stay."

Victoria offered a silent nod and returned to the chair, but soon noticed Shea straining to sit up. She rushed to Shea's side and gently pressed her hand against her shoulders to ease her back to the pillow.

"You probably shouldn't do that," she said. "Did you need anything, or were you just feeling ambitious?"

"Blanket," Shea said, her tone thick with drowsiness. "It's too cold."

Victoria noticed the extra blanket folded at Shea's feet and reached to draw it up over her chest. When she moved to return to the chair, she felt Shea's fingers pinching at her shirt.

"Don't leave," Shea said. "Please, stay. I'm cold."

Victoria hesitated. She glanced at the empty chair across the room and grew increasingly aware of the light pressure of Shea's grip on her shirt. In the next moment she was kicking off her boots and sliding into the narrow space beneath the blanket at Shea's side, nearly holding her breath through each motion. She shifted and felt the weight of Shea's head rest beneath her collarbone; she wondered if Shea could hear her heart pounding inside her rib cage.

"Is this okay?" Shea asked.

Victoria swallowed and trained her eyes on the ceiling.

"Yeah. It's okay."

She felt the chill against the other woman's skin and held her closer, taking a moment to pull up the remaining blankets to cover her shoulders. Shea's hair smelled of their cheap shampoo, while her skin held a tinge of her lavender perfume. Victoria closed her eyes and took a long, steady breath against the fire now burning in her chest. Shea nudged closer against her side and wrapped her arm around her waist.

The two lay together for a few minutes, listening to each other's heartbeat through the dense silence. Victoria closed her eyes and leaned into Shea's warmth, breathing in the scent of her and letting her limbs and mind relax. It was strange to find a moment of peace like that after what she'd done to the Trinity operatives; to experience so much quiet and stillness after so much brutal violence.

A lingering, buried memory subtly crept into Victoria's mind. It was from her last cycle of service before the arrest. The mission was simple enough; her and her Valkyrie sisters were deployed to rescue hostages from an in-bound shuttle from Apex. She could still hear Iris's voice through the earpiece, instructing them that each passenger had been exposed to the Ink by their Forsaken stowaways:

"They need to be put down. For the greater good and all of Odin Prime."

And like a disciplined, loyal Valkyrie, Victoria had obeyed the order and squeezed the trigger. Within an hour after her debrief, she'd been sobbing in Cossette's arms. Sleep had eventually come to her, after Cosette had held her, kissed her, and stroked her hair. She'd fallen asleep not with stench of hot, coppery blood on her mind, but with the sweet scent of Cosette's skin.

And you killed her.

Victoria jerked out of her half-asleep daze. Her heart pounded in her chest, her hands and brow dampened with sweat. She blinked, gritted her jaw, and slowed her breath.

Shea shifted against her and groaned. "My elbow didn't work."

Victoria settled back despite her prickling nerves and wiped a bead of sweat from her temple. "Your elbow?"

"You taught me how to use my elbow, remember?" Shea sounded as though she was waking more now, with her voice steadier and clearer. "I tried to hit him with my elbow when he attacked me. It didn't work. I missed and he punched me."

"I figured, by that gnarly black eye you've got. Maybe you should've paid better attention to my lessons."

Shea pinched Victoria's side. "Are you seriously giving me shit right now? I was going to suggest that maybe your training methods need some work."

"Far from it. Proper stance, rotation, and strike… all quite simple if you pay attention and practice."

"How dare you—demeaning me, and in my fragile condition? How heartless are you?" Shea pinched her again and let out a pained chuckle.

Victoria subdued a smile. "Completely heartless, I assure you. My chest is a vacant husk."

"Clearly."

Silence settled between them again. Victoria closed her eyes and took a breath.

"Do you want to talk about it?" she asked. Shea's demeanor changed with that single question. She grew still, then shook her head. Victoria felt her shirt beneath Shea's eyes dampen with tears; she reached up to gently pet her hair. "Okay. That's fine, you don't have to if you don't want to."

"I don't even want to think about it anymore. But I can't stop. It just… keeps happening in my mind, over and over again. I keep seeing his face. The fear won't go away." Shea's voice cracked in her throat through her chocked sobs.

"Hey, hey." Victoria scooted down the mattress and shifted to level with Shea's face. There were tears in Shea's eyes, which Victoria reached to wipe from her bruised cheek. "It's alright. It's over, you're okay. You're safe."

"I killed him, Victoria," she said through her tears. "He's dead and I killed him."

"Shh, you did what you had to, alright? You defended yourself and you're still here. That's all that matters. It's over, you're safe." Victoria spoke in a kind whisper and wiped each fallen tear from Shea's cheeks. She caressed her dark hair and pulled herself closer to press a kiss against Shea's forehead. "You're okay, you're okay…"

They lay in a warm embrace as Victoria pressed another kiss on Shea's temple, and again on her flushed cheek. Shea's sobs and breathing quieted with each kiss and caress, and she found herself with eyes closed and chin lifting to meet Victoria's lips with her own.

All sense of time seemed to suspend in that moment. Her heartbeat pounded in her ears as Shea's lips pressed against hers again, this time in earnest and yearning, with her hands pressed against her back, holding Victoria tight. Her breath hitched in her chest when she tried to breathe; her stomach felt as though it'd flipped. She ran her fingers through Shea's hair and kissed her again.

Shea dropped her chin and steadied her shaken breath. "Can you stay with me tonight? I don't want to be alone."

Victoria steadied her own breath, nodded, and pressed a kiss to her forehead. She pulled the blanket up to tuck around Shea's shoulders and held her in a warm embrace.

"Promise to be here when I wake up?" Shea asked.

Victoria rested her cheek against Shea's hair. "I promise."

Shea was asleep within minutes. Victoria drifted to sleep shortly after with the scent of lavender on her mind.

Chapter 41

The rickshaw jostled over security road divots as it passed through one of the Dome borough gates. Harriet slid the black leather inter-borough badge back into her jacket pocket and flipped her hood up over her dreadlocks. She turned her attention to Victoria, who sat in silence beside her. She was dressed in a tailored black business suit, and her hair looked uncomfortably tight in its bun.

"Relax, won't ya? You look like you got a stick lodged up your ass."

Victoria adjusted the collar to her suit jacket. "I don't like being in the Dome any longer than I have to be. And I feel like a fucking peacock in this thing." She shifted in her seat. "You should've listened to your son. This is a bad idea."

Harriet's gaze lingered ahead of them as they drew deeper into the Dome. She'd said goodbye to Simon inside the church that morning; her heart had broken when she hugged him. Her embrace had been tighter and longer than usual, and there was concern behind his dark eyes when she pulled away.

"You good, Ma?" he had asked.

Harriet had cupped his cheek, smiled, and simply said,

"I'm always good, baby."

A sudden flash of neon light from a nearby advertisement snapped her out of her daze. She glanced up at the expansive hull windows and stared at the swirl of blood-orange clouds beyond the glass. Her gaze lingered there as if entranced by its slow, unyielding motion. A bump of the rickshaw brought her back and she blinked.

"Sometimes the only option you have is a bad one," she said before tugging her handkerchief from her sleeve. She lifted it to her lips, let out a bellowing cough, and wiped her lips with a deep, raspy breath. "You of all people should understand that. He'll learn that lesson soon enough, too."

"You got something you need to tell me before this meeting?" Victoria asked. "Because you're sounding rather cryptic, and I don't much care for it." She scrutinized their surroundings and paused to turn a cautious eye to Harriet.

Harriet brushed her question aside with a dismissive wave of her hand. "Nothing of consequence." She glanced down at the blood speckled on her handkerchief before tucking it away.

"Uh-huh." Victoria returned her attention to the road and eyed their approaching destination: a tall, slender building that nearly reached the upper limit of the Dome's ceiling.

Harriet peered over at Victoria and smirked. "By the way, how'd the doctor look this morning?"

Victoria's body stiffened beside her. She avoided Harriet's gaze.

"Banged up, but fine."

"Theresa told me this morning that you took her place watchin' her last night. And that you didn't leave her room until this morning."

A beat passed, then Victoria responded curtly, "Your point?"

"Awful nice of you, I think. Didn't expect you'd ever go out of your way for someone you seemingly couldn't stand a few lunars ago. I distinctly remember you being the one asking to kill her after she escaped. Funny that, isn't it?" Harriet grinned and adjusted her hood. Victoria remained silent, eyes and jawline hardened, as the rickshaw slowed to a halt on the curb. "Well, let's not keep them waiting."

***

Shea peered at herself in the mirror and examined the dark ring marking her left eye. Her swollen, bruised jaw throbbed. She traced her fingertips along the purpled, battered skin of her cheek and winced at the pain. Her ribs ached with each breath and turn of her torso. The tracing of her fingertips led to her mouth, where they lingered, passing over her bottom lip.

Victoria had kissed her. Or had she kissed Victoria? Shea couldn't quite remember through the fog of her sleep medication. The thoughts came in hazy pieces, almost disjointed in their sequence. But what she did remember was Victoria holding her, reassuring her, and then...

She was warm. God, her lips were so warm.

Shea's heart gave a start behind her rib cage and she smiled despite the twinge in her cheek. Victoria had already left by the time she'd awoke, but she placed the palm of her hand against the pillow and still felt its lingering warmth.

She winced stepping down the spiral steps of the church, sensing each footfall rattle her bruised bones. She glanced around and felt unnerved by the quiet stillness of the place. Peering up at a wall clock she realized that it was well past noon, and her belly growled despite its lingering unease; it'd been over a day since she'd last eaten.

Shea yawned and met Tony's eyes when she stepped into the kitchen. He'd taken a seat at the table for his lunch of toast, dried meat, and a cheap bottle of brew.

"Mornin' sunshine. You look like shit." He uncorked the bottle and tipped it back against his lips.

Shea smiled and reached for the bag of bread on the counter. "It's good to see you too." She popped two slices into the toaster and felt her stomach growl again at the scent of it.

Tony took a bite from his own toast and turned to look her up and down. "How're ya holdin' up?"

Shea shrugged and tapped her nail against the counter. "How'd you say I looked?"

"Like shit?"

"That more or less covers it."

Tony waved a hand at her. "Eh, you're already walkin' it off. You'll be good in no time."

"We'll see." Shea plopped the warm toast onto a plate, poured herself a glass of water, and joined Tony at the table. She took a sip and looked around again. "Where is everybody?"

"Vic is escortin' Ma to a meetin', and Simon and my sister are downstairs in the trainin' room." His voice grated with irritation.

"I don't get why you're so opposed to Theresa getting trained. Don't you want her being able to defend herself?" Shea bit into a slice of toast.

"Good bit of luck it did for you, eh? All those one-on-ones with Vic?"

Shea glared over her toast. "Be nice."

Tony rolled his eyes. "See, it ain't about her *defendin'* herself. Of course I want that for her. But you know that girl is stubborn as shit and will wanna use that when she gets older to go out on errands for Mama."

"Is that a problem? You don't seem to mind the work."

"You don't get it." Tony shook his head and took another swig of brew. Shea could smell the bitter odor of the drink from across the table and recoiled, focusing instead on her toast. "Our mom died havin' her; Pop had to work for Mama Wilder to support us. But he died a while back fuckin' around with the Trinities, and we've been here ever since." His voice trailed off as he glanced down at the bottle in his hands. "This shit is hard work, man. I've been stabbed, shot, bones broken… this job don't exactly lead to retirement, if ya get me. I just don't want that for her, ya know? She's my baby sis."

"That's really sweet, Tony," Shea said with a smile. She reached out to put her hand over his and squeezed. "You're a good big brother."

He looked at Shea's hand resting on his and shot her a charming grin. He cocked his eyebrow and leaned in closer. "So, uh… would you maybe wanna—"

"Nope." Shea retracted her hand and focused her attention back on her toast. "Not in a million cycles, Tony. You ruined the moment."

Tony scoffed. "So, what'cha sayin' is I gotta shot the cycle after a million cycles. Alright, alright." Shea laughed through a mouthful of toast and reached across the table to slug him in the arm. He chuckled and shrugged his shoulder. "Anyway, Theresa should train under you instead. Seems like safer work bein' a doctor than some goon."

Shea gestured to her bruised face. "You think so? I missed that memo."

Tony snickered and clinked his bottle against Shea's class of water. "You're alright, Doc. Oh and by the way, don't think I forgot that you still owe me for lettin' you borrow Melody for the night."

Shea smiled at him as he took another drink.

***

Victoria was the first to enter the elegant meeting room on the top floor of a Dome office building. An expansive window stretched along the adjacent wall, which offered them an impressive view of the Dome skyline, with its bright neon hue and cosmic ceiling.

Her eyes trailed over the attendees waiting at the conference table in the center of the room. Rubio seated himself at the end farthest from the window, flanked by two hulking male guards in navy-blue suits. Julep's absence was noted, especially considering that she was Rubio's niece and successor to his enterprise. Victoria felt a pang of disappointment, if only because she would've loved to entertain herself eyeing up the bruises she'd left across her face. That day hadn't been her first run-in with Julep, and she had found pleasure in breaking a chair against her skull.

Rubio, a tall, older gentleman in a tailored gray suit, rose from his seat when Harriet entered the room behind her. "Welcome, Ms. Wilder." He smiled through a salt-and-pepper goatee before gesturing for her to sit. "Pleasant commute, I hope?"

"Pleasant enough," Mama Wilder said.

She took her seat across from him nearest to the window.

Victoria followed, but her attention lingered on the open skyline outside. A sense of unease crept up her spine, as though there were eyes beyond the window staring back at her. Her nerves stood on-edge and her pulse quickened.

Victoria leaned in to whisper into Mama Wilder's ear. "Might I suggest we move your chair closer inside the room? Away from the window?"

"Why, somethin' wrong?" Harriet replied, her voice as much as a whisper as her raspy throat could manage. Victoria could hear the irritation laced in her words.

"I have—" She hesitated, trying to decipher the restlessness creeping across her skin. "Certain *reservations* about this."

"Is everything alright?" Rubio asked, his tone still polite but now impatient. He took his own seat and undid his single jacket button, offering an uncertain eye across the table.

"Yes, quite," Mama Wilder responded. Rebuffed, Victoria's jaw tensed as she stood in silence, tall and stoic, at the old woman's side.

"I must say, Harriet, I was rather surprised when you called this meeting. It's quite unlike you to be so forthcoming." Rubio offered a cunning smile as he spoke.

A sly grin curled at Mama Wilder's lips. "Well, given our recent altercations, I figured it best to at least *try* to negotiate, at least before we kill each other, that is."

Rubio snickered. "Fair enough. Let's speak plainly with one another, then."

"By all means."

"I am unaware of how familiar you are with the situation. The Trinities have been forced into a terribly concerning position as of late."

"Is that so?"

"It is. You can imagine our surprise when we discovered that your organization has been holding a high-level state member, a relative to the Chancellor for that matter, against her will," Rubio said through hardening eyes. "Not only is that extremely irresponsible on your part, but it puts my people in the middle in a *very* compromising position. We have a delicate, tenuous understanding with the officials in our borough, you see, and there are certain agreements that have been put upon us to maintain this relationship."

"Let's get one thing very clear, Rubio—Dr. Tristan is not held against her will. It may come as a surprise to you, but Dr. Tristan is, in fact, a welcome member of Shadow. Vital to it, as it were. She can come and go as she pleases; no one is forcing her to stay. She is no hostage of ours, I assure you. No crime has been committed, unless you wish to forcibly remove her against her will? I believe that falls within the definition of kidnapping."

Victoria clenched her fists behind her back.

Rubio watched Mama Wilder with a cautious eye. "I'm disinclined to believe you."

"And I'm disinclined to give a shit about what you do or don't believe," she countered. "She is our physician of her own free will. And, if I might add, had you not murdered our last physician, we wouldn't have even be in the market for a replacement in the first place."

"Regardless," his voice was flat and hallow. "You understand the arrangement we have with the authorities in our borough. What is or isn't a crime doesn't much matter when, at the end of the day, the State gets what it wants. We don't have the liberty to remain neutral when the chancellor's missing niece comes wandering into our territory. Especially when such an intrusion ends in a… confrontation." These last few words he nearly spat in irritation with his cheeks flushed and knuckles tightened. He shot a menacing glare to Victoria, who merely stared him down with cold indifference.

"I understand, and I apologize for my son's carelessness. And"—Harriet gestured to Victoria at her side—"certain acts of violence committed against your niece during the exchange."

"Carelessness doesn't begin to describe it, Harriet." Rubio leaned forward over the table, resting his weight onto his elbows. "We could've kept a turned, blind eye had the girl stayed put in your borough. I honestly don't give much of a shit if she spent the rest of her days growing old and fat in that disgusting church of yours. But she came into our territory, and that altercation your son started has us involved now. The POs *know*. We can't play dumb anymore; they're forcing our hand against you."

"I knew you had an agreement with the POs, Rubio, but I never knew how much of a lapdog you've become. It's pathetic," she snapped.

Rubio's nostrils flared, his face flushed hot. "Harriet, I'm *serious*. We don't want this conflict any more than you do. Don't get me wrong, I have no concern over your welfare, but I do over my own and that of my men. Surely you feel the same of yours. It's in both our interests to settle this."

"What the hell would you suggest, then?"

"Hand the girl over. Lieutenant Wiles assures me that this ends once Dr. Tristan returns to the Dome. We can continue as we were, no harm no foul. We can go back to hating one another from the safety of our own boroughs."

Mama Wilder laughed and crossed her arms over her chest, shaking her head in disbelief. "Such talk about turning a blind eye and letting bygones be bygones from a man who snitches so easily to the POs about our business," she said, still stifling a chuckle. "I knew you were an asshole, Rubio, but I never knew you were such a hypocrite."

"Excuse me?" Rubio asked, taken aback. "I have to cooperate with the POs when, and only when, I absolutely have to. But I'm no fucking snitch."

The woman glared at him from across the table. "Oh, don't play stupid. You think we didn't know that one of your boys snitched about our supply runs? To what—disrupt our operation just enough for you to make a move? To get some upper hand?" Rubio stared at her, his mouth agape, as she continued. "I'm almost impressed by the size of the balls you must have to still look me in the face and talk about *bygones*."

"What the hell are you talking about?" Rubio stood from his seat, pressed his knuckles onto the table, and stared her down. "We'd be stupid not to think you didn't have some kind of logistic connection with the Dome, but what the fuck makes you think we knew anything substantial?"

Victoria unclasped her hands from behind her back and shifted her shoulders, to which Rubio's guards responded in-kind. Harriet raised a hand palm in front of Victoria, a signal to restrain herself.

"We have it on good authority that one of your operatives, Robert Bunker, snitched to the chief of security's personal assistant, a man named Philip McGovern. His information led the POs to our driver and, after interrogating him, directly compromised our operation. You sayin' that didn't happen?" Her voice was stern and cold.

"What I'm sayin' is that if it *did* happen, it didn't come from us. Robert Bunker was a shitty operative who killed himself over some stupid fucking girl. He couldn't be trusted to supervise paint drying, let alone what you're accusing us of. Even if I *did* want to move against you—which I don't, you can keep your shitty borough—you think I'd be stupid enough to rely on *that* piece of shit?"

Mama Wilder rose from her chair with a fervor and pointed a heated glare across the table when the window behind her shattered.

Chapter 42

THWAP.

"Good job," Simon said, shifting the punching mat against his chest. He adjusted his grip on the handles. "Now give me sixty seconds just *wailin'* on me."

Theresa's face, already flushed and slick with sweat, crimsoned further. She let out an awkward laugh, smiled, and did as he instructed, landing punch after punch, throwing in a mix of elbow strikes, in succession for a full sixty seconds. Her braided pigtails bobbed with each thrown fist, and she began to huff as the seconds ticked away.

"Come on, five more seconds!"

THWAP-THWAP-THWAP.

Her knuckles beat against the mat against his chest, slowing as her arms grew heavy and fatigued.

"And… time! Great job, go grab some water."

Theresa let out a loud, exasperated groan.

"That felt longer than a minute." Theresa breathed heavy and rested her palms against her knees. After a moment, she shook out her hands, knuckles aching, and sauntered to the side of the mat to reach for her water bottle.

"It'll get easier the more we practice." Simon trailed his fingertips along his bandaged ear, feeling along the rough edges of the medical tape. He patted around his ear with a towel, brushing away sweat beading along his scalp. When he lifted his gaze, he found Theresa staring at him, her cheeks rosy. "You alright?"

Theresa choked down the gulp of water in her mouth and coughed. "Y-Yeah, I'm fine. I just…" she faltered and placed the water bottle back onto the floor. She stepped back onto the mat and cleared her throat. "Thank you, Simon. I know you'd rather not be down here training me, but… I appreciate it."

Simon smiled at her and tossed his towel aside. "Of course, I'm more than happy to help."

"So now that my knuckles are good and sore, what's next?"

"Well." Simon rested his hands on his hips. "We've done choke holds, breaking choke holds, wrist grabs… what about—"

Two black-clad figures slipped through the training room's doorway. The first raised the barrel of their pistol to Theresa and squeezed the trigger, releasing a dart into the base of her throat. She let out a gasp, staggered on her feet, and collapsed to the mat beneath her.

Simon had only enough time to charge forward before taking a dart to the chest. He screamed against the sharpness now splitting through his ribs, and stumbled against the weight of his unsteady legs. He lifted his fist, now suddenly too heavy to hoist above his shoulder, and swung toward the two men before dropping to the floor, unconscious.

✳✳✳

It happened quick. There was little more Victoria could do after hearing the window burst behind her than brace herself between Mama Wilder and the scattering fragments of glass. There was a clatter of metal against the floor, then the blinding, disorienting blast of a concussive grenade.

Victoria blinked. There were muted, distant screams reaching her past the deafening high-pitched tone in her ears. Acrid, bitter smoke filled her nose and stinging eyes. She breathed in and her lungs seized: riot gas.

She clutched Harriet's shoulders and pushed her, heavy and staggering, toward the door. Gunshots fired behind her. Two rounds struck her in the back and dropped her to her knees. Harriet collapsed forward onto the floor, gasping for air. Victoria coughed and tasted copper against her tongue, felt warmth trail down her lips and chin. She looked back to see a tall, dark figure emerge from the thick cloud of gas.

A Valkyrie.

Victoria's heart stopped when she eyed the black matte body armor and sleek, dark helmet. Her blood ran cold. It was looking at a shadow of her past self, as though her dreams had manifested and followed her to that conference room. She could almost still feel the press of the body armor against her skin and the way the helmet sat against her ears.

A sudden realization struck her. Valkyrie operations were, by nature, heavily classified and controlled at the highest level. The unit was designed for the specific task of handling the most sensitive, dangerous missions that posed a direct threat to Odin Prime and its interests. Only one person, other than the chancellor himself, could authorize a Valkyrie operation: Chief Hammond.

A hot, manic rage churned deep inside her gut. It drowned out the radiating pain from her back, the burning of her lungs and chest. She spat a wad of blood to the floor, gritted her teeth, and silently cursed her mother.

The dark figure stepped closer and adjusted her rifle against her shoulder. "Stay down," a woman's voice muffled voice commanded from behind the helmet. "I'd rather not kill you."

"You can try," Victoria snarled and, after a beat, charged at her.

The Valkyrie stepped back and fired a single warning shot into her thigh. Victoria, unfazed, snatched the barrel of her weapon and twisted. She leveled a solid, heavy blow to the Valkyrie's ribs. The woman let out a grunt, but wasted no time jutting forward to crack the mask of her helmet against Victoria's nose.

Seconds later, the weapon was wrenched from the Valkyrie's grasp and the two tumbled together to the floor. Victoria slammed her elbow into the woman's throat. The woman choked, gagging, as Victoria pivoted to press her knee hard against her chest. She trained the rifle's barrel on the Valkyrie's forehead and wrapped her finger around the trigger.

"Subject Raven! *Stand down!*"

***

Shea threw back the remainder of her water and placed her dirty dishes into the kitchen sink. Tony had also finished the last drops of his brew and slid the empty bottle beside her dishes in the basin. She felt his body sway a bit, the alcohol already taking affect, as he placed an arm around her shoulders. He towered over her, and when she glanced up at him, she saw a wide grin across his face.

"So, uh… how was it?"

Shea raised an eyebrow. "How was… what?"

"You know what I'm talkin' about. You and Mel'!" He

poked her side with his thick forefinger and nearly giggled. "I wanna hear all about it."

Shea wriggled out from under his arm and stepped away, shooting him an incredulous look. "Gross, Tony."

"Aw, come on!" He let out an exaggerated, offended shoulder shrug. "I figured we both play for the same team now, or at a lil' bit right?"

Shea laughed and took a breath to speak but was silenced by a deafening detonation from the church's main room. The two staggered as the walls rattled and dust cascaded from the ceiling. Shea and Tony exchanged a panicked glance before darting out of the kitchen into a billow of blinding smoke.

The smoke tasted pungent. Shea braced her arm over her stinging eyes. She inhaled and felt her lungs constrict inside her chest, choking her with each desperate gasp of air. Gunshots erupted, and screams echoed against the tall pillars surrounding them.

Tony reached through the haze and snatched her wrist, pulling her back toward the basement stairs. The rattle of gunfire followed them down the stairs, into the darkness.

"God!" Shea choked and hunched lower. "Tony, what—"

"We gotta find Theresa!" Tony's coughed between haggard breaths. His fingers fumbled clumsily with a wall locker and, after a few tense moments, turned back to her with a shotgun and pistol in each hand. The pistol he handed to Shea. "We gotta get you guys outta here."

Shea stared, eyes hollow, at the pistol resting in her hands. She felt the weight of the metal against her skin. A cold, paralyzing fear gripped her. Her eyes and skin burned; her lungs gasped desperately for air as her heart quickened and sweat broke across her skin. She was beckoned to move only by the yank of Tony's grasp at her shirt.

They found the training room dark and empty.

Tony stood, mouth ajar and eyes wide, searching the room for any sign of either his sister or Simon. When his eyes fell to her water bottle, tipped over on the mat, he anxiously ran his fingers through his sweat-slicked hair. He took a breath and bit at his lip before turning to pace along the length of the mat. Shea saw tears in his eyes when he turned in her direction.

"Okay." His voice cracked in his throat. "It's… it's okay. She's with Simon, right? She'll be safe with him." He turned his gaze to Shea, and her heart broke at the desperation lingering in his eyes.

"Tony—"

He turned away from her and gestured at the exercise equipment in the far corner. There was a slight tremor in his voice when he spoke again. "We'll post down here, take them out when they come through that door. One by one, like target practice, ya know? Then we'll go find her. Yeah?"

Shea nodded with hot tears welling in her stinging eyes. He approached her and placed a reassuring hand on her shoulder; all the warmth from his skin seemed to have slipped away, leaving only a chill in its place. He squeezed and offered her a strained, tense smile.

"Just stay next to me, 'kay? I got you."

Footsteps clattered down the basement steps. Shea posted herself behind the free-weight rack, the butt of her pistol resting on a dumbbell. Her hands trembled, and when she turned her gaze to Tony, she could see dread shadowing his face. He cocked the shotgun and aimed the barrel at the door, taking one last moment to turn his attention back to Shea.

"Shoot anythin' that comes through that door. Keep shootin' until there's nothin' movin'." He returned his focus to the door and muttered under his breath, "I'll be damned if I go out like this."

***

Victoria's joints locked. She froze, her body suddenly rigid like a statue. She held the rifle in her grasp, paralyzed, desperately beckoning herself to move. She willed herself to squeeze the trigger, but remained still in the frenzied panic. Her breath quickened and an older gentleman wearing a gasmask stepped into view. She recognized the familiarity of his cold eyes and peppered dark hair.

"Subject Raven, drop your weapon."

No.

The rifle slipped from her slack fingers. The Valkyrie snatched the weapon, wiggled free with little resistance, and scrambled to her feet.

"Subject Raven, lie face down on the floor."

No!

She closed her eyes, jaw taut and set below quivering lips, and lowered herself to the floor. Her body began to tremble, her mind gripped by the voice she'd heard so often whisper in her nightmares. She strained to keep her breath level and calm, to reel in the terror creeping up her spine.

Footsteps moved past her to where Mama Wilder still lay coughing. She heard the old woman give out a cry, resisting when dragged to her feet and slammed hard against the conference table.

The Valkyrie restrained the woman's wrists and yanked

her back onto her feet. "You are hereby under arrest by the supreme authority of the State. Resist and I will not hesitate to use lethal means to subdue you. Anything you say can and will be used against you in State court."

The older gentleman strode casually across the conference room and crouched at Victoria's side. "Have you missed me, Raven?" Victoria could hear the smile behind his gasmask. He reached out to caress her cheek and wiped a smear of blood from her lips. "Because I sure have missed you…"

***

The first buckshot erupted inside the training room. Shea nearly jumping through her skin with a shriek. The shot blasted the armored Valkyrie operative in the gut, who stumbled backward through the open doorway and collapsed. A moment later she was rising to her feet again, undeterred.

"Shit!" Tony shouted, and recharged the shotgun. His voice cracked with fear. "Valkyries!"

Another figure emerged from the shadows beyond the doorway with their rifle at the ready. Shea panicked. She couldn't help but close her eyes when she squeezed the trigger. The round struck the doorframe. She held her breath as the Valkyrie knelt and fired a single round, striking Tony in the abdomen. He let out a cry, fell back against the wall, and lost grip of his shotgun.

"Tony!" Shea dropped the pistol and scrambled to his side. She pressed her trembling hands over his wound. Fear overcame her as his blood seeped through his shirt and between her fingers. "No, Tony, stay with me!"

Arms wrapped around her waist and dragged her away. She screamed and thrashed, struggling with all her strength against the Valkyrie's firm grasp. Tears burned her eyes and streamed down her cheeks as she hollered and kicked. She writhed in protest, coughing and gasping through the acrid gas, up the stairs and across the main floor of the church. A few bodies lay cast across the floor, familiar faces of regular visitors to the church whom she'd seen before. Old Bern, ever watchful at the main door, lay dead with his outstretched fingertips reaching for his fallen rifle. She met his cold, vacant gaze before the Valkyrie lugged her outside and ushered her inside an armored black transport.

Shea gasped for breath. She stared at her bloodstained hands, feeling her body now begin to shiver violently against the cold metal floor of the van. The vehicle lurched forward, knocking her back against the wall.

"Good afternoon, Dr. Tristan."

Shea turned her attention to Chief Hammond, who sat on the opposite side of the van dressed neatly in her formal blue uniform. Her green eyes were devoid of empathy or warmth. She instead looked almost bored, unamused by the young, bloodied woman trembling on the floor before her.

"What—" Shea breathed, tears dripping from her chin. Her lip quivered as she spoke. "What have you done?"

"What was necessary," Iris stated with an ambivalent shrug. "I must admit, you're taking this far worse than I thought you would. You wanted to be rescued nearly half a cycle ago, did you not? Better late than never?"

Shea fell silent. She stared at her, aghast, and suppressed the sudden urge to vomit.

Iris scoffed, disgusted. "Don't tell me you grew *attached* to them?"

A hot, bitter rage roiled in Shea's chest. Her lips curled to a snarl. "How could you?"

"They were *criminals*!" Iris snapped, silencing Shea in her moment of fury. "You think they didn't kill innocent people, citizen *and* non-citizen alike, in pursuit their own interests? Are you still so naive?" Silence fell over them inside the transport. Iris continued firmly, "We need to get our story straight before you're taken to your uncle."

"Why the fuck should I listen to you?"

"Would you instead prefer to have Simon and Victoria share the same fate?" Iris asked, nodding her head back toward the church. Shea's jaw grew taut, her nostrils flared as she bit back her spite. She remained silent and dropped her gaze to the floor. "I thought not," Iris continued, casually crossing her legs. "Now, let's start from the beginning."

Chapter 43

Simon stirred. He groaned, peeked one aching eye open, and stared at a plain, white ceiling above him. He tried to sit up, to lift his hand to his throbbing head and ear, but found his ankles, wrists, and chest strapped down. Panic struck him, and he was suddenly wide awake. He raised his head from the pillow and glanced around the unadorned bedroom. In the far corner, he saw another small bed; Theresa lay on it, unconscious, her wrists and ankles bound by thick leather straps. His heart lurched, pounding against his ribs. He flexed against the leather straps bound to his wrists, clanking the metal fastenings against the bed frame.

"Don't go hurting yourself trying to break out of those." Jefferson stepped into the room, carrying a steaming teacup in one hand and a cup of water in the other. A colorful bendy straw extended from the mouth of the cup. "You may as well just accept them and take this time to rest."

Simon froze and stared at him with an incredulous, unnerved gaze. Jefferson still wore his tailored suit, but he'd removed his jacket and rolled his shirtsleeves up to his elbows. He was a larger man than Simon remembered, with broad shoulders, tall posture, and strong arms and hands that looked out of place carrying something as delicate and fragile as a teacup. Simon's eye caught the glimmer of an expensive watch and a single, silver ring on his left hand.

Jefferson took a seat beside the bed. He extended the cup to Simon, the straw bobbing close to his lips. A strained smile appeared behind his trimmed beard. "I figured you'd be thirsty when you woke up."

"I don't want it." Simon's voice cracked in his dry throat. Jefferson held the cup there for a few more seconds, waiting, then let out a resigned sigh as he placed the cup on the nearby nightstand.

"You always were stubborn," he said.

"Don't talk like you know me."

"You're my child," Jefferson said. "Don't talk to me like I don't."

Simon's nostrils flared, and his jaw tautened. "What'd you do to Theresa? And what the hell is going on?"

"Your friend is fine. Heavily sedated, is all," Jefferson said before taking a sip of his tea. He leaned back in his chair. "Although she's lucky—we had hoped you would be alone, or at least with someone I wouldn't feel guilty about shooting." He smiled with sadness in his eyes. "But I've got a soft spot for kids."

Simon grimaced and looked away. "How'd you get us past Bern?"

Jefferson's eyes grew sad despite his smile. "I wouldn't have been able to take two steps into that front door without Bern breaking my nose, let alone carry you out like a sack of potatoes on my shoulder. He and I never quite got on well after your mother and I... well, went our separate ways."

"You still haven't answered my question." Simon's gaze

remained fixed on an invisible spot on the ceiling.

Jefferson sipped his tea and shrugged. "The short answer is that I never went past him."

"And the long answer?"

"The long answer is that there is more to that church than you know. I used to live there too, remember?" A moment of tense silence passed between the two before Jefferson continued. "Do you really think your mother is the kind of person who would feel comfortable only having one way in and out of that church? She's cautious to a fault, if not somewhat paranoid."

Simon met his father's gaze, curious. "A secret entrance? Are you serious?" Jefferson said nothing and sipped his tea. "You're lying. Ma would've told me."

Jefferson suppressed a chuckle. "Oh yes, your mother would've told her troublesome, rebellious teenager about her private, secret passage in and out of their home. That would be poor parenting."

"That's rich, coming from you. And I wasn't rebellious," Simon said, incredulous.

"You don't think your mother told me when you stayed out late and got wasted on cheap brew? And then proceeded to light a bag of trash on fire before hurling it at inter-gate security guards?" Jefferson looked amused and grinned. "And what was it that she said you shouted at them?"

Simon cleared his throat and turned his eyes away. "'Elitist fucks.'" Jefferson chuckled. "I didn't think she still spoke to you, let alone talk about me."

"Who'd you think pulled the strings to get security off your back?" Jefferson's gaze lingered on the cup of tea in his hands. "Inter-gate security was pounding on the POs' door in the Middle Borough to arrest you on-sight if you ever crossed over. It took some time, but I convinced them otherwise."

Simon scoffed. "I guess being a lapdog has its perks."

The two sat in silence for a while, listening only to the sound of their breathing and the occasional scrape of teacup against saucer. Jefferson took a breath, placed his teacup onto the nightstand, and leaned forward, hands clasped.

"Simon…" His voice was low, nearly pleading. "You have to understand that just because I wasn't physically there in your life, doesn't mean that I haven't been involved in it. I did what I had to, to protect you."

Simon scoffed. "Is that what you call *this*?" He jerked his arms against his restraints and turned an angry eye on his father. "Protection?"

Jefferson frowned and shook his head. "You don't understand."

"Enlighten me."

"That would be ill-advised," Jefferson said, and stood from his seat. He collected his cup from the nightstand and turned to leave. "I know you're upset and confused. But I promise you, Simon, everything that's happened is for your own good."

Simon stared at him, eyes widening. "Everything that's happened? What're you talking about?" Jefferson lingered in the doorway with his back turned, fingertips tracing along the lip of his teacup. Simon tugged at his restraints again, clattering the metal against the steel bed frame. "Dad! Please, what happened?" His voice was pleading, desperate.

Jefferson leaned against the doorway and bowed his head as though a heavy weight rested against his shoulders. A few silent moments passed before he took a measured breath.

"Shadow is gone." Jefferson's voice was steady, quiet. "A squad of Valkyries raided the church this morning looking for Dr. Tristan, while another intercepted your mother during her meeting with the Trinities. They took them both alive, along with your friend Victoria."

Simon stared at his father's back, frowning and distraught. His vision blurred as fresh, hot tears stung his eyes. His voice hitched in his throat when he finally spoke again. "What have you done?"

"I've saved your life," Jefferson said. He nodded back toward Theresa. "And hers."

***

Iris's boots clicked against the floor as they walked down the long corridor. The noise and echo grated on Shea's shaken nerves. She'd fallen back into passive docility since returning to State authorities in the Dome. She obeyed orders when given, didn't protest or complain when directed. But that didn't make the bitter hatred churning in her chest any less volatile. She followed behind the chief and stared at the back of her head, her short red hair swaying with each step, wondering what it would feel like to bash her skull open with her fists.

She peered down at her hands, scrubbed clean by estate servants. They had been waiting for her arrival at her uncle's estate, and the servants whisked her away the moment the transport doors opened. They washed her in rose-scented bathwater, brushed and assembled her hair, and dressed her in what seemed to be her old clothes. But she had slimmed in her meager lunars residing in the Anchor, and her slacks now hung loose at her narrow waist. The servants attending her furrowed their brows and hurried off to find her a new set of clothes.

She caught a glimpse of herself when she passed a mirror hung on the wall. She didn't recognize the woman in the reflection staring back at her. Everything felt wrong, like an ill-fitted Statesman costume. The makeup applied to her face couldn't hide the bruises, her black eye or swollen jaw. Visible injuries aside, the lunars with Shadow had changed her. No amount of makeup could hide that. Shadow had changed her; Victoria, Simon, Theresa—

Her fingers trembled again recalling the heat from Tony's abdominal wound against her fingertips. She heard the gunshots and screams, the haunting stare of Bern's vacant eyes.

The door at the end of the hall slid open when they approached. Her uncle's office was much as she'd remembered it from her visits as a child: enormous and elegant with a blanket of warm light. She marveled at the hanging plants, vibrant green and blooming with white and red flowers, from the ceiling and walls. The air was fresh and clear, scented with a hint of roses and incense. How remarkable it all was to her now after spending a good part of the cycle in the Anchor, where greenery was rare, and the air hung heavy with the scent of its destitute inhabitants. How could a place this marvelous be something she once thought as common and ordinary?

Shea found her uncle standing beside his desk on the far side of the room, dressed sharply in a navy-blue suit and hand leaned against his chair. She immediately recognized Secretary Herrington standing near him, gesturing to the scattered documents across the desk. The sound of the closing doors drew his attention and he glanced over his shoulder. His tired eyes grew kind when he saw Shea, and a warm smile stretched across his slender face. Shea's heart twisted as she recognized her mother's smile in his.

But something was different about him. Something unusual that left Shea with a sense of unease. He moved away from the desk and walked briskly toward them. It took another moment for Shea for finally identify it, and she faltered when it hit her: he was *walking*. She had heard from Secretary Willis that her wheelchair-bound uncle had started walking again after his stroke, and was dedicating time to physical therapy. But the gentleman who was approaching them now was striding with the confidence of a man who'd never been trapped in a wheelchair. His stride was strong and sure; his spine was tall and straight. The chancellor was practically radiating strength.

Iris clicked her heels, brought the palm of her right fist to her chest, and bowed forward. "His Majesty Guide Us."

"May Strength Remain," Alexander responded, his voice hoarse. "You have my utmost gratitude, Chief Hammond, for bringing my cherished niece back home safely."

"Of course, Chancellor," Iris said, still bowed.

"I'm also told that we've decapitated two of Odin Prime's most dangerous gangs in one raid! Amazing work, truly."

"Thank you, Chancellor. It is an honor to fulfill my duty to you and Odin Prime."

"Indeed, it is." Satisfaction gleamed in his eyes.

Secretary Herrington joined them with an upturned nose and pursed lips. She cleared her throat and adjusted her purple-rimmed glasses. "Has there been any unrest since the operation? And what of our lost asset?"

Iris straightened her posture and clasped her gloved hands behind her back. She avoided Secretary Herrington's gaze. "The asset has been moved to a secure location inside the Ministry of Defense. And as for the gang leaders, our officers stand ready to engage any resistance posed by their supporters. No active resistance has yet been made, but there are reports of unruly gatherings in the Anchor. We're actively monitoring the situation."

"Excellent work." Alexander's grin widened as he stepped forward, arms outstretched to Shea. "It's so good to see you, my dear. I've notified your father on Apex, he's truly relieved that you're safe and well."

"You look well, Uncle. His Fortune Shines." Uttering the words again after so long left a bitter taste on her tongue. She bit the inside of her cheek.

Shea stepped into his open arms. Unease crept across her skin as he wrapped her into a firm hug and rested his chin against her hair. There was a strength in his arms that she'd not felt since she was a child, when he'd lift her from the floor and hold her in his arms. She remembered how much he'd reminded her of her mother when she was young, but she sensed none of her mother in this embrace. It was too close, too binding. Her nerves screamed, begged to pull away and run; but she stayed. There was nowhere to run, no one to help her. Not anymore. She was alone, and so she breathed slow, steady breaths and remained still.

"Your father and I have been worried sick since your disappearance," Alexander said, releasing her. His smile faltered when he examined the injuries marked on her face. "By the Patriarch, what did they do to you? You're beaten black and blue!"

Shea steadied herself and managed a smile. "I'm quite alright, Uncle. I'm sorry to have worried you."

Alexander examined her for a few silent moments, his gaze lingering on each mark on her skin. He offered a nod and extended an arm toward a dining table set on the opposite side of the office. "Please, you must be famished. Join me for supper and let's talk."

"Of course, Uncle."

An enormous dinner was already set and waiting on the corner table. Shea took a seat at her Uncle's side and gazed over the supper set before them: steak, roasted root vegetables, a jug of chilled lavender and honey brew, and warm, steaming dinner rolls.

"Steak," Shea whispered in awe.

"Indeed! A fresh shipment arrived just two days ago from Apex. We've doubled our meat and dairy export over the last cycle alone." Alexander unfolded a cloth napkin and laid it delicately across his lap. "I must admit, your father is an effective governor. And I'm not just saying that because he's my sister's husband. The man has a good head on his shoulders."

"I'm glad to hear that, Uncle."

"My secretaries even inform me that we've started rationing some of it to our citizens in the Middle. Isn't that marvelous?" Alexander skewered a chunk of steak and pulled it onto his empty plate.

Shea strained to smile. "It is, His Fortune Shines."

Despite having had little to eat since the day before, her appetite was nonexistent. She was hollow, like she'd been shelled and husked. Her eyes lingered on the slab on meat at the center of the table. She thought of the dead bodies likely still lying scattered across the church floor and looked away, suddenly nauseated by the odor of warm meat. She instead looked over her shoulder to see Iris and Secretary Herrington speaking to one another, Iris's hands cupped behind her back in the expected stance of a subordinate. The woman's eyes met with hers for a brief moment before looking away again.

"Chief Hammond briefed me on what happened," Alexander said, forking another piece of steak. "Those monsters deserved worse for holding you hostage, for mistreating you as they did. Barbarians…"

Shea reached out to spoon some root vegetables onto her plate. She took one roll and placed it on her napkin. "Yes, I even tried to escape a few times but…" She hesitated, her throat constricting against each word. Her mind went to Victoria, and her eyes suddenly welled with tears. She parted her lips to continue speaking, to recite the lines Iris had given her in the van. But all that came from her lips was a choked, bitter sob.

"No, no dear. You did the best you could, given your unfortunate circumstances." Alexander reached out and placed a loving hand on hers. He smiled and nodded at her, "I can see how hard this has been on you. But you're safe now, there's no need to worry."

Shea strained to return his smile as a tear rolled down her cheek. She brushed it away and cleared her throat. "Indeed, Uncle. His Fortune Shines. It's a relief to be back, surely. I'm looking forward to my reinstatement at the hospital, as Chief Hammond assured me that I would have. I miss my old life, my old duties."

"So eager to serve again, aren't you? Your father would

be so proud, as would my sister. They've raised proper Statesmen, you and your charming brother," Alexander said with a satisfied grin as he cut into his steak. "But I must admit I'm beginning to wonder if the hospital is a right fit for you."

Shea stared at him, bewildered. "Begging your indulgence, Uncle, what do you mean? I'm a doctor. The hospital is my proper place, is it not?"

Alexander chewed on the chunk of steak and gestured with his fork. "You always did remind me of your mother. You both share the same curiosity, inquisitiveness, and *passion* for medicine and research. It's a beautiful sight, I must admit. It makes me miss her even more, seeing you step so effortlessly into her shoes."

He took a sip of chilled brew and looked directly into Shea's eyes with a steeled, knowing gaze. A chill danced up Shea's spin.

"Surely your... *exposure* to our recently returned asset, Subject Raven, shed some light on your mother's work, has it not?"

Shea's pulse quickened. "Subject Raven? You mean the unpleasant red-headed woman?" Shea realized just then that her plate remained untouched. She picked up a fork and took a small bite of her vegetables despite her stomach's protests. The food tasted sour against her tongue, like the churning vitriol in her gut.

"Indeed. The Valkyrie team briefed me on their find in Shadow's medical room during their exit sweep. Quite an intriguing find." He grinned with torn steak between his teeth.

Shea could feel Iris's eyes burning a hole in the back of her skull as she took a bite of bread. The Valkyries hadn't found as much as her Uncle presumed, thanks to Iris's intervention during the raid itself. Had they found her mother's entire box of research documents, they would be having a very different conversation under less amiable circumstances. Iris had taken the box back to her home and burned each sliver of paper, shattered each external drive and disk. Shea knew this, but still felt the shadow of uncertainty looming over her, like an axe just waiting to strike her neck.

"Intriguing, Uncle?" Shea's hands began to sweat against her fork, but she speared a roasted carrot and brought it to her lips as if his words hadn't affected her. Her stomach stirred, urging her to reject each morsel of food she swallowed.

"We know you've been doing research on Cyntrax, or at least doing the best you could with such shit resources. We found a sample of Raven's blood, as well, linking her condition with the outbreak in the lower. You even set up a rudimentary experiment testing rats—it's quite remarkable."

Shea swallowed against a lump in her throat. Her heart pounded like a drum in her chest. "I assure you, Uncle, my intentions were only to test whether the treatments were safe to use on the lower's non-citizen children, as directed by Harriet Wilder. With the outbreak, you see, and—"

Alexander outstretched a hand to silence her. "You misunderstand me, Shea, dear. The fact that you were able to identify the Cyntrax as the source in the first place is outstanding, and then to find the link to Raven? I'm *impressed*. There's so much of your mother in you." He took another sip of brew and leaned closer to her. "How would you like to join our research development division?

To carry on with Project Stronghold where your mother left off? Your mother's old research partner, Dr. Samson, is quite intrigued by you. He asked for you personally."

Shea was struck silent. Her thoughts staggered, mouth agape and tongue tied.

"I..." Her blood was ice in her veins. She thought of Victoria's frail body in her mother's research logs and strained to hold back fresh, hot tears. She bit her lip until she tasted blood and forced a smile. "Thank you, Uncle. I don't know what to say. It would be... an *honor* to continue my mother's work. I will do my best to fulfill my duty to you and Odin Prime."

The look in his eyes softened as he watched her. "Good." His voice was a sigh of relief. "I understand that your passion lies in working in the hospital, but the state could really benefit from a mind as curious and dedicated as yours."

"Of course, Uncle. I will do my best."

"Outstanding, my dear. We have big plans for the station in the near future, and I'd love for you to be by my side every step of the way, carrying on our family's legacy."

Shea couldn't eat another bite. Her uncle continued with his supper, oblivious to her troubles. She took a sip of water and understood what the team must've found in her examination room. She imagined a Valkyrie, clad in her armored suit, opening the lids to Alfred and Benjamin's boxes. If her uncle's excitement indicated anything, it was that Alfred now lay dead, feverishly yellowed and bleeding out in his box, killed by the tainted Cyntrax.

Shea's experiment had been a success, and Dr. Samson had noticed. A cold sweat broke against her brow as a thought struck her: *Why were they not concerned, or even surprised, about tainted Cyntrax? Unless.... they already knew.*

Nausea crept up Shea's throat until the back of her throat sweat. "I can't quite express my gratitude at such a generous offer, Uncle. It would be my honor to work alongside Dr. Samson and to represent our noble family."

"That is very good to hear, Shea." Alexander reached out to take her hand with a warm smile. He squeezed her hand and nodded. "That is very good, indeed."

Chapter 44

Shea fell to her knees in front of the estate's guestroom toilet and vomited. She gasped through the acrid bile in her throat, choked back tears, and reached to wave her palm over the flush sensor. When she closed her eyes, she saw Tony's fear-stricken face the moment the Valkyries burst through the door. She took a breath in a meager attempt to temper her stomach. But a moment later she recalled the bodies strewn about the church congregation space, and her stomach turned again. She lurched forward and dry heaved into the open mouth of the toilet.

How many people were dead because of her? The chancellor spoke endlessly of how similar she was to her mother, but maybe Shea was more like her mother than he realized. How many people had her mother killed throughout the course of her research? And now that Shea was to take up her mother's mantle under her uncle's guidance, how many more would die?

Shea rested her forehead against the toilet seat and wept. She braced her elbows beside her ears and cradled her head. Reality was too bitter and harsh, and every stifled breath she took between sobs ached in her chest. She shut her eyes and begged to open them to the familiar sight of her church bedroom. Patients would be seated in the congregation space, waiting to be seen for whatever ailments brought them to Shadow's door. Simon and Victoria would be training down the hall from her examination room, Theresa most likely watching Simon and blushing. She imagined sitting beside Theresa on her break between appointments. They'd each have a fresh mug of cheap tea, and she'd watch Victoria with a blush of her own.

Her life had been lonely before Shadow. Each day was nothing more than a dry routine of waking, working, eating, and sleeping alone. Her existence was pragmatic and mechanical, each motion set to serve Odin Prime and her uncle. She hadn't the time to read books or develop genuine relationships with others. Shadow was a den of criminals, of men and women accustomed to their ruthless business, but they were her friends in the end. She'd grown to love them despite their flaws, and despite hers.

Love them... Her thoughts lingered on Victoria. Iris was tight-lipped when Shea had asked about Victoria in the transport earlier that morning. Her lip had twitched, and she'd looked away without saying a word. Iris had at least mentioned that Simon and Theresa were safe, as if admitting this would act as a form of insurance for Shea's behavior when they returned to the Dome. But Victoria was now lost to her.

She opened her eyes and took a long, deep breath to steady her heart and nerves. Her fingers trembled as she reached to wipe away tears from her eyes before standing from the floor. She averted her reflection in the bathroom mirror and slipped back into the suite's lounging room, where the station's evening broadcast was about to begin. The lounge's sofa was soft and welcoming. It sank beneath her weight as she stretched out across the length of it and rested her head on a pillow.

She was exhausted; physically, mentally, and emotionally drained and empty. Her mind was a haze of muddled worries and fears, but there was nothing for her to do. At least not tonight. She could at least allow herself to sleep for now, and wake in the morning ready to face her worries. There was little else she could do now that she was alone again in the Dome. Sleep first, then think of something to do.

The entire wall across from her flickered to life. Odin Prime's flag appeared across the wall, waving in an invisible wind, as upbeat music played from the speakers behind the wall-screen. Shea's eyelids grew heavy. She yawned as a young, smiling man in a pressed black suit appeared across the wall.

"Good evening, citizens, and welcome to Prime Evening News. I am your host, Duke Merigold," he spoke in an artificially charismatic tone through a nearly perfect set of white teeth. Shea's heavy eyelids shut, and she shifted comfortably on the sofa. "We begin our broadcast this evening with shocking news from the Anchor Borough, where a daring rescue operation was undertaken by our station's brave Valkyrie agents."

Shea was suddenly awake. She sat erect on the sofa, jaw agape and fingers gripped tight to the edge of the cushion.

"Volume up," she commanded, and the broadcast grew louder inside the lounge room. A moment later, Shea's official Ministry of Health and Wellness photograph appeared in the top right corner of the screen. She stared at her own photo, with her hair in the tight, unyielding bun and clothed in her white lab coat, and felt as though she were seeing a stranger.

Duke Merigold continued. "Doctor Shea Tristan, Chancellor Tristan's niece and resident physician at the Ministry of Health and Wellness, disappeared nine lunars ago after taking sabbatical to volunteer her services to those in need in the Anchor."

The video transitioned to her jowled Ministry supervisor, Dr. Brad Wilson, standing tall in front of the Ministry of Health and Wellness crest in the lobby of the facility. She pictured him loitering outside her miniscule office door after a daunting thirteen-hour shift in his pristine lab coat.

"When Dr. Tristan approached us about the idea of volunteering in the Anchor, we emphasized how dangerous it could be for her. Working with refugees and non-citizens bares a certain magnitude of danger that we naturally advise our best and brightest to steer clear of. But she was persistent, and ensured us that she understood the risks involved and wanted to go anyway." Dr. Wilson gave a warm smile and shrugged. "That's just the sort of person she is—kind to a fault, and tenacious in her drive to help others."

Shea's lip curled in a snarl. "Liar." She now imagined, with a tinge of satisfaction, how it would feel to introduce her elbow to his nose.

The feed cut back to Duke Merigold, while her photo remained in the corner. "Dr. Tristan assumed an alias during her volunteer work to protect her identity. She successfully concealed her identity until a few weeks ago, when Shadow agents intercepted and kidnapped her as she took lunch at a local Middle Borough café. District peace officers attempted to pursue her abductees at the time of the incident, but were met with violent resistance."

Shea stood from the sofa and took slow, steady steps toward the wall-screen. Tears welled in her aching eyes, her fists clenched and trembled.

They're all lying. They're all fucking lying!

"A Valkyrie team carried out the rescue operation earlier this morning. During the raid, agents successfully secured Dr. Tristan and returned her to the safety of State authorities. Chancellor Tristan himself personally thanked those involved in his niece's rescue in an official statement released shortly after news of the operation broke. Additionally, Valkyrie officials remarked on the overwhelming success of the mission, stating that Shadow had been incapacitated in the raid by detaining the terrorist organization's leader, Harriet Wilder, and neutralizing many of its members."

The video feed cut to Iris, clad in her pressed, navy-blue dress uniform, standing at a press briefing podium. Shea noticed the stiffness in Iris's smile as she spoke.

"While we have reason to celebrate today's decisive victory against malicious actors who terrorize our station and its people, what mattered most was ensuring Dr. Tristan's safe return to her loved ones. Citizens like Dr. Tristan, who put service to others and to the State before their own safety, are to be celebrated, honored, and emulated. We cannot stand idly by and permit those who wish to inflict harm on those like her or the innocents she strives to aid. Our mission as Valkyries is to serve and protect, and today we made sure to remind the enemies of the State how dedicated we are to that cause."

"Mute!" Shea barked. The audio dropped, leaving the room in a heavy, piercing silence.

Shea snatched up a nearby vase and hurled it at the wall-screen. It shattered and left a tarnish across Iris's cheek as the inaudible feed continued to roll. There were no more tears left in her eyes. Her fury dispelled any exhaustion clouding her mind before that moment, and her chest burned with it. A swelling rage tangled with helplessness and grief.

She fixed her resolute gaze on Iris as she inaudibly answered questions from an off-screen interviewer. The video feed continued rolling as Shea turned on a heel, strode across the room, and disappeared out the estate's entrance.

***

Iris removed the glass topper from her whiskey decanter and poured herself a drink. She lifted her gaze to the expansive, floor-to-ceiling rendering of a lush green rainforest across her wall. Drops of rain pattered against the leaves, and twittering birds hopped playfully from branch to branch. On any other evening, Iris could have spent an hour or more staring at that scene with a drink in her hand, listening to the birds, the trickling rain, and the occasional rolling thunderstorm. While serene, the scene itself was alien to her. She'd never step foot on Valhalla, let alone walk through its forests. And on any other day it would offer her a quiet reprieve.

She closed her eyes, gritted her teeth, and ran her fingers through her hair. "Change display." The forest vanished. "Display external camera view, stern feed."

Iris opened her eyes and gazed at the expanse of outer space across her wall. The gigantic gaseous orange and crimson of Yggdrasil breached the corner of the camera's panorama. The penetrating black void beyond the vibrancy of the nearby planet beyond seized Iris in a moment of dread.

Iris turned away from the display and raised the glass to her lips, consuming the whiskey in one swallow. She braced against the burn down her throat and stomach, hoping that it would soon coat her nerves. The breath in her lunges hitched, and her knuckles whitened, gripping the drink glass.

Her late husband's peace officer portrait drew her attention. She reached to fiddle with the dog tags hanging round her neck, focusing primarily on one, and traced her fingertips along the edges.

"Don't look at me like that, Daniel," she said, eyeing the photograph. "You would've done the same for her."

She poured herself another drink, tipped it back in one gulp, and turned her gaze back to the vastness of space stretched across her wall. Her eyes hardened as she peered into the empty blackness.

"The son-of-a-bitch better hold up his end of the bargain."

The doorbell rang.

Iris looked at the time: 23:18. She brushed a loose strand of red hair behind her ear and adjusted her shirt collar. The remnants of dread lingering on her nerves fell away.

"This better be fucking important. Open hallway camera screen." A small screen overlay appeared atop the wall-display, revealing the live feed from outside Iris's front door.

Shea, draped in a baggy peace officer jacket, shifted from one foot to the other outside her door. Her hands fidgeted as she stood. Iris watched Shea reach out to press the bell button again, twice in rapid succession.

"Close hallway camera screen." The feed vanished.

Iris strode toward the door and rolled her eyes at the fourth, persistent ring of her doorbell. She snatched up the pulse pistol resting beside her discarded uniform jacket and tucked it into the waistline behind her back.

Iris signaled for the door to open with a wave of her hand. She crossed her arms, tilted her head, and turned an amused eye on Shea. "What a surprise, Doctor. Mind telling me what—"

Shea darted into the apartment. Iris, while startled, let her pass without much resistance and let out a long, exasperated breath. Glancing over her shoulder, she observed Shea holding a pulse pistol of her own, the barrel leveled at her back.

Iris leaned against the doorframe and rubbed her eye with the heel of her wrist. "I don't suppose we could do this tomorrow. It's quite late, you know, and Uncle dearest will wonder where you've gone at this hour."

"Close the door and step away from the intercom." Shea's voice was as cold and steady as her fixed, resolute gaze.

Iris grinned and took a moment to collect herself, adjusting her shirt and collar as she eyed Shea across the room. The girl radiated fury; her face paled against her darkened, bloodshot eyes. The pistol trembled in her grip, her finger hovering in the trigger well. She was a far cry from the polite, polished Statesman Iris had escorted hours before.

"So, let me guess." Iris pushed off the doorframe and waved a hand to shut it behind her. "You caught a glimpse of the news broadcast this evening and would like to lodge a complaint. Is that it?"

"Everything." Shea's voice quivered in her throat as she spoke. "*Everything* was a lie."

"Well of course it was, you foolish girl! What did you expect—the *truth*? Good heavens, no!" Iris nearly laughed as she walked back to her whiskey decanter. She poured herself another drink.

Shea gritted her teeth. "I expected more than what I saw on that broadcast."

"Oh, please." Iris rolled her eyes and swirled the dark whiskey in her glass. "Do you honestly believe the State would openly admit to its own blatant incompetence? Especially when it came to protecting not only a loyal Statesman, but the chancellor's own niece? There would be too many questions."

Shea said nothing.

Iris took a sip of her drink and leaned against the wall. "So, you're going to kill me now?"

"Yes."

"Because the State lies?"

"And because you're a monster, and my friends deserved better than what you did to them. It's the least I can do."

"And what of your life here in the Dome? What of your uncle?"

"None of it matters to me. Not anymore."

"You're willing to throw away the life you have here in the Dome, a life of comfort and privilege, for possible imprisonment or death, for—what? Your *friends*?"

"I'm willing to throw away the life I have here in the Dome because I don't think I could stand to live with myself for one more day knowing the truth while doing nothing about it. And at this point, I'd rather die than pick up my mother's work, to surrender myself to their agenda and hurt more people."

Iris's amusement fell away. She hesitated for a moment with her eyes fixed on Shea. After a while, she returned the glass of whiskey to the table and crossed her arms. When she spoke again, her voice had grown softer.

"And what of my daughter? And Simon? Does this crusade you find yourself on include risking your life for them?"

Shea furrowed her brow, her lips joining in a frown. "You already used them to manipulate me into cooperating with you this morning. You're running out of material."

"I'm asking for your honesty. If you had the opportunity to save them, to offer them a better life at the expense of your own, would you?"

Shea wavered. She remembered the strength of Simon's arms when he hugged her, the sweetness in his laugh; she remembered the warmth of Victoria's body when they lay together, and how her lips felt against her own. Her eyes welled with tears despite the tightness of her jaw, the angry knit of her brow.

"… Yes."

"Well then, I suggest that you put that gun down."

Shea blinked. "Why?"

"Because if you kill me, you won't get that chance." Iris snatched up the glass of whiskey and drank it all in one swig. "I'll pour you a glass while you make yourself comfortable. I have a lot to catch you up on."

Chapter 45

The zero-gravity cell was frigid. Harriet shivered and pulled the itchy wool blanket tighter around her shoulders. It was harder to conserve body heat in the weightlessness. She had no bed to sleep on, no mattress to curl up for warmth beneath her. But she was used to this practice from her youth. She had been one of the first protesters detained after the chancellor enacted his anti-refugee policies. She'd spent most of the first night shouting, banging her fists against the cell door, demanding humane treatment.

"You're ungrateful scum, spitting in the State's face after all it's done for you," the guard had chided. *"Heat and gravity are a service provided to law-abiding citizens and Statesmen, not trash like you. You aren't worth the electricity."*

She was sure the practice was designed to break prisoners, mentally and physically, into submission. There had been plenty of protestors who, after spending only a week in the weightless cold, never returned to the streets. But the experience had only riled her anger and hardened her resolve. It would not be her last time in a State holding facility, and it would be the formative period of Shadow itself.

Her body ached. Each motion was a reminder that she was no longer the vibrant revolutionary of her youth, and she winced with each labored, haggard breath. She slid her fingers across her bald scalp and felt the chill of the air against her skin. The peace officers had taken her wig and man-handled her after the arrest, not caring about her old bones or joints when processing her. She cursed them under her breath and opened her eyes to peer through the darkness of her cell.

The room had a single steel door with a narrow gap beside the wall for nutrient packs for whenever, *if* ever, the guards decided to feed them. She was in no hurry to eat. Nutrient packs were little more than a brick of pulverized crickets and corn meal—she'd nearly vomited the first time she'd eaten one during her first arrest. But after a few days of floating around with an empty belly, she stopped caring. The feeding gap provided the sole source of light from the hallway outside and gave her just enough illumination to make out the corners of her cell. She counted her slow breaths just as she did when she was young, easing the unrest in her mind.

"Hey there, Wilder," a man's voice whispered through the gap.

Harriet gasped with a start. She craned her neck toward the gap and sneered. "Keep that shit up and I'm going to have a heart attack in here long before y'all get the satisfaction of puttin' me up on that Mourning Tower of yours."

The man chuckled. "It's good to see that the cycles haven't changed you. You still got a bite to you."

Harriet's demeanor changed. Her face softened as pulled herself closer to the gap. "Freddy?"

"God, I haven't heard that name in a while. Damn near everyone just calls me Jefferson nowadays." She could hear the smile in his voice.

Harriet hesitated and, after a beat of silence, rested her head against the cold metal wall. She closed her eyes. "How's our baby?"

"Safe," Jefferson said. "*Hostile*, but safe."

Harriet smiled despite the quiver of her lower lip. "That's good, that's good."

"I don't have much time. I just wanted to come by to let you know that everything's goin' as planned. And, you know, to check in on you. To see how you're doing."

Harriet let out a chuckle, which grew to a wheeze. She coughed and tasted blood. "Why—you worried about lil' old me, Freddy?"

"I'm always worried about you, Harriet," Jefferson said. He slid his fingers into the narrow gap between them. "And I always will. You know that."

Reaching into the gap, Harriet touched her fingertips to his. She felt the warmth of his skin against hers and let out a haggard sigh. "Take care of our child, Freddy. You do that, and I'll be more than alright."

"You have my word." His voice was earnest, resolute. "Stay strong, it won't be long now. I'll make sure our kid gets outta here safe and sound."

A weary smile spread across her lips. She closed her eyes against warm, brimming tears. "You'd better. And you'd better tell him his mama loves him before you send him on his way."

***

"You can't be serious." Shea stared at Iris in disbelief. "It's completely mental!"

Iris took a seat across from her on the sofa. "You aren't necessarily wrong in that assessment."

Shea leaned forward in her chair and rested her elbows against her knees. She buried her face in the palms of her hands and took slow, level breaths. "This is insane."

"Well, no one said it was going to be *easy*." Iris dismissed Shea's panic with a casual wave of her hand.

"So, let me get this straight." Shea lifted her eyes to meet Iris's. "You and Harriet worked together to deliberately orchestrate the raids on Shadow with the intent of securing both Victoria and Simon in the Dome—where you will launch them into the empty void of space. This, of course, is after you somehow bypass Ministry of Defense security protocols and reach the escape pods, *with two known criminals*, without being detected and shot first." Shea paused for a beat. "It's basically suicide."

"Yes, essentially. But you're missing a few key elements there," Iris stated pointedly. "We aren't just *launching* them into space. Heavens, that would be a death sentence all on its own."

"Oh no, you're right, how could I forget?" Shea threw her hands in the air, exasperated. "You've got a man on the *outside*! Nothing sounds more reliable than a bribed CoP smuggler you've made this clandestine arrangement with! Well shit, that makes this whole thing foolproof."

"Secondly," Iris said, ignoring Shea's outburst, "while yes, this plan does have significant risk, including you helps our chances considerably."

Shea scoffed. "Is that so? How?"

"When your uncle asked you to continue your mother's

work, you agreed. That alone places you within the Ministry of Defense, working directly with Victoria. Having you there will make it exceedingly easier to move her to the launch deck."

"Isn't your office in the Ministry of Defense as well? Why couldn't you do it?"

"While yes, I work in the facility, I don't have a need for access to the research wing. I'm permitted temporary access for security assessment purposes only, and those are only once a cycle under escort. My previous plan was to steal access credentials, most likely a visitor badge of some sort, and somehow muggle Victoria out—I'd most likely cause a racket, leave more than a few bodies along the way. But with you already there, I can focus my efforts on delaying any triggered security response before meeting you at an agreed-upon location. It's much cleaner, quieter. You prefer that, don't you?"

"What about Simon? Is he already in the holding cells or something?"

"No, he's with his father on the other side of the Dome," Iris said, and let out a sigh. "We tried arranging for his arrest prior to the raid. God knows it'd be exponentially simpler just to have the two of them already inside the Ministry... but his father was concerned that the peace officers, even if given explicit orders to detain the boy through non-lethal means, would possibly have an *accident.* Simon wouldn't have been the first."

Shea shuddered at the thought. She shook the image from her mind and continued, "So how are we bringing him in, then?"

Iris shrugged, unconcerned. "Drug him and bring him in

as an arrest to be processed, most likely. Jefferson operates as a contracted detective under my authority, so no one would question it."

Shea considered Iris with a scrutinizing eye for a few moments before asking, "Fair enough. And the escape pod? Whose escape pod will we be using?"

Iris grinned. "Yours, of course."

"Mine?"

"What, you don't know that you own one? Very few people do, you know—only the highest in our ranks get theirs reserved. Your mother, for example." Iris resisted the satisfied smile behind her lips when she noticed Shea flinch. "After your mother's untimely death, her designated pod was gifted to you by your uncle. I suppose he thought it would be what she would've wanted, after all. Isn't that sweet?"

"Even if I do own one, I don't know how to access or use it," Shea said.

"That's, again, where I come in." Iris leaned forward to pour more brown liquor into her and Shea's glasses on the table. "Pod functionality checks are a routine duty for junior peace officers. I not only have access to every pod's register and deck sequence, but I know the ins and outs of every fucking control panel on that deck. God knows I hated that duty enough when I was young."

Shea frowned. "What exactly was your plan for getting a pod *before* I agree to join this insane suicide mission?"

"You don't want to know," Iris said as she raised her glass to her lips. "It was—*messier,* to say the least."

Shea let out a groan, snatched her glass from the table, and took a sip. The whiskey left a warm coat on her tongue but burned her throat when she swallowed. She let out a cough and contorted her face against the lingering burn. It was a welcome reprieve from her thoughts.

"I have more questions. Apart from this plan, that is," Shea said.

Iris rolled her eyes. "Of course you do."

"Why would Harriet agree on the raids? Why not just take Simon and leave Shadow alone?"

"That was the deal we made." Iris dropped her gaze to the drink in her lap. "I free her child from Odin Prime, offer him a better life elsewhere, and she gives me Shadow."

Shea sneered. "What, so you can come out of this the beloved State hero? 'Rescuing' me and taking down a terrorist organization all in one swoop?"

"Don't be stupid," Iris growled. "It was *leverage*. You really think that your uncle and his arrogant Party secretaries would just let that incident at the café slide? Sure, they suspected your disappearance had something to do with one of the gangs, but didn't have any substantial proof. The State had more than enough proof though after the peace officers submitted their incident reports—which I tried to bury, by the way, and nearly got caught in the process!" Iris's face reddened against the setting veins in her forehead and throat. "This suicide mission, as you call it, hinges on my access to the Ministry of Defense and escape deck—what was I supposed to do when they looked at me with even *one ounce* of suspicion?"

Shea sat frozen in sight of Iris's rage. After a moment, Iris continued.

"Besides, Harriet is dying. Even if Simon did have the capacity to carry on in his mother's place, the Anchor as you know it won't survive your uncle's Peace Accords. Shadow was already on its deathbed; both she and I understood that." Iris's voice gradually calmed; her fury diminished. "So yes, I sent the Valkyries to murder your friends. And to capture my daughter. I returned you to your despot uncle with a false narrative behind your kidnapping and paid off your old boss to lie about it. I've killed for my daughter before, and I didn't hesitate when it was Shadow's turn. I did what I had to, as did Harriet."

The two women sat for the next few minutes in a heavy silence. Iris sat, high posture and legs crossed, nearly motionless except to take sips from her drink. Her attention gradually shifted to the cosmic display across the wall. Shea, meanwhile, kept her gaze fixed to her lap. Her fingers fidgeted around the glass in her hands, and her knee bounced with the tapping of her heel on the floor.

A thought had gnawed at her mind most of the afternoon between fits to crying and anger: Why weren't they surprised by the tainted Cyntrax? Why didn't they care? Why, instead, were they only surprised that she'd discovered the link?

"This... urgency you have to get them out of Odin Prime." Shea's voice was quiet, contemplative. Her eyes remained fixed to her lap, then to the floor ahead of her. "Does it have anything to do with Cyntrax?"

Iris didn't readily respond, and instead let her thoughts turn for a few moments before answering.

"My urgency is for my daughter's sake only. I thought I could buy some time hiding her in the Anchor, but the Peace Accords, whenever they are enacted, will make that difficult." She shifted, finished her drink, and switched crossed legs.

"But I won't lie to you—you're right to be worried about it."

"About the Cyntrax?" Shea asked. "What do you know?"

"Not much, I'm afraid," Iris said. She reached to place her empty glass on the table. "But there is a familiar eeriness hanging in the air, much like when your uncle declared independence from the CoP, and again when he enacted his refugee and morality policies. It's like a thick silence you can almost feel right before an explosion." Iris met Shea's worried gaze and grinned. "But we'll most likely be killed during or after this operation anyway, so why bother worrying about it?"

"Because innocent people will die," Shea uttered through a clenched, taut jaw.

Iris nearly sneered. "And who's going to save them all? You?" The woman snickered and shook her head. "Innocent people die every day on this god-forsaken station. You need to focus on the next few days and let everything else go."

Silence fell over them again. Minutes passed as Shea gradually finished her drink against simmering, muted anger. She would glance up to see Iris staring at the star-riddled display across the wall, almost as if her eyes were searching for something beyond the camera's reach. When the silence grew too heavy to bear, Shea rose from the sofa and made to collect her jacket.

"You'll need to be ready in two days' time," Iris stated flatly. Her gaze never broke from the display.

Shea froze, furrowed her brow, and scoffed. "*Two days?* But... that's too soon, I—"

"In the meantime," Iris interjected, her voice increasing, "I want you to get your measurements taken by the estate's staff in the morning. Tell them you're looking to be fitted for new clothes, seeing as you've lost some weight. Message me your measurements in the afternoon, and return here after the estate staff has retired for the evening."

"What the hell do you need my measurements for?" Shea asked as she snatched her jacket from the back of the sofa.

"If shit hits the fan, and you end up being the only thing standing between my daughter and a lifetime of State custody—" Iris turned and leveled her gaze at Shea. "The least I can do is ensure you've got decent armor."

Chapter 46

It was nearly midnight when Shea returned to her uncle's estate. Darkness blanketed the property except for a soft luminous glow along the garden path. She had sweet-talked the gate guard well enough and evaded suspicion regarding her spontaneous evening tryst, but was still on edge. Every step treaded eggshells. She was lucky to have gotten away with it tonight, but she doubted her chances tomorrow. The pressure of successfully venturing outside the estate unescorted a second time weighed on her.

She scurried through the lush garden's rose-entangled archway and felt a sudden wave of nausea. She slowed to a halt and rested against a nearby shed, closing her eyes against the churning in her gut. It was stupid of her to drink with an agitated, empty belly. Her tongue wetted; her stomach twisted. She took a breath and pressed her damp forehead against the wall; she needed to vomit again, but suppressed the urge. A steadying breath, and then another. The sensation soon passed, and she pushed ahead through the garden.

Shea entered her suite and froze. Unless the whiskey had muddled her thoughts, she'd remembered to turn the living room light off upon leaving. She closed the door behind her and craned her neck to peek around the foyer wall. She closed her eyes and took another breath when the room began to spin beneath her feet. It wasn't the whiskey dragging her down, it was her stomach's relentless refusal to hold down food, the emotional exhaustion. There was nothing more she wanted than sleep. Perhaps in her mental haze she had left the light on and not remembered—

"Shea? Is that you?"

Shea immediately opened her eyes. Her heart lurched in her chest; she recognized the young man's voice almost immediately.

She heard footsteps, and within seconds a young gentleman clothed in a peace officer's formal dress uniform stepped into view. A row of polished awards sat affixed across the breast of his fitted dark blue jacket. In his hands he clutched pristine white gloves, which he now wrung anxiously between his fingers.

"Hey, sis." A coy smile crossed his face as he shrugged. "Surprise?"

"Charles!" Shea rushed to throw her arms around his neck. The high collar of his jacket rubbed against her cheek, and she marveled at how tall he'd grown. She clutched him tight until he let out a choked laugh and squeezed her back. A few moments later she pulled away and scrutinized his smiling face. He was still young, barely twenty-three cycles old, but had begun to come into his features. Features that Shea now noticed included their father's nose and mother's eyes. He looked more like a man than a boy, and he was *handsome*.

"It's been ages! I haven't seen you in so long! What, since…"

His smile waned. "… Since mom's funeral."

"Yeah. Four cycles doesn't feel that long ago, does it?" Shea's heart suddenly grew heavy. She cleared her throat and forced a weak smile across her lips. "What're you doing all the way up here? I thought you were with Dad out in the colony."

"I was—well, I *am*."

The two moved farther into the living room and sat on the sofa. Shea turned her head when she heard the clink of cups to see another uniformed gentleman in the kitchen preparing tea. He scratched at his trimmed, graying beard, noticed her watching him, and offered her a pleasant nod of his head.

"Dad appointed me as convoy attaché to Odin Prime. We were planning on making an official visit next week, but Dad was adamant about sending me as soon as we got word of your rescue."

"Oh god." Shea rested her palm against her cheek. "Is he doing alright with everything?"

Charles scoffed. "Are you kidding? You know how he gets. He started worrying when he hadn't heard from you for a while after his birthday—nice video, by the way, Dad loved it—but Uncle Alexander wouldn't tell us anything specific. He kept emphasizing how busy you were but that everything was fine. Then—BAM! We get this emergency comm about your goddamn rescue mission! Dad is absolutely *livid* about the whole thing—"

The uniformed gentleman in the kitchen loudly cleared his throat as he poured tea. Charles fell silent, collected himself with a straightening of his posture, and continued in a more measured tone.

"Anyway, he insisted I hop on the next shuttle to see you.

We arrived not even an hour ago."

Shea took his hand and squeezed. "I don't think you know how much it means to me to see you again, Charles. Truly, I…" Her thoughts drifted to her meeting with Iris the hour prior. While Charles had been boarding the station to see her, Shea was discussing plans against the State that would likely result in her own death. She hesitated, swallowed hard, and forced a smile. "Thank you so much for coming. I'm sure Uncle Alexander will be pleased to see you as well."

"Indeed. I don't think I've seen him since other's funeral either. Life has just been… well, *life*. You know how it is." Charles shrugged and placed a hand on Shea's knee. "But more importantly, how are *you*? You look pretty banged up."

Shea grazed her black eye with the tip of her finger and swallowed hard. "I'm… alright. Tired, mostly. It's been a hard day."

"I can imagine, but I bet you're relieved to be back in the Dome!"

Shea forced a smile. "Yes, of course. Nothing makes me happier."

"I wish I'd known sooner." Charles shook his head and frowned. "I wish I could've done something. You know that Dad and I would've marched down into the Anchor ourselves and through Shadow's front doors if it meant getting you back safe."

"I know, Charles," Shea said. Her heart sank deep in her chest when she thought of the friends she'd made in Shadow. She swallowed hard and shook Victoria's face from her thoughts. "I'd rather not talk about it if you don't mind. Not yet."

Charles's brow creased. He reached out to lay his hand

on her shoulder. "Yes, of course. You take whatever time you need to recover and clear your head." He squeezed her shoulder and smiled at her. "You know you can lean on us, right? Me and Dad, even Uncle Alexander. We all love you."

Shea smiled at Charles and placed her hand over his. "Thank you, Charles. I love you all, too."

The uniformed gentleman joined them carrying a tray of steaming mint tea. He was taller and stockier than Charles, with dark hair and eyes. Streaks of gray peppered his sideburns and beard. There was an air of steeled maturity and discipline to him in the way he moved, but also of gentleness when he offered Shea a warm smile.

She returned the smile. "Thank you."

"My pleasure." His voice and eyes were kind.

Charles gestured to him. "This is Captain Francis deLeon, head of my security detail and executive officer of Apex security operations."

Francis clicked his heels and bowed slightly to Shea. "It's an honor to finally meet you, Dr. Tristan. I've heard much about you from your father and brother."

"All good things, I hope."

"Of course," he said.

"His Fortune Shines! If you'd heard about me from my brother ten cycles earlier, he would've told you I was evil incarnate." Shea lifted the mug of tea to her lips, took a sip, and begged that the mint would ease her churning stomach. "He was a bit of a brat, you see."

Charles feigned offense. "Oh! A brat? How dare you."

"Well, nevertheless, you would make for a very lovely devil, Dr. Tristan," Francis said as he took his own tea from the tray.

"You hear that, Charles? I believe I've won over the good captain."

"Don't let her charm you, Francis." Charles shot a wink to his sister. "This girl tormented me about my studies when we were children. Never let me have any fun. I remember one time when I was eight, she came outside to fetch me when I was playing with my friends so I could complete my homework. I didn't want to go, obviously, so I tried to run off, but she grabbed me by the scruff of my neck like a dog and literally dragged me back home, with all my friends watching! They never let me hear the end of it. I swear, you were worse than Mother sometimes."

"You forgot to end with, 'Thank you, sister, for your selfless dedication in forming me into the quality man that I am today,'" Shea said.

Charles scoffed. "You were relentless."

Shea tutted. "Tenacious, Charles. *Tenacious*."

Charles and Shea laughed through casual sips of tea. Francis, now seated beside her brother, cracked a hint of a smile before turning his attention to a holo-tablet left on the coffee table. His brow furrowed as he scrolled through lines of text in what appeared to be the next day's schedule and agenda. Soon their laughter died down and the siblings sat together in momentary silence, eyes fixed on the tea in their hands.

"I've missed you guys," Shea said, her voice softened.

"We've missed you, too."

"It hasn't been easy being here alone, not after what happened to Mom." Shea's voice caught in her throat. Her eyes welled with tears. "I wish I could've joined you two at the colony instead of staying here."

Charles's face grew grim. "It isn't safe down there, Shea. Not yet. Dad wouldn't've let you come even if you'd gotten Uncle Alexander's blessing. The Forsaken are… brutal." He took a breath. "What news does the State release about Apex?"

"Not much, really. Only occasional reports about successful farming and mining projects. But to be honest, not much else is really discussed." Shea turned a curious eye to deLeon, then back to her brother. "Why? What's happening?"

"Begging your indulgence, sir, but perhaps this conversation may best be reserved for a more *secure* setting," deLeon said, his voice level and calm. Charles regarded him for a moment and offered a knowing nod.

"Yes, of course." Charles's demeanor had changed, and the smile he forced strained his lips. "Well, we should let you get some rest. It's late, after all, and we still need to prepare for tomorrow's meetings."

Shea smiled and squeezed his hand again. "Not at all, I'm glad you came. It was so good to see you."

He stood and they made their way to the front door. "Tomorrow will be utter chaos for me, but how about we catch lunch the day after? Just the two of us to catch up on things? We can maybe go to that place you liked so much in the square, the one with the egg tarts."

Shea's limbs became rigid, and her heart dropped like a stone in her chest. "I…" The day after next was the day she'd committed to Iris, to her obligation to Victoria and Simon. The day that she wasn't even sure she'd survive. "I'm sorry. I can't do lunch, I'm beginning work with Dr. Samson on that day."

"Oh, that's right. Uncle did mention that in his message."

Charles snapped his fingers. "How about dinner, then? Let's say, after you get outta work?"

Tears stung her eyes. She blinked and smiled through it, gave a nod. "That's be great, Charles. I'd like that."

"Perfect! I'll see you later then. Get some rest, alright?"

Charles made to turn toward the door but halted when Shea wrapped her arms around his waist. She pulled him close and buried her face in his chest, her tears pressing into his jacket. He put his arms around her shoulders and gave her a reassuring squeeze. He kissed her hair through a smile.

"I love you, Charles," she spoke through choked sobs. "I hope you know that."

"Of course I do. I love you too, sis. I'll see you soon, okay?"

She watched them leave without saying another word. She sat on the floor and fixed her gaze to the closed door, wondering if she would live long enough to see her brother again. She closed her eyes and wiped her tear-soaked cheeks. Pulling her knees into her chest, she buried her face in her arms and sobbed.

****

There wasn't much that Victoria remembered after the Peace Officers had seized her that morning. She'd felt the chill of the metal cuffs securing around her wrists before they injected a syringe of milky fluid into her neck. Despite her screams and thrashing, her limbs had grown heavy as darkness overcame her.

There was nothing for a while. No fear, no hatred, no crippling sadness or pain. She was like a mote of dust suspended in the air, passive and small. And in all of it, darkness. Silence. It consumed her and filled each jagged crack of her consciousness. She wondered if this was what death was like; like floating in nothingness, a peaceful vacuum. The notion of it felt compelling, and she almost wished that she were dead. How inviting it was to feel nothing, blanketed in darkness forever. Emptiness was the better alternative to returning to State custody.

She felt a pulling, as if being submerged and drawn back again from thick fluid. She felt the weight of her limbs, the quickening panic of her heart. Her pulse pounded in her skull. Voices came to her in muffled tones; she recognized one and felt a sudden rage ignite in her chest. She'd seen his face in the meeting room, recognized the familiar curve of his lips when he grinned: Dr. Samson.

There were hands on her, holding her down against what might've been a bed, or a table, she wasn't sure. Her wrists were bound and caught when she tugged; her ankles were held down and strapped. She still saw nothing, not even a blur of shadows when she opened her eyes. She sensed a radiating warmth over her, and a breath against her shoulder. Someone had leaned close to her while affixing a restraint across her shoulders. They were close; close enough for her teeth.

Through the haze she tasted hot, bitter copper against her tongue, heard screams and cries of men. Her mouth and nostrils filled, and she choked on the thick liquid that spilled down her throat. There was another sharp pierce in her neck, and she drifted again into nothingness.

Chapter 47

"Dr. Tristan, His Majesty Guide Us and welcome to our Sanctuary!"

Shea recognized the gentleman waiting in the Ministry of Defense lobby almost immediately from her mother's research footage. She smiled despite the heat flushing her cheeks. The same voice that called to her had commanded Victoria to stab herself in the chest. She'd seen the slightest grin curl at his lip when he placed the pistol in front of her to kill the woman she loved. With a polite nod and a wave, she wished him a slow and agonizing death.

"May Strength Remain. It's a pleasure to meet finally meet you, Dr. Samson. The chancellor speaks very highly of you." Shea's cheeks ached from holding the strained smile across her lips.

"Oh, His Fortune Shines! The pleasure is all mine, I assure you." They shook hands and Shea winced at his tight squeeze. "If you follow me, please, I'll take you to the holding level. We've got a very long day ahead of us. I know it's your first day and we're only just showing you around this afternoon, but we're all *extremely* excited to bring you into our program."

"Of course. And I'm excited to be here." Shea gestured for

him to proceed. "After you, Doctor."

He led her to the security entry-port. The facility lobby was open to the public, but admittance into the secured levels were accessible only after passing through a body scan, metal detector, and pat down by a peace officer. This was standard protocol, and she'd done this even on her first day at the Ministry of Health and Wellness. She'd passed each entry-port without any complications; but that was before she'd become a secret enemy of the state. Her thoughts turned to the evacuation pods, *her* pod, waiting ten levels beneath their feet, and became aware of the weakening of her knees.

Dr. Samson passed through the security checks without a hitch. A peace officer motioned for Shea to follow. She entered the body-scan chamber and waited. The archway emitted a red glow for a few seconds before flashing orange. A beep sounded. The peace officer behind the monitor screen cleared her throat and cocked an inquisitive eyebrow.

"Triggered for elevated heart rate and perspiration. Anything to proclaim, ma'am?"

I am an enemy of the state who is actively working to liberate a top-secret medical experiment and killing machine.

Shea faltered and shrugged, indifferent. "Nothing to proclaim. I'm just nervous for my first day with Dr. Samson."

The officer gestured for her to proceed to the metal detector and waited for clearance before patting her down. Once checked, Shea rushed to meet Dr. Samson near the elevators.

"Right," he said as the sliding elevator doors parted. He stepped inside and offered Shea a smile when she followed. "Let's get started. Why don't we start with you filling me in on what you already know?"

The space between them in the elevator felt too narrow. She could feel his closeness, smelled his cologne, and desperately wished she could recoil from it. Shea instead swallowed her anxiety like a dry pill and shifted on her feet.

I know enough to warrant a trip to the executor's platform. Everyone would know my face, telecast across Odin Prime, before a bullet ripped through it. I know that tomorrow won't be like any other day, and I may not live to see the end of it.

"My mother headed a state-sponsored medical research program called Project Stronghold, where you were her partner in trying to find a cure to the Ink epidemic on Valhalla. You've just recently re-secured an escaped subject from that project, and her body somehow displays a remarkable ability to heal. But apart from finding a link between the outbreak in the Anchor and that test subject, I can't say I know much else."

The elevator slowed to a halt. Shea caught a glimpse of herself in the reflection of the golden-mirrored shine of the doors before they parted. She appeared as she had in her day-to-day in the Ministry of Health and Wellness: lab coat, dress slacks, button-up collared shirt, and a tight bun pulling at her scalp. Except she saw something else in her reflection that triggered a chill up her spine. There was someone else in the face gazing back at her: her mother.

"Well I'd say that you're more familiar with our work than most Party members, even with what limited exposure you've had. It's a shame, really—I do love to brag about our successes, but the non-disclosure agreement doesn't exactly leave us room to do so."

Shea feigned disappointment. "What a shame."

Shea followed Dr. Samson when he stepped from the elevator. She glanced at the sign affixed to the wall: *Level 14-B*. She squinted against the abrasive lights and breathed in the stale air. There was a sterility to the floor that unnerved her.

"Project Stronghold's ultimate goal was to understand the Ink pandemic on Valhalla. We'd invested so much on that damned moon that we couldn't afford to just let it take over—hell, we'd cease to exist if we didn't at least have Apex tethering us to its resources. Your mother was set on making sure that each soul residing on Valhalla, regardless of whether they were out on some farm or within Apex itself, was safe from the Ink. A safe Valhalla makes for a safe Odin Prime."

"Understandable," Shea said. "Yet I'm still confused how that research led to your subject's advanced restorative abilities."

"Well—" Dr. Samson halted and turned to grin at her. "Gene mutation therapy. More precisely, stem cell and bone marrow treatments. The thing about the Ink, you see, is that it's got an exceedingly high mortality rate. We couldn't exactly have our entire stock of test subjects die on us; limited supply, you know? So, we had to develop a way to beef up their immune system and resiliency. Toughen them up a bit, made them re-usable in our research."

Shea's jaw clenched against the simmering ire in her chest. She had heard this all before from her mother's tapes, but remained attentive as though it were all new. She silently thanked Iris for destroying her mother's box of research.

"So, you created a test subject who couldn't die, infected them with the deadly Ink strain, observed them, and treated them. Rinse and repeat?"

Dr. Samson shrugged. "Until we developed a vaccine for the Ink, yes, more or less. It was far from ideal, but we had limited resources and had to work with what we had. And it worked out for the best, in more ways than one. While finding the Ink vaccine was remarkable enough on its own, the by-products of our research garnered immense support from the State."

"By-products?" Shea asked, brow creased. "You mean the test subjects?"

Dr. Samson snapped his fingers. "Exactly. Your mother's gene mutation breakthrough was a medical miracle!"

"It was, truly," she began, steadying her voice. "It makes sense: bone marrow being a part of the immune system, hematopoietic stem cells produce white blood cells. But how does that explain the body's elevated capacity to heal? Hematopoietic stem cells can only create blood."

"Ah, see, that's where the *gene* therapy comes into play." Dr. Samson shook a finger at her and winked. The two continued down the hallway toward a security door. "Did you know that CoP researchers had attempted to mutate human skin cell DNA to change them into embryonic stem cells decades ago? Before our liberation? They failed, of course."

Shea scoffed. "Sounds improbable."

"Improbable, yes, but not impossible," Dr. Samson paused before entering a security door. He turned and smiled at her. "You see, your mother mimicked this research and found a way to genetically mutate skin cells to replicate embryonic stem cells. Then, through a series of tests she discovered the method in enabling that same cell generation within *bone marrow* alongside the hematopoietic stem cells. Using a hormone stimulant, we triggered the body to pump out doses of erythropoietin to activate both blood cell creation as well as any cell the body needed. Hematopoietic and embryotic stem cells alike."

A strange, sick sense of curiosity crept into Shea's mind. This study *was* fascinating, as detestable as she knew it was. Despite the very real human cost, the science itself was remarkable. It was a medical breakthrough that could change not only the trajectory of Odin Prime, but the entire colonized territories. This treatment would completely revolutionize medical care: repairing extensive nerve damage, eliminating organ failure, rapidly healing broken bones, restoring inhibited motor functions. The thought alone gave her pause, and she then recalled how tall her uncle had stood in his office after spending cycles bound to a wheelchair.

"That's..." Her voice cracked, faltered. She recalled shooting Victoria in the Ministry of Health and Wellness, and it not even fazing her; it was her first glimpse at her mother's astonishing success. Victoria was a medical triumph, a walking horror of science. "That's extraordinary. What happened with this research?"

"We did a lot of great work, your mother and I. But..." His eyes hardened, and his jaw set. "It was mostly lost in the end. Someone attacked our offices, destroyed almost everything. Cycles of hard research, lost. And then of course, your mother just had to—"

He cut himself off and cleared his throat.

"What about my mother, Dr. Samson?" Shea asked. Her steadied voice masked the anger rising in her chest.

Dr. Samson smiled sweetly at her. "Your mother was the glue that held this project together. With the core data files lost, and her tragic passing, our progress has not only stalled, it's regressed, I'm afraid." He leaned toward the credentials pad beside a secured door. "Michael Samson."

The pad blinked from red to green. "Credentials verified. Good afternoon, Dr. Samson."

The door lock released, and the doors slid open before them. They entered an abrasively bright, spacious laboratory. Dr. Samson continued to speak as they walked past rows of workstations and empty steel beds, their leather restraints dangling to the linoleum flooring below. Shea's eyes lingered on a vacant bed and braced against the shiver trailing up her spine.

"We haven't yet been able to backward-engineer the technique your mother used. We've come close, to be sure, but still haven't quite hit the mark. That's where we're hoping you can help, if only as a new set of eyes to the data."

"Begging your indulgence, Dr. Samson." Shea stopped and lowered her voice. "But may I ask you a question in confidence?"

Dr. Samson's brow furrowed. "Of course, my dear. What is it?"

Shea leaned in closer and nearly whispered, eyes looking about to ensure they were alone. "The last I saw my uncle cycles ago, he was wheelchair-bound from a severe stroke. I saw him yesterday standing and walking with hardly as much as a limp."

A grin curled at the edges of Dr. Samson's mouth. "You're curious if we've tested on him, hm?" Shea offered a nod, and Dr. Samson continued. "You're correct to suspect as much.

It's remarkable, isn't it? The progress he's made."

He led Shea through the laboratory as he went on. "While we couldn't backward-engineer the stem-cell therapy for him, we found a way to use a matching blood-type from one of our subjects to treat his malady. We tested the process on another human test subject first, of course, to ensure that it worked. We pulled a volunteer from the Ministry of Health and Wellness, a sixty-cycle-old man with stage 4 metastasized colon cancer." Dr. Samson clicked his tongue and grinned wider. "Lucky bugger was cancer-free after five treatments."

They entered a darkened hallway. Motion-sensor lights flickered to life and illuminated the white passageway and the doors on either side. Each door had only a single window, and next to the handle was a security pad.

"As remarkable as these treatments are, it isn't sustainable. We could drain our subjects dry to cure any and all disease on this station and there will always be more." He shook his head. "For longer-term success, we need your mother's technique."

"I believe it." Shea's attention trailed to the metallic nameplates fastened to each door they passed.

Hammer... Wolf... Thunder... Horn....

"They each have their own name." Shea swallowed against her drying throat. Her eyes caught a glimpse inside a dark holding cell through the door's window as she passed: there was a tall figure standing in the far corner, obscured by the shadows, peering back at her. She couldn't see their eyes through the darkness, but she could feel their gaze following her. She looked away.

They approached the last door in the passageway and

stopped. Shea's gaze lingered on the nameplate: Raven.

He stepped aside to let Shea approach the door. She glanced inside the holding cell and suppressed the gasp that clawed up from her lungs. A woman lay on the hospital bed with her wrists, ankles, waist, and chest secured by thick leather straps. A blindfold masked her eyes, and a metal wire cage sealed her jaw shut. IV tubes dangled from syringes pierced and taped to each hand and arm, feeding her pale liquid from drip bags suspended beside her. Shea watched the rise and fall of her chest as she breathed steadily against the leather restraint.

Victoria: Subject Raven.

Chapter 48

Shea tucked her hands deep inside her lab coat pockets to hide the tremor creeping into her fingers. Victoria's long, crimson hair was clipped short; not nearly as short as in her mother's video logs, but seeing how much they'd shorn off left Shea's heart aching. Considering the amount of time Victoria had been freed and how long her hair had grown, Shea wondered if she had ever cut her hair once since her rescue. Four cycles… gone.

Shea cleared her throat and straightened her posture.

"That thing did nothing but terrorize me while I was held hostage. I'm relieved you were able to apprehend her before she could do any more damage." She gestured to her black eye, still visibly black and purple beneath a generous layer of flesh-tone makeup.

Dr. Samson tutted and rested a sympathetic hand on her shoulder. "I can't imagine what you went through in the wretched borough. But both you and her are back with us, safe and sound. That is what matters." He turned a side-eye back to Victoria. "Considering how much time, sweat, and tears your mother and I poured into this project and its subjects, having her back feels almost like a miracle itself. His Fortune Shines."

"His Fortune Shines." Shea feigned agreeance. "How was she able to escape in the first place?"

"Our old lab used to be in the Ministry of Health and Wellness. Your mother preferred it that way—she wanted that facility to be the center of all medical research and innovation on the station. But it lacked the security measures we needed, and it was a lesson we learned too late. And we paid for it dearly…" His voice trailed off, mouth downturned. "Someone broke in and set fire to the place, destroying cycles of research. Your mother was absolutely devastated. Some of us think that's why she—"

"Begging your indulgence, Doctor, to refrain from speaking again of the circumstances of my mother's death." Shea turned a hardened gaze at him.

"Yes of course, my apologies." He faltered, cleared his throat, and continued in a softer tone. "Thankfully, we backed up some records for posterity, but not nearly enough. We found that Raven was missing only after we extinguished the fire. Now that we know she was hiding with those Shadow bastards, we can only assume that they were the ones behind the incident. We moved the project here for the extra security afterward and haven't had any problems since. Only a fool would try to infiltrate this facility."

Shea stifled a surge of laughter through choked coughs. Dr. Samson observed her, eyebrow cocked, and patted her back.

"Are you alright, Dr. Tristan?"

Shea coughed once again and nodded, face flushed. "Choked on my own saliva—don't you hate it when that happens? It feels like our own bodies have a secret death wish."

"Shall I fetch you some water?" Dr. Samson asked.

"Oh yes, please. If you do not mind."

"It won't be but a moment." Dr. Samson turned to leave, but was stopped by Shea's outstretched arm.

"May I take a closer look in the meantime?" Shea asked, gesturing toward the door.

He shrugged a shoulder. "If you wish." He pressed his thumb against the security pad. The pad illuminated blue, then flashed green before releasing the heavy lock inside the door. "Just steer clear of her face—that muzzle is there for a reason. She tore a handler's throat out with her teeth after we brought her back."

"Thank you for the warning," Shea grimaced. She offered a polite wave as he continued toward the main laboratory and disappeared around the corner.

A chill brushed against her cheek as she stepped inside the holding cell. The heavy silence around them was broken only by the beeping and wheezing of monitoring devices. Shea approached Victoria's side. Her heart ached the longer her gaze lingered on the leather restraints, on the metal contraption strapped to her jaw. Had her mother restrained Victoria like this when she was her subject? Did she have Victoria blindfolded, restrained, and muzzled like a deranged animal? Was this normal?

She took Victoria's hand into her own. Shea reached and cradled the side Victoria's head with the palm of her hand, her thumb grazing the cold, metal muzzle. She gazed at her for a few brief moments, caressing her temple, before she leaned forward beside Victoria's ear.

"I'm gonna to get you out of here, Victoria. I promise…"

Shea stayed there for a moment longer, cradling the

woman, when she felt the lightest nudge against her fore-head. Victoria, drugged and blindfolded, had turned her head only a matter of centimeters toward Shea so that their temples rested against the other. Shea closed her eyes and held back a swell of tears. The two remained there for a few quiet seconds before the sound of footsteps echoed down the hall. Shea pulled away and brushed the moisture from her eye.

"Your water, Dr. Tristan." Dr. Samson entered the room with a tall glass of chilled water.

Shea smiled as warmly as she could manage before taking the glass from him. "You're too kind."

"Not at all, not at all." He waved a dismissive hand. "Now, shall we continue with the tour?"

"Absolutely," Shea said, and followed him out the door, not turning back to catch another glimpse of Victoria as the door slammed shut.

Shea fiddled with the clutch purse in her hands. Her nail plucked at one glossy black bead as she rocked from one heeled foot to the other. The elevator chimed. The doors slid open to a bright, sweet-smelling hallway with luscious green flora lining the walls and ceiling. Fragrant flowers and tendrils cascaded down the walls. Shea and the two enormous peace officers flanking her stepped from the elevator. She took in a deep breath and let out a pleasant sigh.

"Beautiful place, isn't it?" She remarked as though she were seeing it with fresh eyes. As though she hadn't already been there the night before with a pistol tucked inside her jacket, intent on putting a round between their chief's eyes. She smiled sweetly at one of the officers. "Don't you think so?"

"It is indeed," the officer replied. His voice carried a tinge of boredom. "Albeit a bit too high-brow for my taste."

The other officer mumbled passive assent as they approached the last suite in the hall. He reached to press his fat finger to the suite's doorbell. Shea could sense the bitter annoyance radiate from each of them; neither wanted to be there with her, playing bodyguard and babysitter. They could have been home instead, or out drinking at the very least.

The suite door slid open.

Iris stood in the doorway, clad in a pencil-skirt dress with a convincing smile across her lips.

"Dr. Tristan!" She clicked her heels and bowed forward. "What a pleasure it is to welcome you into my home."

"Good evening Chief Hammond. Thank you for having me." Shea nodded her head politely with her own strained smile. "And thank you for accepting my offer to come see you. It didn't feel altogether right to simply write you a thank-you note for what you've done for me."

"Not at all, Doctor. I was merely doing my duty. And it is a pleasure to have you as my guest for dinner. Please, do come in." Shea entered the suite, and the two officers moved to follow. Iris moved to block in their way. "Thank you for escorting Dr. Tristan this far. You are dismissed for the evening."

One of the officers clicked his heels, standing at attention. "Begging the Chief's indulgence, we were instructed to escort Dr. Tristan for the remainder of the evening until she returned to the estate. To guarantee her safety."

Iris's smile tightened. "Do you think your Chief unfit to

guarantee her guest's safety?"

The officers faltered and froze. "N-No, Ma'am. It's just—"

Iris waved a dismissive hand. "I will personally see to Dr. Tristan's safe return to the estate after our dinner, I assure you. You may direct any irate supervisor my way if they wish to voice a grievance. Now please, you gentlemen go enjoy your evening as you see fit."

"Ma'am." They each pressed a clenched fist to their chest and bowed. Iris dismissed them and stepped back into the suit. The doors slid shut with a motion of her hand, and the air of gentle politeness dropped almost immediately.

"I don't suppose you have any *real* dinner set aside, do you?" Shea asked, tossing the purse onto the nearby sofa. She kicked her heels off across the floor. "Today was such a whirlwind that we ended up skipping lunch entirely."

"You can eat later—we have work to do first. Follow me." Iris started down the corridor with Shea reluctantly following behind. "What's your assessment from your first day with the doctor?"

"Dr. Samson doesn't suspect a thing. I think he was so eager to have me on board that he was ecstatic at even the slightest hint of interest on my part. He was an endless chatterbox for most of the day, rattling on about he and my mother's work."

"Good," Iris said. "He trusts you, and that will be essential tomorrow. What about your uncle?"

"He thought me visiting you this evening as a way to formally offer my thanks was 'proper Statesman etiquette'," Shea rolled her eyes. "So naturally, he was delighted."

"Excellent."

Iris led them to what looked to be a modest training

room. The setup reminded Shea of the sparring area within Shadow's basement, with its padded flooring and smattering of fitness equipment. Of course, all the gear inside Iris's suite was far more expensive, with considerably less duct tape, dents, and rust. Shea's eyes flickered to a shadow the corner of the room, and was startled at the armored figure standing there, stoic and still.

"Someone's a bit jumpy, hm?" Iris asked. "Stand there, don't move." She strode to the armor's side and hoisted it up. A moment later, she had placed it squarely in front of Shea, and ran a scrutinizing eye over each of them. "Hm. Should fit."

Shea blinked. *Fit? This thing? On me?* She scoffed. "You must be joking."

"Do I strike you as the sort of woman who jokes, doctor?" Iris responded, voice deadpan.

Shea shrugged. "Not particularly, no. Or laughing, smiling, experiencing the full, complex spectrum of human emotion."

"Shut up and pay attention." Iris rested her palm against the armor's shoulder and patted it. "This *thing*, as you called it, is a highly classified prototype. Valkyrie medic armor: reinforced nano-shields that can withstand nearly thirty hits from a pulse rifle before needing recharge, helmet equipped with built-in infrared visor, diagnostics heads-up display, and toxin-mesh." Iris dropped her hand to tap on the armor's hip compartments. "Grav-assist litter that can lift and hold over two hundred kilos, non-lethal defensive concussive and riot gas grenades." She pointed to the armor's forearm. "Liquid emergency drug repositories that administer through the user's glove." She motioned to the armor's knees. "Reinforced mechanical suspension joints in knees, shoulders, elbows, and back that allows the user to lift and carry an additional one hundred kilos."

Shea's eyes widened, jaw agape. "You must not have a lot of faith in me if you think I'll need all that to get Victoria out."

"Correct," Iris said as she removed the helmet. "The only consistency in operational planning is that at one point or another, the plan goes to shit. And if you're the only thing standing between my daughter and her freedom, I'm going to make sure that you can at least carry her there."

"I can't argue with that," Shea said. Iris passed the helmet to her, which she held delicately in her hands. "It's incredible. Whoever's wearing it is like a walking, breathing triage center."

"That's the point. It spent cycles in development"

Shea traced her fingertip along the sleek helmet in awe. "Then why is it only a prototype? Why not use it?"

Iris scoffed. "The higher-ups lost interest in pursuing advanced Valkyrie medic armor once they caught wind of your mother's research findings. After all, who needs a medic with expensive gear when your operatives can just heal themselves?" She plucked the helmet from Shea's grasp and placed it on the soft training mat. "Who cares that my girls die in combat in the meantime? I'm sure Dr. Samson is chomping at the bit to replace my teams with his vacant, invincible golems."

"No doubt he is." Shea watched Iris take the armor apart, piece by piece, until each segment lay scattered at her feet. "So, what's the plan?"

"Our plan, for now"—Iris let out a tired sigh and rubbed

the back of her neck—"is to not leave this room until you can suit-up in less than a minute."

458

Chapter 49

Simon awoke the next morning to the sound of the bedroom door creaking shut. He jerked awake, tugged at the restraints, and squinted one eye open through the darkness.

"It's only me." Jefferson's voice was tired, grated. "My apologies, I didn't mean to wake you. I really must get that door fixed."

A moment later, the wall along the floor's edging emitted a low, warm glow. The room filled with a dim light that revealed Jefferson standing in the far corner by the desk, his back turned to Simon.

"Dad, what the hell?" Simon groaned and let his head fall back onto the pillow. He grimaced against the ache in his shoulders, back, and hips—too long spent immobilized on a bed. He closed his eyes and sighed. "What time is it?"

"Nearly 08:00." Jefferson still had his back turned and was busy handling a seemingly delicate task on the desk. He brought something to eye level, tapped his nail, and set it down again. "How're you feeling?"

"Like I'm tired of being kept in this bed," Simon said through gritted teeth.

Jefferson turned toward his son and crossed his arms. A

metallic tray sat behind him on the desk, though it was too dark for Simon to see what lay on it.

"I have no doubt that you're eager to get out of those cuffs. I wanted to speak with you this morning before—" Jefferson faltered and forced a smile. "Before we parted ways again. I didn't feel right just… well, I wanted to offer you some options."

"Options?"

Jefferson turned to pluck a syringe from the tray behind him and strode over to Simon's side. Simon took one look at the needle in his father's hand and wrenched back against the restraints.

"Shh, shh." Jefferson gently patted Simon's shoulder. "Relax. Hear me out."

"What the fuck?" Simon strained to pull back as far as he could manage from his father, his eyes never breaking from the syringe. His hands dampened with sweat, his heart raced. "What the fuck is *that*?"

"A sedative. Rather potent, too," Jefferson said. He placed the syringe on the nightstand beside Simon's bed. "One that will play a vital role in how today will end, depending on how much you're willing to cooperate."

"Cooperate with what?" Simon asked.

Jefferson hesitated for a moment, leaving a thick, heavy silence between them until finally he took a breath and forced out the words.

"We're sending you off Odin Prime today."

Simon fell silent, dumbfounded. He stared at his father, blinked, and nearly chuckled. "You can't be serious."

"We're sending you somewhere the State can't touch you. Somewhere you'll be safer, happier."

Simon gawked at him. "That's insane—I was already happy in the Anchor with Ma. If you want me to be happy, you'll let me go back to the Anchor. That's where my life is. And if Shadow is gone, as you say it is, I need to get back to help get it started again. The people in the Anchor need us."

Jefferson shifted in his chair, turned his eyes away. "And how long do you think you can keep up with that sort of life, hm? You've already been shot—if she'd aimed only a few centimeters closer, you'd be dead."

"Yeah, I got shot. And I might get stabbed, beaten, shot again." Simon gazed at his father with steeled resolve. "But it's my life, and it's what *I* want. We're helping people, we're pushing back against the State. My life had *purpose* with Shadow. You can't just ask me to leave all that behind." Simon shook his head, frowning. "And I can't leave Ma. I won't."

Jefferson met Simon's eyes. "So that's it, then?" Simon didn't respond, and only held his father's gaze. The man let out a long, tired sigh. "I understand, Simon. Truly, I do. You've got fire in your heart, just like your mother." Tears welled in his eyes as he spoke. "I'm sorry I failed you as a father when… when you changed. I was a fool, and it will be my life's regret. But I'm here now, and I won't fail you again. I want you to know that I love you, and that I'm proud of the person you've become. I loved you as Simone, and I still love you as Simon. I always will. Do you hear me?"

Simon fell silent. Tears brimmed and stung his eyes. He gritted his teeth, swallowed against the lump growing in his throat, and blinked the tears away.

"I said, do you hear me?" Jefferson repeated, his voice earnest and nearly pleading.

Simon nodded. "Yeah, Dad. I hear you."

"Good, good…" Jefferson wiped the tears from his cheeks and took a deep breath.

A sudden burst of movement erupted from Jefferson's chair. Simon watched his father snatch the syringe from the nightstand and plunge the needle deep into his arm.

***

"Prepare for gravity!" the guard shouted down the long corridor.

Harriet, half-asleep and floating near the ceiling, startled awake and clutched tight onto the nearest handle. An abrupt heave of force slammed into her, jerking her weight toward the floor. Her fingers strained to keep hold as she swung for a moment, steadied herself, and dropped, albeit unsteadily, onto her feet. She heard countless prisoners down the corridor banging to the floor, cursing and shouting in pain.

"Go to hell, you PO fuck!"

"Give us a little more warning next time, jackass!"

"Agh, I think my fuckin' shoulder's dislocated!"

"Amateurs," Harriet snickered with a shake of her head. She moved and winced at the sudden, sharp ache in her back and shoulders. Time spent in those cells had been exceedingly easier in her thirties.

Footsteps sounded from the corridor's main entrance. Harriet stared at the cell door, jaw taut. She forgot about the pain throbbing across her back, and instead took slow, measured steps back against the wall.

Prison protocol dictated that gravity be initiated when either depositing or withdrawing a prisoner. Harriet heard only two sets of footsteps. Two guards, no prisoner—they were there to take someone, to take *her*. She turned her back toward the door and placed both palms against the chilled metal wall, preparing for what would come next.

The guards stopped outside her door. One rapped his knuckles against the metal.

"Prisoner 199608. Acknowledge," the guard barked through the door.

"Something you need, officer?" Harriet's tone was cavalier despite the sneer across her lips.

"Prisoner 199608, place your hands against the back wall and do not resist. Any sudden movement will be seen as a direct threat and lethal force may be taken against you. Do you understand?"

"Yeah, yeah. Just get your asses in here and get it over with," Harriet groaned.

The heavy lock unhinged, and the two guards were on her within seconds of the door sliding open.

***

Iris stared out her office window, arms crossed and pensive. Her jaw clenched tight as she let out a sigh. Her finger tapped restlessly against her arm. She glanced at the clock affixed to the wall: 09:13. The operation was in motion, and nothing short of an armed peace officer barricade could stop them now.

She closed her eyes, took a breath, and craned her neck to either side. "No use overthinking this. Focus on right now. Stay focused. Treat it like any other mission."

A buzzer rang on her desk, followed by a young man's voice. Her new assistant was just as courteous and sub-servient as Philip had been, but considerably less nosey.

"Chief Hammond, ma'am," the young man's polite, clear voice spoke through the intercom. *"Prisoner 199608 is here*

for interrogation."

"Send her in," Iris commanded. Her eyes flickered to her Valkyrie suit standing in the corner. "And bring in my breakfast as well, while you're at it."

"Coffee, too, ma'am?"

"Yes."

"Black, no sugar?"

"Bring some in case I feel like a change. Cream, as well."

"Right away, ma'am."

Iris plucked up a cigarette case from her desk and tapped out a single stick. The office doors slid open as she placed the cigarette between her lips and ignited it with a lighter built into the case itself. Two armed guards dragged Mama Wilder inside and aggressively tossed her to the floor. She let out a muffled cry and curled into herself, wincing and grimacing with each motion. Iris watched her with indifference as she took a long drag from her cigarette.

"Your breakfast, ma'am," her new assistant announced as he scuttled in behind the guards. He carried a silver platter with an assortment of warm, aromatic breakfast foods and a steaming kettle of hot coffee.

Iris nodded toward the desk. "Leave it and get out. All of you."

"Shall we wait outside, ma'am?" one of the guards asked. "To bring her back to her cell once you've finished with her?"

Iris turned a cold eye on him. "Did I tell you to wait outside, or did I tell you to leave?"

The guard swallowed hard and shifted from one foot to another. "To leave, ma'am."

"Then do as you're told," Iris snapped at him and flicked a speck of ash to the floor. "I will call you if you're needed. I've been waiting decades to personally interrogate this bitch and I aim to take my time with her. Now, *leave us.*"

Both guards snapped to attention and saluted with fists pressed against their chests. They turned on their heels and hurried out the room, followed closely by the young assistant. The doors slid shut. Iris waited a moment, then stepped forward to extend a hand in Mama Wilder's direction.

"Good morning."

"Good morning, my ass," Mama Wilder spat at Iris. She reached out, clasped onto her extended hand, and hoisted herself up from the floor with Iris's help. Groaning, the old woman rotated her shoulders and stretched her back. "This plan had better work. At this rate I'm starting to question if my body can even make it to the finish line."

Iris handed her the lit cigarette. "It will. Care for a headscarf?"

"You're too kind," Mama Wilder said as Iris slipped a hand into her desk and retrieved a black scarf. She tossed it to the woman, who snatched it out of the air, then slid the cigarette between her lips and tied the scarf gracefully around her bald scalp. "Your boys took my wig. Motherfuckers."

"Protocol is inconvenient," Iris stated flatly. "There's been some changes you should know about."

"Oh?" Mama Wilder's gaze steeled. She took a long, satisfying drag from the cigarette. She coughed and licked the corner of her mouth with a blood-speckled tongue. "Enlighten me."

"The charming young doctor came to my home a few nights ago to kill me," Iris said.

Mama Wilder choked out a laugh. *"Did she?* Good for her."

"Indeed. Snuck out with a stolen pistol and stood at my door, ready to blow my head off." Iris had walked around the desk as she spoke and poured herself a cup of coffee. She took a sip and sighed. "A stupid idea, no doubt, but she doesn't lack in tenacity."

"I always found it annoying," the old woman remarked, and followed Iris to the desk.

"Likewise. Regardless, however annoying her tenacity may be, it's useful—as are her accesses."

"She's a connected Statesman, sure. But what could she possibly have that'd you agree to bring her on board?"

Iris nearly laughed. "You know, it's funny. I'd expected the chancellor to welcome her back with open arms and reinstate her at the hospital. I figured she'd finally be out of my hair. I was *not* expecting him to assign her to her mother's old research project."

"No shit? Well, that's convenient. She has direct access to Vic," Mama Wilder said. "Hell, that'll make our day a little less challenging, at least. We can focus more on getting my boy, then."

"The girl also inherited her mother's pod," Iris stated flatly.

Mama Wilder gawked at her. She said nothing for a few moments, then let out a sigh. "I hope you were at least honest with the stupid girl on our odds of survival before committing to using her."

"I was. No hesitation at all. Damn near enthusiastic about it."

A sad, weak smile spread across the woman's lips. "Well, then. That's that, isn't it?"

"Indeed," Iris said, and gestured to the tray. "Coffee?"

Mama Wilder nodded, and Iris poured her a tall mug of

coffee with two squares of white sugar and a splash of cream. The aroma surrounded them, and the woman sighed happily after the first sip.

"God, do you know how long it's been since I've had *good* coffee? With *actual* sugar and cream?" She held the mug in front of her nose for a few moments, and her smile sank away. Her eyes scanned the breakfast platter of fried eggs, toast, bacon, and diced fruit. None of it was rehydrated or nutrient substitute; it was all fresh and authentic, and it sat untouched.

A silence fell between them. Iris stared off out the distant window and took another sip from her black coffee.

"A good last meal to have, don't you think?"

"For me or for you?" Mama Wilder asked.

Iris shrugged. "I'm a Valkyrie—we don't get last meals. This is all I need." She raised her mug of coffee before taking another sip. "I don't make it a habit to eat before missions anyway."

"Well, any last meal is better than the nutrient bricks they toss us in prison," Mama Wilder said as she picked up a butter-slathered wedge of toast. She took a bite and groaned. "Ah fuck, and that's real butter."

Iris gestured with her steaming mug of coffee, then turned her attention to the scenery outside her office window. "Enjoy it. We've got a long day ahead of us, and I need you to be at your best."

***

Simon heard the long, strained groan of his father when the man gently lowered his limp body to the living room sofa. The world was a blur of muffled noise and darkness. He strained to lift his head, but it instead lolled from side to side, eyelids heavy and slowly blinking. He parted his lips to speak, but instead only managed incoherent mumbles and moans.

His father's voice reached him through the haze. "Don't worry, kid. You'll be out of here soon enough. And things'll be better for you. Safer. And don't worry about Theresa, I'll make sure she's taken care of."

Simon tried lifting himself from the sofa, but could barely maintain a grip on the cushion. He let out a frustrated growl and fell limp again, resigned. His head drooped forward, his eyes closed.

"I know this isn't what you want," his father's muffled voice barely reached him as he spoke. "But please try to trust—"

A deafening explosion ripped through the opposite end of room. Simon crumpled to his side on the sofa cushions. He gasped for air and tasted metal and dust; he coughed and wheezed into the cushion beneath him. His heavy eyelids draped his blurred vision, and his hearing was little more than a high-pitched, piercing whistle and the rapid thudding of his own heartbeat.

Voices reached him as though he were submerged in water—murky and distant. He strained to move, to will his muscles to tighten, his joints to bend, but instead lay still and limp. Laughter broke through the fog, and his heart lurched. He recognized that single, amused voice as they stepped closer.

"Sorry about the ear, boy-o. I think this just about makes us even-steven." Julep's sweet, mischievous voice reached him as he gradually slipped into darkness.

Chapter 50

Dr. Samson switched the microphone from red to green on the console, cleared his throat, and touched his lips to the receiver. "Bring in the subject."

His voice projected inside the white, sterile test chamber. Dr. Samson and Shea stood in the control room opposite the chamber, connected only by a ten-centimeter one-way mirror. The doors inside the test chamber slid open, followed by two hulking guards escorting Victoria by both arms. The guards released her with a shove and promptly exited the chamber. Monitors lining the walls flickered to life, displaying a live feed of the subject's vital signs and neuro-imaging. Dr. Samson turned his head to offer Shea an enthusiastic thumbs up. She gripped tight to the clipboard with clammy hands and forced a smile through clenched teeth.

"God, I'm so excited. It feels so surreal, standing where my mother once stood, researching the same subject. It's like a dream, taking over where she left off." *Nightmares are dreams.*

"No doubt, no doubt," Dr. Samson said with a cocky grin. "I can see you're eager to start. Shall we begin?"

Shea swallowed against the dryness against her tongue and throat, but nodded with a smile.

He crouched and touched his lips to the receiver again. "Subject Raven, sit in the chair."

They watched in silence as Victoria, barefoot and dressed only in a long-sleeve white tunic and matching slacks, moved toward the single chair in the center of the room. Her stride was sluggish and unsteady, her feet dragged. She clumsily lowered herself onto the chair and reached to adjust the clear plastic muzzle affixed across her jaw.

"Subject Raven, leave it alone," Dr. Samson snapped through the microphone.

Victoria's hand stilled. Her nostrils flared, and her jaw clamped tight. A beeping from the monitor on the wall indicated an elevated heart rate. Within a few moments her hand, now trembling, returned to her lap.

"Fascinating. She still responds to verbal cues after all these cycles," Shea said.

"Indeed." Dr. Samson crossed his arms and peered at Victoria through the glass. "Our team dedicated a considerable amount of time to their behavioral conditioning. And a *lot* of drugs. You wouldn't believe the volume of narcotics we have to keep stocked for them. But in the end, it was extremely effective, as you can see for yourself. All those cycles spent away from our supervision and she *still* responds to our cues. Granted, she still requires basic, rudimentary commands but—" He breathed a satisfied sigh. "It's magnificent."

Drugs to weaken the mind, make them more suggestible and malleable.

"So, their obedience is based entirely on conditioning? It's all in their head?"

Dr. Samson shrugged. "More or less. The other subjects fully comply with much less input, but act with none of the interference as Raven does. You see there, how her hand is shaking? Her heart rate, perspiration, neural scans? She's drugged all to hell but she's still fighting it."

"She's insufferably strong-willed," Shea said as she watched Victoria shift dozily in her chair. *And I've come to love that about her.* "How long will it take to break her? To remove that interference?"

"Well, that's what we're here to find out," Dr. Samson said, his voice laced with excitement. He turned back to the microphone. "Commencing Project Stronghold Obedience Trial, Series X-01 on Subject Raven. Time is now 09:25 on 06LUN24,C172."

The first series of tests consisted of simple, rudimentary commands. He bid her to complete easy tasks, such as touching her nose, raising each arm and then both over her head, standing to walk across the room, jog in place, and return to her seat again. Dr. Samson burned through nearly thirty minutes on these commands alone, testing Victoria's basic motor functions and her willingness to comply. And Victoria, in spite of the hatred swimming behind her drooping eyes, complied with each command without hesitation.

"It's easy for them to obey when the tasks are simple movement commands. Your mother and I often started each conditioning session this way to get them warmed up and primed to accept instruction." Dr. Samson yawned. "Necessary, but so damned boring."

"When do you graduate to more complicated instruction?" Shea asked. Her eyes flickered to the time displayed across the console monitor: 09:56. *Keep him talking.*

"Well, it all depends." Dr. Samson crossed his arms and regarded Victoria seated in the center of the test chamber. "In the beginning, we often used electric shock to motivate our subjects into following instructions. They'd already survived the marrow therapy treatment, so we could afford to dose them up with enough narcotics that would kill you or me without the fear of overdose. The shock-drug method was remarkably effective. Eventually they no longer needed the electric shock, and needed only the verbal stimuli to comply."

"That's..." Shea's smile was tense, strained. *Barbaric.* "Brilliant."

He yawned again and scratched his trimmed beard. "I think we've observed her response to basic commands long enough. I think it's about time we start having a little fun, hm?"

Shea's brow furrowed. "Fun?"

Dr. Samson grinned as he activated the microphone. "Subject Raven, punch yourself."

The crack of Victoria's knuckles against her skull rang through the intercom. Shea flinched. Dr. Samson laughed.

"Barely any hesitation at all. Outstanding!"

Heat flushed Shea's cheeks, her knuckles whitening as she grasped the clipboard. She spoke through gritted teeth, pacing her words. "Begging your indulgence, Doctor, you could've given me a bit more warning first. I find unnecessary violence... unsightly."

"Oh, you'll be rid of that soon." Dr. Samson dismissed her with a wave. "The first few sessions are always the hardest. Besides, she's a moral offender. I wouldn't lose sleep over any perceived suffering." He leaned toward the microphone. "Subject Raven, break your index finger."

Victoria hesitated. The moment was brief, and Shea wasn't sure if Dr. Samson had even noticed. Victoria flinched, but remained rigid for a passing moment before reaching up to clasp her index finger. She snapped the bone.

Shea closed her eyes and grimaced. "Very impressive, Doctor."

"Subject Raven, set the broken finger."

Victoria complied and, though the pain showed only slightly in her eyes, situated the broken bone back into place. Shea returned her gaze to watch the alignment of the bone straighten. What looked to be an expression of muted relief registered in Victoria's eyes.

"Beautiful, isn't it?" Dr. Samson said through a smile.

Shea bit her tongue and swallowed the vitriol crawling up her chest. She glanced again at the time just as a knock came at the observation room's door.

"What—" Dr. Samson sneered over his shoulder. "This is a *closed* session!"

"Begging the doctors' indulgences." A young intern in a lab coat poked his head inside. His eyes and smile were anxious and apologetic. "I have a delivery here for Dr. Tristan?"

"Oh!" Shea pipped and hurried to the door. "Yes, bring it in, thank you." She flashed a charming smile at Dr. Samson. "My apologies, I forgot to tell you about my side project with Chief Hammond."

Dr. Samson's brow creased, his lips downturned. "Side project?"

"Yes." Shea opened the door further to offer the intern space to push through a waist-high crate on wheels. "I met with Chief Hammond last night for supper. I wanted to personally thank her for rescuing me from the Anchor, and while I was over, she mentioned there was a proto-medic Valkyrie suit she'd been working on. Well, I thought the least I could do was offer my services as a consultant, considering all she'd done for me."

"Oh lord, she's still on about that stupid suit?" Dr. Samson's tense brow eased with a roll of his eyes. "She and I have been going back and forth with the Cabinet about that stupid prototype. I told her that medic suits like hers would be rendered useless after our research was complete."

The intern rolled the crate against the wall before hurrying out again, muttering apologies and closing the door behind him. Shea unfastened the latch on the crate, hoisted the lid, and stared down at the pieces of armor set in molded foam. Shea's mouth ran dry.

"I would agree with you, Dr. Samson," she said. "But I hope you're not bothered by me doing this as a personal favor. I told her to send the armor here, as I do not have an assigned office yet. Do you mind?"

Dr. Samson's scowl eased only slightly as he turned his back to her. "Yes, yes, it's fine. Store it in that facility closet, will you? I don't need that blasted thing cluttering up the place." He massaged the bridge of his nose. "And please try to focus, Dr. Tristan. I understand you want to help Chief Hammond, but don't let your generosity distract you from your primary duties with this project."

"No, of course not." Shea opened the back closet and peered inside; it was just wide enough to squeeze in both herself and crate between stacks of cleaning and office supplies. The crate bumped against a metal rack as she awkwardly shimmied it through. She peeked her head out the door with a contrite smile. "Please continue with the experiment, Dr. Samson. I'm just checking the manifest here to ensure I have all the pieces here that I need."

Dr. Samson grumbled. "Very well. Make it quick—I don't want that thing taking any more time away from our *actual* research."

"Of course, Dr. Samson. I won't be but a moment." Shea pulled the closet door shut behind her and immediately dropped her polite facade. She hurriedly yanked the lab coat from her shoulders and kicked off her shoes as her colleague continued without her. His voice trailed in through the door as she wiggled out of her pants and peeled off her shirt, revealing a tight black skinsuit underneath.

"Subject Raven has successfully complied with rudimentary verbal instruction. Her performance in the last hour demonstrates success in the initial phases of Project Stronghold." Dr. Samson droned on as Shea snatched pieces of armor from the crate. "Subject Raven has operated outside of Project Stronghold supervision for over four cycles, yet still demonstrates prompt responsiveness to early-stage cuing."

Heart pounding, Shea frantically affixed each piece of armor against her body and clipped it into place with its corresponding parts. She silently counted the seconds as they passed and imagined a disgruntled Iris standing beside her with a timer in-hand. Her fingers fidgeted with the clips, and she cursed under her breath when one pinched her knuckle.

Dr. Samson continued. "These initial tests seem to indicate that early initiatives offer prolonged effectiveness with few diminishing effects. Dr. Tristan and I recommend moving ahead with future projects with a similar cognitive conditioning approach."

Completing the final latch, Shea straightened tall in the Valkyrie armor and flexed her shoulders. The armor felt nearly weightless against her body as she moved and twisted. She let out a sigh and plucked the helmet and pulse pistol from inside the crate. Sliding the helmet over her head, the illuminated HUD flickered to life inside her visor, displaying her vitals and shield integrity.

No going back now.

Shea's fingers fidgeted on the pistol's grip as she opened the closet door. Dr. Samson's attention remained fixed on Victoria, his back turned to her.

"Based on current observations, Subject Raven appears to be ready for continued cognitive response development," he stated flatly. "Previous iterations indicate this next phase may take upwards of five lunars, and will result in increased handler capacity to—"

Shea swung wide to crack the base of the pistol grip against his temple. He cried out and fumbled aside, clutching his skull with the palm of his hand. The wall caught him, and he crumpled to the floor. Grimacing through gritted teeth, he peered up to watch Shea aim the pistol between his eyes. She rocked from one boot to the other, her free hand flexing and unflexing in its glove.

"What—" Dr. Samson breathed through the pulsing ache in his head and winced. He squinted at Shea and sneered. "What the fuck do you think you're doing?!"

"Stopping you," Shea's voice trembled.

Dr. Samson let out a haggard breath. "*Stop* me? What are

you talking about? Stop what?"

"What you're doing here, what you have done to all these people, to *Victoria,* is wrong. You should be ashamed of yourself, Dr. Samson," Shea said. Her tone, despite its tremor, carried with it a simmering, bitter anger. "I'm ashamed that my mother enabled this in the first place, enabled *you.*"

"Ashamed?" Dr. Samson's cheeks reddened; his nostrils flared. "What your mother and I accomplished was a medical miracle! Do you know how many lives we've saved from this research? Do you know how many *more* will be saved?"

"At the expense of innocent lives!" Shea snapped. "You physically and psychologically tortured these people!"

Dr. Samson raised his palm to Shea, pleading. "They were criminals, Shea. Criminals and moral offenders. They didn't matter—"

"Of course they mattered, you son-of-a-bitch," Shea growled. "Each one of them mattered. *Victoria* matters!"

"Oh… so there it is, then," Dr. Samson's demeanor chilled. His eyes steadied and peered at Shea with poorly veiled disgust. "She got to you, didn't she? I should have known that Shadow would prey on you like the rats they are… to corrupt you, to *use* you. Those little fucks got into your head—pled their sad, pathetic soliloquies and poisoned you against us. Against your State, your family! You're a Statesman, for Patriarch's sake!"

"I gladly dropped that title a long time ago, Doctor."

Dr. Samson scoffed and shook his head, resigned. "Well, then. That's that, isn't it? What a remarkable disappointment you turned out to be, my dear."

"You couldn't pay me a better compliment."

"So, what're you going to do now? *Shoot* me?" He snarled and drew his fingers back from his temple. A touch of blood smeared across his fingertips.

"I haven't decided yet," Shea said. "I suppose it depends."

"On?"

Shea crouched to level her helmet with his face. Her eyes lay hidden behind the helmet's glossy screen, but Dr. Samson stared through her nonetheless with haughty resolve. The HUD overlay blinked inside her visor; his heart rate, blood pressure, and perspiration readings displayed beside his highlighted outline.

"On how you answer my questions. And don't lie, I'm monitoring your vitals." She adjusted and flexed her fingers around the pistol grip. "First question, yes or no: did the State purposefully tamper with Cyntrax knowing Shadow would smuggle it back to the Anchor?"

A knowing grin curled at Dr. Samson's lips. "Ah. Smart girl."

Shea slid her finger into the pistol's trigger well. "Answer the question."

"Was it intentional? Yes."

His answer struck her like a fist to the chest.

Shea spoke through gritted teeth. "Second question: what contagion was used?"

Dr. Samson's heart rate spiked. His jaw clenched, and sweat dampened his brow. "The Ink," he said and swallowed hard. "A modified, isolated strand of the Ink... strong enough to infect, but innocuous once exposed outside the body."

"Why?" Shea's voice was bitter.

"I don't dictate policy, do I?" Dr. Samson snapped. His

gaze darted from her pistol to the control console, his brow knit and tense. He looked back to Shea, his voice nearly pleading. "How am I supposed to know the State's top-level strategy? They asked if we could do it, and I said yes. It's my job."

"And how many more innocent people had to suffer and die for you to perfect that modified strain?"

Dr. Samson lifted his chin with steely arrogance. "I only did what the State asked. If you're looking for someone to blame, blame *them*. You can't possibly hold me accounta—"

"How many people have died because of you, Dr. Samson?" Shea calmly asked. "That's my final question: How many people have you killed?"

"I- I don't..." He stammered and tripped over his words. Shea observed his pounding heart rate and spiking blood pressure with passive indifference. A tense smile pulled across his lips as he wiped sweat from his cheek. "Dr. Tristan, please, just... put the gun down. Let me explain—"

Dr. Samson blathered on through pleading stutters. His words fell on deaf ears. Shea's attention turned inward as the world around her, and the bumbling man at her feet, seemed to almost fade away. She thought of the children lost to the modified Ink in the Anchor; she remembered every face, every name, and how their parents had wept. She thought of Lauren, and of the tiny baby boy lying lifeless in the crook of her pallid arm. She thought of Victoria now sitting in the testing chamber, awaiting further instruction from the madman who enslaved her again after cycles of freedom. Her mother's research logs circuited in her mind like a recurring nightmare: Victoria was seated again at the metal table, pistol in hand, blood trailed down her white tunic—Cosette sat limp and lifeless across from her. Shea saw all this from her mother's eyes, and she watched a single tear trail down Victoria's cheek as a conceited grin pulled across her research partner's lips.

Dr. Samson was still rambling and begging when Shea squeezed the trigger.

Chapter 51

"...Based on current observations, Subject Raven appears to be ready for continued cognitive response development. Previous iterations indicate this next phase may take upwards of five lunars, and will result in increased handler capacity to—"

Dr. Samson's booming voice cut out.

Victoria shivered in her chair and let out a feeble, trembling breath. She lazily blinked through heavy eyelids; her head lolled as she flexed her hands. The room, while flooded with white light, blurred in her vision when she tried to focus. She gritted her teeth.

It's quiet. Why is it quiet?

She clutched clumsily at her plastic muzzle and tugged. No voice boomed through the microphone telling her to stop this time. Her trembling fingers groped along the strap up her jaw until they touched her shorn hair, where she instantly froze and let out a muffled cry—only about three centimeters of hair remained. Fury burned like a furnace in her chest and skull. She breathed hard into the muzzle, brow furrowed and nostrils flaring, as she fumbled with its straps and locking mechanism. Her balance wavered the more she struggled.

Her strength failed her, and she let her hands drop like

heavy burdens onto her lap. She bowed her head, deflated, and let her shoulders sag. Exhaustion overcame her and tampered her simmering fury. She let out a breath and closed her aching eyes.

An abrupt, muted bang reached her through the observation screen across the room. She paid it no mind, and instead focused on the sound of her own heartbeat and breath. The clear plastic muzzle fogged with each breath, and her cracked, dry lips parted as drowsiness blanketed her. Her heavy skull swayed when she lifted it up and tilted against the back of her chair. She raised her empty gaze to the blank, white ceiling above her and stared.

Patriarch...

Victoria swallowed, throat dry and sore, and blinked through brimming tears. Silence enveloped her.

Or, whatever you're called. If you even exist at all, and are not just another creation of theirs. I haven't prayed to you since Cosette's death. There's not been a point to pray, has there? You either exist and ignore prayers, turn a blind eye to suffering... or you don't exist, and this doesn't matter anyway. But if you do exist, and if you only listen to a single prayer of mine, just, please...

A tear rolled from Victoria's eye as she closed her eyes. Her voice cracked and hitched in her throat.

"... let me die."

An alarm blared inside the chamber. Victoria didn't startle, and calmly peeled open her aching eyes and strained to lift her head. The bright white light inside the room was now a flashing pulse of blinding crimson and darkness. She shifted in the chair, leaning forward to rest her elbows unsteadily onto her knees. The pounding siren ricocheted inside her brain and left her grimacing into her muzzle.

A figure moved toward her from the opened chamber door, disappearing and reappearing closer with each red pulse of light. Victoria squinted through her blurred vision until the dark figure stepped once more into the red light and became clear: a Valkyrie, in fitted matte black armor and helmet. The Valkyrie carried a pulse pistol in her right hand, and a key-fob in the other.

"Subject Raven, remain still."

Victoria nearly laughed, and the sound that escaped her throat was guttural and desperate.

You wasted no time answering that *prayer, did you Patriarch?*

The Valkyrie stepped past a rigid Victoria and pressed the key-fob to the muzzle's locking mechanism. It released with a loud click, and the muzzle straps dangled for a moment before the device fell from Victoria's face. The Valkyrie knocked it aside to the floor and crouched down at her bare feet. Then the Valkyrie reached up, clasped hold of either side of its helmet, and peeled it from its head.

Victoria's heart seized behind her ribs. Shea gazed back at her, tears swimming in her eyes, and smiled. Without a word, Shea leaned in to press a kiss against her lips. Victoria tasted the salt from the woman's tears, and willed herself to move, to throw her arms around Shea's shoulders and hold her. But she still sat immobilized, not yet released from her last command.

Shea pulled away and raised a gloved hand to graze her fingertips across Victoria's temple. Her gaze lingered on Victoria's face through the pulsating red light, scanning every centimeter and detail as she cupped Victoria's jaw in her palm like she was fragile enough to disintegrate.

She brushed the side of her thumb against Victoria's cheek, wiping away a fallen tear.

Shea's voice reached her through the blaring siren. "Don't forget me, okay?"

Panic struck Victoria just as Shea pressed her palm against her throat. A needle pierced her skin, and within seconds there was nothing.

***

Iris froze in the hallway with her grip tight around Mama Wilder's bound wrists. The same alarm siren pierced the previously quiet hall. Flashes of red blinked in and out of their vision; the crimson of Iris's Valkyrie armor nearly darkened to black with each iteration.

"Shit," the old woman uttered under her breath. She glanced over her shoulder to Iris, who was 'escorting' her after their cordial interrogation. "That can't be good."

Iris's eyes hardened behind her helmet. "No, it is not."

"We gotta keep moving," Mama Wilder whispered. Her voice was stern, nearly desperate. "Simon will be here soon. Whatever the hell's going on, we can't let it slow us down—"

Iris's helmet comms-unit crackled to life in her ear. The old woman kept speaking, and Iris raised a hand to silence her.

"Quiet," Iris snapped, and turned her head away to listen. Mama Wilder's lips downturned to sneer.

"… Shots fired! I repeat, shots fired. Alert all security personnel on this channel!" The voice belonged to a frantic young man, and Iris could hear him straining to speak through his weeping. "Oh god, he's dead… Dr. Samson is dead! Someone please, help!"

Iris's heart dropped like a stone in her gut.

"She killed him. She wasn't supposed to kill him."

Mama Wilder fixed her gaze on Iris. "Who killed who?"

"Shea. She killed Dr. Samson, the doctor holding Victoria." Iris shook her head. "She was supposed to knock him out—drug him, not fucking *kill* him. So much for keeping a low profile—God, what the hell was she thinking?"

Mama Wilder took a quick moment to look around them, ensuring no one was watching, and leaned closer to Iris's helmet. "I say good for her and good fucking riddance. But I'd also say this is a good time for us to hurry the hell up and meet her before she's got another chance to be reckless. Our children are relying on us keeping our shit together, understood?"

Iris took a steadying breath and nodded. She unfastened her pulse pistol from her hip holster and flexed her fingers around the grip. "Let's go. Be ready for a fight."

Mama Wilder scoffed. "I'm always ready for a fight. *You* just be ready to take these cuffs off when it comes to that."

***

Simon stirred. His head and heavy eyelids ached; his lower back and shoulders throbbed. He groaned and rolled to his side; lumpy cushions reeking of old musk and dust shifted beneath his weight.

"Mornin', sunshine." *Julep.*

Simon jerked up, fully awake. His joints and muscles screamed as he scrambled up on hands and knees atop the dilapidated sofa. Julep watched him with obsidian eyes, and muted amusement, from a stool across the room. He looked around the room: low-hanging ceiling, cheap carpeted floor, makeshift bar in the corner illuminated by the dull yellow glow of a single bulb. The scent of stale brew and dust lingered in the air.

"Where am I?" Simon asked. His voice cracked, and he winced at the dryness in his mouth and throat. "Where's my father?"

Julep cocked her head. "A Trinity safehouse. And daddy-dearest is safe, taking a bit of a nap. No need to worry." She watched him for a few more moments in silence. Her voice was heated and terse when she spoke again. "I'm sure you have questions—I know *I* sure as shit would if I were you. So, let me just summarize it for you, to save you the trouble: those State bastards raided us both, damn near everyone is dead, and everything is fucked."

Simon stared at her, bewildered. "My father told me about Shadow, but…" He faltered and eased down, deflated, onto the sofa. "Rubio?"

"Dead," Julep stated flatly. She nearly laughed, silenced only after biting her bottom lip, and blinked hard. Scarlet irises flashed against her black eyes before vanishing. "Wasted no time in hangin' him from the Mourning Tower, too. I bet they were proud of that—showin' him off like that in his own goddamn borough."

"I'm sorry, Julep. Truly, I am," Simon said. "Our history aside, your uncle deserved better than the tower."

Julep chuckled. "Yeah, well." She flexed her jaw and smiled bitterly. "I'm gonna make the State regret leaving *this* Trinity alive; leaving *us* alive Simon."

"Is that why you came for me?" Simon asked. "To join you in righteous retribution?"

"Absolutely." A mischievous grin crossed her lips. "Your body was nowhere to be found—I found it odd and asked around. One nosy old woman admitted to seeing you and the girl carried away by two men, one identified as your estranged father. Anyway"—she waved a dismissive hand—"I'm not a body language expert, but being carried unconscious doesn't exactly imply consent. Findin' his address after that was remarkably easy. And, well, the rest is history, ain't it?"

"That still doesn't explain why you came after me," Simon said.

Julep's grin wavered. She strained to hold it in place as she cocked her head to the other side. "We're all that's left, Simon. The State—they've taken *everything* from us, even our rivalry. The Trinities, Shadow… they've purged us. Our friends, our *families*, are dead at their hand. After what's happened, don't you think we're owed justice?"

Simon stared at her, brow furrowed. "What happened, Julep?"

Julep stood from the stool and moved to the makeshift bar. She plucked a bottle of brew from a mini-fridge and popped the top. She dropped her gaze to the floor, refusing to meet Simon's.

"I thought the meeting was a bad idea—I especially didn't want him going alone, without me. I made my case against it, things may have gotten a bit heated between us, and I stormed off. We didn't even say goodbye. I was too fucking stubborn." Julep grew still and bit her lip. Her knuckles whitened, gripping the bottle.

"I'm sorry," Simon spoke in little more than a whisper. His mind turned to that last morning with his mother, when she'd hugged him for what may have been the last time. He clenched his jaw and forced back the tears brimming in his eyes.

Julep cleared her throat. "It's fine. I left our headquarters shortly after he did—I couldn't stand still. Too anxious. I was out with a couple of my guys, runnin' some routine checks and patrols when it happened…" She took a swig from the bottle and strode across the room to hand it to Simon, who took it and took a gracious mouthful of brew. "I was halfway across the borough when I heard gunfire. The Middle was just… chaos. People were freakin' out, screamin'. We were the only ones runnin' toward the fight—everyone was dead by the time we got there."

Simon said nothing, and instead continued drinking the bitter brew. Julep took her seat at the stool again and stifled a laugh.

"And you know what's funny? I thought it was *you guys*, retaliatin' against us for that shit we pulled tryin' to abduct that stupid doctor. You can imagine my surprise when I found everyone dead at your headquarters, too. Well, *mostly* everyone."

"Hey, Julep! How do I change the channel on this fuckin' thing?" a familiar voice called out from a distance behind the closed door. After a beat, Simon propelled himself from the sofa and hurried out the door.

"God, don't encourage him!" Julep called after him.

Simon ran up a narrow set of stairs and emerged into a dimly lit sitting room. Two long sofas and some cushioned chairs sat across from a cracked display wall portraying the State's official broadcasting channel. The well-dressed woman on-screen was in mid-explanation of an Apex import surge when Simon heard a gasp from across the room.

"Simon!" Theresa launched herself from one of the

cushioned chairs. She crashed into him and threw her arms around his chest.

Simon let out a breath of air as she squeezed him. "Good to see you too, T."

"No, sure, it's fine!" a throaty, weary voice called out from the sofa. "Be more excited to see *him* over your own bro! What do I care?"

"Holy shit—Tony?" Simon pried himself from Theresa's embrace and moved toward the sofa.

The light from the display wall flickered and illuminated Tony's frame, his chest and abdomen bound in bandages, lying across the cushions. Sweat coated his pale skin, and dark circles framed his bloodshot eyes.

"You look like shit, man," Simon said, and knelt at Tony's side. "You alright?"

"I mean, I'm alive, if that counts."

"He's lucky," Theresa said before plopping down by her brother's feet. She slapped his shin. "Julep found him just in time, ain't that right?"

Tony sneered. "I saved myself, thank you."

Simon turned a curious eye to Theresa, brow furrowed. He mouthed, *How?* to her when Tony closed his eyes to shift against the cushion. Theresa rolled her eyes, indignant, and mouthed back, *Just go with it.*

"Tony, what happened in the church?" Simon asked.

Tony's demeanor shifted in the light of the news broadcast. His forehead creased as he seemed to sink deeper into the sofa.

"Valkyries," he nearly whispered. "They sent Valkyries."

Simon stilled and stared at him. "You can't be serious. You're sure they were *Valkyries?*"

"Of course I'm fuckin' sure! I saw 'em with my own eyes!" Tony snapped in a flurry of rage. Theresa gently shushed him and massaged the length of his shin until he settled back again. His voice quieted as he spoke. "I was with the doc in the kitchen when it all went down. They threw concussive grenades, riot gas… I panicked; I didn't know what to do. I just knew I needed to find Theresa, and get the doc out while I could. But when I went downstairs to find y'all—" Theresa offered a reassuring squeeze on his ankle. He faltered for a moment before continuing. "They found us in the training room. I took one down, but they caught me in the gut and left me for dead."

"What happened to Shea?" Simon asked.

"They took her," Tony said. He let out a cough and winced, then closed his eyes and hissed through clenched teeth. His palm slid over his bandaged wound. "She tried helpin' me… she ran over after I was shot, but they grabbed her and left. I barely had enough in me to drag myself to her office—tried to stop the bleedin' best I could. Eventually passed out, then woke up here."

"Shit." Simon ran his fingers across his scalp. "I'm glad you made it out in one piece, Tony."

"I'm not so sure I did," Tony scoffed, and closed his bloodshot eyes. "Now, would you mind leavin' me alone so I can get some fuckin' sleep?"

Simon moved away from Tony's side and watched him for a few moments, frowning. His thoughts turned to his mother, and his heart sank like a stone in his chest. He closed and rubbed his eyes with the heels of his palms.

"So," Julep poked the tip of her finger against Simon's temple. A mischievous grin curled at her lips. "Now that you're awake and all caught up—why don't we have a talk with dear ol' dad?"

Chapter 52

I wasn't supposed to kill him. Iris told me to just knock him out, take his badge...

The piercing siren blared and red alert lights pulsed as Shea pulled the clumsily awkward load behind her.

It doesn't matter anymore. Just get her to the service elevator. Just get her to Iris!

She took a split second to glance back over her shoulder, to make sure that Victoria was still securely strapped to the grav-litter. Victoria appeared asleep, with thick straps binding her ankles, legs, waist, and shoulders to the metal plate beneath her. Half-orbs affixed underneath the litter emitted a low hum and vibrated the air around it, supposedly replicating localized zero-gravity. All Shea knew was that the litter was difficult to control, and often swayed inelegantly with each tug from her arm.

POP.

A pulse round struck the back of Shea's nano-shield. The round deflected and send shock waves through her spine and rib cage. She stifled a scream, stumbled forward a few steps, and frantically groped for the riot gas grenade fastened to her belt.

"Turn around!" a voice barked from far behind her. "Put

your hands on your head!"

Shea turned her attention toward the voice and found five peace officers, weapons drawn and at the ready, down the hall from where she came. Her own breath inside the helmet and heartbeat drumming in her ears drowned out the sirens and advancing officers. She activated the infrared HUD across her visor, turning her vision onto a sea of darkness pocked with shifting masses of heat and color.

POP.

Another round struck her shoulder's nano-shield. She winced and hissed through clenched teeth before unclipping the grenade from her belt and yanking out the pin. Smoke billowed from the canister as she hurled it down the hall. The vivid humanoid masses of color recoiled, buckled to the floor covering their mouths and eyes. Shea could barely hear their haggard gasping as she grabbed hold of the grav-litter and sprinted in the opposite direction. Her visor HUD reverted back to standard view.

Shea rounded the corner and caught sight of the service elevator at the end of the corridor. She breathed a sigh of relief, allowing herself a brief moment's reprieve, and pressed forward through the sirens and flashing lights. The grav-litter bobbled from side-to-side with each stride and bumped against the walls, dipped down toward the floor and up again as if riding an invisible wave. The localized gravity simulators groaned beneath Victoria's weight. Each awkward sway of the litter pulled her off-balance and left her stumbling.

"Stupid prototype," she growled as her momentum was again disrupted by the litter's sway.

Voices called out from behind her when she reached the

service elevator. She didn't dare look back, and instead pulled Dr. Samson's access badge from a storage compartment on her thigh's armor before slapping it against the control panel. Bright green holo-keys illuminated on the panel.

POP POP POP.

Pulse rounds struck the elevator frame, wall, and floor around her. Shea pressed the glowing summon key on the control panel and braced as another volley of rounds cracked around her. Fear gripped her, seeped into her rattled nerves like poison.

"Come on!" She slammed the key again with her fist. "Hurry up!"

A round hit her square in the thigh, and two others connected with her lower back and shoulder. Her nano-shields protected her from the penetrating rounds, but the shock still clattered her bones and sent ripples of lightning pain coursing through her limbs. The grav-litter tugged against her grip, and when Shea turned to look, she noticed a splatter of blood against Victoria's white tunic. Open, seeping wounds marking Victoria's torso and neck bled onto the litter beneath her.

"No!" Shea's fear slipped away as she snatched her pistol at her side. Rage consumed her, boiled over her thoughts as she raised the weapon and blindly returned fire. She drew Victoria back, positioning the woman in between herself and the elevator doors. In the next moment, she'd unclipped and lobbed another riot-gas canister down the hall. Thick, acrid smoke blanketed the peace officers down the corridor and left them gasping for air; some still managed to train their fire on her.

Pulse rounds cracked against her abdomen, hip, and knee as she continued firing. She gritted her teeth, subdued the scream crawling up her throat, and fell to one knee. An alert flashed across her visor notifying her of her armor's rapidly depleting nano-shields. She glanced back to see the elevator doors still closed.

"Shit." Shea braced herself against the grav-litter after another hit to the gut.

There was a moment of silence as the peace officer ceased fire. Shea hesitated, her pistol still raised and trembling in her hand. A sudden deafening clamor ricocheted down the corridor as a bludgeoning force slammed into her shoulder. Shea's pistol slipped from her weakening fingers and fell with a clatter to her feet. She strained to breathe and dropped her other knee to the floor. A throbbing agony reached across her chest, gripped her lungs like a strangling fist. It took all her strength to not buckle forward and succumb to the pain.

Shea reached with trembling fingers to gingerly touch the stinging wound at the narrow space between her pieces of armor. A notification flashed inside her helmet visor HUD, warning her of traumatic bodily harm, and to seek immediate medical aid. Instead, Shea weakly reached with her uninjured arm to collect the fallen pistol. She leaned back on her heels, swayed, and inelegantly raised the pistol down the hall.

A Valkyrie, clad in dark armor, emerged from the thick cloud of acrid smoke and stood motionless in the pulsing red lights of the corridor. She yanked back the hammer of her specialized sniper rifle, recharging the weapon, and leveled it against her shoulder. Shea watched the Valkyrie slide her finger into the sniper rifle's trigger well. She fired her pistol one final time.

***

A canister grenade clattered along the tile at the Valkyrie's feet before an explosion of blinding white light ripped across the corridor. Shea cried out and shielded her eyes as Iris snatched the back of her armor to drag her back into the service elevator. Harriet strained to navigate the lumbering grav-litter inside before the doors slid shut. The elevator shivered, registered its destination, and descended.

An electric silence clung to the air before Iris removed her helmet and turned on Shea. She shoved her against the wall with a sneer.

"What the fuck were you thinking?" Iris wrested Shea's helmet from her head and glared at her pallid, sweat-slick face. "You *killed* Samson. What the hell is wrong with you? What part of 'quietly subdue' did you not comprehend? Now every peace officer and Valkyrie in the sector will be gunning for us!"

"Maybe should'a pushed your girl here instead of pulling," Mama Wilder said as she bent forward to examine Victoria's closing wounds. "She's fine, of course. Doubt she even felt anything."

Iris's lips curled in a snarl. "What a fucking mess."

Shea winced, closing her eyes. "I—" She strained to breathe, grimaced, and sagged her shoulder. "I'm not good at this sorta thing."

"Clearly! I can't imagine how much worse this would've been if I hadn't given you that armor—most likely killed before even reaching the damn elevator." Iris moved closer and peered at Shea's sagging shoulder. Her brow creased.

"My nano-shields were still up. Twenty percent left, I think." Shea breathed and rested her head back against the wall. "She still got me."

"Shield-piercing rounds," Iris stated flatly and unfastened a storage pack on Shea's hip. She fished out a tube of sealant paste. "Valkyrie-issued, very expensive. Looks like they wanted to capture you alive. Can't imagine why."

Shea grit her teeth when Iris pressed the tip to her wound and squeezed; she made no attempt to be gentle. "What makes you say that?"

Iris spread the paste with the tip of her finger and turned Shea around to repeat the process on the exit-wound. Shea pressed her damp forehead against the cool metallic wall and strained to steady her breath.

"She could've easily shot you in the head. But she knows Valkyrie armor—its weaknesses and vulnerable spots. And she caught you in a good one. I'm sure they had prepared plenty of questions for you before your execution."

"Well, it's a good thing you showed up when you did, then," Shea said through feigned gratitude. Iris turned her back around with a roll of her eyes.

"We aren't finished." Iris handed Shea her helmet. "Patch yourself up. I recommend a shot of morphine—don't worry about antibiotics, you won't be needing them after they catch up with us."

Shea said nothing further and moved across the elevator to stand at Victoria's side. Iris watched Shea press the palm of her hand against her neck and hold her breath. A second later she winced and exhaled.

"Well that's convenient," Harriet remarked, eyebrow cocked.

"Yes, it is." Shea rested her hand on Victoria's bare ankle and leaned against the back wall. Shea extended her hand with a weak smile. "You want a hit before this all goes down?"

Mama Wilder snickered and appeared to consider the offer.

"We'll be arriving at the pod deck soon," Iris said as she watched the numbers cascade up the elevator's display monitor. "Get ready to move."

***

They arrived to a silent and vacant pod deck. The elevator doors opened into a seemingly endless dark corridor that smelled of stale dust and poorly recycled air. Not even the wailing alarm sirens could be heard through the thirty levels of reinforced fiberglass and steel. Slender windows along the ceiling spanned the length of the deck, revealing the unsettling emptiness of space within arm's reach. Escape pod chambers lined the wall, accessible only by their accompanying security panels. Each panel glowed red and created a strangely beautiful string of lights down the otherwise black passageway.

Iris hurriedly stepped out onto the landing. "Let's go. We don't have much time."

Shea and Mama Wilder followed closely behind, pulling Victoria along between them. Track-lights flickered to life above one-by-one as they moved, manifesting a moving train of illumination that followed them down the corridor.

"We shouldn't be the first ones here, Iris," Mama Wilder said. She coughed, cleared her throat, and spat a wad of blood to the floor. Her lips stained red as she continued, her voice becoming increasingly strained. "My boys should'a triggered these lights, not us."

Iris said nothing in return and instead focused on examining each secured pod chamber they passed. She recognized the names of Odin Prime's most prominent and powerful Statesmen as she rushed past them, disregarding each name that wasn't a *Tristan*. Her heart pounded like a drum in her chest, her eyes desperately scanning one name after the next. A sinking dread settled in her gut when she heard the sound of the service elevator doors shut far behind them; it rattled before ascending to whomever had summoned it.

Shea, having also heard the elevator, glanced back with a frown. "Iris—"

"Found it!" Iris called out and snatched the pistol from her side. She gestured to the chamber beside her and redirected her attention back toward the far end of the corridor. "Shea, get your ass over here and open it. We gotta hurry."

Mama Wilder swiveled her head around, squinting down the passageway and back again. "Where the hell are they?"

"Maybe they're the ones who called the elevator," Shea said as she hurried to Iris's side. She faltered when she read the name etched across the chamber's ownership nameplate: *Shea Tristan (Dedicated on Behalf of Chancellor Tristan, In Loving Memory of Lilly Tristan).*

Iris charged her pistol. "Let's hope that's the case. And for fuck's sake, hurry it up!"

Shea rushed to pry open the security panel's protective cover. She struggled with the fastening latch for a few moments until it finally gave way and slid open with ease.

"I'm going to assume this works like every other secured room in the Dome," Shea said as she grimaced and rotated her shoulder. "I don't exactly have a great track record with these."

Harriet inelegantly drew the grav-litter closer to the chamber door and wiped a bead of sweat from her brow. Her breath was beginning to catch in her lungs with each inhale. "Well, let's hope it works or this'll have all been for nothin'."

Shea squatted to level herself with the panel and cleared her throat. She spoke loud and clear: "Shea. Tristan."

A beat of silence and stillness—the red indicator flipped to green. The heavy locking mechanism inside the chamber door released with an audible click that resonated down the corridor. Shea breathed a sigh of relief and waved a hand over the panel to trigger the door to open. It slid back to reveal a narrow space beside the open pod, and a single light sputtered to life on the ceiling.

"Good, good." Iris turned back and hurried into the chamber. "Harriet, keep an eye on that elevator while I help secure Victoria."

"I don't like this, Iris," Harriet said with a shake of her head. She crossed her arms, peered back toward the elevator, and rocked from one foot to the other. "My boys should fuckin' be here by now. Something's not right, I can feel it. Something went wrong."

"Just keep an eye out!" Iris barked back. "Shea, follow me."

She hoisted Victoria from the grav-litter and carried her into the pod chamber. The grey and black vehicle was akin to an upright egg, with a rear entrance hatch that opened above two sizable engine nozzles. A bulbous front-window peered down through an open chute that launched the pod, and its two occupants, into the freezing vacuum of space.

Shea entered the pod behind Iris, ducking a bit to step inside the central compartment.

"What do we do if Simon doesn't show?"

"That's not a priority of mine right now." Iris gently lowered Victoria onto one of the bucket seats inside the compartment. She removed her helmet and reached into a storage pouch on her thigh to withdraw a sealed, folded envelope.

Shea glared at her in disbelief. "What the hell do you mean? Of *course* it's a priority. The whole point of this operation was to get *both* of them off the station, not just Victoria."

Iris ignored Shea and tucked the envelope beneath Victoria's leg, pinning it snug against the seat. She hesitated for a moment, hand resting on Victoria's knee, and looked into her daughter's slumbering face. There were no more words to say, nothing more to do but to let go. Iris reached out to touch Victoria's cheek and leaned in to press a kiss on her forehead. She lingered there, hearing nothing but the rhythm of her own heartbeat in her ears, and let out a haggard breath.

"Be good, baby girl," Iris whispered, and broke away without looking back. Her face hardened, jaw set, when she met Shea's gaze. "Make sure she's secure for launch. I'm getting the pod ready. If Jefferson finally decides to arrive with his son, then all the better. But I won't let their absence deter this mission."

"Good luck telling Harriet that," Shea said as she moved to Victoria's side. "There's no way she's going to let this pod launch without Simon strapped in that spare seat. She'd sooner kill you than let that happen."

"She's welcome to try," Iris said. She took a moment to regard the empty bucket seat across from Victoria and found herself drawn to it. An idea struck her: an empty seat on her daughter's escape pod, on a path to new beginnings and real, genuine hope for a better life. That spare seat represented an opportunity to make things right, to make up for lost time with her daughter. There was still hope for her, and that spare seat was her way out. A smile tugged at her lips.

Shea's shuffling pulled her from her reverie, and the smile fell from her face. Iris watched Shea in the corner of her vision; the girl cradled Victoria's jaw in her hand and gingerly tugged at the seat's restraints to ensure its integrity. She leaned forward and pressed a kiss on Victoria's cheek, then stood and wiped moisture from her eye.

"Iris!" Mama Wilder shouted from the corridor. "The elevator. I think they're here."

Iris and Shea exchanged glances and dashed out of the pod. They reached Mama Wilder's side and peered down the passageway.

"Is it Simon?" Shea asked as she watched Iris slip her helmet back over her head and clumsily followed suit.

Mama Wilder let out a shaken sigh. "It'd better fuckin' be."

The three women watched the distant end of the corridor as the elevator shuddered to a stop. The doors parted and smile immediately dropped.

Chapter 53

Simon peered down at his father's bruised, weary face. The blast that morning had left abrasions across his cheek and forehead, and his puffed left eye squinted back from the dim closet floor.

"Your plan didn't pan out too well, did it?" Simon said.

"Indeed. I hope you're quite proud of yourselves," Jefferson said. He rotated his shoulders and spine against bound wrists. He closed his eyes and rested his head on the wall behind him.

"I am, actually," Julep pleasantly quipped over Simon's shoulder.

Jefferson coughed and winced. "And what is it, exactly, that you hope to do next?"

"I'm glad you asked." Simon squatted to the floor to level with him. "Shadow is gone, sure. But *we're* still here. And if the State has Mama, then we're going to get her out."

Jefferson strained to stifle his laughter but failed. It tumbled out between his lips as he shook his head.

"*Then* what?" he asked.

Simon's brow creased as he shifted on his feet. "We carry on where we left off—return to the Anchor and rebuild Shadow." Julep cleared her throat, and Simon turned his ear toward her. "And help get the Trinities back up and running. With realigned partnership, of course."

"I see. I guess you have it all figured out, then." Jefferson hesitated a moment before continuing. "And your mama?"

"We get her out."

"How?"

Simon stammered, "I… we haven't figured it out yet, but—"

"Don't bother," Jefferson stated flatly. "It's already over. It's too late."

Simon stared at him, bewildered.

"What do you mean? Why is it too late?" When his father said nothing, Simon pressed on with anger lacing his voice. "What the hell aren't you telling me, Dad?"

Jefferson let out a resigned groan.

"There are a few things you need to know first, Simon." He turned his gaze to his son. "You aren't going to like what you hear."

"I don't care—tell me," Simon said.

Jefferson took a shaky breath and exhaled. He closed his eyes.

"Your mama was the one who sold Shadow out in the first place. She's been working with Chief Hammond for cycles now, ever since you rescued her daughter from that lab. Your mama…. she's sick—*real* sick. Didn't have much time left anyhow, and knew it. She didn't want you taking over for her, she wanted better for you—we *both* did. Hammond approached Harriet with a proposition… to get you off Odin Prime entirely, to ensure your safety, as well as her daughter's—at the cost of Shadow. Your mama accepted."

"You're lying." Simon's voice was cold and bitter. His eyes swam with tears. "You're fuckin' lying. Ma would *never* agree to that—*ever!* Shadow was her people—she wouldn't betray their loyalty like that, she wouldn't!"

"To save you? Absolutely, she would. And she did. She would burn down this entire station if it meant you were safe."

Simon rose to his feet and turned his back to his father, fists clenched tight and knuckles paling.

"This operation was all or nothing, Simon. Your mama knew what she was doing—we all did. You were our primary goal—you and Victoria. Nothing else mattered... *we* didn't matter."

Simon faced his father again with tears trailing down his cheeks. "What are you saying?"

Jefferson faltered and wiped away tears brimming in his eyes. "I'm saying... that it's already too late. I was supposed to bring you to the ministry building, where I'd meet with Hammond and your mama in the escape pod deck. They might be able to get Victoria out, but—" He paused and dropped his gaze to the floor. "We had no expectation of surviving the mission, Simon. Even if we managed to reach the deck without drawing attention, the State would detect a launch initiation and would've sent security forces after us."

"Maybe she escaped with the pod," Simon said, his voice quieting. "Or found another way out."

"Simon." Jefferson shook his head. "She's likely already dead—you have to accept that."

"No!" Simon lunged forward and snatched Jefferson's collar. He hauled his father up from the floor and slammed him hard against the closet wall. "I'm not accepting shit!"

"I'm so sorry." Jefferson's voice choked against Simon's

pressing grip. "It wasn't supposed to end like this."

"She's alive, goddamnit," Simon growled, and pressed harder against his father's throat. "And so is Shadow. They can't fucking get rid of us that easily, you understand me?"

Simon released Jefferson and let him drop to the floor. Jefferson crouched low on his knees and coughed, gasped for air, as Simon stomped out of the room without saying another word.

***

A cluster of peace officers spilled from the service elevator at the end of the corridor. There were seven of them, readily armed with pulse rifles and shotguns. One spoke into a comms-unit affixed to his shoulder and signaled for the elevator to ascend again.

"Those aren't my boys." Mama Wilder casually stepped behind Shea's armored frame. "The fuck do we do now?"

Shea's heart lurched up her throat when the first shot fired and connected with Iris's nano-shield. Iris staggered back with a grunt. Mama Wilder snatched the pulse pistol from Shea's hip and shunted her into the pod chamber beside them. Iris and Mama Wilder mercilessly returned fire as officers ducked and hugged the walls for cover. Iris unclipped a riot gas grenade from her belt, primed it, and hurled it down the passageway, where it exploded in a thick, blanketing cloud of acrid smoke. Both women darted inside the open chamber.

Iris braced her shoulder against the door frame. She pivoted to fire three successive shots down the corridor before pulling back inside.

"We have to launch! Now!"

"No!" Mama Wilder barked. She stepped out and fired two

shots before slipping back. "We aren't launching without my son."

Iris fired three more rounds into the cloud of smoke and turned to face the old woman.

"Simon isn't here. What else can we do? Hold out until whenever the fuck they decide to show up?"

"We had an agreement, goddammit!"

"Bullshit—we both agreed to put our own children first if shit ever went sideways. You and I both know that!"

Shea heard the officers coughing and gasping for air down the corridor. They drew nearer, albeit slowly. She loitered near the pod's rear hatch, immobilized, and watched the two women with an increasingly potent sense of dread and panic.

How could everything unravel so mind numbingly fast?

Iris primed a pulse grenade and tossed it down the passageway, where it disappeared within the billowing swirl of smoke. A peace officer cried out just as the grenade detonated; the corridor trembled and Harriet buckled forward, covering her ears. A piercing silence followed. Mama Wilder recovered, her balance wavering, and aimed the pistol at Iris's helmet.

"Fuck you, Iris. The pod stays."

"You would do the same if it were Simon in that chair instead of my daughter," Iris said, ignoring the pistol trained unsteadily at her face. "Harriet, that group of officers was just a scouting team. They sent the elevator back—they know we're here. And the next group to storm out those elevator doors won't be officers. It'll be Valkyries."

"I'm not leaving my son!"

"I'm not asking you to." She dipped her fingers inside a

storage pouch on her belt and extracted a small key-fob. "Take this and find your son—it'll unlock the utility vent at the other end of this deck. It'll be a tight fit, but it'll lead you outside this facility. Where you decide to go, or how you'll get there, is up to you."

"Where the hell'd you get that?" Shea asked, baffled.

Iris shrugged. "You'd be surprised what you can get when you're in a position of authority and ask the right people. It was my contingency plan."

Mama Wilder narrowed her gaze. "Why should I trust you?"

"Would you rather you die here and never see your son again?" Iris asked, and gestured with the fob. "Take it and get out. Leave the pistol—it'll make you look even more suspicious than you already are."

The two women held each other's gaze for a beat before Mama Wilder snatched the fob from Iris's palm. She tossed the pistol back to Shea, who shrieked and fumbled to catch it.

"Should I go with her?" Shea asked after composing herself. "I might be able to help get Simon out if—"

"No. I can't launch the pod on my own with Valkyries breathing down our necks," Iris said. She and Mama Wilder watched one another for a few moments, silent and immobile, until the old woman extended an open hand.

"You're still a cunt."

"Likewise." Iris took her hand and squeezed. "Go find your boy."

Mama Wilder glanced at Shea with a grin. "It's been a hell of a ride, Doctor. Give em' hell for me."

"Only if you give Simon my regards," Shea said through

a diluted smile. Tears swam in her eyes and blurred her vision. She felt Iris watching her, but paid her no mind. "And Theresa, if you find her."

Mama Wilder said nothing more as she met Iris's eyes one final time and disappeared around the doorway. Shea and Iris could hear her hurried footfalls grow faint in the distance.

Tears trailed down Shea's flushed cheeks. Her chest constricted like a vice around her pounding heart, and her nerves prickled with erratic electricity. Everything they had planned and prepared for, all of their effort and strife had led them here: they had reached the end. There was nowhere left to go, nothing left to do but initiate the launch and wait for the end. Shea had expected herself to be crippled with fear knowing what was to come. Instead, she found a strange resoluteness to her thoughts. Fear rattled her body, but her mind remained steady and prepared. Shea exhaled, and her warm tears sank away.

"What do you need me to do, Iris?"

Iris stared at the escape pod. Shea approached and rested a hand on her shoulder.

"Iris," she repeated louder. "What do you need me to do? The Valkyries will be here any minute."

Seconds passed in silence before the woman spoke again. She refused to meet Shea's eyes.

"You're nothing like your mother, are you? You turned out to be much better in the end." Her tone was distant, almost curious.

Shea blinked, bewildered. "I... don't quite know how to respond to that, if I'm being honest." She waited for Iris to explain, and continued when met with only silence. "Iris, I need you to tell me what to do right now, okay?"

"Right." Iris broke away from the daze that consumed her and gestured toward the corridor. There was a stern finality to her voice when she spoke. "Stand guard by the door and don't take your eyes off that elevator. You start shooting as soon as those doors open. There's one last thing I have to do. Do you understand?"

"I do," Shea said, and moved back to the open doorway. "Just hurry it up—we don't have much time left."

Iris vanished inside the escape pod. Shea posted at the door, shoulder pad pressed against the frame and pistol trained down the corridor. Bodies of peace officers lay scattered along the hall as the last of the riot gas dissipated in a lingering haze. Her eyes ached from crying and straining to focus on the elevator doors. Knots twisted deep inside her gut, and her palms dampened with sweat inside her gloves.

Nearly a minute passed before Shea heard the shuddering elevator descend to their deck and come to a halt behind the doors. Her heart nearly stopped.

"Iris!" Shea called out. "Iris, they're here! I need you back—"

A hand snatched the back of Shea's armor and pulled; she lost balance and tumbled backward to fall hard to the floor. The chamber doors slid shut, locking her inside. Shea scrambled to her feet and rushed to the door. She peered out the narrow window and went cold.

"No! What are you doing?"

Iris stood barefoot and armor-less in the corridor, clad only in leggings and an undershirt, typing onto the security panel with one hand and clutching her pistol with the other. A stoic, hardened expression etched across her face.

"You have thirty seconds to get inside the pod. I would hurry, if I were you," Iris's voice came through the panel as static inside the chamber.

"Why?" Shea cried and slammed her fists against the door. "Come with us!"

Iris's face remained calm despite the tears welling in her eyes. *"Someone has to stay to hold them off while you launch."* A tear rolled down her cheek. She lifted her gaze to meet Shea's eyes one final time. *"Look after my daughter, Shea."*

Red warning lights flashed inside the chamber. Shea broke away from the door and sprinted inside the escape pod. The rear hatch beeped and gradually shut behind her as she threw herself into the spare seat and frantically grasped at the harness buckles. The rear engines roared to life and rattled the vehicle.

***

The elevator doors parted. Three Valkyries swiftly emerged with their pulse rifles raised. Iris stood, spine erect and chin high, in the center of the passageway.

She blinked and could think of nothing but the morning of Victoria's birth. Her husband Daniel had pressed a kiss against her dampened hair and caressed her shoulder in an embrace she never wanted to end. Victoria, nothing but a warm bundle in her arms, wiggled against her and filled Iris' heart with more love than she could ever imagine possible. She clutched onto that memory as she gripped tighter onto her pistol.

"A proper Valkyrie's death, and my baby is safe," Iris muttered to herself. She let out a deep breath and found that her tears had dried; her fear had melted away. A satisfied grin crossed her lips. "Good enough for me."

511

Iris raised her pistol and fired. Bellowing engines drowned the sounds of death inside the passageway. The pod's engines ignited inside the secured chamber and rocketed the vehicle through the open chute into the empty vacuum of space.

Chapter 54

Shea awoke with a start. She gasped inside her helmet as panic gripped her; her frantic gaze darted around the inside of the escape pod. The vehicle's control panel offered a warm glow in the otherwise inky blackness. Her breath caught in her lungs as she fumbled with her seat buckles.

"Computer!" she hollered, and clumsily unclipped herself. "Gravity!"

Weightlessness pulled at her limbs and guided her from the seat. A green indicator light flashed on the control panel as a beep resonated inside the pod. An abrupt heaviness planted Shea's feet onto the grate floor beneath her; she collapsed to her knees and pried the helmet from her head.

Nausea roiled in her gut, and her hands and brow dampened with sweat. She strained to steady her breathing, to force air through her strangled lungs. Tears trailed down her cheeks and she found herself shivering inside her armor. The morphine shot was losing potency, and the dull ache of her shoulder returned with a heavy throb.

She closed her eyes and saw Iris standing opposite the chamber's doors. The last moments inside the chamber had been a blur to her—her body seemingly acted on its own when it carried her into the escape pod and threw her into the spare seat. She'd barely finished buckling the safety straps when the vehicle launched. She had no memory of exiting the chute; there was only ignition, a sudden rush, and then nothing.

Her breath hitched in her throat. She scrambled to her seat and desperately searched for an evacuation capsule. Her tongue wetted and heat swelled beneath her cheeks as her fingers found the sealed pouch and tore it open. She pressed the opening around her lips, hunched over, and vomited with a forceful heave.

Moments passed in silence.

Her heartbeat soon steadied as she cradled herself, arms wrapped around her chest and shoulders, and pressed her forehead against the seat. She sealed the pouch and tossed it aside. Her nerves and breath settled.

Shea's attention turned to Victoria, who lay unconscious in the other bucket seat. She stared at her for what felt like minutes, watching the rise and fall of her chest as she breathed, until she pulled herself up by the arm of her seat. She closed the space between them and caught sight of the envelope tucked beneath Victoria's leg. After only a moment's hesitation, she slid the envelop free and regarded it in her hands. She lifted her gaze out the front window and noticed Yggdrasil, now only a tiny orange marble floating on a black canvas, far in the distance.

Her fingers traced along the rough edges of the envelope and the stiff, flat pieces sealed inside. When she shifted her attention toward the narrow rear of the vehicle, she caught sight of Iris's crimson Valkyrie armor, cast apart in pieces, strewn across the floor. She stepped into the space and knelt beside the helmet. She collected it into her hands, frowned, and looked over her shoulder at Victoria with an ache in her chest.

She dropped the helmet and returned to her seat with a long, tired sigh. Her fingers idly toyed with the envelope as she gazed out the window into the empty void of space. She looked sidelong at Victoria for a brief moment, hesitated, and peeled open the envelope's seal; inside she found a set of dog tags, a data chip, and a folded sheet of paper. The two dog tags, attached to a single chain, displayed two etched names: *Daniel Hammond* on one, and *Iris Hammond* on the other. When she unfolded the sheet of paper, a photograph slipped out and fell to her lap. She took the photograph in her hands and squinted through the dim lighting to see a young Iris, with long red hair, holding a baby girl in her arms. A taller blonde man stood beside her—both smiling and happy. A crease marked the center of the photograph, and its edges were worn with age.

"Computer—light," Shea commanded before an overhead light flickered to life above her seat. She examined the photo a moment longer, her heart sinking deeper into her chest, and tucked it back inside the envelope with the dog tags and data chip. Her gaze dropped to the handwritten letter:

Victoria,

If you are reading this letter, it means our mission was a success. You and Simon are free. I know you will have questions and are most likely confused or angry—you have every right to be. I unfortunately cannot answer your questions, but god help me, I wish I could. This letter will have to suffice.

Here is what I can tell you—

A CoP smuggler named Conner will be meeting you shortly. He will take you to a CoP outpost, where you will likely be debriefed by their agents—they will want the deliverables I promised in exchange for your safe passage and protection. The data is loaded on the chip in this envelop. Comply with their requests (and please, Victoria, be polite).

I know you have no reason to trust me after what I have done to you, after all the suffering I have caused. But please believe me when I say that I have felt no greater regret or sorrow than betraying your trust and subjecting you to that woman's tests. Cowardice got the better of me. I thought that killing her, enacting that revenge for the both of us, would help assuage my guilt. But my cowardice weighs on me every single day, and I will spend every day hating myself until the day I die. I am a broken woman knowing that I have failed you as a mother; failed you by turning you away when you needed me the most.

Freedom is all I have left to give you. I cannot change our past, but I can at least guarantee your future. You are going where I cannot follow, and I do not ask for your forgiveness. My only wish is that you eventually find happiness and peace, and know that I love you with all my heart. I hope you find love again—in others, of course, but mostly in yourself. Wherever life takes you, you will always be my little girl. I am proud of you, Victoria, and I will always love you.

I have carried this photo with me since you were a child, and I have worn your father's tags since his death. Carry us with you—if only for his sake.

- Your mother

***

An unsettling evening fell on Odin Prime. Armored peace officers, led by teams of Valkyries, moved into main gathering areas within all sectors. They had occupied those spaces since the afternoon, and even citizens within the Dome steered clear. Shops in the Middle Borough shuttered early, and citizens hurried home to lock their doors. The Anchor witnessed the strongest State presence, where a curfew was enacted soon after the sirens within the Ministry of Defense went silent. Empty rickshaws lined the vacant streets, quiet except for the scheduled armed security patrols that inspected the area. They found little resistance in their movement.

The artificial sky flickered and went black, covering the different sectors in darkness before a display of Odin Prime's flag flashed across its linking panels. The picture appeared on every display wall and teleprompter on the station.

Harriet dipped her face into the crook of her elbow and released a bellowing cough. She wheezed and spat a mouthful of blood to the ground of the narrow Dome alleyway. Sweat dampened her pallid face and soaked the scarf tied around her head. She'd managed to snag discarded housekeeper's clothing in the garbage after crawling out of the long stretch of venting. The pant leg was torn at the knee, and the stained shirt was far too loose around her shoulders. But it was better than her prisoner's uniform. Her palms and knees were filthy and ached.

She winced and lowered herself to the ground behind a trash receptacle. Her weary gaze lifted to the ceiling projection—she felt weak, and fought against the heaviness pulling at her stinging eyelids.

Odin Prime's flag disappeared and revealed Chancellor Tristan standing behind an elegant podium. His tired face, despite noticeable makeup, revealed dark circles beneath his bloodshot eyes. He sniffed, arranged papers on the podium, and cleared his throat with intent. His hardened gaze lifted to peer directly into the camera. When he spoke, his voice boomed throughout the station. Harriet grimaced.

"To all my brothers and sisters on Odin Prime, citizen and non-citizen alike—good evening, and His Majesty Guide Us.

I address you this evening with a heavy, burdened heart. And while I prefer to leave official announcements to the revered Secretary Harrington, recent events have obligated me to speak directly and candidly to you, my brothers and sisters."

He faltered. His gaze remained fixed on the camera as his grip tightened on the sides of the podium.

"It saddens me to bring you news this evening of a failed coup against our station's administration. The coup was organized and carried out by corrupt, secessionist Statesmen—and rest assured, those responsible have met swift, righteous judgement for their crimes. And while the attempt failed, His Fortune Shines, innocent lives were lost; I pray the Patriarch welcome them into His mighty dominion."

Chancellor Tristan's bottom lip quivered as he turned his eyes down to his papers. Harriet watched this with an increasingly deep furrow lining her brow.

His voice broke and warbled.

"One victim of this needless violence includes my own beloved niece, Dr. Shea Tristan. My niece, who only a few days ago was rescued from Shadow captivity, was killed honorably serving the people of Odin Prime. Her death has broken me, but I will persevere for you, my beloved people."

Harriet's heart shuddered. She swallowed and lowered her gaze to stare ahead at the wall across from her. "I really hoped that girl would've made it..." She covered her eyes with the palm of her hand as a silent tear rolled down her cheek.

***

The chancellor's speech projected on the display wall inside the Trinity safe house. Tony still lay across the sofa, half awake and grumbling, with Theresa seated at his feet.

"No, not Shea!" Theresa cried out with hands clasped across her mouth. Tears spilled from her eyes as she shook her head in disbelief.

Simon stared numbly at the display and leaned against the nearest wall. His jaw hung open, aghast, as he ran his palm across his scalp. He said nothing and slid down to sit on the carpeted floor. Julep crossed the room and sat by his side; her expression was devoid of its usual humor.

Chancellor Tristan continued, his voice now growing increasingly hostile.

"... *Shadow captivity. My niece was not the only victim of Shadow's cruelty, of their toxic grasp over the weak and desperate of our station. Those of you who have turned to them in your greatest hour of darkness, I understand your plight; but by doing so you have given power to evil itself! It angers me to bring you this shocking news, brothers and sisters: Upon my niece's rescue, our investigators discovered evidence of an emerging spread of the Ink throughout the Anchor—and Shadow's attempts to bury and mask these cases, Shadow hid these cases from us, prevented access to proper medical care, and by doing so put our entire beloved station at risk.*"

"Bullshit!" Simon blurted out. He gestured to the screen with a sneer. "Everything he's saying is a fuckin' lie."

Julep scoffed. "Of course it is."

"*But why?*" Chancellor Tristan went on. "*Why have these crooked secessionists and immoral thugs acted with such reckless abandon? Why have they chosen to sacrifice innocent lives in pursuit of their selfish ambitions?"* He paused for dramatic effect and leaned over the podium. *"Fear. They feared the change that my Peace Accords would bring, and would stoop to feckless violence and bioterrorism as a last, dying gasp of consolidating power. Our unity is their undoing!*

"Brothers and sisters, we are a station of survivors—and the cost of that survival has been high. That cost has left us a divided, broken people. All my actions as your Chancellor have been to make us a stronger, more resilient people. Many of my edicts and policies have been controversial, and were met with violence and anger—wounds have been carved into the fabric of our society that shall linger long after we are gone. But we cannot allow these wounds to prevent progress, *to hinder us from seeking* unity. *We cannot allow fear of change to cripple the advancement of our society, and a peaceful future!*

"That is why I am announcing this evening that my administration has enacted the Peace Accords, effective immediately. Our offices will release official guidance within the new few hours, but I want to personally announce major overhauls to our citizenship protocols."

Theresa gulped through choked sobs. "I don't like this, guys." She squeezed her brother's ankle. "I'm scared."

Tony, in his half-conscious state, reached down to take his sister's hand into his own.

"It's alright, peanut. We'll be alright—don't worry."

Theresa sniffled and lowered herself beside her brother, who wrapped his muscular arm around her trembling shoulders.

"We have approved a clear pathway for non-citizens to earn their citizenship, even if they have previously been exiled. There

are multiple options, including conscription into either our new labor collective or armed services, or applying for our Family Management Program. These volunteers will work to repopulate, occupy, and enrich territory on Valhalla for the betterment of not only themselves, but of the whole community. Upon ten cycles of service, volunteers may choose to reside as a citizen on either Odin Prime or Valhalla, where they may apply to own property.

"These Peace Accords are a major shift in domestic policy, and I understand your hesitation and skepticism. But let me assure you that our intentions are genuine, and my interests are only for the betterment of our noble society. My dear brothers and sisters, you have suffered long enough. I ask you, in the light of these violent events, to come together in unity under our beloved Station's banner and cast aside sadistic dissenters who seek to divide us; and instead, join us in our strive toward a shared, peaceful future!"

Chancellor Tristan offered a kind smile and breathed steadily. *"I pray that the Patriarch bless each and every one of you. Goodnight, and May Strength Remain."*

***

The feed abruptly cut and left the station blanketed in dark silence. In that silence, peace officers strung a new body up to the Mourning Tower. As the artificial sky flickered and sputtered back to its typical orange sunset, an announcement broke over the intercom:

"Be advised, scheduled rainfall set to begin in ten minutes. Be advised, scheduled rainfall set to begin in ten minutes."

Not a single pedestrian unlocked their doors that evening. Security forces continued their periodic patrols despite the downpour that came shortly after, drenching them and the new red-headed body on display in a bitter, cold rain.

Epilogue

Time had stopped.

Or, if it hadn't, it had at least ceased to be a real, tangible thing that mattered. Shea wasn't sure if it had been minutes, hours, or days since reading the letter; she had sat gazing blankly out the front window ever since.

An alert beeped from the console. The sharp noise pierced the silence and instantly drew her from her daze. She sat tall in her chair and realized only then that Iris's handwritten letter remained in her hand, crumbled within a tight fist. Her knuckles and forearm ached as she released it.

"I thought that killing her, enacting that revenge for the <u>both</u> of us, would help assuage my guilt." Written in Iris's own script. The woman's confession to her mother's murder.

Shea closed her eyes and braced against the memory of her mother's bloodied wrists dangling lifeless in the murky crimson bathwater.

"Fuck," Shea whispered through gritted teeth. She wiped her disheveled dark hair from her face and let out a deep breath. She glanced over to Victoria's sleeping face and swallowed the ire crawling up her chest. After a beat, Shea had smoothed the paper out again, folded it, and hidden it away inside her belt pouch.

"Computer." She stood from her chair and squinted out the window. "Display alert."

A message flashed in red across the control panel's HUD: *Incoming Unidentified Vessel. Prepare For Docking.*

Shea snatched her helmet from the floor and affixed it over her head. She grabbed hold of her pistol and peered again at Victoria—she saw more of Iris in Victoria's face than ever before, and it twisted in her gut like a knife.

The vehicle rocked to the side with a bang, sending Shea off-balance against the far wall. She charged her pistol and raised it toward the rear hatch, wincing at the sharp twinge of pain pulling at her wounded shoulder.

A hiss of air spilled through the hatch as it broke open. Her heart pounded like a drum behind her ribs as she adjusted the pistol in her hands. The hatch lowered, opening the back of the pod into a poorly lit cargo bay. The pod had been swallowed up by a larger ship, and the adjusting air pressure left her ears popping.

A silhouette emerged from the rear of the bay with an ambling limp.

Shea steeled herself and moved to position herself between Victoria and the stranger.

"Identify yourself!" she called out. "Identify yourself or I'll shoot!"

The figure let out a throaty laugh and lifted his meaty hands into the air. The heavier-set older man stepped into the light and smiled at her through a scruffy grey beard. He dressed in what appeared to be an old mechanic's uniform with a patchwork of shoddy sewn repairs and oil stains.

"Name's Conner, ma'am." He offered a wave with one of his hands. "The Coalition of Provinces sends their regards."

Shea lowered her pistol and gaped at him. *"You're* Conner?"

"Indeed I am, last I checked." He limped closer and rested his hands on his hips. "Let's get you and your friend outta that pod and into some better accommodations, eh? We got a week's ride to the Bastion."

"The Bastion?" Shea asked. "What's that?"

"Yikes, you don't get out much on that station, do ya?" Conner nearly laughed as Shea stared at him. He offered her a reassuring smile. "It's the political capital for the Coalition of Provinces. And let me tell you, ma'am, they are just *itching* to talk to ya."

Afterword

This novel has been over five years in the making- and I could not have done it without the consistent love and support of my friends and family. As this is my first novel, I had periods of extreme doubt and uncertainty and your kind words and (sometimes) critical criticisms kept me going. Thank you to my friends and beta readers - Greta, Feli, Autumn, Johanna, and Regina- I love you guys.

I'd like to thank my amazing and patient editor, Dylan Garity! Thank you and I'm sorry for all my wonky POV changes and lack of section breaks. Thank you also to my cover artist, Satine Zillah! You continue to astound me with your talent.

To my family— I love you! Thank you for your love, support, and acceptance. (Maybe wait until Madison is a bit older before letting her read this one) Bridget, I always look forward to coming home for drunken push-ups with you.

Most of all I'd like to thank my wife, my rock, my first developmental editor and reader- Rachel. Thank you for the endless re-reads, the brutal but necessary feedback (tough love!), and endless encouragement during my darkest and most challenging periods. I wouldn't be here without you. I love you and I like you, Rachel. (I'm not going to thank my cats- they can't read)

About the Author

Meg knew she wanted to be a writer ever since she wrote Sailor Moon fanfiction in her middle school notebooks. She has spent the last twenty years daydreaming and writing bits of fiction until deciding to write her first novel in 2015. Five years later she is preparing to release her first novel, Valkyrie. (She guarantees it is better than hand-written Sailor Moon fanfiction)

Meg is from Cleveland, Ohio and majored in History with a minor in Asian Studies at Bowling Green State University. She studied Japanese and spent one glorious year abroad in Hiroshima, Japan in 2007. She also earned a MA in History from Texas A&M- Central Texas and a graduate certificate in Cybersecurity Technology from the University of Maryland Global Campus Europe. All this means is that Meg is a huge history and computer nerd with a few expensive pieces of paper.

Unable to stay in one place for very long, Meg calls wherever her wife, Rachel, and their two cats- Anakin and Padme- her home.

You can connect with me on:
🌐 https://www.megludwa.com

9 781735 639437